FOR GRAHAM
who first suggested the hunt
for the American rivals

Contents

	Acknowledgement	8
	Introduction	9
1	Cinderella's Slipper *Hugh C. Weir*	19
2	The Nameless Man *Rodriguez Ottolengui*	57
3	The Montezuma Emerald *Rodriguez Ottolengui*	71
4	Found Guilty *Josiah Flynt and Francis Walton*	86
5	The Scarlet Thread *Jacques Futrelle*	100
6	The Man Higher Up *William MacHarg and Edwin Balmer*	137
7	The Axton Letters *William MacHarg and Edwin Balmer*	169
8	The Man Who Spoke Latin *Samuel Hopkins Adams*	208
9	The Cloud-Bursters *Francis Lynde*	230
10	The Affair of Lamson's Cook *Charles Felton Pidgin and J. M. Taylor*	279
11	The Campaign Grafter *Arthur B. Reeve*	302
12	The Infallible Godahl *Frederick Irving Anderson*	334
13	The Frame-Up *Richard Harding Davis*	373

Acknowledgement

My thanks are due to Refna Wilkin for her invaluable research work in New York and Washington.

Some copyright holders have been difficult to trace. If in any case I have failed I offer my apologies.

Introduction

The reputation of American writers of detective short stories who were working at about the turn of the century has never recovered from Howard Haycraft's pronouncement in his generally admirable history of the detective story, *Murder For Pleasure*. 'It can not be pretended,' says Haycraft, 'that the American detective story revealed any thing like the quantity or the level of quality of its English counterpart in the years up to the first world conflagration.'

This has been quoted since by many other writers on the history of the detective story, and so far as quantity is concerned Haycraft was undoubtedly right. Apart from Arthur B. Reeve America produced no writers anything like as prolific as William Le Queux, E. Phillips Oppenheim and Dick Donavan, and even Reeve cannot quite compete in their league.

One of the interesting things about the American detective story at the time is how many writers produced only one or two collections of detective stories and were otherwise involved in quite different professions or other types of writing. Most of the writers were amateurs in this field and there were no great professionals like Conan Doyle, Arthur Morrison and R. Austin Freeman.

The fact that the American writers were comparatively unknown, left no great body of work behind them and were seldom reprinted poses considerable problems for collectors. It is very hard to find their books outside the main American public libraries. Only a few are available in the British Museum Library as many were never published in England. If it had not been for a stroke of luck I doubt whether I should have persevered in the search. Just as I was about to give up a leading second-hand bookseller in London suddenly offered a large batch – at very high prices.

So far as quality is concerned there is also something in what Haycraft says. But what he overlooks is that, although there is no great body of excellent work by any one author, many writers had it in them to produce one or two stories which, in their very different way, will stand comparison with the work of their English contemporaries. This added to the excitement of the chase. One would plough through one dull and stodgily-written story after another, often in the agonizingly facetious style which was then fashionable in America, and suddenly one would come on a single story with an ingenious twist of plot or an insight into the life of the time which made it stand out and demand to be rescued from oblivion. One can also say that this collection includes six writers who escaped even Haycraft's net.

I mentioned how different the American stories seem from those written in England at the same time. This gives them their interest from the point of view of social history. Sometimes one realizes with a sense of shock how modern these differences make them appear. We find a brutal and corrupt police force, corrupt politicians, bugging, big and wealthy corporations using their power to cheat the Federal Government or to put small competitors out of business, methods used by political parties in elections which are extraordinarily reminiscent of Nixon's CREEP. In this jungle some of the detectives also take on a different character. In addition to the usual private detectives we find Government undercover agents fighting against the criminal methods used by the big corporations and their bosses. Marlowe and Sam Spade could have walked into some of the situations and felt themselves instantly at home – apart from the absence of any sexual interest. Even more than in England at the time it is a man's world, although we do have one very competent female detective.

With her I shall begin, giving the lady first place: Miss Madelyn Mack, Detective. She deserves the place of honour for the first sentence in the story: 'Raymond Rennick might have been going to his wedding instead of to his death.' So far as can be established her creator Hugh C. Weir (1884–1934) never wrote any other detective stories, though he was the author of several books about the building of the Panama Canal. He was a journalist who also did a lot of work in films as a scenario writer. *Miss Madelyn Mack, Detective* was filmed and the first edition was illustrated with film stills. It would be interesting to track down a print. The book was dedicated to a lady called Mary Holland who was evidently a detective in real life.

The other stories I give in order of publication and we come first to Dr Rodriguez Ottolengui, an eminent dentist, who is one of my personal favourites. He writes well in a straightforward way without the pretentiousness which afflicts many of his contemporaries, and in his one volume of short detective stories he creates an interesting relationship between his professional detective Mr Barnes and the rich amateur Mr Mitchel. This book, *The Final Proof*, was never published in England, but four stories from it appeared in 1895 in the *Idler* magazine, which seldom printed detective stories. I have included two of these stories because some extra space is needed to illustrate the interaction between Ottolengui's two detectives. I was much tempted by another story, not included in the *Idler*, in which Mr Mitchel murders the

Missing Link and is found out by Mr Barnes, but, unfortunately, the originality of the idea is not matched by the execution. When Ottolengui, who was born in 1861, died in 1937 his obituary in the *New York Times* was almost entirely devoted to his work as a dentist and to his mastery of such abstruse techniques as orthodontia and root canal therapy. There is no copy of *The Final Proof* in the British Museum Library, but any dentists who may read this introduction will find there the book which Ottolengui probably regarded as his masterpiece, *Methods of Filling Teeth*.

The next book from which I have taken a story, *Powers that Prey* by Josiah Flynt and Francis Walton, is something of a curiosity. It is set in the New York underworld and the authors argue in their introduction that the really effective detectives are the spies and traitors in the ranks of the criminals and that without their help the police would never make an arrest. There is certainly no exaggerated respect for the New York police force which is shown as both incompetent and unscrupulous. The stories are written in a curiously stilted style, but somehow succeed in conveying an authentic atmosphere. I came to the conclusion that one at least of the authors must have been a member of the underworld himself. I was not too far out. Research revealed that Josiah Flynt was the pseudonym of Josiah Flynt Willard (1869–1907). He was employed as a railway policeman by the Pennsylvania Railroad Company on the lines west of Pittsburgh and he also wrote a book called *Notes of an Itinerant Policeman*, published in 1900, which sounds interesting. His collaborator's real name was Alfred Hodder (1866–1907). He graduated in law at Harvard and studied municipal conditions in New York as secretary to a reforming District Attorney, William Travers Jerome. With Josiah Flynt Willard he investigated the New York slums before they joined in writing *Powers That Prey*. That their short lives ended in the same year is a curious coincidence.

About Jacques Futrelle (1875–1912) I have written in the introduction to *More Rivals of Sherlock Holmes.** Since then I have seen in the *New York Times* of 12 April 1912 an account of his death in the Titanic disaster. He helped his wife to a place in a lifeboat and declined the chance to save himself. He is one of the few professional writers of crime stories in this collection, and his detective Professor S. F. X. Van Dusen, the Thinking Machine, has never been entirely forgotten.

I have included two stories by William MacHarg (1872–1951) and Edwin Balmer (1893–1959) because both on merit and rarity they seem to deserve it. Their detective Luther Trant was one of the first psychologist detectives and his use of a lie detector in *The Man Higher Up* was, so far as I know, the first in detective fiction. In the same story we have an instance of the collaboration between a private detective and Federal agents to uncover big business crime, and there is real passion against the bosses who usually remain untouched and leave their underlings to take the rap. Ellery Queen in his bibliography *Queen's Quorum* relates that on two occasions Luther Trant stories had to be dropped from previous anthologies because of 'production difficulties'. So I am now making up for that omission. Both Balmer and MacHarg were professional novelists whose work does not otherwise seem to have survived. MacHarg created a 'good-hearted cop' called O'Malley who appeared for many years in the pages of *Collier's* and the *Saturday Evening Post* – obviously a very different character from Captain Brigstock in *Powers that Prey*. The Balmer–MacHarg partnership extended to Balmer marrying MacHarg's sister as his first wife.

Samuel Hopkins Adams (1871–1958) was another one-

* American title *Cosmopolitan Crimes.*

book man so far as crime writing is concerned. Although his writing is somewhat marred by the contemporary American disease of facetiousness one can agree with Howard Haycraft in regretting that his ingenious book *Average Jones* was his only attempt at detective fiction. He was a busy journalist specializing in health subjects and his articles about tuberculosis, typhoid and yellow fever were considered authoritative in their time. In 1906–7 he conducted a campaign under the title of the Great American Fraud against patent medicine companies and this led to the inclusion of a patent medicine clause in a pure food bill passed by the House of Representatives. So he was a bit of a detective in real life. He also wrote science fiction and was compared in his day with Jules Verne.

Francis Lynde (1856–1930) wrote a number of novels, short stories and magazine articles, but *Scientific Sprague* is his only collection of detective short stories. Like Canon Whitechurch in England whose book *Thrilling Stories of the Railway* appeared in the same year, 1912, as *Scientific Sprague*, Lynde is one of the earliest specialists in railway detection. But the settings are very different. Lynde's trains run through the mountains and deserts of Nevada instead of along English branch lines. His stories deal with a campaign of violence by a 'stock-jobbing gang' in New York to put a small independent railroad, the Nevada Short Line, out of business. The detective, Calvin Sprague, is a Federal agent who uses the cover of a Department of Agriculture chemist. Like the Federal agents in *The Man Higher Up* he is deeply involved in the struggle against the 'big money' crooks whom he describes as 'buccaneers neatly labelled with the dollar-mark instead of the skull and cross-bones.' Robert Louis Stevenson had written about the big railroad men as 'gentlemen in frock coats with a view to nothing more extraordinary than a fortune and a subsequent visit to Paris', and it is a matter of historical fact that the building of the great railroads spanning the continent was accompanied by fraud, bribery and violence on an enormous scale. Four directors of the Central Pacific, for instance, milked their railroad by fraudulent methods of more than sixty million dollars. No Calvin Sprague caught up with them and each left over forty millions at his death.

Another amateur crime writer was Charles Felton Pidgin (1844–1923). He was better known in his own time as an inventor and statistician. As a child he had received an injury to his hip which paralysed one of his legs and forced him to use an artificial support for the rest of his life. In 1873 he was appointed Chief Clerk at the Massachusetts Bureau of Statistics of Labour and assembled one of the earliest mechanical tabulation machines. He also invented 'visible speech' which is described somewhat obscurely as 'a system designed to make possible the photographing of words as if issuing from the mouths of motion-picture actors'. In his middle fifties the unfortunate Pidgin suffered from cataract and this turned him from statistics to writing. He dictated a novel called *Quincy Adams Sawyer* about New England life which was published in 1900. This was followed by several other books about two generations of Quincy Adams Sawyers. Only the last is, strictly speaking, of detective interest, though its hero, Quincy Adams Sawyer junior, had in an earlier book married a girl called Mary Dana who worked in a detective agency. Pidgin's stories have a quality of gentleness, even when blood is shed, and quiet humour rare in American stories of the time. I have no information about his collaborator J. M. Taylor.

With Arthur B. Reeve (1880–1936) we come at last to a thoroughly professional writer of detective short stories. He turned out a long series of books beginning with

The Silent Bullet* in 1912 which were immensely popular
in their day. On the whole the professional has worn less
well than the amateurs, and I had to read an enormous
number of Reeve stories before I found one which seemed
to deserve reprinting. His most famous creation was
Craig Kennedy, a 'scientific' detective, who employed
various mechanical wonders drawn from popular science
magazines. Inevitably Kennedy's achievements are now
somewhat dated. The story I have chosen justifies its
inclusion through the curiously modern political skuldug-
gery which it describes rather than through Kennedy's
methods of detection. Some of Reeve's other books, including *The Exploits of Elaine*, were turned into famous
film serials of the silent era. There is some doubt about
the publishing history of *The Poisoned Pen* from which I
have taken my story. The book was brought out in the
same year, 1913, by three different publishers Dodd Mead,
Harper and Van Rees. The last two editions were illustrated by two different artists. The green cloth Dodd
Mead edition, which is not illustrated, is the only one
recorded in the Library of Congress and must be recognized as the first.

The episode from *Adventures of the Infallible Godahl*
seems to me to be the most original and ingenious story
in this collection. Who is the detective? Who is the
criminal? Frederick Irving Anderson (1877–1947) had a
small and select output of detective short stories. Apart
from Godahl he wrote *The Notorious Sophie Lang* which
for some reason was published only in England and *The
Book of Murder* about Deputy Parr and the writer
Oliver Armiston who also appears in the Godahl story I
have chosen. Anderson is a master of misdirection and of
the double-cross and one feels that he had it in him to be
the best of all American detective story writers until the
days of Hammett and Chandler. But he seems to have

* Published in England as *The Black Hand*.

had only an intermittent urge to write and preferred farming in Vermont.

Richard Harding Davis (1864–1916) would probably be surprised and angry to find himself in this company. He would never have thought of himself as a detective story writer and I must admit that the story I have chosen about District Attorney Wharton is very much of a borderline case. In his day Richard Harding Davis was one of the most famous of American journalists, novelists and playwrights regularly earning his 100,000 dollars a year – and nevertheless leaving his widow almost penniless. It is clear that he was a very arrogant and disagreeable man. Even the usually sober pages of the biographical dictionary *Twentieth Century Authors* breathe an intense dislike of him though it was published a quarter of a century after his death. He was 'a bit of a prig and a bit of a poseur'. He 'lived in a bright day dream'. He was divorced once and was 'Charles D. Gibson's model for the upstanding, handsome young men who squired the famous Gibson girls'. Yet he appears to have been unpleasantly prudish about the failings of other people. The entry in *Twentieth Century Authors* concludes with obvious satisfaction that 'he is deservedly forgotten now'. This is not quite fair. He covered almost all the wars of his time and his reports from the Greco-Turkish, the Boer, the Spanish-American, the Russo-Japanese and the World Wars can still be read with pleasure though they are high-flown and emotional by modern standards. Some of his short stories and his novel of Latin American adventure *Soldiers of Fortune* are still very readable. So is his short thriller *In the Fog*, of which the illustrated first edition is a delightful piece of book-making. All the same I would not deny that in much of his writing there is an unpleasant tinge of vulgarity and self-satisfaction.

There is one quite well-known author, Melville Davisson Post, whose omission from this collection I should explain. His most famous character Uncle Abner solves mysteries in the mountains of West Virginia in Jefferson's time and he cannot, by any stretch of the imagination, be described as a rival of Sherlock Holmes. His unscrupulous lawyer Randolph Mason turned from defeating the ends of justice to defending them in a book called *The Corrector of Destinies* but, like some other rogues, lost a lot of his appeal in the process.

I

Cinderella's Slipper

Hugh C. Weir

I

Raymond Rennick might have been going to his wedding instead of to his death.

Spick and span in a new spring suit, he paused just outside the broad, arched gates of the Duffield estate and drew his silver cigarette case from his pocket. A self-satisfied smile flashed across his face as he struck a match and inhaled the fragrant odour of the tobacco. It was good tobacco, very good tobacco – and Senator Duffield's private secretary was something of a judge!

For a moment Rennick lingered. It was a day to banish uncomfortable thoughts, to smooth the rough edges of a man's problems – and burdens. As the secretary glanced up at the soft blue sky, the reflection swept his mind that his own future was as free from clouds. It was a pleasing reflection. Perhaps the cigarette, perhaps the day helped to deepen it as he swung almost jauntily up the winding driveway toward the square, white house commanding the terraced lawn beyond.

Just ahead of him a maple tree, standing alone, rustled gaily in its spring foliage like a woman calling attention to her new finery. It was all so fresh and beautiful and innocent! Rennick felt a tingling thrill in his blood. Unconsciously he tossed away his cigarette. He reached the rustling maple and passed it …

From behind the gnarled trunk, a shadow darted. A figure sprang at his shoulders, with the long blade of a dagger awkwardly poised. There was a flash of steel in the sunlight ...

It was perhaps ten minutes later that they found him. He had fallen face downward at the edge of the driveway, with his body half across the velvet green of the grass. A thin thread of red, creeping from the wound in his breast, was losing itself in the sod.

One hand was doubled, as in a desperate effort at defense. His glasses were twisted under his shoulders. Death must have been nearly instantaneous. The dagger had reached his heart at the first thrust. One might have fancied an expression of overpowering amazement in the staring eyes. That was all. The weapon had caught him squarely on the left side. He had evidently whirled toward the assassin almost at the instant of the blow.

Whether in the second left him of life he had recognized his assailant, and the recognition had made his death-blow the quicker and the surer, were questions that only deepened the horror of the noon-day crime.

As though to emphasize the hour, the mahogany clock in Senator Duffield's library rang out its twelve monotonous chimes as John Dorrence, his valet, beat sharply on the door. The echo of the nervous tattoo was lost in an unanswering silence. Dorrence repeated his knock before he brought an impatient response from beyond the panels.

'Can you come, sir?' the valet burst out. 'Something awful has happened, sir. It's, it's –'

The door was flung open. A ruddy-faced man with thick, white hair and grizzled moustache, and the hints of a nervous temperament showing in his eyes and voice, sprang into the hall. Somebody once remarked that Senator Duffield was Mark Twain's double. The Senator took the comparison as a compliment, perhaps because it was a woman who made it.

Dorrence seized his master by the sleeve, which loss of dignity did more to impress the Senator with the gravity of the situation than all of the servant's excitable words.

'Mr Rennick, sir, has been stabbed, sir, on the lawn, and Miss Beth, sir –'

Senator Duffield staggered against the wall. The valet's alarm swerved to another channel.

'Shall I get the brandy, sir?'

'Brandy?' the Senator repeated vaguely. The next instant, as though grasping the situation anew, he sprang down the hall with the skirts of his frock coat flapping against his knees. At the door of the veranda, he whirled.

'Get the doctor on the 'phone, Dorrence – Redfield, if Scott is out. Let him know it's a matter of minutes! And, Dorrence –'

'Yes, sir!'

'Tell the telephone girl that, if this leaks to the newspapers, I will have the whole office discharged!'

A shifting group on the edge of the lawn, with that strange sense of awkwardness which sudden death brings, showed the scene of the tragedy.

The circle fell back as the Senator's figure appeared. On the grass, Rennick's body still lay where it had fallen – suggesting a skater who has ignominiously collapsed on the ice rather than a man stabbed to the heart. The group had been wondering at the fact in whispered monosyllables.

A kneeling girl was bending over the secretary's body. It was not until Senator Duffield had spoken her name twice that she glanced up. In her eyes was a grief so wild that for a moment he was held dumb.

'Come, Beth,' he said, gently, 'this is no place for you.'

At once the white-faced girl became the central figure of the situation. If she heard him, she gave no sign. The Senator caught her shoulder and pushed her slowly away. One of the woman-servants took her arm. Curiously enough, the two were the only members of the family that had been called to the scene.

The Senator swung on the group, with a return of his aggressiveness.

'Some one, who can talk fast and to the point, tell me the story. Burke, you have a ready tongue. How did it happen?'

The groom – a much-tanned young fellow in his early twenties – touched his cap.

'I don't know, sir. No one knows. Mr Rennick was lying here, stabbed, when we found him. He was already dead.'

'But surely there was some cry, some sound of a scuffle?'

The groom shook his head. 'If there was, sir, none of us heard it. We all liked Mr Rennick, sir. I would have gone through fire and water if he needed my help. If there had been an outcry loud enough to reach the stable, I would have been there on the jump!'

'Do you mean to tell me that Rennick could have been struck down in the midst of fifteen or twenty people with no one the wiser? It's ridiculous, impossible!'

Burke squared his shoulders, with an almost unconscious suggestion of dignity.

'I am telling you the truth, sir!'

The Senator's glance dropped to his secretary's body and he looked up with a shudder. Then, as though with an effort, his eyes returned to the huddled form, and he stood staring down at the dead man, with a frown knitting his brow. Once he jerked his head towards the gardener with the curt question, 'Who found him?'

Jenkins shambled forward uneasily. 'I did, sir. I hope you don't think I disturbed the body?'

The Senator shrugged his shoulders impatiently. He did not raise his head again until the sound of a motor in the driveway broke the tension. The surgeon had arrived. Almost at the same moment there was a cry from Jenkins.

The gardener stood perhaps a half a dozen yards from the body, staring at an object hidden in the grass at his feet. He stooped and raised it. It was a woman's slipper!

As a turn of his head showed him the eyes of the group turned in his direction, he walked across to Senator Duffield, holding his find at arm's length, as though its dainty outlines might conceal an adder's nest.

The slipper was of black suede, high-heeled and slender, tied with a broad, black ribbon. One end of the ribbon was broken and stained as though it had tripped its owner. On the thin sole were cakes of the peculiar red clay of the driveway.

It might have been unconscious magnetism that caused the Senator suddenly to turn his eyes in the direction of his daughter. She was swaying on the arm of the servant.

Throwing off the support of the woman, she took two quick steps forward, with her hand flung out as though to tear the slipper from him. And then, without a word, she fell prone on the grass.

2

The telephone in my room must have been jangling a full moment before I struggled out of my sleep and raised myself to my elbow. It was with a feeling of distinct rebellion that I slipped into my kimono and slippers and shuffled across to the sputtering instrument in the corner. From eight in the morning until eight in the evening, I had been on racking duty in the Farragut poison trial, and the belated report of the wrangling jury, at an hour which made any sort of a meal impossible until after ten, had left me worn out physically and mentally. I glanced at my watch as I snapped the receiver to my ear. It lacked barely fifteen minutes of midnight. An unearthly hour to call a woman out of bed, even if she is past the age of sentimental dreams!

'Well?' I growled.

A laugh answered me at the other end of the wire. I would have flung the receiver back to the hook and myself back to bed had I not recognized the tones. There is only one person in the world, excepting the tyrant at our city editor's desk, who would arouse me at midnight. But I had thought this person separated from me by twelve hundred miles of ocean.

'Madelyn Mack!' I gasped.

The laughter ceased. 'Madelyn Mack it is!' came back the answer, now reduced to a tone of decorous gravity. 'Pardon my merriment, Nora. The mental picture of your huddled form –'

'But I thought you in Jamaica!' I broke in, now thoroughly awake.

'I was – until Saturday. Our steamer came out of quarantine at four o'clock this afternoon. As it develops, I reached here at the psychological moment.'

I kicked a rocker to my side and dropped into it with a rueful glance at the rumpled sheets of the bed. With Madelyn Mack at the telephone at midnight, only one conclusion was possible; and such a conclusion shattered all thought of sleep.

'Have you read the evening dispatches from Boston, Nora?'

'I have read nothing – except the report of the Farragut jury!' I returned crisply. 'Why?'

'If you had, you would perhaps divine the reason of my call. I have been retained in the Rennick murder case. I am taking the one-thirty sleeper for Boston. I secured our berths just before I telephoned.'

'Our berths!'

'I am taking you with me. Now that you are up, you may as well dress and ring for a taxicab. I will meet you at the Roanoke hotel.'

'But,' I protested, 'don't you think –'

'Very well, if you don't care to go! That settles it!'

'Oh, I will be there!' I said with an air of resignation. 'Ten minutes to dress, and fifteen minutes for the taxi!'

'I will add five minutes for incidentals,' Madelyn replied and hung up the receiver.

The elevator boy at 'The Occident', where I had my modest apartment, had become accustomed to the strange hours and strange visitors of a newspaper woman during my three years' residence. He opened the door with a grin of sympathy as the car reached my floor. As though to give more active expression to his feelings he caught up my bag and gave it a place of honour on his own stool.

'Going far?' he queried as I alighted at the main corridor.

'I may be back in twenty-four hours and I may not be back for twenty-four days,' I answered cautiously – I knew Madelyn Mack!

As I waited for the whir of the taxicab, I appropriated the evening paper on the night clerk's desk. The Rennick murder case had been given a three-column head on the front page. If I had not been so absorbed in the Farragut trial, it could not have escaped me. I had not finished the headlines, however, when the taxi, with a promptness almost uncanny, rumbled up to the curb.

I threw myself back against the cushions, switched on the electric light, and spread my paper over my knee, as the chauffeur turned off toward Fifth Avenue. The story was well written and had made much of a few facts. Trust my newspaper instinct to know that! I had expected a fantastic puzzle – when it could spur Madelyn into action within six hours after her landing – but I was hardly anticipating a problem such as I could read between rather than in the lines of type before me. Long before the 'Roanoke' loomed into view, I had forgotten my lost sleep.

The identity of Raymond Rennick's assassin was as

baffling as in the first moments of the discovery of the tragedy. There had been no arrests – nor hint of any. From the moment when the secretary had turned into the gate of the Duffield yard until the finding of his body, all trace of his movements had been lost as effectually as though the darkness of midnight had enveloped him, instead of the sunlight of noon. More than ten minutes could not have elapsed between his entrance into the grounds and the discovery of his murder – perhaps not more than five – but they had been sufficient for the assassin to effect a complete escape.

There was not even the shadow of a motive. Raymond Rennick was one of those few men who seemed to be without an enemy. In an official capacity, his conduct was without a blemish. In a social capacity, he was admittedly one of the most popular men in Brookline – among both sexes. Rumour had it, apparently on unquestioned authority, that the announcement of his engagement to Beth Duffield was to have been an event of the early summer. This fact was in my mind as I stared out into the darkness.

On a sudden impulse, I opened the paper again. From an inside page the latest photograph of the Senator's daughter, taken at a fashionable Boston studio, smiled up at me. It was an excellent likeness as I remembered her at the inaugural ball the year before – a wisp of a girl, with a mass of black hair, which served to emphasize her frailness. I studied the picture with a frown. There was a sense of familiarity in its outlines, which certainly our casual meeting could not explain. Then, abruptly, my thoughts flashed back to the crowded courtroom of the afternoon – and I remembered.

In the prisoner's dock I saw again the figure of Beatrice Farragut, slender, fragile, her white face, her sombre gown, her eyes fixed like those of a frightened lamb on the jury which was to give her life – or death.

'*She* poison her husband?' had buzzed the whispered comments at my shoulders during the weary weeks of the trial. 'She couldn't harm a butterfly!' Like a mocking echo, the tones of the foreman had sounded the answering verdict of murder – in the first degree. And in New York this meant –

Why had Beatrice Farragut suggested Beth Duffield? Or was it Beth Duffield who had suggested – I crumpled the paper into a heap and tossed it from the window in disgust at my morbid imagination. B-u-r-r-h! And yet they say that a New York newspaper woman has no nerves!

A voice hailed us from the darkness and a white-gowned figure sprang out on to the walk. As the chauffeur brought the machine to a halt, Madelyn Mack caught my hands.

Her next two actions were thoroughly characteristic.

Whirling to the driver, she demanded shortly. 'How soon can you make the Grand Central Station?'

The man hesitated. 'Can you give me twenty minutes?'

'Just! We will leave here at one sharp. You will wait, please!'

Having thus disposed of the chauffeur – Madelyn never gave a thought to the matter of expense! – she seized my arm and pushed me through the entrance of the 'Roanoke' as nonchalantly as though we had parted six hours before instead of six weeks.

'I hope you enjoyed Jamaica?' I ventured.

'Did you read the evening papers on the way over?' she returned as easily as though I had not spoken.

'One,' I answered shortly. Madelyn's habit of ignoring my queries grated most uncomfortably at times.

'Then you know what has been published concerning the case?'

I nodded. 'I imagine that you can add considerably.'

'As a matter of fact, I know less than the reporters!'

Madelyn threw open the door of her room. 'You have interviewed Senator Duffield on several occasions, have you not, Nora?'

'You might say on several *delicate* occasions if you cared to!'

'You can tell me then whether the Senator is in the habit of polishing his glasses when he is in a nervous mood?'

A rather superior smile flashed over my face.

'I assure you that Senator Duffield never wears glasses on any occasion!'

Something like a chuckle came from Madelyn.

'Perhaps you can do as well on another question. You will observe in these newspapers four different photographs of the murdered secretary. Naturally, they bear many points of similarity – they were all taken in the last three years – but they contain one feature in common which puzzles me. Does it impress you in the same way?'

I glanced at the group of photographs doubtfully. Three of them were obviously newspaper 'snapshots', taken of the secretary while in the company of Senator Duffield. The fourth was a reproduction of a conventional cabinet photograph. They showed a clean shaven, well built young man of thirty or thereabouts; tall, and I should say inclined to athletics. I turned from the newspapers to Madelyn with a shrug.

'I am afraid I don't quite follow you,' I admitted ruefully. 'There is nothing at all out of the ordinary in any of them that I can catch.'

Madelyn carefully clipped the pictures and placed them under the front cover of her black morocco note-book. As she did so, a clock chimed the hour of one. We both pushed back our chairs.

As we stepped into the taxicab, Madelyn tapped my arm. 'I wonder if Raymond Rennick polished *his* glasses when he was nervous?' she asked musingly.

3

Boston, from the viewpoint of the South Station at half-past seven in the morning, suggests to me a rheumatic individual climbing stiffly out of bed. Boston distinctly resents anything happening before noon. I'll wager that nearly every important event that she has contributed to history occurred after lunch-time!

If Madelyn Mack had expected to have to find her way to the Duffield home without a guide, she was pleasantly disappointed. No less a person than the Senator, himself, was awaiting us at the train-gate – a somewhat dishevelled Senator, it must be confessed, with the stubble of a day-old beard showing eloquently how his peace of mind and the routine of his habits had been shattered. As he shook hands with us, he made an obvious attempt to recover something of his ease of manner.

'I trust that you had a pleasant night's rest,' he ventured, as he led the way across the station to his automobile.

'Much pleasanter than you had, I fear,' replied Madelyn.

The Senator sighed. 'As a matter of fact, I found sleep hopeless; I spent most of the night with my cigar. The suggestion of meeting your train came as a really welcome relief.'

As we stepped into the waiting motor, a leather-lunged newsboy thrust a bundle of heavy-typed papers into our faces. The Senator whirled with a curt dismissal on his tongue when Madelyn thrust a coin towards the lad and swept a handful of flapping papers into her lap.

'There is absolutely nothing new in the case, Miss Mack, I assure you,' the Senator said impatiently. 'The reporters have pestered me like so many leeches. The sight of a headline makes me shiver.'

Madelyn bent over her papers without comment. As I settled into the seat by her side, however, and the machine whirled around the corner, I saw that she was not even making a pretence of reading. I watched her with a frown as she turned the gates. There was no question of her interest, but it was not the type that held her attention. I doubted if she was perusing a line of the closely-set columns. It was not until she reached the last paper that I solved the mystery. It was the illustrations that she was studying!

When she finished the heap of papers, she began slowly and even more thoughtfully to go through them again. Now I saw that she was pondering the various photographs of Senator Duffield's family that the newspapers had published. I turned away from her bent form and tapping finger, but there was a magnetism in her abstraction that forced my eyes back to her in spite of myself. As my gaze returned to her, she thrust her gloved hand into the recesses of her bag and drew out her black morocco note-book. From its pages she selected the four newspaper pictures of the murdered secretary that she had offered me the night before. With a twinkle of satisfaction, she grouped them about a large, black-bordered picture which stared up at her from the printed page in her lap.

Our ride to the Duffield gate was not a long one. In fact I was so absorbed by my furtive study of Madelyn Mack that I was startled when the chauffeur slackened his speed, and I realized from a straightening of the Senator's bent shoulders that we were nearing our destination.

At the edge of the driveway, a quietly dressed man in a grey suit, who was strolling carelessly back and forth from the gate to the house, eyed us curiously as we passed, and touched his hat to the Senator. I knew at once he was a detective. (Trust a newspaper woman to 'spot' a plain clothes man, even if he has left his police uniform at home!) Madelyn did not look up and the Senator made no comment.

As we stepped from the machine, a tall girl with severe, almost classical features and a profusion of nut-brown hair which fell away from her forehead without even the suggestion of a ripple, was awaiting us.

'My daughter, Maria,' Senator Duffield announced formally.

Madelyn stepped forward with extended hand. It was evident that Miss Duffield had intended only a brief nod. For an instant she hesitated, with a barely perceptible flush. Then her fingers dropped limply into Madelyn Mack's palm. (I chuckled inwardly at the ill grace with which she did it!)

'This must be a most trying occasion for you,' Madelyn said with a note of sympathy in her voice, which made me stare. Effusiveness of any kind was so foreign to her nature that I frowned as we followed our host into the wide front drawing-room. As we entered by one door, a black-gowned, white-haired woman, evidently Mrs Duffield, entered by the opposite door.

In spite of the reserve of the society leader, whose sway might be said to extend to three cities, she darted an appealing glance at Madelyn Mack that melted much of the newspaper cynicism with which I was prepared to greet her. Madelyn crossed the room to her side and spoke a low sentence, that I did not catch, as she took her hand. I found myself again wondering at her unwonted friendliness. She was obviously exerting herself to gain the good will of the Duffield household. Why?

A trim maid, who stared at us as though we were museum freaks, conducted us to our rooms – adjoining apartments at the front of the third floor. The identity of Madelyn Mack had already been noised through the house and I caught a saucer-eyed glance from a second servant as we passed down the corridor. If the atmosphere of suppressed curiosity was embarrassing my companion, however, she gave no sign of the fact. Indeed, we had hardly time to remove our hats when the breakfast gong rang.

The family was assembling in the old-fashioned dining-room when we entered. In addition to the members of the domestic circle whom I have already indicated, my attention was at once caught by two figures who entered just before us. One was a young woman whom it did not need a second glance to tell me was Beth Duffield. Her white face and swollen eyes were evidence enough of her over-wrought condition, and I caught myself speculating why she had left her room.

Her companion was a tall, slender young fellow with just the faintest trace of a stoop in his shoulders. As he turned toward us, I saw a handsome, though self-indulgent face, to a close observer suggesting evidences of more dissipation than was good for its owner. And, if the newspaper stories of the doings of Fletcher Duffield were true, the facial index was a true one. If I remember rightly, Senator Duffield's son more than once had made prim old Boston town rub her spectacled eyes at the tales of his escapades!

Fletcher Duffield bowed rather abstractedly as he was presented to us, but during the eggs and chops he brightened visibly, and put several curious questions to Madelyn as to her methods of work, which enlivened what otherwise would have been a rather dull half hour.

As the strokes of nine rang through the room, my companion pushed her chair back.

'What time is the coroner's inquest, Senator?'

Mr Duffield raised his eyebrows at the change in her attitude. 'It is scheduled for eleven o'clock.'

'And when do you expect Inspector Taylor of head-quarters?'

'In the course of an hour, I should say, perhaps less. His man, Martin, has been here since yesterday afternoon – you probably saw him as we drove into the yard. I can telephone Mr Taylor, if you wish to see him sooner.'

'That will hardly be necessary, thank you.'

Madelyn walked across to the window. For a moment she stood peering out on to the lawn. Then she stooped, and her hand fumbled with the catch. The window swung open with the noiselessness of well-oiled hinges, and she stepped out on to the veranda, without so much as a glance at the group about the table.

I think the Senator and I rose from our chairs at the same instant. When we reached the window, Madelyn was half across the lawn. Perhaps twenty yards ahead of her, towered a huge maple, rustling in the early morning breeze.

I realized that this was the spot where Raymond Rennick had met his death.

In spite of his nervousness, Senator Duffield did not forget his old-fashioned courtliness, which I believe had become second nature to him. Stepping aside with a slight bow, he held the window open for me, following at my shoulder. As we reached the lawn, I saw that the scene of the murder was in plain view from at least one of the principal rooms of the Duffield home.

Madelyn was leaning against the maple when we reached her. Senator Duffield said gravely, as he pointed to the gnarled trunk, 'You are standing just at the point where the woman waited, Miss Mack.'

'Woman?'

'I refer to the assassin,' the Senator rejoined a trifle impatiently. 'Judging by our fragmentary clues, she must have been hidden behind the trunk when poor Rennick appeared on the driveway. We found her slipper somewhat to the left of the tree – a matter of eight or ten feet, I should say.'

'Oh!' said Madelyn listlessly. I fancied that she was somewhat annoyed that we had followed her.

'An odd clue, that slipper,' the Senator continued with

33

an obvious attempt to maintain the conversation. 'If we were disposed to be fanciful, it might suggest the childhood legend of Cinderella.'

Madelyn did not answer. She stood leaning back against the tree with her eyes wandering about the yard. Once I saw her gaze flash down the driveway to the open gate, where the detective, Martin, stood watching us furtively.

'Nora,' she said, without turning, 'will you kindly walk six steps to your right?'

I knew better than to ask the reason for the request. With a shrug, I faced towards the house, and came to a pause at the end of the stipulated distance.

'Is Miss Noraker standing where Mr Rennick's body was found, Senator?'

'She will strike the exact spot, I think, if she takes two steps more.'

I had hardly obeyed the suggestion when I caught the swift rustle of skirts behind me. I whirled to see Madelyn's lithe form darting toward me with her right hand raised as though it held a weapon.

'Good!' she cried. 'I call you to witness, Senator, that I was fully six feet away when she turned! Now I want you to take Miss Noraker's place. The instant you hear me behind you – the *instant*, mind you – I want you to let me know.'

She walked back to the tree as the Senator reluctantly changed places with me. I could almost picture the murderess dashing upon her victim as Madelyn bent forward. The Senator turned his back to us with a rather ludicrous air of bewilderment.

My erratic friend had covered perhaps half of the distance between her and our host when he spun about with a cry of discovery. She paused with a long breath.

'Thank you, Senator. What first attracted your attention to me?'

'The rustle of your dress, of course!'

Madelyn turned to me with the first smile of satisfaction I had seen since we entered the Duffield gate.

'Was the same true in your case, Nora?'

I nodded. 'The fact that you are a woman hopelessly betrayed you. If you had not been hampered by petti-coats –'

Madelyn broke in upon my sentence with that peculiar freedom which she always reserves to herself. 'There are two things I would like to ask of you, Senator, if I may.'

'I am at your disposal, I assure you.'

'I would like to borrow a Boston directory, and the services of a messenger.'

We walked slowly up the driveway, Madelyn again relapsing into her preoccupied silence and Senator Duffield making no effort to induce her to speak.

4

We had nearly reached the veranda when there was the sound of a motor at the gate, and a red touring car swept into the yard. An elderly, clean-shaven man, in a long frock coat and a broad-brimmed felt hat, was sharing the front seat with the chauffeur. He sprang to the ground with extended hand as our host stepped forward to greet him. The two exchanged half a dozen low sentences at the side of the machine, and then Senator Duffield raised his voice as they approached us.

'Miss Mack, allow me to introduce my colleague, Senator Burroughs.'

'I have heard of you, of course, Miss Mack,' the Senator said genially, raising his broad-brimmed hat with a flourish. 'I am very glad, indeed, that you are able to give us the benefit of your experience in this, er – unfortunate affair. I presume that it is too early to ask if you have developed a theory?'

'I wonder if you would allow me to reverse the question?' Madelyn responded as she took his hand.

'I fear that my detective ability would hardly be of much service to you, eh, Duffield?'

Our host smiled faintly as he turned to repeat to a servant Madelyn's request for a directory and a messenger. Senator Burroughs folded his arms as his chauffeur circled on toward the garage. There was an odd suggestion of nervousness in the whole group. Or was it fancy?

'Have you ever given particular study to the legal angle in your cases, Miss Mack?' The question came from Senator Burroughs as we ascended the steps.

'The legal angle? I am afraid I don't grasp your meaning.'

The Senator's hand moved mechanically toward his cigar case. 'I am a lawyer, and perhaps I argue unduly from a lawyer's viewpoint. We always work from the question of motive, Miss Mack. A professional detective, I believe – or at least, the average professional detective – tries to find the criminal first and establish his motive afterward.'

'Now, in a case such as this, Senator –'

'In a case such as this, Miss Mack, the trained legal mind would delve first for the motive in Mr Rennick's assassination.'

'And your legal mind, Senator, I presume, has delved for the motive. Has it found it?'

The Senator turned his unlighted cigar reflectively between his lips. 'I have not found it! Eliminating the field of sordid passion and insanity, I divide the motives of the murderer under three heads – robbery, jealousy, and revenge. In the present case, I eliminate the first possibility at the outset. There remain then only the two latter.'

'You are interesting. You forget, however, a fourth

motive – the strongest spur to crime in the human mind!'

Senator Burroughs took his cigar from his mouth.

'I mean the motive of – fear!' Madelyn said abruptly, as she swept into the house. When I followed her, Senator Burroughs had walked over to the railing and stood staring down at the ground below. He had tossed his cigar away.

In the rooms where we had breakfasted, one of the stable boys stood awkwardly awaiting Madelyn Mack's orders, while John Dorrence, the valet, was just laying a city directory on the table.

'Nora,' she said, as she turned to the boy, 'will you kindly look up the list of packing houses?'

'Pick out the largest and give me the address,' she continued, as I ran my finger through the closely typed pages. With a growing curiosity, I selected a firm whose prestige was advertised in heavy letters. Madelyn's fountain pen scratched a dozen lines across a sheet of her note-book, and she thrust it into an envelope and extended it to the stable lad.

As the youth backed from the room, Senator Duffield appeared at the window.

'I presume it will be possible for me to see Mr Rennick's body, Senator?' Madelyn Mack asked.

Our host bowed.

'Also, I would like to look at his clothes – the suit he was wearing at the time of his death, I mean – and, when I am through, I want twenty or thirty minutes alone in his room. If Mr Taylor should arrive before I am through, will you kindly let me know?'

'I can assure you, Miss Mack, that the police have been through Mr Rennick's apartment with a microscope.'

'Then there can be no objection to my going through it with mine! By the way, Mr Rennick's glasses – the pair that was found under his body – were packed with his clothes, were they not?'

'Certainly,' the Senator responded.

I did not accompany Madelyn into the darkened room where the corpse of the murdered man was reposing. To my surprise, she rejoined me in less than five minutes.

'What did you find?' I queried as we ascended the stairs.

'A five-inch cut just above the sixth rib.'

'That is what the newspapers said.'

'You are mistaken. They said a three-inch cut. Have you ever tried to plunge a dagger through five inches of human flesh?'

'Certainly not.'

'I have.'

Accustomed as I was to Madelyn Mack's eccentricities, I stood stock still and stared into her face.

'Oh, I'm not a murderess! I refer to my dissecting room experiences.'

We had reached the upper hall when there was a quick movement at my shoulder, and I saw my companion's hand dart behind my waist. Before I could quite grasp the situation, she had caught my right arm in a grip of steel. For an instant I thought she was trying to force me back down the stairs. Then the force of her hold wrung a low cry of pain from my lips. She released me with a rueful apology.

'Forgive me, Nora! For a woman, I pride myself that I have a strong wrist!'

'Yes, I think you have!'

'Perhaps now you can appreciate what I mean when I say that even I haven't strength enough to inflict the wound that killed Raymond Rennick!'

'Then we must be dealing with an Amazon.'

'Would Cinderella's missing slipper fit an Amazon?' she answered drily.

As she finished her sentence, we paused before a closed door which I rightly surmised led into the room of the murdered secretary. Madelyn's hand was on the knob when there was a step behind us, and Senator Duffield joined us with a rough bundle in his hands.

'Mr Rennick's clothes,' he explained. Madelyn nodded.

'Inspector Taylor left them in my care to hold until the inquest.'

Madelyn flung the door open without comment and led the way inside. Slipping the string from the bundle, she emptied the contents out on to the counterpane of the bed. They comprised the usual warm weather outfit of a well-dressed man, who evidently avoided the extremes of fashion, and she deftly sorted the articles into small, neat piles. She glanced up with an expression of impatience.

'I thought you said they were here, Mr Duffield!'

'What?'

'Mr Rennick's glasses! Where are they?'

Senator Duffield fumbled in his pocket. 'I beg your pardon, Miss Mack. I had overlooked them,' he apologized, as he produced a thin paper parcel.

Madelyn carried it to the window and carefully unwrapped it.

'You will find the spectacles rather badly damaged, I fear. One lens is completely ruined.'

Madelyn placed the broken glasses on the sill, and raised the blind to its full height. Then she dropped to her knees and whipped out her microscope. When she arose, her small, black-clad figure was tense with suppressed excitement.

A fat oak chiffonier stood in the corner nearest her. Crossing to its side, she rummaged among the articles that littered its surface, opened and closed the top drawer, and stepped back with an expression of annoyance. A writing table was the next point of her search, with results which I judged to be equally fruitless. She glanced uncertainly from the bed to the three chairs, the only other articles of furniture that the room contained. Then her eyes lighted again as they rested on the broad, carved mantel that spanned the empty fireplace.

It held the usual collection of bric-a-brac of a bachelor's room. At the end farthest from us, however, there was a narrow, red case, of which I caught only an indistinct view when Madelyn's hand closed over it.

She whirled toward us. 'I must ask you to leave me alone now, please!'

The Senator flushed at the peremptory command. I stepped into the hall and he followed me, with a shrug. He was closing the door when Madelyn raised her voice. 'If Inspector Taylor is below, kindly send him up at once!'

'And what about the inquest, Miss Mack?'

'There will be no inquest – today!'

Senator Duffield led the way down-stairs without a word. In the hall below, a ruddy-faced man, with grey hair, a thin grey beard and moustache, and a grey suit – suggesting any army officer in civilian clothes – was awaiting us. I could readily imagine that Inspector Taylor was something of a disciplinarian in the Boston police department. Also, relying on Madelyn Mack's estimate, he was one of the three shrewdest detectives on the American continent.

Senator Duffield hurried toward him with a suggestion of relief. 'Miss Mack is up-stairs, Inspector, and requested me to send you to her the moment you arrived.'

'Is she in Mr Rennick's room?'

The Senator nodded. The Inspector hesitated as though about to ask another question and then, as though thinking better of it, bowed and turned to the stairs.

Inspector Taylor was one of those few policemen who had the honour of being numbered among Madelyn Mack's personal friends, and I fancied that he welcomed the news of her arrival.

Fletcher Duffield was chatting somewhat aimlessly with Senator Burroughs as we sauntered out into the yard again. None of the ladies of the family were visible. The plain clothes man was still lounging disconsolately in the vicinity of the gate. There was a sense of unrest in the scene, a vague expectancy. Although no one voiced the suggestion, we might all have been waiting to catch the first clap of distant thunder.

As Senator Duffield joined the men, I wandered across to the dining-room window. I fancied the room was deserted, but I was mistaken. As I faced about toward the driveway, a low voice caught my ear from behind the curtains.

'You are Miss Mack's friend, are you not? No, don't turn around, please!'

But I had already faced toward the open door. At my elbow was a white-capped maid – with her face almost as white as her cap – whom I remembered to have seen at breakfast.

'Yes, I am Miss Mack's friend. What can I do for you?'

'I have a message for her. Will you see that she gets it?'

'Certainly.'

'Tell her that I was at the door of Senator Duffield's library the night before the murder.'

My face must have expressed my bewilderment. For an instant I fancied the girl was about to run from the room. I stepped through the window and put my arm about her shoulders. She smiled faintly.

'I don't know much about the law, and evidence, and that sort of thing – and I am afraid! You will take care of me, won't you?'

'Of course, I will, Anna. Your name is Anna, isn't it?'

The girl was rapidly recovering her self-possession. 'I thought you ought to know what happened Tuesday night. I was passing the door of the library – it was fairly late, about ten o'clock, I think – when I heard a man's voice inside the room. It was a loud, angry voice like that of a person in a quarrel. Then I heard a second voice, lower and much calmer.'

'Did you recognize the speakers?'

'They were Mr Rennick and Senator Duffield!'

I caught my breath. 'You said one of them was angry. Which was it?'

'Oh, it was the Senator! He was very much excited and worked up. Mr Rennick seemed to be speaking very low.'

'What were they saying, Anna?' I tried to make my tones careless and indifferent, but they trembled in spite of myself.

'I couldn't catch what Mr Rennick said. The Senator was saying some dreadful things. I remember he cried, "You swindlers!" And then a bit later "I have evidence that should put you and your thieving crew behind the bars!" I think that is all. I was too bewildered to –'

A stir on the lawn interrupted the sentence. Madelyn Mack and Inspector Taylor had appeared. At the sound of their voices, the girl broke from my arm and darted toward the door.

Through the window, I heard the Inspector's heavy tones, as he announced curtly, 'I am telephoning the coroner, Senator, that we are not ready for the inquest today. We must postpone it until tomorrow.'

5

The balance of the day passed without incident. In fact, I found the subdued quiet of the Duffield home becoming irksome as evening fell. I saw little of Madelyn Mack. She disappeared shortly after luncheon behind the door of her room, and I did not see her again until the dressing bell rang for dinner. Senator Duffield left for the city with Mr Burroughs at noon, and his car did not bring him back until dark. The women of the family remained in their apartments during the entire day, nor could I wonder at the fact. A morbid crowd of curious sight-seers was massed about the gates almost constantly, and it was necessary to send a call for two additional policemen to keep them back. In spite of the vigilance, frequent groups of newspaper men managed to slip into the grounds, and, after half a dozen experiences in frantically dodging a battery of cameras, I decided to stick to the shelter of the house.

It was with a feeling of distinct relief that I heard the door of Madelyn's room open and her voice calling to me to enter. I found her stretched on a lounge before the window, with a mass of pillows under her head.

'Been asleep?' I asked.

'No – to tell the truth, I've been too busy.'

'What? In this room!'

'This is the first time I've been here since noon!'

'Then where –'

'Nora, don't ask questions!'

I turned away with a shrug that brought a laugh from the lounge. Madelyn rose and shook out her skirts. I sat watching her as she walked across to the mirror and stood patting the great golden masses of her hair.

A low tap on the door interrupted her. Dorrence, the valet, stood outside as she opened it, extending an envelope. Madelyn fumbled it as she walked back. She let the envelope flutter to the floor and I saw that it contained only a blank sheet of paper. She thrust it into her pocket without explanation.

'How would you like a long motor ride, Nora?'

'For business or pleasure?'

'Pleasure! The day's work is finished! I don't know whether you agree with me or not, but I am strongly of the opinion that a whirl out under the elms of Cambridge, and then on to Concord and Lexington would be delightful in the moonlight. What do you say?'

The clock was hovering on the verge of midnight and the household had retired when we returned. Madelyn was in singularly cheery spirits. The low refrain which she was humming as the car swung into the grounds – 'Schubert's Serenade', I think it was – ceased only when we stepped on to the veranda, and realized that we were entering the house of the dead.

I turned off my lights in silence, and glanced undecidedly from the bed to the rocker by the window. The cool night breeze beckoned me to the latter, and I drew the chair back a pace and cuddled down among the cushions. The lawn was almost silver under the flood of the moonlight, recalling vaguely the sweep of the ocean on a mid-summer night. Back and forth along the edge of the gate the figure of a man was pacing like a tired sentinel. It was the plain-clothes officer from headquarters. His figure suggested a state of siege. We might have been surrounded by a skulking enemy. Or was the enemy within, and the sentinel stationed to prevent his escape? I stumbled across to the bed and to sleep, with the question echoing oddly through my brain.

When I opened my eyes, the sun was throwing a yellow shaft of light across my bed, but it wasn't the sun that had awakened me. Madelyn was standing in the doorway, dressed, with an expression on her face which brought me to my elbow.

'What has happened now?'

'Burglars!'

'Burglars?' I repeated dully.

'I am going down to the library. Some one is making news for us fast, Nora! When will it be our turn?'

I dressed in record-breaking time, with my curiosity whetted by sounds of suppressed excitement which forced their way into the upper hall. The Duffield home not only was early astir, but was rudely jarred out of its customary routine.

When I descended, I found a nervous group of servants clustered about the door of the library. They stood aside to let me pass, with attitudes of uneasiness which I surmised would mean a wholesale series of 'notices' if the strange events in the usually well regulated household continued.

Behind the closed door of the library were Senator Duffield, his son, Fletcher, and Madelyn Mack. It was easy to appreciate at a glance the unusual condition of the room. At the right, one of the long windows, partly raised, showed the small, round hole of a diamond cutter just over the latch. It was obvious where the clandestine entrance and exit had been obtained. The most noticeable feature of the apartment, however, was a small, square safe in the corner, with its heavy lid swinging awkwardly ajar, and the rug below littered with a heap of papers, that had evidently been torn from its neatly tabulated series of drawers. The burglarious hands either had been very angry or very much in a hurry. Even a number of unsealed envelopes had been ripped across, as though the pillager had been too impatient to extract their contents in the ordinary manner. To a man of Senator Duffield's methodical habits, it was easy to imagine that the scene had been a severe wrench.

Madelyn was speaking in her quick, incisive tones as I entered.

'Are you quite sure of that fact, Senator?' she asked sharply, as I closed the door and joined the trio.

'Quite sure, Miss Mack!'

'Then nothing is missing, absolutely nothing?'

'Not a single article, valuable or otherwise!'

'I presume then there were articles of more or less value in the safe?'

'There was perhaps four hundred dollars in loose bills in my private cash drawer, and, so far as I know, there is not a dollar gone.'

'How about your papers and memoranda?'

The Senator shook his head.

'There was nothing of the slightest use to a stranger. As a matter of fact, just two days ago, I took pains to destroy the only portfolio of valuable documents in the safe.'

Madelyn stooped thoughtfully over the litter of papers on the rug. 'You mean three evenings ago, don't you?'

'How on earth, Miss Mack –'

'You refer to the memoranda that you and Mr Rennick were working on the night before his death, do you not?'

'Of course!' And then I saw Senator Duffield was staring at his curt questioner as though he had said something he hadn't meant to.

'I think you told me once before that the combination of your safe was known only to yourself and Mr Rennick?'

'You are correct.'

'Then, to your knowledge, you are the only living person who possesses this information at the present time?'

'That is the case. It was a rather intricate combination, and we changed it hardly a month ago.'

Madelyn rose from the safe, glanced reflectively at a huge leather chair, and sank into its depths with a sigh.

'You say nothing has been stolen, Senator, that the burglar's visit yielded him nothing. For your peace of mind, I would like to agree with you, but I am sorry to inform you that you are mistaken.'

'Surely, Miss Mack, you are hasty! I am confident that I have searched my possessions with the utmost care.'

'Nevertheless, you have been robbed!'

Senator Duffield glanced down at her small, lithe figure impatiently. 'Then, perhaps, you will be good enough to tell me of what my loss consists?'

'I refer to the article for which your secretary was murdered! It was stolen from this room last night.'

Had the point of a dagger pressed against Senator Duffield's shoulders, he could not have bounded forward in greater consternation. His composure was shattered like a pane of glass crumbling.

He sprang toward the safe with a cry like a man in sudden fear or agony. Jerking back its door, he plunged his hand into its lower left compartment. When he straightened, he held a long, wax phonograph record.

His dismay had vanished in a quick blending of relief and anger, as his eyes swept from the cylinder to the grave figure of Madelyn Mack.

'I fail to appreciate your joke, Miss Mack – if you call it a joke to frighten a man without cause as you have me!'

'Have you examined the record in your hand, Senator?'

Fletcher Duffield and I stared at the two. There was a suggestion of tragedy in the scene as the impatience and irritation gradually faded from the Senator's face.

'It is a substitute!' he groaned. 'A substitute! I have been tricked, victimized, robbed!'

He stood staring at the wax record as though it were a heated iron burning into his flesh. Suddenly it slipped from his fingers and was shattered on the floor.

But he did not appear to notice the fact as he burst out, 'Do you realize that you are standing here inactive while the thief is escaping? I don't know how your wit surprised my secret, and don't care now, but you are throwing away your chances of stopping the burglar while he may be putting miles between himself and us! Are you made of ice, woman? Can't you appreciate what this means? In the name of heaven, Miss Mack –'

'The thief will not escape, Mr Duffield!'

'It seems to me that he has already escaped.'

'Let me assure you, Senator, that your missing property is as secure as though it were locked in your safe at this moment!'

'But do you realize that, once a hint of its nature is known, it will be almost worthless to me?'

'Better perhaps than you do – so well that I pledge myself to return it to your hands within the next half hour!'

Senator Duffield took three steps forwards until he stood so close to Madelyn that he could have reached over and touched her on the shoulder.

'I am an old man, Miss Mack, and the last two days have brought me almost to a collapse. If I have appeared unduly sharp, I tender you my apologies – but do not give me false hopes! Tell me frankly that you cannot encourage me. It will be a kindness. You will realize that I cannot blame you.'

Senator Duffield's imperious attitude was so broken that I could hardly believe it possible that the same man who ruled a great political party, almost by the swaying of his finger, was speaking. Madelyn caught his hand with a grasp of assurance.

'I will promise even more.' She snapped open her watch. 'If you will return to this room at nine o'clock, not only will I restore your stolen property – but I will deliver the murderer of Raymond Rennick!'

'Rennick's murderer?' the Senator gasped.

Madelyn bowed. 'In this room at nine o'clock.'

I think I was the first to move toward the door. Fletcher Duffield hesitated a moment, staring at Madelyn; then he turned and hurried past me down the hall.

His father followed more slowly. As he closed the door, I saw Madelyn standing where we had left her, leaning back against her chair, and staring at a woman's black slipper. It was the one which had been found by Raymond Rennick's dead body.

I made my way mechanically toward the dining-room, and was surprised to find that the members of the

Duffield family were already at the table. With the exception of Madelyn, it was the same breakfast group as the morning before. In another house, this attempt to maintain the conventions in the face of tragedy might have seemed incongruous; but it was so thoroughly in keeping with the self-contained Duffield character that, after the first shock, I realized it was not at all surprising. I fancy that we all breathed a sigh of relief, however, when the meal was over.

We were rising from the table, when a folded note, addressed to the Senator, was handed to the butler from the hall. He glanced through it hurriedly, and held up his hand for us to wait.

'This is from Miss Mack. She requests me to have all of the members of the family, and those servants who have furnished any evidence in connection with the, er – murder' – the Senator winced as he spoke the word – 'to assemble in the library at nine o'clock. I think that we owe it both to ourselves and to her to obey her instructions to the letter. Perkins, will you kindly notify the servants?'

As it happened, Madelyn's audience in the library was increased by two spectators she had not named. The tooting of a motor sounded without, and the tall figure of Senator Burroughs met us as we were leaving the dining-room. Senator Duffield took his arm with a glance of relief, and explained the situation as he forced him to accompany us.

6

In the library, we found for the first time that Madelyn was not alone. Engaged in a low conversation with her, which ceased as we entered, was Inspector Taylor. He had evidently been designated as the spokesman of the occasion.

'Is everybody here?' he asked.

'I think so,' Senator Duffield replied. 'There are really only five of the servants who count in the case.'

Madelyn's eyes flashed over the circle. 'Close the door, please, Mr Taylor. I think you had better lock it also.'

'There are fourteen persons in this room,' she continued, 'counting, of course, Inspector Taylor, Miss Noraker and myself. We may safely be said to be outside the case. There are then eleven persons here connected in some degree with the tragedy. It is in this list of eleven that I have searched for the murderer. I am happy to tell you that my search has been successful!'

Senator Duffield was the first to speak. 'You mean to say, Miss Mack, that the murderer is in this room at the present time?'

'Correct.'

'Then you accuse one of this group –'

'Of dealing the blow which killed your secretary, and, later, of plundering your safe.'

Inspector Taylor moved quietly to a post between the two windows. Escape from the room was barred. I darted a stealthy glance around the circle in an effort to surprise a trace of guilt in the faces before me, and was startled to find my neighbours engaged in the same furtive occupation. Of the women of the family, the Senator's wife had compressed her lips as though, as the mistress of the house, she felt the need of maintaining her composure in any situation, Maria was toying with her bracelet, while Beth made no effort to conceal her agitation.

Senator Burroughs was studying the pattern of the carpet with a face as inscrutable as a mask. Fletcher Duffield was sitting back in his chair, his hands in his pockets. His father was leaning against the locked door, his eyes flashing from face to face. With the exception of Dorrence, the valet, and Perkins, the butler, who I do not think would have been stirred out of their stolidness had the ceiling fallen, the servants were in an utter panic. Two of the maids were plainly bordering on hysterics.

Such was the group that faced Madelyn in the Duffield library. One of the number was a murderer, whom the next ten minutes were to brand as such. Which was it? Instinctively my eyes turned again toward the three women of the Duffield family, as Madelyn walked across to a portiere which screened a corner of the apartment.

Jerking it aside, she showed, suspended from a hook in the ceiling, a quarter of fresh veal.

On an adjoining stand was a long, thin-bladed knife, which might have been a dagger, ground to a razor-edge. Madelyn held it before her as she turned to us.

'This is the weapon which killed Mr Rennick.'

I fancied I heard a gasp as she spoke. Although I whirled almost on the instant, however, I could detect no signs of it in the faces behind me.

'I propose to conduct a short experiment, which I assure you is absolutely necessary to my chain of reasoning,' Madelyn continued. 'You may or may not know that the body of a calf practically offers the same degree of resistance to a knife as the body of a man. Dead flesh, of course, is harder and firmer than living flesh, but I think that, adding the thickness of clothes, we may take it for granted that in the quarter of veal before us, we have a fair substitute for the body of Raymond Rennick. Now watch me closely, please!'

Drawing back her arm, she plunged her knife into the meat with a force which sent it spinning on its hook. She drew the knife out, and examined it reflectively.

'I have made a cut of only a little more than three and a half inches. The blow which killed Mr Rennick penetrated at least five inches.

'Here we encounter a singularly striking feature of our case, involving a stratagem which I think I can safely say is the most unique in my experience. To all intents, it was a woman who killed Mr Rennick. In fact, it has been taken for granted that he met his death at the hand of a female assassin. We must dispose of this conclusion at the outset, for the simple reason that it was physically impossible for a woman to have dealt the death blow!'

I chanced to be gazing directly at Fletcher Duffield as Madelyn made the statement. An expression of such relief flashed into his face that instinctively I turned about and followed the direction of his glance. His eyes were fixed on his sister, Beth.

Madelyn deposited the knife on the stand.

'Indeed, I may say there are few men – perhaps not one in ten – with a wrist strong enough to have dealt Mr Rennick's death blow,' she went on. 'There is only one such person among the fourteen in this room at the present time.

'Again you will recall that the wound was delivered from the rear just as Mr Rennick faced about in his own defense. Had he been attacked by a woman, he would have heard the rustle of her dress several feet before she possibly could have reached him. I think you will recall my demonstration of that fact yesterday morning, Mr Duffield.

'Obviously then, it is a man whom we must seek if we would find the murderer of your secretary, and a man of certain peculiar characteristics. Two of these I can name now. He possessed a wrist developed to an extraordinary degree, and he owned feet as small and shapely as a woman's. Otherwise, the stratagem of wearing a woman's slippers and leaving one of them near the scene of the crime to divert suspicion from himself, would never have occurred to him!'

Again I thought I heard a gasp behind me, but its owner escaped me a second time.

'There was a third marked feature among the physical characteristics of the murderer. He was near-sighted – so much so that it was necessary for him to wear glasses of the kind known technically as a "double lens". Unfortunately for the assassin, when his victim fell, the latter caught the glasses in his hand and they were broken under his body. The murderer may have been thrown into a panic, and feared to take the time to recover his spectacles; but it was a fatal blunder. Fortune, however, might have helped him even then in spite of this fact, for those who found the body fell into the natural error of considering the glasses to be the property of the murdered man. Had it not been for two minor details, this impression might never have been contradicted.'

Madelyn held up a packet of newspaper illustrations. Several of them I recognized as the pictures of the murdered secretary that she had shown me at the 'Roanoke'. The others were also photographs of the same man.

'If Mr Rennick hadn't been fond of having his picture taken, the fact that he never wore glasses on the street might not have been noticed. None of his pictures, not even the snapshots, showed a man in spectacles. It is true that he did possess a pair, and it is here where those who discovered the crime went astray. But they were for reading purposes only, the kind termed a ·125 lens, while those of his assailant were a ·210 lens. To clinch the matter, I later found Mr Rennick's own spectacles in his room where he had left them the evening before.'

Madelyn held up the red leather case she had found on the mantel-piece, and tapped it musingly as she gave a slight nod to Inspector Taylor.

'We have now the following description of the murderer – a slenderly built man, with an unusual wrist, possibly an athlete at one time, who possesses a foot capable of squeezing into a woman's shoe, and who is handicapped by near-sightedness. Is there an individual in this room to whom this description applies?'

There was a new glitter in Madelyn's eyes as she continued.

'Through the co-operation of Inspector Taylor, I am

enabled to answer this question. Mr Taylor has traced the glasses of the assassin to the optician who gave the prescription for them. I am not surprised to find that the owner of the spectacles tallies with the owner of these other interesting articles.'

With the words, she whisked from the stand at her elbow, the long, narrow-bladed dagger, and a pair of soiled, black suede slippers.

There was a suggestion of grotesque unreality about it all. It was much as though I had been viewing the denouement of a play from the snug vantage point of an orchestra seat, waiting for the lights to flare up and the curtain to ring down. A shriek ran through my ears, jarring me back to the realization that I was not a spectator, but a part, of the play.

A figure darted toward the window. It was John Dorrence, the valet.

The next instant Inspector Taylor threw himself on the fleeing man's shoulders, and the two went to the floor.

'Can you manage him?' Madelyn called.

'Unless he prefers cold steel through his body to cold steel about his wrists,' was the rejoinder.

'I think you may dismiss the other servants, Senator,' Madelyn said. 'I wish, however, that the family would remain a few moments.'

As the door closed again, she continued, 'I promised you also, Senator, the return of your stolen property. I have the honour to make that promise good.'

From her stand, which was rapidly assuming the proportions of a conjurer's table, she produced a round, brown paper parcel.

'Before I unwrap this, have I your permission to explain its contents?'

'As you will, Miss Mack.'

'Perhaps the most puzzling feature of the tragedy is the motive. It is this parcel which supplies us with the answer.

'Your secretary, Mr Duffield, was an exceptional young man. Not only did he repeatedly resist bribery such as comes to few men, but he gave his life for his trust.

'At any time since this parcel came into his possession, he could have sold it for a fortune. Because he refused to sell it, he was murdered for it. Perhaps every reader of the newspapers is more or less familiar with Senator Duffield's investigations of the ravages of a certain great Trust. A few days ago, the Senator came into possession of evidence against the combine of such a drastic nature that he realized it would mean nothing less than the annihilation of the monopoly, imprisonment for the chief officers, and a business sensation such as this country has seldom known.

'Once the officers of the Trust knew of his evidence, however, they would be fore-armed in such a manner that its value would be largely destroyed. The evidence was a remarkable piece of detective work. It consisted of a phonographic record of a secret directors' meeting, laying bare the inmost depredations of the corporation.'

Madelyn paused as the handcuffed valet showed signs of a renewed struggle. Inspector Taylor without comment calmly snapped a second pair of bracelets about his feet.

'The Trust was shrewd enough to appreciate the value of a spy in the Duffield home. Dorrence was engaged for the post, and from what I have learned of his character, he filled it admirably. How he stumbled on Senator Duffield's latest *coup* is immaterial. The main point is that he tried to bribe Mr Rennick so persistently to betray his post that the latter threatened to expose him. Partly in the fear that he would carry out his threat, and partly in the hope that he carried memoranda which might lead to the discovery of the evidence that he sought, Dorrence planned and carried out the murder.

'In the secretary's pocket he discovered the combination of the safe, and made use of it last night. I found the stolen phonograph record this morning behind the register of the furnace pipe in Dorrence's room. I had already found that this was his cache, containing the dagger which killed Rennick, and the second of Cinderella's slippers. The pair was stolen some days ago from the room of Miss Beth Duffield.'

*

The swirl of the day was finally over. Dorrence had been led to his cell; the coroner's jury had returned its verdict; and all that was mortal of Raymond Rennick had been laid in its last resting place.

Madelyn and I had settled ourselves in the homeward bound Pullman as it rumbled out of the Boston station in the early dusk.

'There are two questions I want to ask,' I said reflectively.

Madelyn looked up from her newspaper with a yawn.

'Why did John Dorrence bring you back a blank sheet of paper when you dispatched him on your errand?'

'As a matter of fact, there was nothing else for him to bring back. Mr Taylor kept him at police headquarters long enough to give me time to carry my search through his room. The message was a blind.'

'And what was the quarrel that the servant girl, Anna, heard in the Duffield library?'

'It wasn't a quarrel, my dear girl. It was the Senator preparing the speech with which he intended to launch his evidence against the Trust. The Senator is in the habit of dictating his speeches to a phonograph. Some of them, I am afraid, are rather fiery.'

The Nameless Man

Rodriguez Ottolengui

Mr Barnes was sitting in his private room, with nothing of special importance to occupy his thoughts, when his office boy announced a visitor.

'What name?' asked Mr Barnes.

'None!' was the reply.

'You mean,' said the detective, 'that the man did not give you his name. He must have one, of course. Show him in.'

A minute later the stranger entered, and, bowing courteously, began the conversation at once.

'Mr Barnes, the famous detective, I believe?' said he.

'My name is Barnes,' replied the detective. 'May I have the pleasure of knowing yours?'

'I sincerely hope so,' continued the stranger. 'The fact is, I suppose I have forgotten it.'

'Forgotten your name?' Mr Barnes scented an interesting case, and became doubly attentive.

'Yes!' said the visitor. 'That is precisely my singular predicament. I seem to have lost my identity. That is the object of my call. I wish to discover who I am. As I am evidently a full-grown man, I can certainly claim that I have a past history, but to me that past is entirely a blank. I awoke this morning in this condition, yet apparently in possession of all my faculties, so much so that I at once saw the advisability of consulting a first-class detective, and, upon inquiry, I was directed to you.'

'Your case is most interesting, from my point of view, I mean. To you, of course, it must seem unfortunate. Yet it is not unparalleled. There have been many such cases recorded, and, for your temporary relief, I may say that sooner or later, complete restoration of memory usually occurs. But now, let us try to unravel your mystery as soon as possible, that you may suffer as little inconvenience as there need be. I would like to ask you a few questions.'

'As many as you like, and I will do my best to answer.'

'Do you think that you are a New Yorker?'

'I have not the least idea, whether I am or not.'

'You say you were advised to consult me. By whom?'

'The clerk at the Waldorf Hotel, where I slept last night.'

'Then, of course, he gave you my address. Did you find it necessary to ask him how to find my offices?'

'Well, no, I did not. That seems strange, does it not? I certainly had no difficulty in coming here. I suppose that must be a significant fact, Mr Barnes?'

'It tends to show that you have been familiar with New York, but we must still find out whether you live here or not. How did you register at the hotel?'

'M. J. G. Remington, City.'

'You are sure that Remington is not your name?'

'Quite sure. After breakfast this morning I was passing through the lobby when the clerk called me twice by that name. Finally, one of the hall-boys touched me on the shoulder and explained that I was wanted at the desk. I was very much confused to find myself called "Mr Remington", a name which certainly is not my own. Before I fully realized my position, I said to the clerk, "Why do you call me Remington?" and he replied, "Because you registered under that name." I tried to pass it off, but I am sure that the clerk looks upon me as a suspicious character.'

'What baggage have you with you at the hotel?'

'None. Not even a satchel.'

'May there not be something in your pockets that would help us; letters, for example?'

'I am sorry to say that I have made a search in that direction but found nothing. Luckily I did have a pocket-book though.'

'Much money in it?'

'In the neighbourhood of five hundred dollars.'

Mr Barnes turned to his table and made a few notes on a pad of paper. While he was so engaged his visitor took out a fine gold watch, and after a glance at the face, was about to return it to his pocket when Mr Barnes wheeled around in his chair, and said:

'That is a handsome watch you have there. Of a curious pattern too. I am rather interested in old watches.'

The stranger seemed confused for an instant, and quickly put up his watch, saying:

'There is nothing remarkable about it. Merely an old family relic. I value it more for that than anything else. But about my case, Mr Barnes, how long do you think it will take to restore my identity to me? It is rather awkward to go about under a false name.'

'I should think so,' said the detective. 'I will do my best for you, but you have given me absolutely no clue to work upon, so that it is impossible to say what my success will be. Still I think forty-eight hours should suffice. At least in that time I ought to make some discoveries for you. Suppose you call again on the day after tomorrow at noon precisely. Will that suit you?'

'Very well, indeed. If you can tell me who I am at that time I shall be more than convinced that you are a great detective, as I have been told.'

He arose and prepared to go, and upon the instant Mr Barnes touched a button under his table with his foot, which caused a bell to ring in a distant part of the building, no sound of which penetrated the private office. Thus anyone could visit Mr Barnes in his den, and might leave unsuspicious of the fact that a spy would be awaiting him out in the street who would shadow him persistently day and night until recalled by his chief. After giving the signal, Mr Barnes held his strange visitor in conversation a few moments longer to allow his spy opportunity to get to his post.

'How will you pass the time away, Mr Remington?' said he. 'We may as well call you by that name, until I find your true one.'

'Yes, I suppose so. As to what I shall do during the next forty-eight hours, why, I think I may as well devote myself to seeing the sights. It is a remarkably pleasant day for a stroll, and I think I will visit your beautiful Central Park.'

'A capital idea. By all means, I would advise occupation of that kind. It would be best not to do any business until your memory is restored to you.'

'Business. Why, of course, I can do no business.'

'No! If you were to order any goods, for example, under the name of Remington, later on when you resume your proper identity, you might be arrested as an impostor.'

'By George, I had not thought of that. My position is more serious than I had realized. I thank you for the warning. Sight-seeing will assuredly be my safest plan for the next two days.'

'I think so. Call at the time agreed upon, and hope for the best. If I should need you before then, I will send to your hotel.'

Then, saying 'Good morning', Mr Barnes turned to his desk again, and, as the stranger looked at him before stepping out of the room, the detective seemed engrossed with some papers before him. Yet scarcely had the door closed upon the retreating form of his recent visitor, when Mr Barnes looked up, with an air of expectancy. A moment later a very tiny bell in a drawer of his desk rang, indicating that the man had left the building, the signal having been sent to him by one of his employés, whose business it was to watch all departures, and notify his chief. A few moments later Mr Barnes himself emerged, clad in an entirely different suit of clothing, and with such an alteration in the colour of his hair, that more than a casual glance would have been required to recognize him.

When he reached the street the stranger was nowhere in sight, but Mr Barnes went to a doorway opposite, and there he found, written in blue pencil, the word 'up', whereupon he walked rapidly up town as far as the next corner, where once more he examined a doorpost, upon which he found the word 'right', which indicated the way the men ahead of him had turned. Beyond this he could expect no signals, for the spy shadowing the stranger did not know positively that his chief would take part in the game. The two signals which he had written on the doors were merely a part of a routine, and intended to aid Mr Barnes should he follow; but if he did so, he would be expected to be in sight of the spy by the time the second signal were reached. And so it proved in this instance, for as Mr Barnes turned the corner to the right, he easily discerned his man about two blocks ahead, and presently was near enough to see 'Remington' also.

The pursuit continued until Mr Barnes was surprised to see him enter the Park, thus carrying out his intention as stated in his interview with the detective. Entering at the Fifth Avenue gate he made his way towards the menagerie, and here a curious incident occurred. The stranger had mingled with the crowd in the monkey-house, and was enjoying the antics of the mischievous little animals, when Mr Barnes, getting close

behind him, deftly removed a pocket-handkerchief from
the tail of his coat and swiftly transferred it to his own.

On the day following, shortly before noon, Mr Barnes
walked quickly into the reading-room of the Fifth
Avenue Hotel. In one corner there is a handsome mahogany cabinet, containing three compartments, each of
which is entered through double doors, having glass
panels in the upper half. About these panels are draped
yellow silk curtains, and in the centre of each appears a
white porcelain numeral. These compartments are used
as public telephone stations, the applicant being shut in,
so as to be free from the noise of the outer room.

Mr Barnes spoke to the girl in charge, and then
passed into the compartment numbered '2'. Less than
five minutes later Mr Leroy Mitchel came into the
reading-room. His keen eyes peered about him, scanning
the countenances of those busy with the papers or writing, and then he gave the telephone girl a number, and
went into the compartment numbered '1'. About ten
minutes elapsed before Mr Mitchel came out again, and,
having paid the toll, he left the hotel. When Mr Barnes
emerged, there was an expression of extreme satisfaction upon his face. Without lingering, he also went out.
But instead of following Mr Mitchel through the main
lobby to Broadway, he crossed the reading-room and
reached 23rd Street through the side door. Thence he
proceeded to the station of the Elevated Railroad, and
went up town. Twenty minutes later he was ringing
the bell of Mr Mitchel's residence. The buttons, who
answered his summons, informed him that his master
was not at home.

'He usually comes in to luncheon, however, does he
not?' asked the detective.

'Yes, sir,' responded the boy.

'Is Mrs Mitchel at home?'

'No, sir.'

'Miss Rose?'

'Yes, sir.'

'Ah! Then I'll wait. Take my card to her.'

Mr Barnes passed into the luxurious drawing-room, and was soon joined by Rose, Mr Mitchel's adopted daughter.

'I am sorry papa is not at home, Mr Barnes,' said the little lady, 'but he will surely be in to luncheon, if you will wait.'

'Yes, thank you, I think I will. It is quite a trip up, and, being here, I may as well stop awhile and see your father, though the matter is not of any great importance.'

'Some interesting case, Mr Barnes? If so, do tell me about it. You know I am almost as much interested in your cases as papa is.'

'Yes, I know you are, and my vanity is flattered. But I am sorry to say I have nothing on hand at present worth relating. My errand is a very simple one. Your father was saying, a few days ago, that he was thinking of buying a bicycle, and yesterday, by accident, I came across a machine of an entirely new make, which seems to me superior to anything yet produced. I thought he might be interested to see it, before deciding what kind to buy.'

'I am afraid you are too late, Mr Barnes. Papa has bought a bicycle already.'

'Indeed! What style did he choose?'

'I really do not know, but it is down in the lower hall, if you care to look at it.'

'It is hardly worth while, Miss Rose. After all, I have no interest in the new model, and if your father has found something that he likes, I won't even mention the other to him. It might only make him regret his bargain. Still, on second thoughts, I will go down with you, if you will take me, into the dining-room and show me the head of that moose which your father had been bragging about killing. I believe it has come back from the taxidermist's?'

'Oh, yes! He is just a monster. Come on!'

They went down to the dining-room, and Mr Barnes expressed great admiration about the moose's head, and praised Mr Mitchel's skill as a marksman. But he had taken a moment to scrutinize the bicycle which stood in the hall-way, while Rose was opening the blinds in the dining-room. Then they returned to the drawing-room, and after a little more conversation Mr Barnes departed, saying that he could not wait any longer, but he charged Rose to tell her father that he particularly desired him to call at noon on the following day.

Promptly at the time appointed, Remington walked into the office of Mr Barnes, and was announced. The detective was in his private room. Mr Leroy Mitchel had been admitted but a few moments before.

'Ask Mr Remington in,' said Mr Barnes to his boy, and when that gentleman entered, before he could show surprise to find a third party present, the detective said:

'Mr Mitchel, this is the gentleman whom I wish you to meet. Permit me to introduce to you, Mr Mortimer J. Goldie, better known to the sporting fraternity as G. J. Mortimer, the champion short-distance bicycle rider, who recently rode a mile in the phenomenal time of 1.56, on a quarter-mile track.'

As Mr Barnes spoke, he gazed from one to the other of his companions, with a half-quizzical, and wholly pleased expression on his face. Mr Mitchel appeared much interested, but the newcomer was evidently greatly astonished. He looked blankly at Mr Barnes a moment, then dropped into a chair with the query:

'How in the name of conscience did you find that out?'

'That much was not very difficult,' replied the detective. 'I can tell you more; indeed I can supply your whole past history, provided your memory has been sufficiently restored for you to recognize my facts as true.'

Mr Barnes looked at Mr Mitchel and winked one eye

in a most suggestive manner, at which that gentleman burst out into hearty laughter, finally saying:

'We may as well admit that we are beaten, Goldie. Mr Barnes has been too much for us.'

'But I want to know how he has done it,' persisted Mr Goldie.

'I have no doubt that Mr Barnes will gratify you. Indeed, I am as curious as you are to know by what means he has arrived at his quick solution of the problem which we set him.'

'I will enlighten you as to detective methods with pleasure,' said Mr Barnes. 'Let me begin with the visit made to me by this gentleman two days ago. At the very outset his statement aroused my suspicion, though I did my best not to let him think so. He announced to me that he had lost his identity, and I promptly told him that his case was not uncommon. I said that, in order that he might feel sure that I did not doubt his tale. But truly his case, if he were telling the truth, was absolutely unique. Men have lost recollection of their past, and even have forgotten their names. But I have never before heard of a man who had forgotten his name, *and at the same time knew that he had done so.*'

'A capital point, Mr Barnes,' said Mr Mitchel. 'You were certainly shrewd to suspect fraud so early.'

'Well, I cannot say that I suspected fraud so soon, but the story was so unlikely, that I could not believe it immediately. I therefore was what I might call analytically attentive during the rest of the interview. The next point worth noting which came out was that although he had forgotten himself, he had not forgotten New York, for he admitted having come to me without special guidance.'

'I remember that,' interrupted Mr Goldie, 'and I think I even said to you at the time that it was significant.'

'And I told you that it at least showed that you had

been familiar with New York. This was better proven
when you said that you would spend the day at Central
Park, and when, after leaving here, you had no difficulty to find your way thither.'

'Do you mean to say that you had me followed? I
made sure that no one was after me.'

'Well, yes, you were followed,' said Mr Barnes, with a
smile. 'I had a spy after you, and I followed you as far
as the Park myself. But let me come to the other points
in your interview and my deductions. You told me that
you had registered as "M. J. G. Remington". This helped
me considerably, as we shall see presently. A few minutes
later you took out your watch, and in that little mirror
over my desk, which I use occasionally when I turn my
back upon a visitor, I noted that there was an inscription
on the outside of the case. I turned and asked you something about the watch, when you hastily returned it to
your pocket, with the remark that it was "an old family
relic". Now can you explain how you could have known
that, supposing that you had forgotten who you were?'

'Neatly caught, Goldie,' laughed Mr Mitchel. 'You
certainly made a mess of it there.'

'It was an asinine slip,' said Mr Goldie, laughing also.

'Now then,' continued Mr Barnes, 'you readily see that
I had good reason for believing that you had not forgotten your name. On the contrary, I was positive that
your name was a part of the inscription on the watch.
What, then, could be your purpose in pretending otherwise? I did not discover that for some time. However, I
decided to go ahead, and find you out if I could. Next I
noted two things. Your coat opened once, so that I saw,
pinned to your vest, a bicycle badge, which I recognized
as the emblem of the League of American Wheelmen.'

'Oh! Oh!' cried Mr Mitchel. 'Shame on you, Goldie,
for a blunderer.'

'I had entirely forgotten the badge,' said Mr Goldie.

'I also observed,' the detective went on, 'little indentations on the sole of your shoe, as you had your legs crossed, which satisfied me that you were a rider even before I observed the badge. Now, then, we come to the name, and the significance thereof. Had you really lost your memory, the choosing of a name when you registered at the hotel, would have been a haphazard matter of no importance to me. But as soon as I decided that you were imposing upon me, I knew that your choice of a name had been a deliberate act of the mind; one from which deductions could be drawn.'

'Ah! Now we come to the interesting part,' said Mr Mitchel. 'I love to follow a detective when he uses his brains.'

'The name as registered, and I examined the registry myself to make sure, was odd. Three initials are unusual. A man without memory, and therefore not quite sound mentally, would hardly have chosen so many. Then why had it been done in this instance? What more natural than that these initials represented the true name? In assuming an alias, it is the most common method to transpose the real name in some way. At least it was a working hypothesis. Then the last name might be very significant. "Remington". The Remingtons make guns, sewing-machines, typewriters, and bicycles. Now, this man was a bicycle rider, I was sure. If he chose his own initials as a part of the alias, it was possible that he selected "Remington" because it was familiar to him. I even imagined that he might be an agent for Remington bicycles, and I had arrived at that point during our interview, when I advised him not to buy anything until his identity was restored. But I was sure of my quarry, when I stole a handkerchief from him at the park, and found the initials "M.J.G." upon the same.'

'Marked linen on your person!' exclaimed Mr Mitchel. 'Worse and worse! We'll never make a successful criminal of you, Goldie.'

'Perhaps not! I shan't cry over it.'

'I felt sure of my success by this time,' continued Mr Barnes, 'yet at the very next step I was baulked. I looked over a list of L.A.W. members and could not find a name to fit my initials, which shows, as you will see presently, that, as I may say, "too many clues spoil the broth." Without the handkerchief I would have done better. Next I secured a catalogue of the Remingtons, which gave a list of their authorized agents, and again I failed. Returning to my office I received information from my spy, sent in by messenger, which promised to open a way for me. He had followed you about, Mr Goldie, and I must say you played your part very well, so far as avoiding acquaintances is concerned. But at last you went to a public telephone, and called up someone. My man saw the importance of discovering to whom you had spoken, and bribed the telephone attendant to give him the information. All that he learned, however, was that you had spoken to the public station at the Fifth Avenue Hotel. My spy thought that this was inconsequent, but it proved to me at once that there was collusion, and that your man must have been at the other station by previous appointment. As that was at noon, a few minutes before the same hour on the following day, that is to say, yesterday, I went to the Fifth Avenue Hotel telephone and secreted myself in the middle compartment, hoping to hear what your partner might say to you. I failed in this, as the boxes are too well made to permit sound to pass from one to the other; but imagine my gratification to see Mr Mitchel himself go into the box.'

'And why?' asked Mr Mitchel.

'Why, as soon as I saw you, I comprehended the whole scheme. It was you who had concocted the little diversion to test my ability. Thus, at last, I understood the reason for the pretended loss of identity. With the knowledge that you were in it, I was more than ever determined to get at the facts. Knowing that you were out, I hastened to your house, hoping for a chat with little Miss Rose, as the most likely member of your family to get information from.'

'Oh, fie! Mr Barnes,' said Mr Mitchel, 'to play upon the innocence of childhood! I am ashamed of you!'

'All's fair, etc. Well, I succeeded. I found Mr Goldie's bicycle in your hall-way, and, as I suspected, 'twas a Remington. I took the number and hurried down to the agency, where I readily discovered that wheel number 5,086 is ridden by G. J. Mortimer, one of their regular racing team. I also learned that Mortimer's private name is Mortimer J. Goldie. I was much pleased at this, because it showed how good my reasoning had been about the alias, for you observe that the racing name is merely a transposition of the family name. The watch, of course, is a prize, and the inscription would have proved that you were imposing upon me, Mr Goldie, had you permitted me to see it.'

'Of course. That was why I put it back in my pocket.'

'I said just now,' said Mr Barnes, 'that without the stolen handkerchief I would have done better. Having it, when I looked over the L.A.W. list I went through the "G's" only. Without it I should have looked through the "G's", "J's", and "M's", not knowing how the letters may have been transposed. In that case I should have found "G. J. Mortimer", and the initials would have proved that I was on the right track.'

'You have done well, Mr Barnes,' said Mr Mitchel. 'I asked Goldie to play the part of a nameless man for a few days, to have some fun with you. But you have had fun with us, it seems. Though, I am conceited enough to say, that had it been possible for me to play the principal part, you would not have pierced my identity so soon.'

'Oh! I don't know,' said Mr Barnes. 'We are both of us a little egotistical, I fear.'

'Undoubtedly. Still, if I ever set another trap for you, I will assign myself the chief role.'

'Nothing would please me better,' said Mr Barnes. 'But,

gentlemen, as you have lost in this little game, it seems to me that some one owes me a dinner, at least!'

'I'll stand the expense with pleasure,' said Mr Mitchel.

'Not at all,' interrupted Mr Goldie. 'It was through my blundering that we lost, and I'll pay the piper.'

'Settle it between you,' cried Mr Barnes. 'But let us walk on. I am getting hungry.'

Whereupon they adjourned to Delmonico's.

3

The Montezuma Emerald

Rodriguez Ottolengui

'Is the Inspector in?'

Mr Barnes immediately recognized the voice, and turned to greet the speaker. The man was Mr Leroy Mitchel's English valet. Contrary to all precedent and tradition, he did not speak in cockney dialect, not even stumbling over the proper distribution of the letter 'h' throughout his vocabulary. That he was English, however, was apparent to the ear, because of a certain rather attractive accent, peculiar to his native island, and to the eye because of a deferential politeness of manner, too seldom observed in American servants. He also always called Mr Barnes 'Inspector', oblivious of the fact that he was not a member of the regular police, and mindful only of the English application of the word to detectives.

'Step right in, Williams,' said Mr Barnes. 'What is the trouble?'

'I don't rightly know, Inspector,' said Williams. 'Won't you let me speak to you alone? It's about the master.'

'Certainly. Come into my private room.' He led the way and Williams followed, remaining standing, although Mr Barnes waved his hand toward a chair, as he seated himself in his usual place at his desk. 'Now then,' continued the detective; 'what's wrong? Nothing serious, I hope?'

'I hope not, sir, indeed! But the master's disappeared!'

'Disappeared, has he!' Mr Barnes smiled slightly. 'Now,

Williams, what do you mean by that? You did not see him vanish, eh?'

'No, sir, of course not. If you'll excuse my presumption, Inspector, I don't think this is a joke, sir, and you're laughing.'

'All right, Williams,' answered Mr Barnes, assuming a more serious tone. 'I will give your tale my sober consideration. Proceed!'

'Well, I hardly know where to begin, Inspector. But I'll just give you the facts, without any unnecessary opinions of my own.'

Williams rather prided himself upon his ability to tell what he called 'a straight story'. He placed his hat on a chair, and, standing behind it, with one foot resting on a rung, checked off the points of his narrative, as he made them, by tapping the palm of one hand with the index finger of the other.

'To begin then,' said he. 'Mrs Mitchel and Miss Rose sailed for England, Wednesday morning of last week. That same night, quite unexpected, the master says to me, says he, "Williams, I think you have a young woman you're sweet on down at Newport?" "Well, sir," says I, "I do know a person as answers that description," though I must say to you, Inspector, that how he ever came to know it beats me. But that's aside, and digression is not my habit. "Well, Williams," the master went on, "I shan't need you for the rest of this week, and if you'd like to take a trip to the sea-shore, I shan't mind standing the expense, and letting you go." Of course, I thanked him very much, and I went, promising to be back on Monday morning as directed. And I kept my word, Inspector; though it was a hard wrench to leave the young person last Sunday in time to catch the boat; the moon being bright and everything most propitious for a stroll, it being her Sunday off and all that. But as I said, I kept my word, and was up to the house Monday morning only a little after seven, the boat having got in at six. I was a little surprised to find the master was not at home, but then it struck me as how he must have gone out of town over Sunday, and I looked for him to be in for dinner. But he did not come to dinner, nor at all that night. Still, I did not worry about it. It was the master's privilege to stay away as long as he liked. Only I could not help thinking I might just as well have had that stroll in the moonlight, Sunday night. But when all Tuesday and Tuesday night went by, and no word from the master, I must confess that I got uneasy; and now here's Wednesday noon, and no news; so I just took the liberty to come down and ask your opinion in the matter, seeing as how you are a particular friend of the family, and an Inspector to boot.'

'Really, Williams,' said Mr Barnes, 'all I see in your story is that Mr Mitchel, contemplating a little trip off somewhere with friends, let you go away. He expected to be back by Monday, but, enjoying himself, has remained longer.'

'I hope that's all, sir, and I've tried to think so. But this morning I made a few investigations of my own, and I'm bound to say what I found don't fit that theory.'

'Ah! You have some more facts! What are they?'

'One of them is this cablegram that I found only this morning under a book on the table in the library.' He handed a blue paper to Mr Barnes, who took it and read the following, on a cable blank:

'Emerald. Danger. Await letter.'

For the first time during the interview, Mr Barnes's face assumed a really serious expression. He studied the dispatch silently for a full minute, and then, without raising his eyes, said:

'What else?'

'Well, Inspector, I don't know that this has anything to do with the affair, but the master had a curious sort of jacket, made of steel links, so tight and so closely put together, that I've often wondered what it was for. Once I made so bold as to ask him, and he said, said he: "Williams, if I had an enemy, it would be a good idea to wear that, because it would stop a bullet or a knife." Then he laughed, and went on, "Of course, I shan't need it for myself. I bought it when I was abroad once, merely as a curiosity." Now, Inspector, that jacket's disappeared also.'

'Are you quite sure?'

'I've looked from dining-room to garret for it. The master's derringer is missing, too. It's a mighty small affair. Could be held in the hand without being noticed, but it carries a nasty-looking ball.'

'Very well, Williams, there may be something in your story. I'll look into the matter at once. Meanwhile, go home, and stay there so that I may find you if I want you.'

'Yes, sir; I thank you for taking it up. It takes a load off my mind to know you're in charge, Inspector. If there's harm come to the master, I'm sure you'll track the party down. Good morning, sir!'

'Good morning, Williams.'

After the departure of Williams, the detective sat still for several minutes, lost in thought. He was weighing two ideas. He seemed still to hear the words which Mr Mitchel had uttered after his success in unravelling the mystery of Mr Goldie's lost identity. 'Next time I will assign myself the chief rôle,' or words to that effect, Mr Mitchel had said. Was this disappearance a new riddle for Mr Barnes to solve? If so, of course, he would undertake it, as a sort of challenge which his professional pride could not reject. On the other hand, the cable dispatch and the missing coat-of-mail might portend ominously. The detective felt that Mr Mitchel was somewhat in the position of the fabled boy who cried 'Wolf' so often, that when at last the wolf really appeared, no assistance was sent to him. Only Mr Barnes decided that he must chase the 'wolf', whether it be real or imaginary. He wished, though, that he knew which.

Ten minutes later he decided upon a course of action, and proceeded to a telegraph office, where he found that, as he had supposed, the dispatch had come from the Paris firm of jewellers from which Mr Mitchel had frequently bought gems. He sent a lengthy message to them, asking for an immediate reply.

While waiting for the answer, the detective was not inactive. He went direct to Mr Mitchel's house, and once more questioned the valet, from whom he obtained an accurate description of the clothes which his master must have worn, only one suit being absent. This fact alone, seemed significantly against the theory of a visit to friends out of town. Next, Mr Barnes interviewed the neighbours, none of whom remembered to have seen Mr Mitchel during the week. At the sixth house below, however, he learned something definite. Here he found Mr Mordaunt, a personal acquaintance, and member of one of Mr Mitchel's clubs. This gentleman stated that he had dined at the club with Mr Mitchel, on the previous Thursday, and had accompanied him home, in the neighbourhood of eleven o'clock, parting with him at the door of his own residence. Since then he had neither seen nor heard from him. This proved that Mr Mitchel was at home one day after Williams went to Newport.

Leaving the house, Mr Barnes called at the nearest telegraph office and asked whether a messenger summons had reached them during the week, from Mr Mitchel's house. The record slips showed that the last call had been received at twelve-thirty a.m. on Friday. A cab had been demanded, and was sent, reaching the house at one o'clock. At the stables, Mr Barnes questioned the cab-driver, and learned that Mr Mitchel alighted at Madison Square.

'But he got right into another cab,' added the driver. 'It was just a chance I seen him, 'cause he made as if he was goin' into the Fifth Avenoo; but luck was again him, for I'd scarcely gone two blocks back, when I had to get down to fix my harness, and while I was doin' that, who should I see but my fare go by in another cab.'

'You did not happen to know the driver of that vehicle?' suggested Mr Barnes.

'That's just what I did happen to know. He's always by the Square, along the curb by the Park. His name's Jerry. You'll find him easy enough, and he'll tell you where he took that fly bird.'

Mr Barnes went down town again, and did find Jerry, who remembered driving a man at the stated time, as far as the Imperial Hotel; but beyond that the detective learned nothing, for at the hotel no one knew Mr Mitchel, and none recollected his arrival early Friday morning.

From the fact that Mr Mitchel had changed cabs, and doubled on his track, Mr Barnes concluded that he was after all merely hiding away for the pleasure of baffling him, and he felt much relieved to divest the case of its alarming aspect. However, he was not long permitted to hold this opinion. At the telegraph office he found a cable dispatch awaiting him, which read as follows:

'Montezuma Emerald forwarded Mitchel tenth. Previous owner murdered London eleventh. Mexican suspected. Warned Mitchel.'

This assuredly looked very serious. Casting aside all thought of a practical joke, Mr Barnes now threw himself heart and soul into the task of finding Mitchel, dead or alive. From the telegraph office he hastened to the Custom House, where he learned that an emerald, the invoiced value of which was no less than twenty thousand dollars, had been delivered to Mr Mitchel in person, upon payment of the custom duties, at noon of the previous

Thursday. Mr Barnes, with this knowledge, thought he knew why Mr Mitchel had been careful to have a friend accompany him to his home on that night. But why had he gone out again? Perhaps he felt safer at a hotel than at home, and, having reached the Imperial, taking two cabs to mystify the villain who might be tracking him, he might have registered under an alias. What a fool he had been not to examine the registry, as he could certainly recognize Mr Mitchel's handwriting, though the name signed would of course be a false one.

Back, therefore, he hastened to the Imperial, where, however, his search for familiar chirography was fruitless. Then an idea occurred to him. Mr Mitchel was so shrewd that it would be unlikely that, meditating a disappearance to baffle the men on his track, he had registered at the hotel several days prior to his permanently stopping there. Turning the page over, Mr Barnes still failed to find what he sought, but a curious name caught his eye.

'Miguel Palma – City of Mexico.'

Could this be the London murderer? Was this the suspected Mexican? If so, here was a bold and therefore dangerous criminal who openly put up at one of the most prominent hostelries. Mr Barnes was turning this over in his mind, when a diminutive newsboy rushed into the corridor, shouting:

'Extra Sun! Extra Sun! All about the horrible murder. Extra!'

Mr Barnes purchased a paper and was stupefied at the headlines.

ROBERT LEROY MITCHEL DROWNED!
His Body Found Floating in the East River.
A DAGGER IN HIS BACK INDICATES
MURDER.

Mr Barnes rushed out of the hotel, and, quickly finding a cab, instructed the man to drive rapidly to the Morgue.

On the way, he read the details of the crime as recounted in the newspaper. From this he gathered that the body had been discovered early that morning by two boatmen, who towed it to shore and handed it over to the police. An examination at the Morgue had established the identity by letters found on the corpse and the initials marked on the clothing. Mr Barnes was sad at heart, and inwardly fretted because his friend had not asked his aid when in danger.

Jumping from the cab almost before it had fully stopped in front of the Morgue, he stumbled and nearly fell over a decrepit-looking beggar, upon whose breast was a printed card soliciting alms for the blind. Mr Barnes dropped a coin, a silver quarter, into his outstretched palm, and hurried into the building. As he did so he was jostled by a tall man who was coming out, and who seemed to have lost his temper, as he muttered an imprecation under his breath in Spanish. As the detective's keen ear noted the foreign tongue an idea occurred to him which made him turn and follow the stranger. When he reached the street again he received a double surprise. The stranger had already signalled the cab which Mr Barnes had but just left, and was entering it, so that he had only a moment in which to observe him. Then the door was slammed, and the driver whipped up his horses and drove rapidly away. At the same moment the blind beggar jumped up, and ran in the direction taken by the cab. Mr Barnes watched them till both cab and beggar disappeared around the next corner, and then he went into the building again, deeply thinking over the episode.

He found the Morgue-keeper, and was taken to the corpse. He recognized the clothing at once, both from the description given by Williams, and because he now remembered to have seen Mr Mitchel so dressed. It was evident that the body had been in the water for several days, and the marks of violence plainly pointed to mur-

der. Still sticking in the back was a curious dagger
of foreign make, the handle projecting between the
shoulders. The blow must have been a powerful stroke,
for the blade was so tightly wedged in the bones of the
spine that it resisted ordinary efforts to withdraw it.
Moreover, the condition of the head showed that a crime
had been committed, for the skull and face had been
beaten into a pulpy mass with some heavy instrument.
Mr Barnes turned away from the sickening sight to
examine the letters found upon the corpse. One of these
bore the Paris post-mark, and he was allowed to read it.
It was from the jewellers, and was the letter alluded to in
the warning cable. Its contents were:

'Dear Sir – As we have previously advised you, the Montezuma emerald was shipped to you on the tenth instant. On
the following day the man from whom we had bought it was
found dead in Dover Street, London, killed by a dagger-thrust
between the shoulders. The meagre accounts telegraphed to
the papers here, state that there is no clue to the assassin.
We were struck by the name, and remembered that the
deceased had urged us to buy the emerald, because, as he declared, he feared that a man had followed him from Mexico,
intending to murder him to get possession of it. Within an
hour of reading the newspaper story, a gentlemanly-looking
man, giving the name of Miguel Palma, entered our store,
and asked if we had purchased the Montezuma emerald. We
replied negatively, and he smiled and left. We notified the
police, but they have not yet been able to find this man. We
deemed it our duty to warn you, and did so by cable.'

The signature was that of the firm from which Mr
Barnes had received the cable in the morning. The plot
seemed plain enough now. After the fruitless murder of
the man in London, the Mexican had traced the emerald
to Mr Mitchel, and had followed it across the water. Had
he succeeded in obtaining it? Among the things found on
the corpse was an empty jewel-case, bearing the name of

the Paris firm. It seemed from this, that the gem had been stolen. But if so, this man, Miguel Palma, must be made to explain his knowledge of the affair.

Once more visiting the Imperial, Mr Barnes made inquiry, and was told that Mr Palma had left the hotel on the night of the previous Thursday, which was just a few hours before Mr Mitchel had undoubtedly reached there alive. Could it be that the man at the Morgue had been he? If so, why was he visiting that place to view the body of his victim? This was a problem over which Mr Barnes puzzled, as he was driven up to the residence of Mr Mitchel. Here he found Williams, and imparted to that faithful servant the news of his master's death, and then inquired the address of the family abroad, that he might notify them by cable, before they might read the bald statement in a newspaper.

'As they only sailed a week ago today,' said Williams, 'they're hardly more than due in London. I'll go up to the master's desk and get the address of his London bankers.'

As Williams turned to leave the room, he started back amazed at the sound of a bell.

'That's the master's bell, Inspector! Someone is in his room! Come with me!'

The two men bounded upstairs, two steps at a time, and Williams threw open the door of Mr Mitchel's boudoir, and then fell back against Mr Barnes, crying:

'The master himself!'

Mr Barnes looked over the man's shoulders, and could scarcely believe his eyes when he observed Mr Mitchel, alive and well, brushing his hair before a mirror.

'I've rung for you twice, Williams,' said Mr Mitchel, and then, seeing Mr Barnes, he added: 'Ah, Mr Barnes! You are very welcome. Come in. Why, what is the matter, man? You are as white as though you had seen a ghost.'

'Thank God you are safe,' fervently ejaculated the detective, going forward and grasping Mr Mitchel's hand. 'Here, read this, and you will understand.' He drew out the afternoon paper and handed it to him.

'Oh, that!' said Mr Mitchel carelessly. 'I've read that. Merely a sensational lie, worked off upon a guileless public. Not a word of truth in it, I assure you.'

'Of course not, since you are alive; but there is a mystery about this which is yet to be explained.'

'What? A mystery, and the great Mr Barnes has not solved it! I am surprised. I am, indeed. But then, you know, I told you after Goldie made a fizzle of our little joke that if I should choose to play the principal part you would not catch me. You see, I have beaten you this time. Confess. You thought that was my corpse which you gazed upon at the Morgue?'

'Well,' said Mr Barnes reluctantly, 'the identification certainly seemed complete, in spite of the condition of the face, which made recognition impossible.'

'Yes; I flatter myself the whole affair was artistic.'

'Do you mean that this whole thing is nothing but a joke? That you went so far as to invent cables and letters from Paris just for the trifling amusement of making a fool of me?'

Mr Barnes was evidently slightly angry, and Mr Mitchel, noting this fact, hastened to mollify him.

'No! No! It is not quite so bad as that,' he said. 'I must tell you the whole story, for there is yet important work to do, and you must help me. No, Williams, you need not go out. Your anxiety over my absence entitles you to a knowledge of the truth. A short time ago I heard that a very rare gem was in the market, no less a stone than the original Emerald which Cortez stole from the crown of Montezuma. The Emerald was offered in Paris, and I was notified at once by the dealer, and authorized the purchase by cable. A few days later I received a dispatch warning me that there was danger. I understood at once, for similar danger has lurked about other large stones which are now in my collection. The warning meant that I should not attempt to get the Emerald from the Custom House until further advices reached me, which would indicate the exact nature of the danger. Later, I received the letter which was found on the body now at the Morgue, and which I suppose you have read?'

Mr Barnes nodded assent.

'I readily located the man Palma at the Imperial, and from his openly using his name I knew that I had a dangerous adversary. Criminals who disdain aliases have brains, and use them. I kept away from the Custom House until I satisfied myself that I was being dogged by a veritable cut-throat, who, of course, was the tool hired by Palma to rob, perhaps to kill me. Thus acquainted with my adversaries, I was ready for the enterprise.'

'Why did you not solicit my assistance?' asked Mr Barnes.

'Partly because I wanted all the glory, and partly because I saw a chance to make you admit that I am still the champion detective baffler. I sent my wife and daughter to Europe that I might have time for my scheme. On the day after their departure I boldly went to the Custom House and obtained the Emerald. Of course I was dogged by the hireling, but I had arranged a plan which gave him no advantage over me. I had constructed a pair of goggles which looked like simple smoked glasses, but in one of these I had a little mirror so arranged that I could easily watch the man behind me, should he approach too near. However, I was sure that he would not attack me in a crowded thoroughfare, and I kept in crowds until time for dinner, when, by appointment, I met my neighbour Mordaunt, and remained in his company until I reached my own doorway late at night. Here he left me, and I stood on the stoop until he disappeared into his own house. Then I turned, and apparently had much trouble to place my latch-key in the lock. This offered the assassin the chance he had hoped for, and, gliding stealthily forward, he made a vicious stab at me. But, in the first place, I had put on a chain-armour vest, and, in the second, expecting the attack to occur just as it did, I turned swiftly and with one blow with a club I knocked the weapon from the fellow's hand, and with another I struck him over the head so that he fell senseless at my feet.'

'Bravo!' cried Mr Barnes. 'You have a cool nerve.'

'I don't know. I think I was very much excited at the crucial moment, but with my chain armour, a stout loaded club in one hand and a derringer in the other, I never was in any real danger. I took the man down to the wine cellar and locked him in one of the vaults. Then I called a cab, and went down to the Imperial, in search of Palma; but I was too late. He had vanished.'

'So I discovered,' interjected Mr Barnes.

'I could get nothing out of the fellow in the cellar. Either he cannot or he will not speak English. So I have merely kept him a prisoner, visiting him at midnight only, to avoid Williams, and giving him rations for another day. Meanwhile, I disguised myself and looked for Palma. I could not find him. I had another card, however, and the time came at last to play it. I deduced from Palma's leaving the hotel on the very day when I took the Emerald from the Custom House, that it was prearranged that his hireling should stick to me until he obtained the gem, and then meet him at some rendezvous, previously appointed. Hearing nothing during the past few days, he has perhaps thought that I left the city, and that his man was still upon my track. Meanwhile I was perfecting my grand *coup*. With the aid of a physician, who is a confidential friend, I obtained a corpse from one of the hospitals, a man about my size whose face was battered beyond recognition. We dressed him in my clothing, and fixed the dagger which I had taken from my would-be assassin so tightly in the backbone that it would not drop out. Then one night we took our dummy to the river and securely anchored it in the water. Last night I simply cut it loose and let it drift down the river.'

'You knew of course that it would be taken to the Morgue,' said Mr Barnes.

'Precisely. Then I dressed myself as a blind beggar, posted myself in front of the Morgue, and waited.'

'You were the beggar?' ejaculated the detective.

'Yes! I have your quarter, and shall prize it as a souvenir. Indeed, I made nearly four dollars during the day. Begging seems to be lucrative. After the newspapers got on the street with the account of my death, I looked for developments. Palma came in due time, and went in. I presume that he saw the dagger, which was placed there for his special benefit, as well as the empty jewel-case, and at once concluded that his man had stolen the gem, and meant to keep it for himself. Under these circumstances he would naturally be angry, and therefore less cautious, and more easily shadowed. Before he came out, you turned up and stupidly brought a cab, which allowed my man to get a start of me. However, I am a good runner, and he only rode as far as Third Avenue, and then took the Elevated Railroad, I easily followed him to his lair. Now I will explain what I wish you to do, if I may count on you?'

'Assuredly!'

'You must go into the street, and when I release the man in the cellar, you must track him. I will go to the other place, and we will see what happens when the men meet. We will both be there to see the fun.'

An hour later, Mr Barnes was skilfully dogging a

sneaking Mexican, who walked rapidly through one of the lowest streets on the East side, until finally he dodged into a blind alley, and before the detective could make sure which of the many doors had allowed him ingress, he had disappeared. A moment later a low whistle attracted his attention, and across in a doorway he saw a figure which beckoned to him. He went over and found Mr Mitchel.

'Palma is here. I have seen him. You see I was right. This is the place of appointment, and the cut-throat has come here straight. Hush! what was that?'

There was a shriek, followed by another, and then silence.

'Let us go up,' said Mr Barnes. 'Do you know which door?'

'Yes; follow me.'

Mr Mitchel started across, but just as they reached the door footsteps were heard rapidly descending the stairs. Both men stood aside and waited. A minute later a cloaked figure bounded out, only to be gripped instantly by those in hiding. It was Palma, and he fought like a demon, but the long, powerful arms of Mr Barnes encircled him, and, with a hug that would have made a bear envious, the scoundrel was soon subdued. Mr Barnes then manacled him, while Mr Mitchel ascended the stairs to see about the other man. He lay sprawling on the floor, face downward, stabbed in the heart.

4

Found Guilty

Josiah Flynt and Francis Walton

I

Among the grave misfortunes in the Under World is that of being in the right in a contest with the Powers That Rule. When a man adds to this misfortune the sheer folly of pressing his rights offensively, the gods have abandoned him. The gods had abandoned Howard Slifer even in the hour of his triumph; from the first his humiliation was a certainty; the precise time and manner of it only were left in doubt.

Howard Slifer was a gentleman of the Under World who allowed it to be generally known that any one who asked him for a fight would get it. A sensitive recognition of the claims of other people and an austere respect for them does not belong to the point of honour in the Under World; the point of honour in the Under World is for the most part concerned with a man's sensitive recognition of his own claims and his determination to have other people austerely respect them; and Howard Slifer was punctiliously honourable. He was possessed of considerable sums of ready money, kept with some trifling exceptions, in strong-boxes, the formula for opening which invariably included a drill and a bit of dynamite. The trifling exceptions were small matters of loose coin and broken rolls of banknotes which people of fortune, who had no previous acquaintance with Mr Slifer, stood and delivered to him 'at sight' and 'on demand', and by a solecism in their business habits asked no quittance or receipt. His physique was a patent of nobility in which all who stood might read a power to levy taxes and to assume possession of his personal estate wherever he might find it. He was of the build that led men to follow him with their eyes and to speculate upon the amount of 'punishment' he could take and could inflict, and while they speculated they respected him greatly – him and his man servant, and his maid servant, his ox and his ass, and everything that was his.

Captain Brigstock, of the — Precinct, was not a man; he was a deputy divinity, and respected nothing except the arch-deputies, his official superiors. Technically there were sharp limitations to his constitutional powers over mere mortals, but in practice technical distinctions so seldom obtruded themselves upon his notice that his sense of them was apt to become quite vague. What the precise occasion was of his entering Mr Slifer's domicile, nobody in the outer world ever plucked up courage to ask him. When Slifer was asked, he said that the captain had dropped in unofficially, on 'private business', and added no comment beyond a malign grin. There was an impression in the outer world that the captain made his visit expressly at a time when he knew Mr Slifer was not at home, and that Mr Slifer had returned unexpectedly; what was certain is that the captain made his exit from the Slifer domicile in unconventional haste, and that no mention of the incident was ever made in the public prints. He had reached the street from a second-storey window through which he had backed with such violence as to bring away the sash. This was the hour of the haughty Slifer's triumph, and the hour when the gods abandoned him.

Three weeks afterward there occurred a manifestation of *esprit de corps* among the Powers That Rule which it was not pleasant to contemplate. Patrolman Hooper, of Captain Brigstock's precinct, had been murdered overnight while on duty; and not only in Brigstock's precinct but throughout the city the force was of one mind. It was not only that if an officer on duty is not safe, not a man of them was safe; there was an element of insult and effrontery in an attack upon a patrolman that stirred something more in his associates than personal fear; it touched their corporate pride.

'Somebody's got to croak for this,' Detective Swinton declared sententiously to a group of his brother 'sleuths'. 'I don't care if Hooper was only a flatty. He was a copper, and we fly cops have got to send some bloke to the chair for blastin' him. There's a push o' guns in this town that thinks flatties don't count, that there won't be much of a kick when one of 'em's keeled over, an' they'll croak some of us fly cops before long if we don't learn 'em a lesson. It was a great bull somebody wasn't croaked for the killin' o' Patrolman Stimson two years ago. Stimson was a fool 'right enough to go up against the gang that did him, but if one of 'em had croaked for bastin' him, Hooper 'ud be alive now. I tell you guns are just like kids when it comes to learnin' 'em anything. If they see 't ye mean business they'll crawl, but if ye monkey with 'em, they'll t'row ye down. There's some that thinks that guns'll act on the level with coppers whether they got to or not. That's damn rot. 'Course there's some squarer than others, but I've known all kinds for twenty-five years, an' I give it to ye straight, they ain't built to like us. They got the same class feelin' 't we have, an' if we don't croak one of 'em for doin' Hooper they'll get so nervy that coppers'll be droppin' in their tracks every month. They got to be called down.'

The law for the Powers That Prey is that it is better ninety-nine guilty men should escape than that one innocent man should suffer; the law for the Powers That

Rule is that an example must be made. The Powers That Prey must suffer as a clan for an offense against the Powers That Rule. The clan must give up its offending member or must stand in terror and uncertainty of where precisely the hand of the force will strike. That it will strike somewhere there must not be the slightest doubt.

The orders of Captain Brigstock were laconic and smacked of his divine authority. He recognized no impossibility in the case; he spoke with the accent of omnipotence; he said simply: 'Find him; I don't want to hear a word about difficulties; damn the difficulties; I want him found.' There were for the moment but the slightest indications to go upon. Hooper must have been struck from behind, must have turned upon his assailant and in the scuffle lost his helmet. At least he had been stabbed twice in the back and had received a heavy downward blow in the temple, from which his helmet would have saved him. The mainspring of his watch had been broken and the hands marked five minutes past four – thus determining almost with exactness the moment when he was assaulted. His assailant had been hurt and could be traced by blood-stains to a sheltered doorway half a block distant, where he had seemingly bound up his wounds and changed his clothes. A hundred other details were reported, but for three days these remained, in spite of the command of deputed omnipotence, the only ones that were significant. Then came a statement that a short time before his death Patrolman Hooper had had a difficulty with Howard Slifer, and that high words had been exchanged.

It is said that Slifer attempted to break away when he found himself safe within the walls of the station-house in the — Precinct; he was, at all events, soundly clubbed before he was locked in his cell. The blows given were accurately measured according to his power for taking punishment. It may be doubted whether Captain Brigstock had been more thoroughly bruised when he measured his length in the street. It is, perhaps, a chance coincidence that the captain was present while Slifer was being taught the power of the law.

The evidence against the prisoner was worked up with systematic vigour. The negative evidence especially was significant: it could not be discovered that at the time Patrolman Hooper was struck down the prisoner was not near at hand. Patrolman Gundy, in a misguided moment, opined that almost at the precise time of the murder he had seen the prisoner enter a house a dozen blocks distant from the scene of the affair. The outburst of disapproval with which this statement was received made Patrolman Gundy uncertain first about the precise time, then about the precise man, and finally about whether or not he had seen any one. Patrolman Conard opined that at a quarter to five he had passed a man, who might be the prisoner, within a block of the scene of the affair. The captain asked him what in the name of things unprintable 'his glims were for', and told him pointblank that any one not an ass could say whether a man that he had passed was the prisoner or not; and Patrolman Conard became certain that he was not an ass, and certain that he had passed the prisoner, and not at all certain that the hour was a quarter to five or a quarter to four or to three. A safe had been blown open in the building immediately in front of which Patrolman Hooper's body was found, and the prisoner's method of collecting the living that the world owed him was well known. There were a number of other people who employed the same method, but that is a detail. The abandoned clothes were much too short in the arms and legs for the prisoner, and much too small to have been drawn on over a second suit; but clad in his underclothing only it was just possible he could squeeze into them; and the less perfectly they fitted him, the better the disguise. And at the time he was stripped and

examined in his cell he had so many recent wounds that
the only difficulty was to decide which of them his captors
had not given him.

The indictment before the grand jury was secured by
evidence which, as the newspaper said, was so 'over-
whelmingly convincing' that murder in the first degree
was the only charge permissible. The district attorney
publicly complimented the police on their handling of
the case, and declared that never before during his
activity as public prosecutor had he known of a murderer
who was not actually seen committing the crime being
brought to the bar of justice with proof of guilt so
thoroughly established and ably presented. In an interview with a representative of the press, he said: 'Captain
Brigstock's men have not only avenged the murder of
their brother officer, they have demonstrated afresh the
remarkable ability of the city's police force. It is no light
matter to protect a city as large as ours, which in the very
nature of things becomes a Mecca and Medina for criminals, and it is gratifying to know that our safety is looked
after by so conscientious a band of officers.'

The patrolmen ordered before the grand jury not only
distinctly remembered seeing Slifer in the near neighbourhood of the scene of the crime soon after it was committed, but they produced the weapon with which
Hooper had been struck down, and showed the jury
several rolls of bills, taken from Slifer's pockets, which
there was no doubt were part of the plunder he had
secured in the safe robbery. Free to indulge his imagination as to how the struggle between Hooper and Slifer
took place, the prosecuting attorney portrayed the villain
discovered by the virtuous Hooper in the act of blowing
open the safe, or in the act of endeavouring to escape, no
matter which. The intellectual and wholly impatient
jury, who had business of their own, which they were not
attending to, saw in their mind's eye the prosecuting

attorney's vivid picture, saw the villain Slifer blow open the safe, saw him make his escape, saw the devoted Hooper attempt to arrest him, saw the struggle, the blows, the gleam of the knife. Finally they saw in private, with eyes not of the mind, Slifer's mishandled body. To add force to these specific arguments, Slifer's record, both as 'peter-man' and convict, was produced, and he was declared to be one of the most desperate offenders in the country. There was nothing for the intellectual and wholly impatient jury to do but indict him, and he was bound over till the next term of court.

2

Francis Pirie and James Schell were two travellers of the Under World who had just returned from Europe to secure fresh letters of credit. They had made the fashionable grand tour of the Continent, had 'blown themselves' at the Monte Carlo 'crib', had seen wonderful things in forbidden Paris, and had come back to 'God's country' to attend to business until their bank accounts should permit of another trip abroad. Schell had suggested while they were in Paris that they recoup their fortunes on the spot and avoid the seasickness and miscellaneous locomotion, but Pirie's counsel had prevailed, and they arrived in 'God's country' about three weeks previous to the murder of Patrolman Hooper.

'There's dough on this side all right,' Pirie admitted in reply to Schell's suggestion that they establish themselves in the French capital, 'but it ain't our kind o' dough. I been rubberin' round pretty strong since I been on this side, an' I'm next to how the money market stands over here. You remember that fellow from Vienna 't I borrowed a hundred from in Rome, an' how he kept tellin' me to be sure an' return it by the time I said I would? Well, he shows up the whole business. He was a nice

enough bloke, an' had the rocks an' all that, but he ain't
the kind o' bloke that lets you an' me live an' take trips
abroad. When he figures up his accounts at the end o'
the year, everything must balance. He'll have a whole
string o' items jus' called "man ain't made o' wood", but
he knows where them contributions went. See? Well, it's
the same all over Europe; they all got to know where and
how their dough went, who got it, and what they got for
it. It 'ud kill 'em to figure up one o' the columns in their
account books, and have to write after it: "Gone, an'
damn me if I know where." They've got dough, but they
ain't got no dough to lose without makin' a hell of a beef
about it. See what they did with Bidwell when he made
that Bank o' England touch in the early seventies. Gave
him life! W'y, them Englishmen thinks money is somethin' sacred, holy, religious like. I gamble a thousand
that old bank could be touched up again for a million or
two, but they'd hang the bloke that done it. It's not like
that on the other side: ev'ry year there's just so much
dough lyin' around loose to be swiped, an' if it ain't
swiped it's put down in the profit column. It's the same
kind o' dough that's lookin' for circulation in poker
games. It wants to keep movin' an' changin' hands, an'
guns is there to give it rope. See? It's a kind o' Providence!'

'An' the coppers is there to make the guns trouble,' retorted Schell. 'It's all right about the loose dough, but
how about the loose fly cops? I'd rather take my chanst
with ten o' these Rube coppers here in Paris'n with one
o' the fly elbows in York.'

'Aw, everybody's a copper on this side,' urged Pirie.
'You remember that gun in Berlin tryin' to make a get-
away after he'd picked the Moll's pocket, an' how the
whole street sprinted after him? That's the way they do
things on this side – the crowd is in sympathy with the
copper an' not with the gun. In the States they give a

gun a runnin' chance, an' let the copper do the chasin'. That's what's what an' the way it ought to be.'

*

The morning of the day following the murder of Patrolman Hooper, two men were in earnest conversation in a gaudily furnished room in an up-town hotel. One lay on the bed with a bandage around his head; and from the blood-stains on the clothes it was evident that he was nursing a wound; the other sat at the bedside. The two were registered on the hotel's books as coming from Sydney, Australia, and had signed the names Richard Wamperson and Jackson Mather.

'You put his light out all right,' the man at the bedside remarked. 'They picked him up croaked.'

'Serves the duffer right,' mumbled the invalid. 'Anybody been copped out yet?'

'The "pipers" say – jes' listen to my furrin eddication! – that the police have pinched that Michigan bloke, Slifer. We done a bit with him in Cherry Hill eight years back – remember? The bloke 'at made old Brigstock take that quick sneak out of his flat one day. They're goin' to railroad him for fair. The *World* says the police found the weapon on him, an' the *Journal* claims 't he had some o' the bank's dough in his pockets.'

'Them newspapers is gettin' real wise. What a lot they do know. Seems like a gun can't do nothin' any more 'thout bein' pinched for somethin' else!'

This comment was certainly ungrateful, the invalid not having been pinched of late for anything. More than that, it was unintelligent: the invalid did not understand the arrangement of things which makes imaginative 'news' columns indispensable.

'I'd sooner be pinched for what I didn't do 'n what I done; it riles a bloke's sense o' justice to be accused false an' helps him put up a front,' declared the other. 'But you kicked in Payree about everybody bein' a copper in Europe an' a gun havin' no chance; what do you call the newspapers in this country but coppers?'

'Fly ones, ain't they! They ain't copped out you an' me; they're as dead as the stiffs in the Front Office!'

'They say Slifer got away with the full fifty thousand 'cause they only found a few rolls on him. They're smart, they are! They think he's made a plant somewheres.'

'Shows you how dead they are. They know about's much who copped that coin as Slifer does. 'Course the police 'a' got to put up a bluff an' 'r' glad to pinch anybody; but you'd think them papers might take a tumble to themselves once in a while.'

'Good job for us 't we wasn't mugged that time that old Freckleton got 'is glims on us. Three years ago, ain't it?'

'Longer'n that; an' besides old Freck's croaked. He's the only man on the force 't knew us.'

'Oh, I ain't leary, I ain't; but it's pie to take your constitutional without everybody rubberin'. Say, I guess I'll take a bit of a leg-loosener an' see 'bout bankin' that dough in London. That's where we need it in our business, an' the sooner we get it there the quicker. We want to mooch soon as you can stand for the ante!'

'A'right, but don't be long – I'm dead to the world up here alone. So-long!'

'So-long.'

*

The night of the beginning of the eighth week after the murder of Patrolman Hooper, Francis Pirie and James Schell were sitting 'at whisky' in a fashionable midnight resort on Sixth Avenue. Pirie should have been at home and in bed; almost any layman could have told him that he was gravely ill. He was a dime-novel spectre, and the flesh had drawn back on his bones till they began to stand out in sharp angles. The inference of an outsider would have been that he was another of the victims which the life in fashionable midnight resorts sometimes demands, but inferences made by outsiders show their wit and not their knowledge. The only person present who really knew what was what was James Schell, but he would not have admitted this even to Pirie. There was a look of disgust in his face while he watched the sick man reach feebly for his glass.

'It's wonder you wouldn't take a bracer. You've been belly-aching around these joints for the last two months, an' I'm gettin' tired o' lookin' at you! I want to mooch to the other side. Any one 'ud think that that copper had hit you with a baseball bat the way you play the baby act. He jus' gave you a love tap with his mace, that's all.'

'A couple o' love taps like that 'ud 'a' put out my light then and there,' Pirie answered wearily. 'I'm a sick man, Schell.'

'Sick nothin'. Why the devil don't you stay to home if you're sick? You been followin' me about for the last eight weeks like a cur pup. I never asked you to. Stay to home an' nurse yourself if you're so knocked up; I'm agreeable; I'm gettin' bally tired o' hearin' you whine. You don't need to be afraid o' me; I ain't goin' to knock against you; nobody'll ever find out from me 't you an' that flatty couldn't hit it off together; I can keep as dead about that as you can. An' I ain't goin' to do you out o' the dough either. You'll get all that's comin' to you when we get to London. It's banked there, an' half of it is yourn. But I give it to you straight, I'm goin' to give you the chilly mit if you don't stop doggin' me round to all these joints.'

'You give me the chilly mit?'

Pirie sat upright in his chair with an obvious effort. The hand of death was upon the man really, but he had his grit with him.

'That's what I said. You're all right when you want to be, but I won't stand for any more o' this shadowin' me about – see? What I think is, you're bughouse.'

Merely to acknowledge that he was sick was a confession which, in the circumstances, it had cost Pirie more than Schell realized to make; to sit at a table with a man whom he had looked upon as his pal and hear that he was 'bughouse' was a challenge which even his weakened state could not keep him from accepting.

'Take that, you duffer!' he hissed between his teeth, and threw his beer-glass with all his might at Schell's head.

The fight was over before the attendants could interfere. Schell tried to throw Pirie to the floor, and Pirie sent a bullet through his heart. His light went out without a flicker.

3

A man lay dying in the hospital ward of — Prison. Captain Brigstock of — Precinct sat beside his couch.

'Scheduled to croak all right – ain't I? Raise me up a bit, Cap. Thanks.'

'That's what they call it, Pirie.'

'Well, Cap, I might as well tell you now as later. You got the wrong bloke in that Hooper business. Slifer didn't do Hooper. Give me some more o' that dope there – quick – I – I – *am* – dyin'. Lord but it's a dirty job to die: an' me too – I die bad. That's why I'm tellin' you.'

The stimulant revived him for a moment.

'Say, Cap – me an' Schell – you listenin'? – put it on paper, blokey; I'm gettin' kind o' weak in me tubes; got the pencil there? – Me an' Schell, we croaked – gettin' it down? we croaked Hooper; me in front with a billy when his helmet dropped off, an' him behind with a knife. That stuff in the papers was rot. An' Schell, I put his light out, damn him: he tried to do me out o' the dough. That's why I'm here. See?'

His mind was wandering.

Brigstock's pencil paused and Brigstock himself took it for a sign of some special care of Providence for him that Pirie's confession had been made to no one else. What kind of Providence would naturally choose him out to care for, and whether in highest heaven or deepest the other place, he had not leisure at the moment to inquire.

'Where's the dough planted?' he asked.

The sick man's eyelids fluttered open, but with no recognition of Captain Brigstock or of his question; there was a great light of anger and pain in the eyes, and the lips drew back from the strong discoloured teeth.

'You give me the chilly mit!' he almost shouted, half rising in bed: 'Take that, you duffer!' and he flung himself bodily on Captain Brigstock.

It was quite true Pirie died bad.

That evening Brigstock in his lodgings meditated afresh on the special care of Providence. At the end of his meditations, which he had assisted by striding up and down the room, he knelt by the open fire and tore out and burned certain leaves from his notebook.

*

The night of New Year's day, some ten months after the murder of Patrolman Hooper, Howard Slifer sat in his cell in — Prison, and talked through the bars of the cell door with his 'death-watch'. The evidence given at the time of his indictment had been repeated with additions at the time of his trial, and among those additions the confession of Francis Pirie was not found.

'You hear what I'm tellin' you, Jackson,' Slifer said that night; 'I ain't turnin' soft an' kickin' 'bout goin' to the chair: not me! It's up to me to sit in it, that's straight. An' I've done enough to deserve croakin' ten times over;

but, Jackson, it ain't up to me to stand for the killin' o' Hooper. I didn't do it. Course the evidence don't look that way, an' they think that they've got me dead to rights; but that jus' shows how bughouse some o' the things in this world are. Jackson, if Hooper could get up out of his grave now, he'd say, "Slifer didn't do it." I don't mind croakin' for anythin' I done, but I hate like hell to croak for somethin' I didn't.'

5

The Scarlet Thread

Jacques Futrelle

I

The Thinking Machine – Professor Augustus S. F. X. Van Dusen, Ph.D., LL.D., F.R.S., M.D., etc., scientist and logician – listened intently and without comment to a weird, seemingly inexplicable story. Hutchinson Hatch, reporter, was telling it. The bowed figure of the savant lay at ease in a large chair. The enormous head with its bushy yellow hair was thrown back, the thin, white fingers were pressed tip to tip and the blue eyes, narrowed to mere slits, squinted aggressively upward. The scientist was in a receptive mood.

'From the beginning, every fact you know,' he had requested.

'It's all out in the Back Bay,' the reporter explained. 'There is a big apartment house there, a fashionable establishment, in a side street, just off Commonwealth Avenue. It is five storeys in all, and is cut up into small suites, of two and three rooms with bath. These suites are handsomely, even luxuriously furnished, and are occupied by people who can afford to pay big rents. Generally these are young unmarried men, although in several cases they are husband and wife. It is a house of every modern improvement, elevator service, hall boys, liveried door men, spacious corridors and all that. It has both the gas and electric systems of lighting. Tenants are at liberty to use either or both.

'A young broker, Weldon Henley, occupies one of the handsomest of these suites, being on the second floor, in front. He has met with considerable success in the Street. He is a bachelor and lives there alone. There is no personal servant. He dabbles in photography as a hobby, and is said to be remarkably expert.

'Recently there was a report that he was to be married this Winter to a beautiful Virginia girl who has been visiting Boston from time to time, a Miss Lipscomb – Charlotte Lipscomb, of Richmond. Henley has never denied or affirmed this rumor, although he has been asked about it often. Miss Lipscomb is impossible of access even when she visits Boston. Now she is in Virginia, I understand, but will return to Boston later in the season.'

The reporter paused, lighted a cigarette and leaned forward in his chair, gazing steadily into the inscrutable eyes of the scientist.

'When Henley took the suite he requested that all the electric lighting apparatus be removed from his apartments,' he went on. 'He had taken a long lease of the place, and this was done. Therefore he uses only gas for lighting purposes, and he usually keeps one of his gas jets burning low all night.'

'Bad, bad for his health,' commented the scientist.

'Now comes the mystery of the affair,' the reporter went on. 'It was five weeks or so ago Henley retired as usual – about midnight. He locked his door on the inside – he is positive of that – and awoke about four o'clock in the morning nearly asphyxiated by gas. He was barely able to get up and open the window to let in the fresh air. The gas jet he had left burning was out, and the suite was full of gas.'

'Accident, possibly,' said The Thinking Machine. 'A draught through the apartments; a slight diminution of gas pressure; a hundred possibilities.'

'So it was presumed,' said the reporter. 'Of course it would have been impossible for –'

'Nothing is impossible,' said the other, tartly. 'Don't say that. It annoys me exceedingly.'

'Well, then, it seems highly improbable that the door had been opened or that anyone came into the room and did this deliberately,' the newspaper man went on, with a slight smile. 'So Henley said nothing about this; attributed it to accident. The next night he lighted his gas as usual, but he left it burning a little brighter. The same thing happened again.'

'Ah,' and The Thinking Machine changed his position a little. 'The second time.'

'And again he awoke just in time to save himself,' said Hatch. 'Still he attributed the affair to accident, and determined to avoid a recurrence of the affair by doing away with the gas at night. Then he got a small night lamp and used this for a week or more.'

'Why does he have a light at all?' asked the scientist, testily.

'I can hardly answer that,' replied Hatch. 'I may say, however, that he is of a very nervous temperament, and gets up frequently during the night. He reads occasionally when he can't sleep. In addition to that he has slept with a light going all his life; it's a habit.'

'Go on.'

'One night he looked for the night lamp, but it had disappeared – at least he couldn't find it – so he lighted the gas again. The fact of the gas having twice before gone out had been dismissed as a serious possibility. Next morning at five o'clock a bell boy, passing through the hall, smelled gas and made a quick investigation. He decided it came from Henley's place, and rapped on the door. There was no answer. It ultimately developed that it was necessary to smash in the door. There on the bed they found Henley unconscious with the gas pouring into the room from the jet which he had left lighted. He was revived in the air, but for several hours was deathly sick.'

'Why was the door smashed in?' asked The Thinking Machine. 'Why not unlocked?'

'It was done because Henley had firmly barred it,' Hatch explained. 'He had become suspicious, I suppose, and after the second time he always barred his door and fastened every window before he went to sleep. There may have been a fear that someone used a key to enter.'

'Well?' asked the scientist. 'After that?'

'Three weeks or so elapsed, bringing the affair down to this morning,' Hatch went on. 'Then the same thing happened a little differently. For instance, after the third time the gas went out Henley decided to find out for himself what caused it, and so expressed himself to a few friends who knew of the mystery. Then, night after night, he lighted the gas as usual and kept watch. It was never disturbed during all that time, burning steadily all night. What sleep he got was in daytime.

'Last night Henley lay awake for a time; then, exhausted and tired, fell asleep. This morning early he awoke; the room was filled with gas again. In some way my city editor heard of it and asked me to look into the mystery.'

That was all. The two men were silent for a long time, and finally The Thinking Machine turned to the reporter.

'Does anyone else in the house keep gas going all night?' he asked.

'I don't know,' was the reply. 'Most of them, I know, use electricity.'

'Nobody else has been overcome as he has been?'

'No. Plumbers have minutely examined the lighting system all over the house and found nothing wrong.'

'Does the gas in the house all come through the same meter?'

'Yes, so the manager told me. This meter, a big one, is just off the engine room. I supposed it possible that some one shut it off there on these nights long enough to extinguish the lights all over the house, then turned it on again. Do you think it was an attempt to kill Henley?'

'It might be,' was the reply. 'Find out for me just who in the house uses gas; also if anyone else leaves a light burning all night; also what opportunity anyone would have to get at the meter, and then something about Henley's love affair with Miss Lipscomb. Is there anyone else? If so, who? Where does he live? When you find out these things come back here.'

*

That afternoon at one o'clock Hatch returned to the apartments of The Thinking Machine, with excitement plainly apparent on his face.

'Well?' asked the scientist.

'A French girl, Louise Regnier, employed as a maid by Mrs Standing in the house, was found dead in her room on the third floor today at noon,' Hatch explained quickly. 'It looks like suicide.'

'How?' asked The Thinking Machine.

'The people who employed her – husband and wife – have been away for a couple of days,' Hatch rushed on. 'She was in the suite alone. This noon she had not appeared, there was an odour of gas and the door was broken in. Then she was found dead.'

'With the gas turned on?'

'With the gas turned on. She was asphyxiated.'

'Dear me, dear me,' exclaimed the scientist. He arose and took up his hat. 'Let's go see what this is all about.'

2

When Professor Van Dusen and Hatch arrived at the apartment house they had been preceded by the Medical Examiner and the police. Detective Mallory, whom both knew, was moving about in the apartment where the girl had been found dead. The body had been removed and a telegram sent to her employers in New York.

'Too late,' said Mallory, as they entered.

'What was it, Mr Mallory?' asked the scientist.

'Suicide,' was the reply. 'No question of it. It happened in this room,' and he led the way into the third room of the suite. 'The maid, Miss Regnier, occupied this, and was here alone last night. Mr and Mrs Standing, her employers, have gone to New York for a few days. She was left alone, and killed herself.'

Without further questioning The Thinking Machine went over to the bed, from which the girl's body had been taken, and, stooping beside it, picked up a book. It was a novel by 'The Duchess'. He examined this critically, then, standing on a chair, he examined the gas jet. This done, he stepped down and went to the window of the little room. Finally The Thinking Machine turned to the detective.

'Just how much was the gas turned on?' he asked.

'Turned on full,' was the reply.

'Were both the doors of the room closed?'

'Both, yes.'

'Any cotton, or cloth, or anything of the sort stuffed into the cracks of the window?'

'No. It's a tight-fitting window, anyway. Are you trying to make a mystery out of this?'

'Cracks in the doors stuffed?' The Thinking Machine went on.

'No.' There was a smile about the detective's lips.

The Thinking Machine, on his knees, examined the bottom of one of the doors, that which led into the hall. The lock of this door had been broken when employees burst into the room. Having satisfied himself here and at the bottom of the other door, which connected with the bedroom adjoining, The Thinking Machine again climbed on a chair and examined the doors at the top.

'Both transoms closed, I suppose?' he asked.

'Yes,' was the reply. 'You can't make anything but suicide out of it,' explained the detective. 'The Medical Examiner has given that as his opinion – and everything I find indicates it.'

'All right,' broke in The Thinking Machine abruptly. 'Don't let us keep you.'

After a while Detective Mallory went away. Hatch and the scientist went down to the office floor, where they saw the manager. He seemed to be greatly distressed, but was willing to do anything he could in the matter.

'Is your night engineer perfectly trustworthy?' asked The Thinking Machine.

'Perfectly,' was the reply. 'One of the best and most reliable men I ever met. Alert and wide-awake.'

'Can I see him a moment? The night man, I mean?'

'Certainly,' was the reply. 'He's downstairs. He sleeps there. He's probably up by this time. He sleeps usually till one o'clock in the daytime, being up all night.'

'Do you supply gas for your tenants?'

'Both gas and electricity are included in the rent of the suites. Tenants may use one or both.'

'And the gas all comes through one meter?'

'Yes, one meter. It's just off the engine room.'

'I suppose there's no way of telling just who in the house uses gas?'

'No. Some do and some don't. I don't know.'

This was what Hatch had told the scientist. Now together they went to the basement, and there met the night engineer, Charles Burlingame, a tall, powerful, clean-cut man, of alert manner and positive speech. He gazed with a little amusement at the slender, almost childish figure of The Thinking Machine and the grotesquely large head.

'You are in the engine room or near it all night every night?' began The Thinking Machine.

'I haven't missed a night in four years,' was the reply.

'Anybody ever come here to see you at night?'

'Never. It's against the rules.'

'The manager or a hall boy?'

'Never.'

'In the last two months?' The Thinking Machine persisted.

'Not in the last two years,' was the positive reply. 'I go on duty every night at seven o'clock, and I am on duty until seven in the morning. I don't believe I've seen anybody in the basement here with me between those hours for a year at least.'

The Thinking Machine was squinting steadily into the eyes of the engineer, and for a time both were silent. Hatch moved about the scrupulously clean engine room and nodded to the day engineer, who sat leaning back against the wall. Directly in front of him was the steam gauge.

'Have you a fireman?' was The Thinking Machine's next question.

'No. I fire myself,' said the night man. 'Here's the coal,' and he indicated a bin within half a dozen feet of the mouth of the boiler.

'I don't suppose you ever had occasion to handle the gas meter?' insisted The Thinking Machine.

'Never touched it in my life,' said the other. 'I don't know anything about meters, anyway.'

'And you never drop off to sleep at night for a few minutes when you get lonely? Doze, I mean?'

The engineer grinned good-naturedly.

'Never had any desire to, and besides I wouldn't have the chance,' he explained. 'There's a time check here,' – and he indicated it. 'I have to punch that every half hour all night to prove that I have been awake.'

'Dear me, dear me,' exclaimed The Thinking Machine irritably. He went over and examined the time check –

a revolving paper disc with hours marked on it, made to move by the action of a clock, the face of which showed in the middle.

'Besides there's the steam gauge to watch,' went on the engineer. 'No engineer would dare go to sleep. There might be an explosion.'

'Do you know Mr Weldon Henley?' suddenly asked The Thinking Machine.

'Who?' asked Burlingame.

'Weldon Henley?'

'No-o,' was the slow response. 'Never heard of him. Who is he?'

'One of the tenants, on the second floor, I think.'

'Lord, I don't know any of the tenants. What about him?'

'When does the inspector come here to read the meter?'

'I never saw him. I presume in daytime, eh Bill?' and he turned to the day engineer.

'Always in daytime – usually about noon,' said Bill from his corner.

'Any other entrance to the basement except this way – and you could see anyone coming here this way I suppose?'

'Sure I could see 'em. There's no other entrance to the cellar except the coal hole in the sidewalk in front.'

'Two big electric lights in front of the building, aren't there?'

'Yes. They go all night.'

A slightly puzzled expression crept into the eyes of The Thinking Machine. Hatch knew from the persistency of the questions that he was not satisfied; yet he was not able to fathom or to understand all the queries. In some way they had to do with the possibility of someone having access to the meter.

'Where do you usually sit at night here?' was the next question.

'Over there where Bill's sitting. I always sit there.'

The Thinking Machine crossed the room to Bill, a typical, grimy-handed man of his class.

'May I sit there a moment?' he asked.

Bill arose lazily, and The Thinking Machine sank down into the chair. From this point he could see plainly through the opening into the basement proper – there was no door – the gas meter of enormous proportions through which all the gas in the house passed. An electric light in the door made it bright as daylight. The Thinking Machine noted these things, arose, nodded his thanks to the two men and, still with the puzzled expression on his face, led the way upstairs. There the manager was still in his office.

'I presume you examine and know that the time check in the engineer's room is properly punched every half-hour during the night?' he asked.

'Yes. I examine the dial every day – have them here, in fact, each with the date on it.'

'May I see them?'

Now the manager was puzzled. He produced the cards, one for each day, and for half an hour The Thinking Machine studied them minutely. At the end of that time, when he arose and Hatch looked at him inquiringly, he saw still the perplexed expression.

After urgent solicitation, the manager admitted them to the apartments of Weldon Henley. Mr Henley himself had gone to his office in State Street. Here The Thinking Machine did several things which aroused the curiosity of the manager, one of which was to minutely study the gas jets. Then The Thinking Machine opened one of the front windows and glanced out into the street. Below fifteen feet was the sidewalk; above was the solid front of the building, broken only by a flagpole which, properly roped, extended from the hall window of the next floor above out over the sidewalk a distance of twelve feet or so.

'Ever use that flagpole?' he asked the manager.

'Rarely,' said the manager. 'On holidays sometimes – Fourth of July and such times. We have a big flag for it.'

From the apartments The Thinking Machine led the way to the hall, up the stairs and to the flagpole. Leaning out of this window, he looked down toward the window of the apartments he had just left. Then he inspected the rope of the flagpole, drawing it through his slender hands slowly and carefully. At last he picked off a slender thread of scarlet and examined it.

'Ah,' he exclaimed. Then to Hatch: 'Let's go, Mr Hatch. Thank you,' this last to the manager, who had been a puzzled witness.

Once on the street, side by side with The Thinking Machine, Hatch was bursting with questions, but he didn't ask them. He knew it would be useless. At last The Thinking Machine broke the silence.

'That girl, Miss Regnier, *was murdered*,' he said suddenly, positively. 'There have been four attempts to murder Henley.'

'How?' asked Hatch, startled.

'By a scheme so simple that neither you nor I nor the police have ever heard of it being employed,' was the astonishing reply. '*It is perfectly horrible in its simplicity.*'

'What was it?' Hatch insisted, eagerly.

'It would be futile to discuss that now,' was the rejoinder. 'There has been murder. We know how. Now the question is – who? What person would have a motive to kill Henley?'

3

There was a pause as they walked on.

'Where are we going?' asked Hatch finally.

'Come up to my place and let's consider this matter a bit further,' replied The Thinking Machine.

Not another word was spoken by either until half an hour later, in the small laboratory. For a long time the scientist was thoughtful – deeply thoughtful. Once he took down a volume from a shelf and Hatch glanced at the title. It was 'Gases: Their Properties'. after a while he returned this to the shelf and took down another, on which the reporter caught the title, 'Anatomy'.

'Now, Mr Hatch,' said The Thinking Machine in his perpetually crabbed voice, 'we have a most remarkable riddle. It gains this remarkable aspect from its very simplicity. It is not, however, necessary to go into that now. I will make it clear to you when we know the motives.

'As a general rule, the greatest crimes never come to light because the greatest criminals, their perpetrators, are too clever to be caught. Here we have what I might call a great crime committed with a subtle simplicity that is wholly disarming, and a greater crime even than this was planned. This was to murder Weldon Henley. The first thing for you to do is to see Mr Henley and warn him of his danger. Asphyxiation will not be attempted again, but there is a possibility of poison, a pistol shot, a knife, anything almost. As a matter of fact, he is in great peril.

'Superficially, the death of Miss Regnier, the maid, looks to be suicide. Instead it is the fruition of a plan which has been tried time and again against Henley. There is a possibility that Miss Regnier was not an intentional victim of the plot, but the fact remains that she was murdered. Why? Find the motive for the plot to murder Mr Henley and you will know why.'

The Thinking Machine reached over to the shelf, took a book, looked at it a moment, then went on:

'The first question to determine positively is: Who hated Weldon Henley sufficiently to desire his death? You say he is a successful man in the Street. Therefore there is a possibility that some enemy there is at the bottom of the affair, yet it seems hardly probable. If by his operations Mr Henley ever happened to wreck another man's fortune find this man and find out all about him. He may be the man. There will be innumerable questions arising from this line of inquiry to a man of your resources. Leave none of them unanswered.

'On the other hand there is Henley's love affair. Had he a rival who might desire his death? Had he any rival? If so, find out all about him. He may be the man who planned all this. Here, too, there will be questions arising which demand answers. Answer them – all of them – fully and clearly before you see me again.

'Was Henley ever a party to a liaison of any kind? Find that out, too. A vengeful woman or a discarded sweetheart of a vengeful woman, you know, will go to any extreme. The rumour of his engagement to Miss – Miss –'

'Miss Lipscomb,' Hatch supplied.

'The rumor of his engagement to Miss Lipscomb might have caused a woman whom he had once been interested in or who was once interested in him to attempt his life. The subtler murders – that is, the ones which are most attractive as problems – are nearly always the work of a cunning woman. I know nothing about women myself,' he hastened to explain; 'but Lombroso has taken that attitude. Therefore, see if there is a woman.'

Most of these points Hatch had previously seen – seen with the unerring eye of a clever newspaper reporter – yet there were several which had not occurred to him. He nodded his understanding.

'Now the centre of the affair, of course,' The Thinking Machine continued, 'is the apartment house where Henley lives. The person who attempted his life either lives there or has ready access to the place, and frequently spends the night there. This is a vital question for you to answer. I am leaving all this to you because you know better how to do these things than I do. That's all, I think. When these things are all learned come back to me.'

The Thinking Machine arose as if the interview were at an end, and Hatch also arose, reluctantly. An idea was beginning to dawn in his mind.

'Does it occur to you that there is any connection whatever between Henley and Miss Regnier?' he asked.

'It is possible,' was the reply. 'I had thought of that. If there is a connection it is not apparent yet.'

'Then how – how was it she – she was killed, or killed herself, whichever may be true, and –'

'The attempt to kill Henley killed her. That's all I can say now.'

'That all?' asked Hatch, after a pause.

'No. Warn Mr Henley immediately that he is in grave danger. Remember the person who has planned this will probably go to any extreme. I don't know Mr Henley, of course, but from the fact that he always had a light at night I gather that he is a timid sort of man – not necessarily a coward, but a man lacking in stamina – therefore, one who might better disappear for a week or so until the mystery is cleared up. Above all, impress upon him the importance of the warning.'

The Thinking Machine opened his pocketbook and took from it the scarlet thread which he had picked from the rope of the flagpole.

'Here, I believe, is the real clew to the problem,' he explained to Hatch. 'What does it seem to be?'

Hatch examined it closely.

'I should say a strand from a Turkish bath robe,' was his final judgement.

'Possibly. Ask some cloth expert what he makes of it, then if it sounds promising look into it. Find out if by any possibility it can be any part of any garment worn by any person in the apartment house.'

'But it's so slight –' Hatch began.

'I know,' the other interrupted, tartly. 'It's slight, but I believe it is a part of the wearing apparel of the person, man or woman, who has four times attempted to kill Mr Henley and who did kill the girl. Therefore, it is important.'

Hatch looked at him quickly.

'Well, how – in what manner – did it come where you found it?'

'Simple enough,' said the scientist. 'It is a wonder that there were not more pieces of it – that's all.'

Perplexed by his instructions, but confident of results, Hatch left The Thinking Machine. What possible connection could this tiny bit of scarlet thread, found on a flagpole, have with someone shutting off the gas in Henley's rooms? How did anyone go into Henley's rooms to shut off the gas? How was it Miss Regnier was dead? What was the manner of her death?

A cloth expert in a great department store turned his knowledge on the tiny bit of scarlet for the illumination of Hatch, but he could go no further than to say that it seemed to be part of a Turkish bath robe.

'Man or woman's?' asked Hatch.

'The material from which bath robes are made is the same for both men and women,' was the reply. 'I can say nothing else. Of course there's not enough of it to even guess at the pattern of the robe.'

Then Hatch went to the financial district and was ushered into the office of Weldon Henley, a slender, handsome man of thirty-two or three years, pallid of face and nervous in manner. He still showed the effect of the gas poisoning, and there was even a trace of a furtive fear – fear of something, he himself didn't know what – in his actions.

Henley talked freely to the newspaper man of certain things, but of other things was resentfully reticent. He admitted his engagement to Miss Lipscomb, and finally even admitted that Miss Lipscomb's hand had been sought by another man, Reginault Cabell, formerly of Virginia.

'Could you give me his address?' asked Hatch.

'He lives in the same apartment house with me – two floors above,' was the reply.

Hatch was startled; startled more than he would have cared to admit.

'Are you on friendly terms with him?' he asked.

'Certainly,' said Henley. 'I won't say anything further about this matter. It would be unwise for obvious reasons.'

'I suppose you consider that this turning on of the gas was an attempt on your life?'

'I can't suppose anything else.'

Hatch studied the pallid face closely as he asked the next question.

'Do you know Miss Regnier was found dead today?'

'Dead?' exclaimed the other, and he arose. 'Who – what – who is she?'

It seemed a distinct effort for him to regain control of himself.

The reporter detailed then the circumstances of the finding of the girl's body, and the broker listened without comment. From that time forward all the reporter's questions were either parried or else met with a flat refusal to answer. Finally Hatch repeated to him the warning which he had from The Thinking Machine, and feeling that he had accomplished little, went away.

At eight o'clock that night – a night of complete darkness – Henley was found unconscious, lying in a little used walk in the Common. There was a bullet hole through his left shoulder, and he was bleeding profusely. He was removed to the hospital, where he regained consciousness for just a moment.

'Who shot you?' he was asked.

'None of your business,' he replied, and lapsed into unconsciousness.

4

Entirely unaware of this latest attempt on the life of the broker, Hutchinson Hatch steadily pursued his investigations. They finally led him to an intimate friend of Reginault Cabell. The young Southerner had apartments on the fourth floor of the big house off Commonwealth Avenue, directly over those Henley occupied, but two flights higher up. This friend was a figure in the social set of the Back Bay. He talked to Hatch freely of Cabell.

'He's a good fellow,' he explained, 'one of the best I ever met, and comes of one of the best families Virginia ever had – a true F.F.V. He's pretty quick tempered and all that, but an excellent chap, and everywhere he has gone here he has made friends.'

'He used to be in love with Miss Lipscomb of Virginia, didn't he?' asked Hatch, casually.

'Used to be?' the other repeated with a laugh. 'He *is* in love with her. But recently he understood that she was engaged to Weldon Henley, a broker – you may have heard of him? – and that, I suppose, has dampened his ardor considerably. As a matter of fact, Cabell took the thing to heart. He used to know Miss Lipscomb in Virginia – she comes from another famous family there – and he seemed to think he had a prior claim on her.'

Hatch heard all these things as any man might listen to gossip, but each additional fact was sinking into his mind, and each additional fact led his suspicions on deeper into the channel they had chosen.

'Cabell is pretty well to do,' his informant went on, 'not rich as we count riches in the North, but pretty well to do, and I believe he came to Boston because Miss Lipscomb spent so much of her time here. She is a beautiful young woman of twenty-two and extremely popular in the social world everywhere, particularly in Boston. Then there was the additional fact that Henley was here.'

'No chance at all for Cabell?' Hatch suggested.

'Not the slightest,' was the reply. 'Yet despite the heartbreak he had, he was the first to congratulate Henley on winning her love. And he meant it, too.'

'What's his attitude toward Henley now?' asked Hatch. His voice was calm, but there was an underlying tense note imperceptible to the other.

'They meet and speak and move in the same set. There's no love lost on either side, I don't suppose, but there is no trace of any ill feeling.'

'Cabell doesn't happen to be a vindictive sort of man?'

'Vindictive?' and the other laughed. 'No. He's like a big boy, forgiving, and all that; hot-tempered, though. I could imagine him in a fit of anger making a personal matter of it with Henley, but I don't think he ever did.'

The mind of the newspaper man was rapidly focusing on one point; the rush of thoughts, questions and doubts silenced him for a moment. Then:

'How long has Cabell been in Boston?'

'Seven or eight months – that is, he has had apartments here for that long – but he has made several visits South. I suppose it's South. He has a trick of dropping out of sight occasionally. I understand that he intends to go South for good very soon. If I'm not mistaken, he is trying now to rent his suite.'

Hatch looked suddenly at his informant; an idea of seeing Cabell and having a legitimate excuse for talking to him had occurred to him.

'I'm looking for a suite,' he volunteered at last. 'I wonder if you would give me a card of introduction to him? We might get together on it.'

Thus it happened that half an hour later, about ten minutes past nine o'clock, Hatch was on his way to the big apartment house. In the office he saw the manager.

'Heard the news?' asked the manager.

'No,' Hatch replied. 'What is it?'

'Somebody's shot Mr Henley as he was passing through the Common early tonight.'

Hatch whistled his amazement.

'Is he dead?'

'No, but he is unconscious. The hospital doctors say it is a nasty wound, but not necessarily dangerous.'

'Who shot him? Do they know?'

'He knows, but he won't say.'

Amazed and alarmed by this latest development, an accurate fulfilment of The Thinking Machine's prophecy, Hatch stood thoughtful for a moment, then recovering his composure a little asked for Cabell.

'I don't think there's much chance of seeing him,' said the manager. 'He's going away on the midnight train – going South, to Virginia.'

'Going away tonight?' Hatch gasped.

'Yes; it seems to have been rather a sudden determination. He was talking to me here half an hour or so ago, and said something about going away. While he was here the telephone boy told me that Henley had been shot; they had 'phoned from the hospital to inform us. Then Cabell seemed greatly agitated. He said he was going away tonight, if he could catch the midnight train, and now he's packing.'

'I suppose the shooting of Henley upset him considerably?' the reporter suggested.

'Yes, I guess it did,' was the reply. 'They moved in the same set and belonged to the same clubs.'

The manager sent Hatch's card of introduction to Cabell's apartments. Hatch went up and was ushered into a suite identical with that of Henley's in every respect save in minor details of furnishings. Cabell stood in the middle of the floor, with his personal belongings scattered about the room; his valet, evidently a Frenchman, was busily engaged in packing.

Cabell's greeting was perfunctorily cordial; he seemed agitated. His face was flushed and from time to time he ran his fingers through his long, brown hair. He stared at Hatch in a preoccupied fashion, then they fell into conversation about the rent of the apartments.

'I'll take almost anything reasonable,' Cabell said hurriedly. 'You see, I am going away tonight, rather more suddenly than I had intended, and I am anxious to get the lease off my hands. I pay two hundred dollars a month for these just as they are.'

'May I look them over?' asked Hatch.

He passed from the front room into the next. Here, on a bed, was piled a huge lot of clothing, and the valet, with deft fingers, was brushing and folding, preparatory to packing. Cabell was directly behind him.

'Quite comfortable, you see,' he explained. 'There's room enough if you are alone. Are you?'

'Oh, yes,' Hatch replied.

'This other room here,' Cabell explained, 'is not in very tidy shape now. I have been out of the city for several weeks, and – What's the matter?' he demanded suddenly.

Hatch had turned quickly at the words and stared at him, then recovered himself with a start.

'I beg your pardon,' he stammered. 'I rather thought I saw you in town here a week or so ago – of course I didn't know you – and I was wondering if I could have been mistaken.'

'Must have been,' said the other easily. 'During the time I was away a Miss —, a friend of my sister's, occupied the suite. I'm afraid some of her things are here. She hasn't sent for them as yet. She occupied this room, I think; when I came back a few days ago she took another place and all her things haven't been removed.'

'I see,' remarked Hatch, casually. 'I don't suppose

there's any chance of her returning here unexpectedly if I should happen to take her apartments?'

'Not the slightest. She knows I am back, and thinks I am to remain. She was to send for these things.'

Hatch gazed about the room ostentatiously. Across a trunk lay a Turkish bath robe with a scarlet stripe in it. He was anxious to get hold of it, to examine it closely. But he didn't dare to, then. Together they returned to the front room.

'I rather like the place,' he said, after a pause, 'but the price is –'

'Just a moment,' Cabell interrupted. 'Jean, before you finish packing that suit case be sure to put my bath robe in it. It's in the far room.'

Then one question was settled for Hatch. After a moment the valet returned with the bath robe, which had been in the far room. It was Cabell's bath robe. As Jean passed the reporter an end of the robe caught on a corner of the trunk, and, stopping, the reporter unfastened it. A tiny strand of thread clung to the metal; Hatch detached it and stood idly twirling it in his fingers.

'As I was saying,' he resumed, 'I rather like the place, but the price is too much. Suppose you leave it in the hands of the manager of the house –'

'I had intended doing that,' the Southerner interrupted.

'Well, I'll see him about it later,' Hatch added.

With a cordial, albeit preoccupied, handshake, Cabell ushered him out. Hatch went down in the elevator with a feeling of elation; a feeling that he had accomplished something. The manager was waiting to get into the lift.

'Do you happen to remember the name of the young lady who occupied Mr Cabell's suite while he was away?' he asked.

'Miss Austin,' said the manager, 'but she's not young. She was about forty-five years old, I should judge.'

'Did Mr Cabell have his servant Jean with him?'

'Oh, no,' said the manager. 'The valet gave up the suite to Miss Austin entirely, and until Mr Cabell returned occupied a room in the quarters we have for our own employees.'

'Was Miss Austin ailing any way?' asked Hatch. 'I saw a large number of medicine bottles upstairs.'

'I don't know what was the matter with her,' replied the manager, with a little puzzled frown. 'She certainly was not a woman of sound mental balance – that is, she was eccentric, and all that. I think rather it was an act of charity for Mr Cabell to let her have the suite in his absence. Certainly we didn't want her.'

Hatch passed out and burst in eagerly upon The Thinking Machine in his laboratory.

'Here,' he said, and triumphantly he extended the tiny scarlet strand which he had received from The Thinking Machine, and the other of the identical colour which came from Cabell's bath robe. 'Is that the same?'

The Thinking Machine placed them under the microscope and examined them immediately. Later he submitted them to a chemical test.

'*It is the same,*' he said, finally.

'Then the mystery is solved,' said Hatch, conclusively.

5

The Thinking Machine stared steadily into the eager, exultant eyes of the newspaper man until Hatch at last began to fear that he had been precipitate. After a while, under close scrutiny, the reporter began to feel convinced that he had made a mistake – he didn't quite see where, but it must be there, and the exultant manner passed. The voice of The Thinking Machine was like a cold shower.

'Remember, Mr Hatch,' he said, critically, 'that unless every possible question has been considered one cannot boast of a solution. Is there any possible question lingering yet in your mind?'

The reporter silently considered that for a moment, then:

'Well, I have the main facts, anyway. There may be one or two minor questions left, but the principal ones are answered.'

'Then tell me, to the minutest detail, what you have learned, what has happened.'

Professor Van Dusen sank back in his old, familiar pose in the large arm chair and Hatch related what he had learned and what he surmised. He related, too, the peculiar circumstances surrounding the wounding of Henley, and right on down to the beginning and end of the interview with Cabell in the latter's apartments. The Thinking Machine was silent for a time, then there came a host of questions.

'Do you know where the woman – Miss Austin – is now?' was the first.

'No,' Hatch had to admit.

'Or her precise mental condition?'

'No.'

'Or her exact relationship to Cabell?'

'No.'

'Do you know, then, what the valet, Jean, knows of the affair?'

'No, not that,' said the reporter, and his face flushed under the close questioning. 'He was out of the suite every night.'

'Therefore might have been the very one who turned on the gas,' the other put in testily.

'So far as I can learn, nobody could have gone into that room and turned on the gas,' said the reporter, somewhat aggressively. 'Henley barred the doors and windows and kept watch, night after night.'

'Yet the moment he was exhausted and fell asleep the

gas was turned on to kill him,' said The Thinking Machine; 'thus we see that *he was watched more closely than he watched.*'

'I see what you mean now,' said Hatch, after a long pause.

'I should like to know what Henley and Cabell and the valet knew of the girl who was found dead,' The Thinking Machine suggested. 'Further, I should like to know if there was a good-sized mirror – not one set in a bureau or dresser – either in Henley's room or the apartments where the girl was found. Find out this for me and – never mind. I'll go with you.'

The scientist left the room. When he returned he wore his coat and hat. Hatch arose mechanically to follow. For a block or more they walked along, neither speaking. The Thinking Machine was the first to break the silence:

'You believe Cabell is the man who attempted to kill Henley?'

'Frankly, yes,' replied the newspaper man.

'Why?'

'Because he had the motive – disappointed love.'

'How?'

'I don't know,' Hatch confessed. 'The doors of the Henley suite were closed. I don't see how anybody passed them.'

'And the girl? Who killed her? How? Why?'

Disconsolately Hatch shook his head as he walked on. The Thinking Machine interpreted his silence aright.

'Don't jump at conclusions,' he advised sharply. 'You are confident Cabell was to blame for this – and he might have been, I don't know yet – but you can suggest nothing to show how he did it. I have told you before that imagination is half of logic.'

At last the lights of the big apartment house where Henley lived came in sight. Hatch shrugged his shoulders. He had grave doubts – based on what he knew

– whether The Thinking Machine would be able to see Cabell. It was nearly eleven o'clock and Cabell was to leave for the South at midnight.

'Is Mr Cabell here?' asked the scientist of the elevator boy.

'Yes, just about to go, though. He won't see anyone.'

'Hand him this note,' instructed The Thinking Machine, and he scribbled something on a piece of paper. 'He'll see us.'

The boy took the paper and the elevator shot up to the fourth floor. After a while he returned.

'He'll see you,' he said.

'Is he unpacking?'

'After he read your note twice he told his valet to unpack,' the boy replied.

'Ah, I thought so,' said The Thinking Machine.

With Hatch, mystified and puzzled, following, The Thinking Machine entered the elevator to step out a second or so later on the fourth floor. As they left the car they saw the door of Cabell's apartment standing open; Cabell was in the door. Hatch traced a glimmer of anxiety in the eyes of the young man.

'Professor Van Dusen?' Cabell inquired.

'Yes,' said the scientist. 'It was of the utmost importance that I should see you, otherwise I should not have come at this time of night.'

With a wave of his hand Cabell passed that detail.

'I was anxious to get away at midnight,' he explained, 'but, of course, now I shan't go, in view of your note. I have ordered my valet to unpack my things, at least until tomorrow.'

The reporter and the scientist passed into the luxuriously furnished apartments. Jean, the valet, was bending over a suitcase as they entered, removing some things he had been carefully placing there. He didn't look back or pay the least attention to the visitors.

'This is your valet?' asked The Thinking Machine.

'Yes,' said the young man.

'French, isn't he?'

'Yes.'

'Speak English at all?'

'Very badly,' said Cabell. 'I use French when I talk to him.'

'Does he know that you are accused of murder?' asked The Thinking Machine, in a quiet, conversational tone.

The effect of the remark on Cabell was startling. He staggered back a step or so as if he had been struck in the face, and a crimson flush overspread his brow. Jean, the valet, straightened up suddenly and looked around. There was a queer expression, too, in his eyes; an expression which Hatch could not fathom.

'Murder?' gasped Cabell, at last.

'Yes, he speaks English all right,' remarked The Thinking Machine. 'Now, Mr Cabell, will you please tell me just who Miss Austin is, and where she is, and her mental condition? Believe me, it may save you a great deal of trouble. What I said in the note is not exaggerated.'

The young man turned suddenly and began to pace back and forth across the room. After a few minutes he paused before The Thinking Machine, who stood impatiently waiting for an answer.

'I'll tell you, yes,' said Cabell, firmly. 'Miss Austin is a middle-aged woman whom my sister befriended several times – was, in fact, my sister's governess when she was a child. Of late years she has not been wholly right mentally, and has suffered a great deal of privation. I had about concluded arrangements to put her in a private sanitarium. I permitted her to remain in these rooms in my absence, South. I did not take Jean – he lived in the quarters of the other employees of the place, and gave the apartment entirely to Miss Austin. It was simply an act of charity.'

'What was the cause of your sudden determination to go South tonight?' asked the scientist.

'I won't answer that question,' was the sullen reply.

There was a long, tense silence. Jean, the valet, came and went several times.

'How long has Miss Austin known Mr Henley?'

'Presumably since she has been in these apartments,' was the reply.

'Are you sure *you* are not Miss Austin?' demanded the scientist.

The question was almost staggering, not only to Cabell, but to Hatch. Suddenly, with flaming face, the young Southerner leaped forward as if to strike down The Thinking Machine.

'That won't do any good,' said the scientist, coldly. 'Are you sure you are not Miss Austin?' he repeated.

'Certainly I am not Miss Austin,' responded Cabell, fiercely.

'Have you a mirror in these apartments about twelve inches by twelve inches?' asked The Thinking Machine, irrelevantly.

'I – I don't know,' stammered the young man. 'I – have we, Jean?'

'*Oui*,' replied the valet.

'Yes,' snapped The Thinking Machine. 'Talk English, please. May I see it?'

The valet, without a word but with a sullen glance at the questioner, turned and left the room. He returned after a moment with the mirror. The Thinking Machine carefully examined the frame, top and bottom and on both sides. At last he looked up; again the valet was bending over a suitcase.

'Do you use gas in these apartments?' the scientist asked suddenly.

'No,' was the bewildered response. 'What is all this, anyway?'

Without answering, The Thinking Machine drew a chair up under the chandelier where the gas and electric fixtures were and began to finger the gas tips. After awhile he climbed down and passed into the next room, with Hatch and Cabell, both hopelessly mystified, following. There the scientist went through the same process of fingering the gas jets. Finally, one of the gas tips came out in his hand.

'Ah,' he exclaimed, suddenly, and Hatch knew the note of triumph in it. The jet from which the tip came was just on a level with his shoulder, set between a dressing table and a window. He leaned over and squinted at the gas pipe closely. Then he returned to the room where the valet was.

'Now, Jean,' he began, in an even, calm voice, 'please tell me *if you did or did not kill Miss Regnier purposely?*'

'I don't know what you mean,' said the servant sullenly, angrily, as he turned on the scientist.

'You speak very good English now,' was The Thinking Machine's terse comment. 'Mr Hatch, lock the door and use this 'phone to call the police.'

Hatch turned to do as he was bid and saw a flash of steel in young Cabell's hand, which was drawn suddenly from a hip pocket. It was a revolver. The weapon glittered in the light, and Hatch flung himself forward. There was a sharp report, and a bullet was buried in the floor.

6

Then came a fierce, hard fight for possession of the revolver. It ended with the weapon in Hatch's hand, and both he and Cabell blowing from the effort they had expended. Jean the valet, had turned at the sound of the shot and started toward the door leading into the hall. The Thinking Machine had stepped in front of him, and now stood there with his back to the door. Physically he would have been a child in the hands of the valet, yet there was a look in his eyes which stopped him.

'Now, Mr Hatch,' said the scientist quietly, a touch of irony in his voice, 'hand me the revolver, then 'phone for Detective Mallory to come here immediately. Tell him we have a murderer – and if he can't come at once get some other detective whom you know.'

'Murderer!' gasped Cabell.

Uncontrollable rage was blazing in the eyes of the valet, and he made as if to throw The Thinking Machine aside, despite the revolver, when Hatch was at the telephone. As Jean started forward, however, Cabell stopped him with a quick, stern gesture. Suddenly the young Southerner turned on The Thinking Machine; but it was with a question.

'What does it all mean?' he asked, bewildered.

'It means that that man there,' and The Thinking Machine indicated the valet by a nod of his head, 'is a murderer – that he killed Louise Regnier; that he shot Weldon Henley on Boston Common, and that, with the aid of Miss Regnier, he had four times previously attempted to kill Mr Henley. Is he coming, Mr Hatch?'

'Yes,' was the reply. 'He says he'll be here directly.'

'Do you deny it?' demanded The Thinking Machine of the valet.

'I've done nothing,' said the valet sullenly. 'I'm going out of here.'

Like an infuriated animal he rushed forward. Hatch and Cabell seized him and bore him to the floor. There, after a frantic struggle, he was bound and the other three men sat down to wait for Detective Mallory. Cabell sank back in his chair with a perplexed frown on his face. From time to time he glanced at Jean. The flush of anger which had been on the valet's face was gone now; instead there was the pallor of fear.

'Won't you tell us?' pleaded Cabell impatiently.

'When Detective Mallory comes and takes his prisoner,' said The Thinking Machine.

Ten minutes later they heard a quick step in the hall outside and Hatch opened the door. Detective Mallory entered and looked from one to another inquiringly.

'That's your prisoner, Mr Mallory,' said the scientist, coldly. 'I charge him with the murder of Miss Regnier, whom you were so confident committed suicide; I charge him with five attempts on the life of Weldon Henley, four times by gas poisoning, in which Miss Regnier was his accomplice, and once by shooting. He is the man who shot Mr Henley.'

The Thinking Machine arose and walked over to the prostrate man, handing the revolver to Hatch. He glared down at Jean fiercely.

'Will you tell me how you did it or shall I?' he demanded.

His answer was a sullen, defiant glare. He turned and picked up the square mirror which the valet had produced previously.

'That's where the screw was, isn't it?' he asked, as he indicated a small hole in the frame of the mirror. Jean stared at it and his head sank forward hopelessly. 'And this is the bath robe you wore, isn't it?' he demanded again, and from the suit case he pulled out the garment with the scarlet stripe.

'I guess you got me all right,' was the sullen reply.

'It might be better for you if you told the story then?' suggested The Thinking Machine.

'You know so much about it, tell it yourself.'

'Very well,' was the calm rejoinder. 'I will. If I make any mistake you will correct me.'

For a long time no one spoke. The Thinking Machine had dropped back into a chair and was staring through his thick glasses at the ceiling; his finger tips were pressed tightly together. At last he began:

'There are certain trivial gaps which only the imagination can supply until the matter is gone into more fully. I should have supplied these myself, but the arrest of this man, Jean, was precipitated by the attempted hurried departure of Mr Cabell for the South tonight, and I did not have time to go into the case to the fullest extent.

'Thus, we begin with the fact that there were several clever attempts to murder Mr Henley. This was by putting out the gas which he habitually left burning in his room. It happened four times in all; thus proving that it was an attempt to kill him. If it had been only once it might have been accident, even twice it might have been accident, but the same accident does not happen four times at the same time of night.

'Mr Henley finally grew to regard the strange extinguishing of the gas as an effort to kill him, and carefully locked and barred his door and windows each night. He believed that someone came into his apartments and put out the light, leaving the gas flow. This, of course, was not true. Yet the gas was put out. How? My first idea, a natural one, was that it was turned off for an instant at the meter, when the light would go out, then turned on again. This, I convinced myself, was not true. Therefore still the question – how?

'It is a fact – I don't know how widely known it is – but it is a fact that every gas light in this house might be extinguished at the same time from this room without leaving it. How? Simply by removing the gas jet tip and blowing into the gas pipe. It would not leave a jet in the building burning. It is due to the fact that the lung power is greater than the pressure of the gas in the pipes, and forces it out.

'Thus we have the method employed to extinguish the light in Mr Henley's rooms, and all the barred and locked doors and windows would not stop it. At the same time it threatened the life of every person in the house – that is, every person who used gas. It was probably for this reason that the attempt was always made late at night, I should say three or four o'clock. That's when it was done, isn't it?' he asked suddenly of the valet.

Staring at The Thinking Machine in open-mouthed astonishment the valet nodded his acquiescence before he was fully aware of it.

'Yes, that's right,' The Thinking Machine resumed complacently. 'This was easily found out – comparatively. The next question was how was a watch kept on Mr Henley? It would have done no good to extinguish the gas before he was asleep, or to have turned it on when he was not in his rooms. It might have led to a speedy discovery of just how the thing was done.

'There's a spring lock on the door of Mr Henley's apartment. Therefore it would have been impossible for anyone to peep through the keyhole. There are no cracks through which one might see. How was this watch kept? How was the plotter to satisfy himself positively of the time when Mr Henley was asleep? How was it the gas was put out at no time of the score or more nights Mr Henley himself kept watch? Obviously he was watched through a window.

'No one could climb out on the window ledge and look into Mr Henley's apartments. No one could see into that apartment from the street – that is, could see whether Mr Henley was asleep or even in bed. They could see the light. Watch was kept with the aid offered by the flagpole, supplemented with a mirror – this mirror. A screw was driven into the frame – it has been removed now – it was swung on the flagpole rope and pulled out to the end of the pole, facing the building. To a man standing in the hall window of the third floor it offered precisely the angle necessary to reflect the interior of Mr Henley's suite, possibly even showed him in bed through a narrow opening in the curtain. There is no shade on the windows of that suite; heavy curtains instead. Is that right?'

Again the prisoner was surprised into a mute acquiescence.

'I saw the possibility of these things, and I saw, too, that at three or four o'clock in the morning it would be perfectly possible for a person to move about the upper halls of this house without being seen. If he wore a heavy bath robe, with a hood, say, no one would recognize him even if he were seen, and besides the garb would not cause suspicion. This bath robe has a hood.

'Now, in working the mirror back and forth on the flagpole at night a tiny scarlet thread was pulled out of the robe and clung to the rope. I found this thread; later Mr Hatch found an identical thread in these apartments. Both came from that bath robe. Plain logic shows that the person who blew down the gas pipes worked the mirror trick; the person who worked the mirror trick left the thread; the thread comes back to the bath robe – that bath robe there,' he pointed dramatically. 'Thus the person who desired Henley's death was in these apartments, or had easy access to them.'

He paused a moment and there was a tense silence. A great light was coming to Hatch, slowly but surely. The brain that had followed all this was unlimited in possibilities.

'Even before we traced the origin of the crime to this room,' went on the scientist, quietly now, 'attention had been attracted here, particularly to you, Mr Cabell. It was through the love affair, of which Miss Lipscomb was the centre. Mr Hatch learned that you and Henley had been rivals for her hand. It was that, even before this scarlet thread was found, which indicated that you might have some knowledge of the affair, directly or indirectly.

'You are not a malicious or revengeful man, Mr Cabell. But you are hot-tempered – extremely so. You demonstrated that just now, when, angry and not understanding, but feeling that your honour was at stake, you shot a hole in the floor.'

'What?' asked Detective Mallory.

'A little accident,' explained The Thinking Machine quickly. 'Not being a malicious or revengeful man, you are not the man to deliberately go ahead and make elaborate plans for the murder of Henley. In a moment of passion you might have killed him – but never deliberately as the result of premeditation. Besides you were out of town. Who was then in these apartments? Who had access to these apartments? Who might have used your bath robe? Your valet, possibly Miss Austin. Which? Now, let's see how we reached this conclusion which led to the valet.

'Miss Regnier was found dead. It was not suicide. How did I know? Because she had been reading with the gas light at its full. If she had been reading by the gas light, how was it then that it went out and suffocated her before she could arise and shut it off? Obviously she must have fallen asleep over her book and left the light burning.

'If she was in this plot to kill Henley, why did she light the jet in her room? There might have been some slight defect in the electric bulb in her room which she had just discovered. Therefore she lighted the gas, intending to extinguish it – turn it off entirely – later. But she fell asleep. Therefore when the valet here blew into the pipe, intending to kill Mr Henley, he unwittingly killed the woman he loved – Miss Regnier. It was perfectly possible, meanwhile, that she did not know of the attempt to be made that particular night, although she had participated in the others, knowing that Henley had night after night sat up to watch the light in his rooms.

'The facts, as I knew them, showed no connection between Miss Regnier and this man at that time – nor any connection between Miss Regnier and Henley. It might have been that the person who blew the gas out of the pipe from these rooms knew nothing whatever of Miss Regnier, just as he didn't know who else he might have killed in the building.

'But I had her death and the manner of it. I had eliminated you, Mr Cabell. Therefore there remained Miss Austin and the valet. Miss Austin was eccentric – insane, if you will. Would she have any motive for killing Henley? I could imagine none. Love? Probably not. Money? They had nothing in common on that ground. What? Nothing that I could see. Therefore, for the moment, I passed Miss Austin by, after asking you, Mr Cabell, if you were Miss Austin.

'What remained? The valet. Motive? Several possible ones, one or two probable. He is French, or says he is. Miss Regnier is French. Therefore I had arrived at the conclusion that they knew each other as people of the same nationality will in a house of this sort. And remember, I had passed by Mr Cabell and Miss Austin, so the valet was the only one left; he could use the bath robe.

'Well, the motive. Frankly that was the only difficult point in the entire problem – difficult because there were so many possibilities. And each possibility that suggested itself suggested also a woman. Jealousy? There must be a woman. Hate? Probably a woman. Attempted extortion? With the aid of a woman. No other motive which would lead to so elaborate a plot of murder would come forward. Who was the woman? Miss Regnier.

'Did Miss Regnier know Henley? Mr Hatch had reason to believe he knew her because of his actions when informed of her death. Knew her how? People of such relatively different planes of life can know each other – or do know each other – only on one plane. Henley is a typical young man, fast, I dare say, and liberal. Perhaps, then, there had been a liaison. When I saw this possibility I had my motives – all of them – jealousy, hate and possibly attempted extortion as well.

'What was more possible than Mr Henley and Miss Regnier had been acquainted? All liaisons are secret ones. Suppose she had been cast off because of the engagement to a young woman of Henley's own level? Suppose she had confided in the valet here? Do you see? Motives enough for any crime, however diabolical. The attempts on Henley's life possibly followed an attempted extortion of money. The shot which wounded Henley was fired by this man, Jean. Why? Because the woman who had cause to hate Henley was dead. Then the man? He was alive and vindictive. Henley knew who shot him, and knew why, but he'll never say it publicly. He can't afford to. It would ruin him. I think probably that's all. Do you want to add anything?' he asked of the valet.

'No,' was the fierce reply. 'I'm sorry I didn't kill him, that's all. It was all about as you said, though God knows how you found out,' he added, desperately.

'Are you a Frenchman?'

'I was born in New York, but lived in France for eleven years. I first knew Louise there.'

Silence fell upon the little group. Then Hatch asked a question:

'You told me, Professor, that there would be no other attempt to kill Henley by extinguishing the gas. How did you know that?'

'Because one person – the wrong person – had been killed that way,' was the reply. 'For this reason it was hardly likely that another attempt of that sort would be made. You had no intention of killing Louise Regnier, had you, Jean?'

'No, God help me, no.'

'It was all done in these apartments,' The Thinking Machine added, turning to Cabell, 'at the gas jet from which I took the tip. It had been only loosely replaced and the metal was tarnished where the lips had dampened it.'

'It must take great lung power to do a thing like that,' remarked Detective Mallory.

'You would be amazed to know how easily it is done,' said the scientist. 'Try it some time.'

The Thinking Machine arose and picked up his hat; Hatch did the same. Then the reporter turned to Cabell.

'Would you mind telling me why you were so anxious to get away tonight?' he asked.

'Well, no,' Cabell explained, and there was a rush of red to his face. 'It's because I received a telegram from Virginia – Miss Lipscomb, in fact. Some of Henley's past had come to her knowledge and the telegram told me that the engagement was broken. On top of this came the information that Henley had been shot and – I was considerably agitated.'

The Thinking Machine and Hatch were walking along the street.

'What did you write in the note you sent to Cabell that made him start to unpack?' asked the reporter curiously.

'There are some things that it wouldn't be well for everyone to know,' was the enigmatic response. 'Perhaps it would be just as well for you to overlook this little omission.'

'Of course, of course,' replied the reporter, wonderingly.

6

The Man Higher Up

William MacHarg and Edwin Balmer

The first real blizzard of the winter had burst upon New
York from the Atlantic. For seventy-two hours – as
Rentland, file clerk in the Broadway offices of the American Commodities Company, saw from the record he was
making for President Welter – no ship of any of the
dozen expected from foreign ports had been able to make
the Company's docks in Brooklyn, or, indeed, had been
reported at Sandy Hook. And for the last five days, during
which the weather bureau's storm signals had stayed
steadily set, no steamer of the six which had finished
unloading at the docks the week before had dared to try
for the open sea except one, the *Elizabethan Age*, which
had cleared the Narrows on Monday night.

On land the storm was scarcely less disastrous to the
business of the great importing company. Since Tuesday
morning Rentland's reports of the car and train-load
consignments which had left the warehouses daily had
been a monotonous page of trains stalled. But until that
Friday morning, Welter – the big, bull-necked, thick-
lipped master of men and money – had borne all the
accumulated trouble of the week with serenity, almost
with contempt. Only when the file clerk added to his
report the minor item that the 3,000-ton steamer *Elizabethan Age*, which had cleared on Monday night, had
been driven into Boston, something suddenly seemed to
'break' in the inner office. Rentland heard the president's

secretary telephone to Brooklyn for Rowan, the dock superintendent; he heard Welter's heavy steps going to and fro in the private office, his hoarse voice raised angrily; and soon afterwards Rowan blustered in. Rentland could no longer overhear the voices. He went back to his own private office and called the station master at the Grand Central Station on the telephone.

'The seven o'clock train from Chicago?' the clerk asked in a guarded voice. 'It came in at 10.30, as expected? Oh, at 10.10! Thank you.' He hung up the receiver and opened the door to pass a word with Rowan as he came out of the president's office.

'They've wired that the *Elizabethan Age* couldn't get beyond Boston, Rowan,' he cried curiously.

'The – hooker!' the dock superintendent had gone strangely white; for the imperceptible fraction of an instant his eyes dimmed with fear, as he stared into the wondering face of the clerk, but he recovered himself quickly, spat offensively, and slammed the door as he went out. Rentland stood with clenching hands for a moment; then he glanced at the clock and hurried to the entrance of the outer office. The elevator was just bringing up from the street a red-haired, blue-grey-eyed young man of medium height, who, noting with a quick, intelligent glance the arrangement of the offices, advanced directly toward President Welter's door. The chief clerk stepped forward quickly.

'You are Mr Trant?'

'Yes.'

'I am Rentland. This way, please.' He led the psychologist to the little room behind the files, where he had telephoned the moment before.

'Your wire to me in Chicago, which brought me here,' said Trant, turning from the inscription 'File Clerk' on the door to the dogged, decisive features and wiry form of his client, 'gave me to understand that you wished to have me investigate the disappearance, or death, of two of your dock scale-checkers. I suppose you were acting for President Welter – of whom I have heard – in sending for me?'

'No,' said Rentland, as he waved Trant to a seat. 'President Welter is certainly not troubling himself to that extent over an investigation.'

'Then the company, or some other officer?' Trant questioned, with increasing curiosity.

'No; nor the company, nor any other officer in it, Mr Trant.' Rentland smiled. 'Nor even am I, as file clerk of the American Commodities Company, overtroubling myself about those checkers,' he leaned nearer to Trant, confidentially, 'but as a special agent for the United States Treasury Department I am extremely interested in the death of one of these men, and in the disappearance of the other. And for that I called you to help me.'

'As a secret agent for the Government?' Trant repeated, with rapidly rising interest.

'Yes; a spy, if you wish to call me, but as truly in the ranks of the enemies to my country as any Nathan Hale, who has a statue in this city. Today the enemies are the big, corrupting, thieving corporations like this company; and appreciating that, I am not ashamed to be a spy in their ranks, commissioned by the Government to catch and condemn President Welter, and any other officers involved with him, for systematically stealing from the Government for the past ten years, and for probable connivance in the murder of at least one of those two checkers so that the company might continue to steal.'

'To steal? How?'

'Customs frauds, thefts, smuggling – anything you wish to call it. Exactly what or how, I can't tell; for that is part of what I sent for you to find out. For a number of years the Customs Department has suspected, upon circumstantial evidence, that the enormous profits of this company upon the thousand and one things which it is importing and distributing must come in part from goods they have got through without paying the proper duty. So at my own suggestion I entered the employ of the company a year ago to get track of the method. But after a year here I was almost ready to give up the investigation in despair, when Ed Landers, the company's checker on the docks in scale house No. 3, was killed – accidentally, the coroner's jury said. To me it looked suspiciously like murder. Within two weeks Morse, who was appointed as checker in his place, suddenly disappeared. The company's officials showed no concern as to the fate of these two men; and my suspicions that something crooked might be going on at scale house No. 3 were strengthened; and I sent for you to help me to get at the bottom of things.'

'Is it not best then to begin by giving me as fully as possible the details of the employment of Morse and Landers, and also of their disappearance?' the young psychologist suggested.

'I have told you these things here, Trant, rather than take you to some safer place,' the secret agent replied, 'because I have been waiting for someone who can tell you what you need to know better than I can. Edith Rowan, the stepdaughter of the dock superintendent, knew Landers well, for he boarded at Rowan's house. She was – or is, if he still lives – engaged to Morse. It is an unusual thing for Rowan himself to come here to see President Welter, as he did just before you came; but every morning since Morse disappeared his daughter has come to see Welter personally. She is already waiting in the outer office.' Opening the door, he indicated to Trant a light-haired, overdressed, nervous girl twisting about uneasily on the seat outside the president's private office.

'Welter thinks it policy, for some reason, to see her a moment every morning. But she always comes out almost at once – crying.'

'This is interesting,' Trant commented, as he watched the girl go into the president's office. After only a moment she came out, crying. Rentland had already left his room, so it seemed by chance that he and Trant met and supported her to the elevator, and over the slippery pavement to the neat electric coupé which was standing at the curb.

'It's hers,' said Rentland, as Trant hesitated before helping the girl into it. 'It's one of the things I wanted you to see. Broadway is very slippery, Miss Rowan. You will let me see you home again this morning? This gentleman is Mr Trant, a private detective. I want him to come along with us.'

The girl acquiesced, and Trant crowded into the little automobile. Rentland turned the coupé skilfully out into the swept path of the street, ran swiftly down Fifth Avenue to Fourteenth Street, and stopped three streets to the east before a house in the middle of the block. The house was as narrow and cramped and as cheaply constructed as its neighbours on both sides. It had lace curtains conspicuous in every window, and impressive statuettes, vases and gaudy bits of bric-a-brac in the front rooms.

'He told me again that Will must still be off drunk; and Will never takes a drink,' she spoke to them for the first time, as they entered the little sitting room.

' "He" is Welter,' Rentland explained to Trant. ' "Will" is Morse, the missing man. Now, Miss Rowan, I have brought Mr Trant with me because I have asked him to help me find Morse for you, as I promised; and I want you to tell him everything you can about how Landers was killed and how Morse disappeared.'

'And remember,' Trant interposed, 'that I know very little about the American Commodities Company.'

'Why, Mr Trant,' the girl gathered herself together, 'you cannot help knowing something about the company! It imports almost everything – tobacco, sugar, coffee, wines, olives, and preserved fruits, oils, and all sorts of table delicacies, from all over the world, even from Borneo, Mr Trant, and from Madagascar and New Zealand. It has big warehouses at the docks with millions of dollars' worth of goods stored in them. My stepfather has been with the company for years, and has charge of all that goes on at the docks.'

'Including the weighing?'

'Yes; everything on which there is a duty when it is taken off the boats has to be weighed, and to do this there are big scales, and for each one a scale house. When a scale is being used there are two men in the scale house. One of these is the Government weigher, who sets the scale to a balance and notes down the weight in a book. The other man, who is an employee of the company, writes the weight also in a book of his own; and he is called the company's checker. But though there are half a dozen scales, almost everything, when it is possible, is unloaded in front of scale No. 3, for that is the best berth for ships.'

'And Landers?'

'Landers was the company's checker on scale No. 3. Well, about five weeks ago I began to see that Mr Landers was troubled about something. Twice a queer, quiet little man with a scar on his cheek came to see him, and each time they went up to Mr Landers's room and talked a long while. Ed's room was over the sitting room, and after the man had gone I could hear him walking back and forth – walking and walking until it seemed as though he would never stop. I told father about this man who troubled Mr Landers, and he asked him about it, but Mr Landers flew into a rage and said it was nothing of importance. Then one night – it was a Wednesday – everybody stayed late at the docks to finish unloading the steamer *Covallo*. About two o'clock father got home, but Mr Landers had not been ready to come with him. He did not come all that night, and the next day he did not come home.

'Now, Mr Trant, they are very careful at the warehouses about who goes in and out, because so many valuable things are stored there. On one side the warehouses open onto the docks, and at each end they are fenced off so that you cannot go along the docks and get away from them that way; and on the other side they open onto the street through great driveway doors, and at every door, as long as it is open, there stands a watchman, who sees everybody that goes in and out. Only one door was open that Wednesday night, and the watchman there had not seen Mr Landers go out. And the second night passed, and he did not come home. But the next morning, Friday morning,' the girl caught her breath hysterically, 'Mr Landers's body was found in the engine room back of scale house No. 3, with the face crushed in horribly!'

'Was the engine room occupied?' said Trant, quickly. 'It must have been occupied in the daytime, and probably on the night when Landers disappeared, as they were unloading the *Covallo*. But on the night after which the body was found – was it occupied that night?'

'I don't know, Mr Trant. I think it could not have been for after the verdict of the coroner's jury, which was that Mr Landers had been killed by some part of the machinery, it was said that the accident must have happened either the evening before, just before the engineer shut off his engines, or the first thing that morning, just after he had started them; for otherwise somebody in the engine room would have seen it.'

'But where had Landers been all day Thursday, Miss Rowan, from two o'clock on the second night before, when your father last saw him, until the accident in the engine room?'

'It was supposed he had been drunk. When his body

was found, his clothes were covered with fibers from the coffee-sacking, and the jury supposed he had been sleeping off his liquor in the coffee warehouse during Thursday. But I had known Ed Landers for almost three years, and in all that time I never knew him to take even one drink.'

'Then it was a very unlikely supposition. You do not believe in that accident, Miss Rowan?' Trant said, brusquely.

The girl grew white as paper. 'Oh, Mr Trant, I don't know! I did believe in it. But since Will – Mr Morse – has disappeared in exactly the same way, under exactly the same circumstances, and everyone acts about it exactly the same way –'

'You say the circumstances of Morse's disappearance were the same?' Trant pressed quietly when she was able to proceed.

'After Mr Landers had been found dead,' said the girl, pulling herself together again, 'Mr Morse, who had been checker in one of the other scale houses, was made checker on scale No. 3. We were surprised at that, for it was a sort of promotion, and father did not like Will; he had been greatly displeased at our engagement. Will's promotion made us very happy, for it seemed as though father must be changing his opinion. But after Will had been checker on scale No. 3 only a few days, the same queer, quiet little man with the scar on his cheek who had begun coming to see Mr Landers before he was killed began coming to see Will, too! And after he began coming, Will was troubled, terribly troubled, I could see; but he would not tell me the reason. And he expected, after that man began coming, that something would happen to him. And I know, from the way he acted and spoke about Mr Landers, that he thought he had not been accidentally killed. One evening, when I could see he had been more troubled than ever before, he said that if anything happened to him I was to go at once to his boarding house and take charge of everything in his room, and not to let anyone into the room to search it until I had removed everything in the bureau drawers; everything, no matter how useless anything seemed. Then, the very next night, five days ago, just as while Mr Landers was checker, everybody stayed overtime at the docks to finish unloading a vessel, the *Elizabethan Age*. And in the morning Will's landlady called me on the phone to tell me that he had not come home. Five days ago, Mr Trant! And since then no one has seen or heard from him; and the watchman did not see him come out of the warehouse that night just as he did not see Ed Landers.'

'What did you find in Morse's bureau?' asked Trant.

'I found nothing.'

'Nothing?' Trant repeated. 'That is impossible, Miss Rowan! Think again! Remember he warned you that what you found might seem trivial and useless.'

The girl, a little defiantly, studied for an instant Trant's clear-cut features. Suddenly she arose and ran from the room, but returned quickly with a strange little implement in her hand.

It was merely a bit of wire, straight for perhaps three inches, and then bent in a half circle for five or six inches, the bent portion of the wire being wound carefully with stout twine, thus:

'Except for his clothes and some blank writing paper and envelopes that was absolutely the only thing in the bureau. It was the only thing at all in the only locked drawer.'

Trant and Rentland stared disappointedly at this strange implement, which the girl handed to the psychologist.

'You have shown this to your stepfather, Miss Rowan, for a possible explanation of why a company checker should be so solicitous about such a thing as this?' asked Trant.

'No,' the girl hesitated. 'Will had told me not to say anything; and I told you father did not like Will. He had made up his mind that I was to marry Ed Landers. In most ways father is kind and generous. He's kept the coupé we came here in for mother and me for two years; and you see,' she gestured a little proudly about the bedecked and badly furnished rooms, 'you see how he gets everything for us. Mr Landers was most generous, too. He took me to the theatre two or three times every week – always the best seats, too. I didn't want to go, but father made me. I preferred Will, though he wasn't so generous.'

Trant's eyes returned, with more intelligent scrutiny, to the mysterious implement in his hand.

'What salary do checkers receive, Rentland?' he asked, in a low tone.

'One hundred and twenty-five dollars a month.'

'And her father, the dock superintendent – how much?' Trant's expressive glance now jumping about from one gaudy extravagant trifle in the room to another, caught a glimpse again of the electric coupé standing in the street, then returned to the tiny bit of wire in his hand.

'Three thousand a year,' Rentland replied.

'Tell me, Miss Rowan,' said Trant, 'this implement – have you by any chance mentioned it to President Welter?'

'Why, no, Mr Trant.'

'You are sure of that? Excellent! Excellent! Now the queer, quiet little man with the scar on his cheek who came to see Morse; no one could tell you anything about him?'

'No one, Mr Trant; but yesterday Will's landlady told me that a man has come to ask for Will every forenoon since he disappeared, and she thinks this may be the man with the scar, though she can't be sure, for he kept the collar of his overcoat up about his face. She was to telephone me if he came again.'

'If he comes this morning,' Trant glanced quickly at his watch, 'you and I, Rentland, might much better be waiting for him over there.'

The psychologist rose, putting the bent, twine-wound bit of wire carefully into his pocket; and a minute later the two men crossed the street to the house, already known to Rentland, where Morse had boarded. The landlady not only allowed them to wait in her little parlour, but waited with them until the end of an hour she pointed with an eager gesture to a short man in a big ulster who turned sharply up the front steps.

'That's him – see!' she exclaimed.

'That man with the scar!' cried Rentland. 'Well! I know him.'

He made for the door, caught at the ulster and pulled the little man into the house by main force.

'Well, Dickey!' the secret agent challenged, as the man faced him in startled recognition. 'What are you doing in this case? Trant, this is Inspector Dickey, of the Customs Office,' he introduced the officer.

'I'm in the case on my own hook, if I know what case you're talking about,' piped Dickey. 'Morse, eh? and the American Commodities Company, eh?'

'Exactly,' said Rentland, brusquely. 'What were you calling to see Landers for?'

'You know about that?' The little man looked up sharply. 'Well, six weeks ago Landers came to me and told me he had something to sell; a secret system for beating the customs. But before we got to terms, he began losing his nerve a little; he got it back, however, and was going to tell me when, all at once, he disappeared, and two days later he was dead! That made it hotter for me; so I went after Morse. But Morse denied he knew anything. Then Morse disappeared, too.'

'So you got nothing at all out of them?' Rentland interposed.

'Nothing I could use. Landers, one time when he was getting up his nerve, showed me a piece of bent wire – with string around it – in his room, and began telling me something when Rowan called him, and then he shut up.'

'A bent wire!' Trant cried, eagerly. 'Like this?' He took from his pocket the implement given him by Edith Rowan. 'Morse had this in his room, the only thing in a locked drawer.'

'The same thing!' Dickey cried, seizing it. 'So Morse had it, too, after he became checker at scale No. 3, where the cheating is, if anywhere. The very thing Landers started to explain to me, and how they cheated the customs with it. I say, we must have it now, Rentland! We need only go to the docks and watch them while they weigh, and see how they use it, and arrest them and then we have them at last, eh, old man?' he cried in triumph. 'We have them at last!'

'You mean,' Trant cut in upon the customs man, 'that you can convict and jail perhaps the checker, or a foreman, or maybe even a dock superintendent – as usual. But the men higher up – the big men who are really at the bottom of this business and the only ones worth getting – will you catch them?'

'We must take those we can get,' said Dickey sharply.

Trant laid his hand on the little officer's arm.

'I am a stranger to you,' he said, 'but if you have followed some of the latest criminal cases in Illinois perhaps you know that, using the methods of modern practical psychology, I have been able to get results where old ways have failed. We are front to front now with perhaps the greatest problem of modern criminal catching, to catch, in cases involving a great corporation, not only the little men low down who perform the criminal acts, but the men higher up, who conceive, or connive at the criminal scheme. Rentland, I did not come here to convict merely a dock foreman; but if we are going to reach anyone higher than that, you must not let Inspector Dickey excite suspicion by prying into matters at the docks this afternoon!'

'But what else can we do?' said Rentland, doubtfully.

'Modern practical psychology gives a dozen possible ways for proving the knowledge of the man higher up in this corporation crime,' Trant answered, 'and I am considering which is the most practicable. Only tell me,' he demanded suddenly, 'Mr Welter I have heard is one of the rich men of New York who make it a fad to give largely to universities and other institutions; can you tell me with what ones he may be most closely interested?'

'I have heard,' Rentland replied, 'that he is one of the patrons of the Stuyvesant School of Science. It is probably the most fashionably patroned institution in New York; and Welter's name, I know, figures with it in the newspapers.'

'Nothing could be better!' Trant exclaimed. 'Kuno Schmalz has his psychological laboratory there. I see my way now, Rentland; and you will hear from me early in the afternoon. But keep away from the docks!' He turned and left the astonished customs officers abruptly. Half an hour later the young psychologist sent in his card to Professor Schmalz in the laboratory of the Stuyvesant School of Science. The German, broad-faced, spectacled, beaming, himself came to the laboratory door.

'Is it Mr Trant – the young, apt pupil of my old friend,

Dr Reiland?' he boomed, admiringly. 'Ach! luck is good to Reiland! For twenty years I, too, have shown them in the laboratory how fear, guilt, every emotion causes in the body reactions which can be measured. But do they apply it? Pouf! No! it remains to them all impractical, academic, because I have only nincompoops in my classes!'

'Professor Schmalz,' said Trant, following him into the laboratory, and glancing from one to another of the delicate instruments with keen interest, 'tell me along what line you are now working.'

'Ach! I have been for a year now experimenting with the plethysmograph and the pneumograph. I make a taste, I make a smell, or I make a noise to excite feeling in the subject; and I read by the plethysmograph that the volume of blood in the hand decreases under the emotions and that the pulse quickens; and by the pneumograph I read that the breathing is easier or quicker, depending on whether the emotions are pleasant or unpleasant. I have performed this year more than two thousand of those experiments.'

'Good! I have a problem in which you can be of the very greatest use to me; and the plethysmograph and the pneumograph will serve my purpose as well as any other instrument in the laboratory. For no matter how hardened a man may be, no matter how impossible it may have become to detect his feelings in his face or bearing, he cannot prevent the volume of blood in his hand from decreasing, and his breathing from becoming different, under the influence of emotions of fear or guilt. By the way, Professor, is Mr Welter familiar with these experiments of yours?'

'What, he!' cried the stout German. 'For why should I tell him about them? He knows nothing. He has bought my time to instruct classes; he has not bought, py chiminey! everything – even the soul Gott gave me!'

'But he would be interested in them?'

'To be sure, he would be interested in them! He would bring in his automobile three or four other fat money-makers, and he would show me off before them. He would make his trained bear – that is me – dance!'

'Good!' cried Trant again, excitedly. 'Professor Schmalz, would you be willing to give a little exhibition of the plethysmograph and pneumograph, this evening, if possible, and arrange for President Welter to attend it?'

The astute German cast on him a quick glance of interrogation. 'Why not?' he said. 'It makes nothing to me what purpose you will be carrying out; no, py chiminey! not if it costs me my position of trained bear; because I have confidence in my psychology that it will not make any innocent man suffer!'

'And you will have two or three scientists present to watch the experiments? And you will allow me to be there also and assist?'

'With great pleasure.'

'But, Professor Schmalz, you need not introduce me to Mr Welter, who will think I am one of your assistants.'

'As you wish about that, pupil of my dear old friend.'

'Excellent!' Trant leaped to his feet. 'Provided it is possible to arrange this with Mr Welter, how soon can you let me know?'

'Ach! it is as good as arranged, I tell you. His vanity will arrange it if I assure the greatest publicity –'

'The more publicity the better.'

'Wait! It shall be fixed before you leave here.'

The professor led the way into his private study, telephoned to the president of the American Commodities Company, and made the appointment without trouble.

A few minutes before eight o'clock that evening Trant again mounted rapidly the stone steps to the professor's laboratory. The professor and two others, who were bending over a table in the centre of the room, turned at his entrance. President Welter had not yet arrived. The young psychologist acknowledged with pleasure the introduction to the two scientists with Schmalz. Both of them were known to him by name, and he had been following with interest a series of experiments which the elder, Dr Annerly, had been reporting in a psychological journal. Then he turned at once to the apparatus on the table.

He was still examining the instruments when the noise of a motor stopping at the door warned him of the arrival of President Welter's party. Then the laboratory door opened and the party appeared. They also were three in number; stout men, rather obtrusively dressed, in jovial spirits, with strong faces flushed now with the wine they had taken at dinner.

'Well, Professor, what fireworks are you going to show us tonight?' asked Welter, patronizingly. 'Schmalz,' he explained to his companions, 'is the chief ring master of this circus.'

The bearded face of the German grew purple under Welter's jokingly overbearing manner; but he turned to the instruments and began to explain them. The Marey pneumograph, which the professor first took up, consists of a very thin flexible brass plate suspended by a cord around the neck of the person under examination, and fastened tightly against the chest by a cord circling the body. On the outer surface of this plate are two small, bent levers, connected at one end to the cord around the body of the subject, and at the other end to the surface of a small hollow drum fastened to the plate between the two. As the chest rises and falls in breathing, the levers press more and less upon the surface of the drum; and this varying pressure on the air inside the drum is transmitted from the drum through an air-tight tube to a little pencil which it drops and lifts. The pencil, as it rises and falls, touching always a sheet of smoked paper traveling over a cylinder on the recording device, traces a line whose rising strokes represent accurately the drawing of air into the chest and whose falling represents its expulsion.

It was clear to Trant that the professor's rapid explanation, though plain enough to the psychologists already familiar with the device, was only partly understood by the big men. It had not been explained to them that changes in the breathing so slight as to be imperceptible to the eye would be recorded unmistakably by the moving pencil.

Professor Schmalz turned to the second instrument. This was a plethysmograph, designed to measure the increase or decrease of the size of one finger of a person under examination as the blood supply to that finger becomes greater or less. It consists primarily of a small cylinder so constructed that it can be fitted over the finger and made air-tight. Increase or decrease of the size of the finger then increases or decreases the air pressure inside the cylinder. These changes in the air pressure are transmitted through an air-tight tube to a delicate piston which moves a pencil and makes a line upon the record sheet just under that made by the pneumograph. The upward or downward trend of this line shows the increase or decrease of the blood supply, while the smaller vibrations up and down record the pulse beat in the finger.

There was still a third pencil touching the record sheet above the other two and wired electrically to a key like that of a telegraph instrument fastened to the table. When this key was in its normal position this pencil made simply a straight line upon the sheet; but instantly when the key was pressed down, the line broke downward also.

This third instrument was used merely to record on the sheet, by the change in the line, the point at which the object that aroused sensation or emotion was displayed to the person undergoing examination.

The instant's silence which followed Schmalz's rapid explanation was broken by one of Welter's companions with the query:

'Well, what's the use of all this stuff, anyway?'

'Ach!' said Schmalz, bluntly, 'it is interesting, curious! I will show you.'

'Will one of you gentlemen,' said Trant, quickly, 'permit us to make use of him in the demonstration?'

'Try it, Jim,' Welter laughed, noisily.

'Not I,' said the other. 'This is your circus.'

'Yes, indeed it's mine. And I'm not afraid of it. Schmalz, do your worst!' He dropped laughing into the chair the professor set for him, and at Schmalz's direction unbuttoned his vest. The professor hung the pneumograph around his neck and fastened it tightly about the big chest. He laid Welter's forearm in a rest suspended from the ceiling, and attached the cylinder to the second finger of the plump hand. In the meantime Trant had quickly set the pencils to bear upon the record sheet and had started the cylinder on which the sheet traveled under them.

'You see, I have prepared for you.' Schmalz lifted a napkin from a tray holding several little dishes. He took from one of these a bit of caviar and laid it upon Welter's tongue. At the same instant Trant pushed down the key. The pencils showed a slight commotion, and the spectators stared at this record sheet:

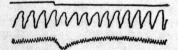

'Ah!' exclaimed Schmalz, 'you do not like caviar.'

'How do you know that?' demanded Welter.

'The instruments show that at the unpleasant taste you breathe less freely – not so deep. Your finger, as under strong sensation or emotion, grows smaller, and your pulse beats more rapidly.'

'By the Lord! Welter, what do you think of that?' cried one of his companions; 'your finger gets smaller when you taste caviar!'

It was a joke to them. Boisterously laughing, they tried Welter with other food upon the tray; they lighted for him one of the black cigars of which he was most fond, and watched the trembling pencils write the record of his pleasure at the taste and smell. Through it all Trant waited, alert watchful, biding the time to carry out his plan. It came when, having exhausted the articles at hand, they paused to find some other means to carry on the amusement. The young psychologist leaned forward suddenly.

'It is no great ordeal after all, is it, Mr Welter?' he said. 'Modern psychology does not put its subjects to torture like' – he halted, meaningly – '*a prisoner in the Elizabethan Age!*'

Dr Annerly, bending over the record sheet, uttered a startled exclamation. Trant, glancing keenly at him, straightened triumphantly. But the young psychologist did not pause. He took quickly from his pocket a photograph, showing merely a heap of empty coffee sacks piled carelessly to a height of some two feet along the inner wall of a shed, and laid it in front of the subject. Welter's face did not alter; but again the pencils shuddered over the moving paper, and the watchers stared with astonishment. Rapidly removing the photograph, Trant substituted for it the bent wire given him by Miss Rowan. Then for the last time he swung to the instrument, and as his eyes caught the wildly vibrating pencils, they flared with triumph.

President Welter rose abruptly, but not too hurriedly.

'That's about enough of this tomfoolery,' he said, with perfect self-possession.

His jaw had imperceptibly squared to the watchful determination of the prize fighter driven into his corner. His cheek still held the ruddy glow of health; but the wine flush had disappeared from it, and he was perfectly sober.

Trant tore the strip of paper from the instrument, and numbered the last three reactions 1, 2, 3. This is the way the records looked:

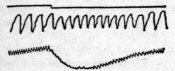

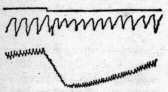

Record of the reaction when Trant said: 'A prisoner in the Elizabethan Age!'

Record made when Welter saw the photograph of a heap of coffee sacks.

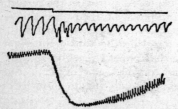

Record made when the spring was shown to Welter.

In each of these diagrams the single break in the upper line shows the point at which an object or words expected to arouse emotion are presented. The wavy line just below it is the record of the subject's breathing. The irregular line at the bottom indicates the alteration of the size of the subject's finger as the blood supply increases or decreases.

'Amazing!' said Dr Annerly. 'Mr Welter, I am curious to know what associations you have with that photograph and bent wire, the sight of which aroused in you such strong emotion.'

By immense self-control, the president of the American Commodities Company met his eyes fairly. 'None,' he answered.

'Impossible! No psychologist, knowing how this record was taken, could look at it without feeling absolutely certain that the photograph and spring caused in you such excessive emotion that I am tempted to give it, without further words, the name of "intense fright"! But if we have inadvertently surprised a secret, we have no desire to pry into it further. Is it not so, Mr Trant?'

At the name President Welter whirled suddenly. 'Trant! Is your name Trant?' he demanded. 'Well, I've heard of you.' His eyes hardened. 'A man like you goes just so far and then – somebody stops him!'

'As they stopped Landers?' Trant inquired.

'Come, we've seen enough, I guess,' said President Welter, including for one instant in his now frankly menacing gaze both Trant and Professor Schmalz; he turned to the door, closely followed by his companions. And a moment later the quick explosions of his automobile were heard. At the sound, Trant seized suddenly a large envelope, dropped into it the photograph and wire he had just used, sealed, signed, and dated it, signed and dated also the record from the instruments and hurriedly handed all to Dr Annerly.

'Doctor, I trust this to you,' he cried, excitedly. 'It will be best to have them attested by all three of you. If possible get the record photograph tonight, and distribute the photographs in safe places. Above all, do not let the record itself out of your hands until I come for it. It is important – extremely important! As for me, I have not a moment to lose!'

The young psychologist sped down the stone steps of the laboratory three at a time, ran at top speed to the nearest street corner, turned it and leaped into a waiting automobile. 'The American Commodities Company's docks in Brooklyn,' he shouted, 'and never mind the speed limits!'

Rentland and the chauffeur, awaiting him in the machine, galvanized at his coming.

'Hot work?' the customs agent asked.

'It may be very hot; but we have the start of him,' Trant replied as the car shot ahead. 'Welter himself is coming to the docks tonight, I think, by the look of him! He left just before me, but must drop his friends first. He suspects, now, that we know; but he cannot be aware that we know that they are unloading tonight. He probably counts on our waiting to catch them at the cheating tomorrow morning. So he's going over tonight himself, if I size him up right, to order it stopped and remove all traces before we can prove anything. Is Dickey waiting?'

'When you give the word he is to take us in and catch them at it. If Welter himself comes, as you think, it will not change the plan?' Rentland replied.

'Not at all,' said Trant, 'for I have him already. He will deny everything, of course, but it's too late now!'

The big car, with unchecked speed, swung down Broadway, slowed after a twenty-minutes' run to cross the Brooklyn Bridge, and, turning to the left, plunged once more at high speed into the narrower and less well-kept thoroughfares of the Brooklyn water front. Two minutes later it overtook a little electric coupé, bobbing excitedly down the sloping street. As they passed it, Trant caught sight of the illuminated number hanging at its rear, and shouted suddenly to the chauffeur, who brought the big motor to a stop a hundred feet beyond. The psychologist, leaping down, ran into the road before the little car.

'Miss Rowan,' he cried to its single occupant, as it came to a stop. 'Why are you coming over here at this time tonight?'

'Oh, it's you, Mr Trant!' She opened the door, showing relief in the recognition. 'Oh, I'm so worried. I'm on my way to see father; for a telegram just came to him from Boston; mother opened it, and told me to take it to him at once, as it was most important. She wouldn't tell me what it was about, but it excited her a great deal. Oh, I'm so afraid it must be about Will and that was why she wouldn't tell me.'

'From Boston?' Trant pressed quickly. Having her confidence, the girl nervously read the telegram aloud by the light of the coupé's side lamps. It read:

> Police have taken your friend out of our hands;
> look out for trouble. Wilson.

'Who is Wilson?' Trant demanded.

'I am not sure it is the man, but the captain of the *Elizabethan Age* is a friend of father's named Wilson!'

'I can't help you then, after all,' said Trant, springing back to his powerful car. He whispered a word to the chauffeur which sent it driving ahead through the drifts at double its former speed, leaving the little electric coupé far behind. Ten minutes later Rentland stopped the motor a block short of a great lighted doorway which suddenly showed in a length of dark, lowering buildings which lay beside the American Commodities Company's Brooklyn docks.

'Now,' the secret agent volunteered, 'it is up to me to find Dickey's ladder!'

He guided Trant down a narrow, dark court which brought them face to face with a blank wall; against this wall a light ladder had been recently placed. Ascending it, they came into the dock inclosure. Descending again by a dozen rickety, disused steps, they reached a darker, covered teamway and hurried along it to the docks. Just short of the end of the open dock houses, where a string of arc lamps threw their white and flickering light upon the huge, black side of a moored steamer, Rentland turned into a little shed, and the two came suddenly upon Customs Officer Dickey.

'This one next to us,' the little man whispered, eagerly, to Trant, as he grasped his hand, 'is the scale house where whatever is being done is done – No. 3.'

In and out of the yawning gangways of the steamer before them struggling lines of sweating men were wheeling trucks loaded with bales of tobacco. Trant looked first to the left, where the bales disappeared into the tobacco warehouse; then to the right, where, close at hand, each truck-load stopped momentarily on a scale platform in front of the low shed which bore the number Dickey indicated in a large white figure.

'Who's that?' asked Trant, as a small figure, hardly five feet tall, cadaverous, beetle-browed, with cold, malignant, red-lidded eyes passed directly under the arc light nearest them.

'Rowan, the dock superintendent!' Dickey whispered.

'I knew he was small,' Trant returned with surprise, 'but I thought surely he must have some fist to be the terror of these dock laborers.'

'Wait!' Rentland, behind them, motioned.

A bloated, menacing figure had suddenly swung clear of the group of dock labourers – a roustabout, goaded to desperation, with a fist raised against his puny superior.

But before the blow had fallen another fist, huge and black, struck the man over Rowan's shoulder with a hammer. He fell, and the dock superintendent passed on without a backward glance, the giant Negro who had struck the blow following in his footsteps like a dog.

'The black,' Rentland explained, 'is Rowan's bodyguard. He needs him.'

'I see,' Trant replied. 'And for Miss Rowan's sake I am glad it was that way,' he added, enigmatically.

Dickey had quietly opened a door on the opposite side of the shed; the three slipped quickly through it and stepped unobserved around the corner of the coffee warehouse to a long, dark, and narrow space. On one side of them was the rear wall of scale house No. 3, and on the other the engine room where Landers's body had been found. The single window in the rear of No. 3 scale house had been whitewashed to prevent anyone from looking in from that side; but in spots the whitewash had fallen off in flakes. Trant put his eye to one of these clear spots in the glass and looked in.

The scale table, supported on heavy posts, extended across almost the whole front of the house, behind a low, wide window, which permitted those seated at the table to see all that occurred on the docks. Toward the right end of the table sat the Government weigher; toward the left end, and separated from him by almost the whole length of the table, sat the company checker. They were the only persons in the scale house. Trant, after his first rapid survey of the scene, fixed his eye upon the man who had taken the place which Landers had held for three years, and Morse for a few days afterwards – the company checker. A truck-load of tobacco bales was wheeled on to the scales in front of the house.

'Watch his left knee,' Trant whispered quickly into Dickey's ear at the pane beside him, as the balance was being made upon the beam before them. As he spoke, the Government weigher adjusted the balance and they saw the left leg of the company checker pressed hard against the post which protected the scale rod at his end. Both men in the scale house then read aloud the weight and each entered it in the book on the table in front of him. A second truckful was wheeled on to the scale; and again, just as the Government weigher fixed his balances, the company checker, so inconspicuously as to make the act undiscoverable by anyone not looking for that precise move, repeated the operation. With the next truck they saw it again. The psychologist turned to the others. Rentland, too, had been watching through the pane and nodded his satisfaction.

Immediately Trant dashed open the door of the scale house, and threw himself bodily upon the checker. The man resisted; they struggled. While the customs men protected him, Trant, wrenching something from the post beside the checker's left knee, rose with a cry of triumph. Then the psychologist, warned by a cry from Rentland, leaped quickly to one side to avoid a blow from the giant Negro. His quickness saved him; still the blow, glancing along his cheek, hurled him from his feet. He rose immediately, blood flowing from a superficial cut upon his forehead where it had struck the scale-house wall. He saw Rentland covering the Negro with a revolver, and the two other customs men arresting, at pistol point, the malignant little dock superintendent, the checker, and the others who had crowded into the scale house.

'You see!' Trant exhibited to the customs officers a bit of bent wire, wound with string, precisely like that the girl had given him that morning and he had used in his test of Welter the hour before. 'It was almost exactly as we knew it must be! This spring was struck through a hole in the protecting post so that it prevented the balance beam from rising properly when bales were put on the platform. A little pressure just at that point takes many pounds from each bale weighed. The checker had only to move his knee, in a way we would never have noticed if we were not watching for it, to work the scheme by which they have been cheating for ten years! But the rest of this affair,' he glanced at the quickly collecting crowd, 'can best be settled in the office.'

He led the way, the customs men taking their prisoners at pistol point. As they entered the office, Rowan first, a girl's cry and the answering oath of her father told Trant that the dock superintendent's daughter had arrived. But she had been almost overtaken by another powerful car; for before Trant could speak with her the outer door of the office opened violently and President Welter, in an automobile coat and cap, entered.

'Ah! Mr Welter, you got here quickly,' said Trant, meeting calmly his outraged astonishment at the scene. 'But a little too late.'

'What is the matter here?' Welter governed his voice commandingly. 'And what has brought *you* here, from your phrenology?' he demanded, contemptuously, of Trant.

'The hope of catching red-handed, as we have just caught them, your company checker and your dock superintendent defrauding the Government,' Trant returned, 'before you could get here to stop them and remove evidences.'

'What raving idiocy is this?' Welter replied, still with excellent moderation. 'I came here to sign some necessary papers for ships clearing, and you –'

'I say we have caught your men red-handed,' Trant repeated, 'at the methods used, with your certain knowledge and under your direction, Mr Welter, to steal systematically from the United States Government for – probably the last ten years. We have uncovered the means by which your company checker at scale No. 3, which, because of its position, probably weighs more cargoes

than all the other scales together, has been lessening the
apparent weights upon which you pay duties.'

'Cheating here under my direction?' Welter now
bellowed indignantly. 'What are you talking about?
Rowan, what is he talking about?' he demanded, boldly,
of the dock superintendent; but the cadaverous little man
was unable to brazen it out with him.

'You need not have looked at your dock superintendent
just then, Mr Welter, to see if he would stand the racket
when the trouble comes, for which you have been paying
him enough on the side to keep him in electric motors
and marble statuettes. And you cannot try now to disown
this crime with the regular president-of-corporation excuse, Mr Welter, that you never knew of it, that it was all
done without your knowledge by a subordinate to make a
showing in his department; and do not expect, either, to
escape so easily your certain complicity in the murder of
Landers, to prevent him from exposing your scheme and
– since even the American Commodities Company
scarcely dared to have two "accidental deaths" of checkers
in the same month – the shanghaiing of Morse later.'

'My complicity in the death of Landers and the disappearance of Morse?' Welter roared.

'I said the murder of Landers,' Trant corrected. 'For
when Rentland and Dickey tell tomorrow before the
grand jury how Landers was about to disclose to the
Customs Department the secret of the cheating in
weights; how he was made afraid by Rowan, and later was
about to tell anyway and was prevented only by a most
sudden death, I think murder will be the word brought
in the indictment. And I said shanghaiing of Morse, Mr
Welter. When we remembered this morning that Morse
had disappeared the night the *Elizabethan Age* left your
docks and you and Rowan were so intensely disgusted at
its having had to put into Boston this morning instead of
going on straight to Sumatra, we did not have to wait for

the chance information this evening that Captain Wilson is a friend of Rowan's to deduce that the missing checker was put aboard, as confirmed by the Boston harbour police this afternoon, who searched the ship under our instructions.' Trant paused a moment; again fixed the now trembling Welter with his eye, and continued: 'I charge your certain complicity in these crimes, along with your certain part in the customs frauds,' the psychologist repeated. 'Undoubtedly, it was Rowan who put Morse out of the way upon the *Elizabethan Age*. Nevertheless, you knew that he was a prisoner upon that ship, a fact which was written down in indelible black and white by my tests of you at the Stuyvesant Institute two hours ago, when I merely mentioned to you "a prisoner in the *Elizabethan Age*".

'I do not charge that you, personally, were the one who murdered Landers; or even that Rowan himself did; whether his Negro did, as I suspect, is a matter now for the courts to decide upon. But that you undoubtedly were aware that he was not killed accidentally in the engine room, but was killed the Wednesday night before and his body hidden under the coffee bags, as I guessed from the fibers of coffee sacking on his clothes, was also registered as mercilessly by the psychological machines when I showed you merely the picture of a pile of coffee sacks.

'And last, Mr Welter, you deny knowledge of the cheating which has been going on, and was at the bottom of the other crimes. Well, Welter,' the psychologist took from his pocket the bent, twine-wound wire, 'here is the "innocent" little thing which was the third means of causing you to register upon the machines such extreme and inexplicable emotion; or rather, Mr Welter, it is the companion piece to that, for this is not the one I showed you, the one given to Morse to use, which, however, he refused to make use of; but it is the very wire I took to-night from the hole in the post where it bore against the balance beam to cheat the Government. When this is made public tomorrow, and with it is made public, too, and attested by the scientific men who witnessed them, the diagram and explanation of the tests of you two hours ago, do you think that you can deny longer that this was all with your knowledge and direction?'

The big, bull neck of the president swelled, and his hands clenched and reclenched as he stared with gleaming eyes into the face of the young man who thus challenged him.

'You are thinking now, I suppose, Mr Welter,' Trant replied to his glare, 'that such evidence as that directly against you cannot be got before a court. I am not so sure of that. But at least it can go before the public tomorrow morning in the papers, attested by the signatures of the scientific men who witnessed the test. It has been photographed by this time, and the photographic copies are distributed in safe places, to be produced with the original on the day when the Government brings criminal proceedings against you. If I had it here I would show you how complete, how merciless, is the evidence that you knew what was being done. I would show you how at the point marked 1 on the record your pulse and breathing quickened with alarm under my suggestion; how at the point marked 2 your anxiety and fear increased; and how at 3, when the spring by which this cheating had been carried out was before your eyes, you betrayed yourself uncontrollably, unmistakably. How the volume of blood in your second finger suddenly diminished, as the current was thrown back upon your heart; how your pulse throbbed with terror; how, though unmoved to outward appearance, you caught your breath, and your labouring lungs struggled under the dread that your wrongdoing was discovered and you would be branded – as I trust you will now be branded, Mr Welter, when the evidence in this case and the testimony of those who witnessed my test are produced before a jury – a deliberate and scheming thief!'

'— you!' The three words escaped from Welter's puffed lips. He put out his arm to push aside the customs officer standing between him and the door. Dickey resisted.

'Let him go if he wants to!' Trant called to the officer. 'He can neither escape nor hide. His money holds him under bond!'

The officer stepped aside, and Welter, without another word, went into the hall. But when his face was no longer visible to Trant, the hanging pouches under his eyes grew leaden grey, his fat lips fell apart loosely, his step shuffled; his mask had fallen!

'Besides, we need all the men we have, I think,' said Trant, turning back to the prisoners, 'to get these to a safe place. Miss Rowan,' he turned then and put out his hand to steady the terrified and weeping girl, 'I warned you that you had probably better not come here tonight. But since you have come and have had pain because of your stepfather's wrongdoings, I am glad to be able to give you the additional assurance, beyond the fact, which you have heard, that your fiancé was not murdered, but merely put away on board the *Elizabethan Age*; that he is safe and sound, except for a few bruises, and, moreover, we expect him here any moment now. The police were bringing him down from Boston on the train which arrives at ten.'

He went to the window and watched an instant, as Dickey and Rentland, having telephoned for a patrol, were waiting with their prisoners. Before the patrol wagon appeared, he saw the bobbing lanterns of a lurching cab that turned a corner a block away. As it stopped at the entrance, a police officer in plain clothes leaped out and helped after him a young man wrapped in an overcoat, with one arm in a sling, pale, and with bandaged head. The girl uttered a cry, and sped through the doorway. For a moment the psychologist stood watching the greeting of the lovers. He turned back then to the sullen prisoners.

'But it's some advance, isn't it, Rentland,' he asked, 'not to have to try such poor devils alone; but, at last, with the man who makes the millions and pays them the pennies – the man higher up?'

7

The Axton Letters

William MacHarg and Edwin Balmer

The sounds in her dressing-room had waked her just before five. Ethel Waldron could still see, when she closed her eyes, every single, sharp detail of her room as it was that instant she sprang up in bed, with the cry that had given the alarm, and switched on the electric light. Instantly the man had shut the door; but as she sat, strained, staring at it to reopen, the hands and dial of her clock standing on the mantel beside the door, had fixed themselves upon her retina like the painted dial of a jeweler's dummy. It could have been barely five, therefore, when Howard Axton, after his first swift rush in her defense had found the window which had been forced open, had picked up the queer Turkish dagger which he found broken on the sill, and crying to the girl not to call the police, as it was surely 'the same man' – the same man, he meant, who had so inexplicably followed him around the world – had rushed to his room for extra cartridges for his revolver and run out into the cold sleet of the March morning.

So it was now an hour or more since Howard had run after the man, revolver in hand; and he had not reappeared or telephoned or sent any word at all of his safety. And however much Howard's life in wild lands had accustomed him to seek redress outside the law, hers still held the city-bred impulse to appeal to the police. She turned from her nervous pacing at the window and seized the telephone from its hook; but at the sound of the operator's voice she remembered again Howard's injunction that the man, whenever he appeared, was to be left solely to him, and dropped the receiver without answering. But she resented fiercely the advantage he held over her which must oblige her, she knew, to obey him. He had told her frankly – threatened her, indeed – that if there was the slightest publicity given to his homecoming to marry her, or any further notoriety made of the attending circumstances, he would surely leave her.

At the rehearsal of this threat she straightened and threw the superfluous dressing gown from her shoulders with a proud, defiant gesture. She was a straight, almost tall girl, with the figure of a more youthful Diana and with features as fair and flawless as any younger Hera, and in addition a great depth of blue in very direct eyes and a crowning glory of thick, golden hair. She was barely twenty-two. And she was not used to having any man show a sense of advantage over her, much less threaten her, as Howard had done. So, in that impulse of defiance, she was reaching again for the telephone she had just dropped, when she saw through the fog outside the window the man she was waiting for – a tall, alert figure hastening toward the house.

She ran downstairs rapidly and herself opened the door to him, a fresh flush of defiance flooding over her. Whether she resented it because this man, whom she did not love but must marry, could appear more the assured and perfect gentleman without collar, or scarf, and with his boots spattered with mud and rain, than any of her other friends could ever appear; or whether it was merely the confident, insolent smile of his full lips behind his small, close-clipped mustache, she could not tell. At any rate she motioned him into the library without speaking; but when they were alone and she had closed the door, she burst upon him.

'Well, Howard? Well? Well, Howard?' breathlessly.

'Then you have not sent any word to the police, Ethel?'

'I was about to – the moment you came. But – I have not – yet,' she had to confess.

'Or to that –' he checked the epithet that was on his lips – 'your friend Caryl?'

She flushed and shook her head.

He drew his revolver, 'broke' it, ejecting the cartridges carelessly upon the table, and threw himself wearily into a chair. 'I'm glad to see you understand that this has not been the sort of affair for anyone else to interfere in!'

'Has been, you mean;' the girl's face went white; 'you – you caught him this time and – and killed him Howard?'

'Killed him, Ethel?' the man laughed, but observed her more carefully. 'Of course I haven't killed him – or even caught him. But I've made myself sure, at last, that he's the same fellow that's been trying to make a fool of me all this year – that's been after me, as I wrote you. And if you remember my letters, even you – I mean even a girl brought up in a city ought to see how it's a matter of honour with me to settle with him alone!'

'If he is merely trying to "make a fool of you", as you say – yes, Howard,' the girl returned hotly. 'But from what you yourself have told me of him, you know he must be keeping after you for some serious reason! Yes; you know it! I can see it! You can't deny it!'

'Ethel – what do you mean by that?'

'I mean that, if you do not think that the man who has been following you from Calcutta to Cape Town, to Chicago, means more than a joke for you to settle for yourself; anyway, *I* know that the man who has now twice gone through the things in *my* room, is something for me to go to the police about!'

'And have the papers flaring the family scandal again?' the man returned. 'I admit, Ethel,' he conceded, carefully calculating the sharpness of his second sting before he delivered it, 'that if you or I could call in the police without setting the whole pack of papers upon us again, I'd be glad to do it, if only to please you. But I told you, before I came back, that if there was to be any more airing of the family affairs at all, I could not come; so if you want to press the point now, of course I can leave you,' he gave the very slightest but most suggestive glance about the rich, luxurious furnishings of the great room, 'in possession.'

'You know I can't let you do that!' the girl flushed scarlet. 'But neither can you prevent me from making the private inquiry I spoke of for myself!' She went to the side of the room and, in his plain hearing, took down the telephone and called a number without having to look it up.

'Mr Caryl, please,' she said. 'Oh, Henry, is it you? You can take me to your – Mr Trant, wasn't that the name – as soon as you can now ... Yes; I want you to come here. I will have my brougham. Immediately!' And still without another word or even a glance at Axton, she brushed by him and ran up the stairs to her room.

He had made no effort to prevent her telephoning; and she wondered at it, even as, in the same impetus of reckless anger, she swept up the scattered letters and papers on her writing desk, and put on her things to go out. But on her way downstairs she stopped suddenly. The curl of his cigarette smoke through the open library door showed that he was waiting just inside it. He meant to speak to her before she went out. Perhaps he was even glad to have Caryl come in order that he might speak his say in the presence of both of them. Suddenly his tobacco's sharp, distinctive odour sickened her. She turned about, ran upstairs again and fled, almost headlong, down the rear stairs and out the servants' door to the alley.

The dull, gray fog, which was thickening as the morning advanced, veiled her and made her unrecognizable except at a very few feet; but at the end of the alley, she shrank instinctively from the glance of the men passing until she made out a hurrying form of a man taller even than Axton and much broader. She sprang toward it with a shiver of relief as she saw Henry Caryl's light hair and recognized his even, open features.

'Ethel!' he caught her, gasping his surprise. 'You here? Why –'

'Don't go to the house!' She led him the opposite way. 'There is a cab stand at the corner. Get one there and take me – take me to this Mr Trant. I will tell you everything. The man came again last night. Auntie is sick in bed from it. Howard still says it is his affair and will do nothing. I had to come to you.'

Caryl steadied her against a house-wall an instant; ran to the corner for a cab and, returning with it, half lifted her into it.

Forty minutes later he led her into Trant's reception-room in the First National Bank Building; and recognizing the abrupt, decisive tones of the psychologist in conversation in the inner office, Caryl went to the door and knocked sharply.

'I beg your pardon, but – can you possibly postpone what you are doing, Mr Trant?' he questioned quickly as the door opened and he faced the sturdy and energetic form of the red-haired young psychologist, who in six months, had made himself admittedly the chief consultant in Chicago on criminal cases. 'My name is Caryl. Henry Howell introduced me to you last week at the club. But I am not presuming upon that for this interruption. I and – my friend need your help badly, Mr Trant, and immediately. I mean, if we can not speak with you now, we may be interrupted – unpleasantly.'

Caryl had moved, as he spoke, to hide the girl behind him from the sight of the man in the inner office, who, Caryl had seen, was a police officer. Trant noted this and also that Caryl had carefully refrained from mentioning the girl's name.

'I can postpone this present business, Mr Caryl,' the psychologist replied quietly. He closed the door, but reopened it almost instantly. His official visitor had left through the entrance directly into the hall; the two young clients came into the inner room.

'This is Mr Trant, Ethel,' Caryl spoke to the girl a little nervously as she took a seat. 'And, Mr Trant, this is Miss Waldron. I have brought her to tell you of a mysterious man who has been pursuing Howard Axton about the world, and who, since Axton came home to her house two weeks ago, has been threatening her.'

'Axton – Axton!' the psychologist repeated the name which Caryl had spoken, as if assured that Trant must recognize it. 'Ah! Of course, Howard Axton is the son!' he frankly admitted his clearing recollection and his comprehension of how the face of the girl had seemed familiar. 'Then you,' he addressed her directly, 'are Miss Waldron, of Drexel Boulevard?'

'Yes; I am that Miss Waldron, Mr Trant,' the girl replied, flushing red to her lips, but raising her head proudly and meeting his eyes directly. 'The stepdaughter – the daughter of the second wife of Mr Nimrod Axton. It was my mother, Mr Trant, who was the cause of Mrs Anna Axton getting a divorce and the complete custody of her son from Mr Axton twenty years ago. It was my mother who, just before Mr Nimrod Axton's death last year, required that, in the will, the son – the first Mrs Axton was then dead – should be cut off absolutely and entirely, without a cent, and that Mr Axton's entire estate be put in trust for her – my mother. So, since you doubtless remember the reopening of all this again six months ago when my mother, too, died, I am now the sole heir and legatee of the Axton properties of upwards of sixty millions, they tell me. Yes; I am that Miss Waldron, Mr Trant.'

'I recall the accounts, but only vaguely – from the death of Mr Axton and, later, of the second Mrs Axton, your mother, Miss Waldron,' Trant replied, quietly, 'though I remember the comments upon the disposition of the estate both times. It was from the pictures published of you and the accompanying comment in the papers only a week or two ago that I recognized you. I mean, of course, the recent comments upon the son, Mr Howard Axton, whom you have mentioned, who has come home at last to contest the will.'

'You do Miss Waldron an injustice – all the papers have been doing her a great injustice, Mr Trant,' Caryl corrected quickly. 'Mr Axton has not come to contest the will.'

'No?'

'No. Miss Waldron has had him come home, at her own several times repeated request, so that she may turn over to him as completely as possible, the whole of his father's estate! If you can recall, in any detail, the provisions of Mr Axton's will, you will appreciate, I believe, why we have preferred to let the other impression go uncorrected. For the second Mrs Axton so carefully and completely cut off all possibility of any of the property being transferred in any form to the son, that Miss Waldron, when she went to a lawyer to see how she could transfer it to Howard Axton, as soon as she had come into the estate, found that her mother's lawyers had provided against every possibility except that of the heir marrying the disinherited son. So she sent for him, offering to establish him into his estate, even at that cost!'

'You mean that you offered to marry him?' Trant questioned the girl directly again. 'And he has come to gain his estate in that way?'

'Yes, Mr Trant; but you must be fair to Mr Axton also,' the girl replied. 'When I first wrote him, almost a year ago, he refused point blank to consider such an offer. In spite of my repeated letters it was not till six weeks ago, after a shipwreck in which he lost his friend who had been traveling with him for some years, that he would consent even to come home. Even now I – I remain the one urging the marriage.'

The psychologist looked at the girl keenly and questioningly.

'I need scarcely say how little urging he would need, entirely apart from the property,' Caryl flushed, 'if he were not gentleman enough to appreciate – partly, at least – Miss Waldron's position. I – her friends, I mean, Mr Trant – have admitted that he appeared at first well enough in every way to permit the possibility of her marrying him if she considers that her duty. But now, this mystery has come up about the man who has been following him – the man who appeared again only this morning in Miss Waldron's room and went through her papers –'

'And Mr Axton cannot account for it?' the psychologist helped him.

'Axton won't tell her or anybody else who the man is or why he follows him. On the contrary, he has opposed in every possible way every inquiry or search made for the man, except such as he chooses to make for himself. Only this morning he made a threat against Miss Waldron if she attempted to summon the police and "take the man out of his hands"; and it is because I am sure that he will follow us here to prevent her consulting you – when he finds that she has come here – that I asked you to see us at once.'

'Leave the details of his appearance this morning to the last then,' Trant requested abruptly, 'and tell me where you first heard of this man following Mr Axton, and how? How, for instance, do you know he was following him, if Mr Axton is so reticent about the affair?'

'That is one of the strange things about it, Mr Trant' – the girl took from her bosom the bundle of letters she had taken from her room – 'he used to write to amuse me with him, as you can see here. I told you I wrote Mr Axton about a year ago to come home and he refused to consider it. But afterwards he always wrote in reply to my letters in the half-serious, friendly way you shall see. These four letters I brought you are almost entirely taken up with his adventures with the mysterious man. He wrote on typewriter, as you see' – she handed them over – 'because on his travels he used to correspond regularly for some of the London syndicates.'

'London?'

'Yes; the first Mrs Axton took Howard to England with her when he was scarcely seven, immediately after she got her divorce. He grew up there and abroad. This is his first return to America. I have arranged those letters, Mr Trant,' she added as the psychologist was opening them for examination now, 'in the order they came.'

'I will read them that way then,' Trant said, and ~~he~~ glanced over the contents of the first hastily; it was post-marked at Cairo, Egypt, some ten months before. He then reread more carefully this part of it:

But a strange and startling incident has happened since my last letter to you, Miss Waldron, which bothers me considerably. We are, as you will see by the letter paper, at Shepheard's Hotel in Cairo, but could not, after our usual custom, get communicating rooms. It was after midnight, and the million noises of this babel-town had finally died into a hot and breathless stillness. I had been writing letters, and when through I put out the lights to get rid of their heat, lighted instead the small night lamp I carry with me, and still partly dressed threw myself upon the bed, without, however, any idea of going to sleep before undressing. As I lay there I heard distinctly soft footsteps come down the corridor on which my room opens and stop apparently in front of the door. They were not, I judged, the footsteps of a European, for the walker was either barefooted or wore soft sandals. I turned my head toward the door, expecting a knock, but none followed. Neither did the door open, though I had not yet locked it. I was on the point of rising to see what was wanted, when it occurred to me that it was probably not at my door that the steps had stopped but at the door directly opposite, across the corridor. Without doubt my opposite neighbour had merely returned to his room and his footsteps had ceased to reach my ears when he entered and closed his door behind him. I dozed off. But half an hour later, as nearly as I can estimate it, I awoke and was thinking of the necessity for getting undressed and into bed, when a slight – a very slight rustling noise attracted my attention. I listened intently to locate the direction of the sound and determine whether it was inside the room or out of it, and then heard in connection with it a slighter and more regular sound which could be nothing else than breathing. Some living creature, Miss Waldron, was in my room. The sounds came from the direction of the table by the window. I turned my head as silently as I was able, and was aware that a man was holding a sheet of paper under the light of the lamp. He was at the table going through the papers in my writing desk. But the very slight noise I had made in turning on the bed had warned him. He rose, with a hissing intake of the breath, his feet pattered softly and swiftly across the floor, my door creaked under his hand, and he was gone before I could jump from the bed and intercept him. I listened, but could hear no movement in any of the rooms near me. I went back and examined the writing desk, but found nothing missing; and it was plain nothing had been touched except some of my letters from you. But, before finally going

to bed, you may well believe, I locked my door carefully; and in the morning I reported the matter to the
hotel office. The only description I could give of the
intruder was that he had certainly worn a turban, and
one even larger it seemed to me than ordinary. The
hotel attendants had seen no one coming from or entering my corridor that night who answered this description. The turban and the absence of European shoes,
of course, determined him to have been an Egyptian,
Turk or Arab. But what Egyptian, Turk or Arab
could have entered my room with any other object
than robbery – which was certainly not the aim of my
intruder, for the valuables in the writing desk were
untouched? That same afternoon, it is true, I had had
an altercation amounting almost to a quarrel with a
Bedouin Arab on my way back from Heliopolis; but
if this were he, why should he have taken revenge on
my writing desk instead of on me? And what reason
on earth can any follower of the Prophet have had for
examining with such particular attention my letters
from you? It was so decidedly a strange thing that I
have taken all this space to tell it to you – one of the
strangest sort of things I've had in all my knocking
about; and Lawler can make no more of it than I.

'Who is this Lawler who was with Mr Axton then?'
Trant looked up interestedly from the last page of the
letter.

'I only know he was a friend Howard made in London
– an interesting man who had traveled a great deal, particularly in America. Howard was lonely after his
mother's death; and as Mr Lawler was about his age,
they struck up a friendship and traveled together.'

'An English younger son, perhaps?'

'I don't know anything else except that he had been in
the English army – in the Royal Sussex regiment – but

was forced to give up his commission on account of charges that he had cheated at cards. Howard always held that the charges were false; but that was why he wanted to travel.'

'You know of no other trouble which this Lawler had?'

'No, none.'

'Then where is he now?'

'Dead.'

'Dead?' Trant's face fell.

'Yes; he was the friend I spoke of that was lost – drowned in the wreck of the *Gladstone* just before Howard started home.'

Trant picked up the next letter, which was dated and postmarked at Calcutta.

'Miss Waldron, I have seen him again,' he read. 'Who, you ask? My Moslem friend with a taste for your correspondence. You see, I can again joke about it; but really it was only last night and I am still in a perfect funk. It was the same man – shoeless and turbaned and enjoying the pleasant pursuit of going through my writing desk for your letters. Did he follow us down the Red Sea, across the Indian Ocean – over three thousand miles of ocean travel? I can imagine no other explanation – for I would take oath to his identity – the very same man I saw at Cairo, but now here in this Great Eastern Hotel at Calcutta, where we have two rooms at the end of the most noisome corridor that ever caged the sounds and odours of a babbling East Indian population, and where the doors have no locks. I had the end of a trunk against my door, notwithstanding the fact that an Indian servant I have hired was sleeping in the corridor outside across the doorway, but it booted nothing; for Lawler in the next room had neglected to fasten his door in any way, trusting to *his* servant, who occupied a like stra-

tegic position outside the threshold, and the door between our two rooms was open. I had been asleep in
spite of everything – in spite of the snores and stertor-
ous breathing of a floorful of sleeping humans, for the
partitions between the rooms do not come within
several feet of the ceilings; in spite of the distant
bellowing of a sacred bull, and the nearer howl of a
very far from sacred dog, and a jingling of elephant
bells which were set off intermittently somewhere close
at hand whenever some living thing in their neighbourhood – animal or human – shifted its position. I
was awakened – at least I believe it was this which
awakened me – by a creaking of the floor boards in
my room, and, with what seemed a causeless, but was
certainly one of the most oppressive feelings of chilling
terror I have ever experienced, I started upright in my
bed. He was there, again at my writing desk, and
rustling the papers. For an instant I remained motionless; and in that moment, alarmed by the slight sound
I had made, he fled noiselessly, pattered through the
door between the rooms and loudly slammed it shut,
slammed Lawler's outer door behind him, and had
gone. I crashed the door open, ran across the creaking floor of the other room – where Lawler, awakened
by the slamming of the doors, had whisked out of
bed – and opened the door into the corridor. Lawler's
servant, aroused, but still dazed with sleep, blubbered
that he had seen no one, though the man must have
stepped over his very body. A dozen other servants,
sleeping before their masters' doors in the corridor,
had awakened likewise, but cried out shrilly that they
had seen no one. Lawler, too, though the noise of the
man's passage had brought him out of bed, had not
seen him. When I examined my writing desk I found,
as before at Cairo, that nothing had been taken. The
literary delight of looking over your letters seems to

be all that draws him – of course, I am joking; for there must be a real reason. What it is that he is searching for, why it is that he follows me, for he has never intruded on anyone else so far as I can learn, I would like to know – I would like to know – I would like to know! The native servants asked in awe-struck whispers whether I noticed if his feet were turned backwards; for it seems they believe that to be one of the characteristics of a ghost. But the man was flesh and blood – I am sure of it; and I am bound that if he comes again I will learn his object, for I sleep now with my pistol under my pillow, and next time – I shall shoot!'

Trant, as he finished the last words, looked up suddenly at Miss Waldron, as though about to ask a question or make some comment, but checked himself, and hastily laying aside this letter he picked up the next one, which bore a Cape Town date line:

'My affair with my mysterious visitor came almost to a conclusion last night, for except for a careless mistake of my own I should have bagged him. Isn't it mystifying, bewildering – yes, and a little terrifying – he made his appearance here last night in Cape Town, thousands of miles away from the two other places I had encountered him; and he seemed to have no more difficulty in entering the house of a Cape Town correspondent, Mr Arthur Emsley, where we are guests, than he had before in entering public hotels, and when discovered he disappeared as mysteriously as ever. This time, however, he took some precautions. He had moved my night lamp so that, with his body in shadow he could still see the contents of my desk; but I could hear his shoulders rubbing on the wall and located him exactly. I slipped my hand noiselessly for my revolver, but it was gone. The slight noise I made in searching for it alarmed him, and he ran. I rushed out into the hall after him. Mr Emsley and Lawler, awakened by the breaking of the glass, had come out of their rooms. They had not seen him, and though we searched the house he had disappeared as inexplicably as the two other times. But I have learned one thing: It is not a turban he wears, it is his coat, which he takes off and wraps around his head to hide his face. An odd disguise; and the possession of a coat of that sort makes it probable he is a European. I know of only two Europeans who have been in Cairo, Calcutta and Cape Town at the same time we were – both travelers like ourselves; a guttural young German named Schultz, a freight agent for the Nord Deutscher Lloyd, and a nasal American named Walcott, who travels for the Seric Medicine Co. of New York. I shall keep an eye on both of them. For, in my mind at least, this affair has come to be a personal and bitter contest between the unknown and myself. I am determined not only to know who this man is and what is the object of his visits, but to settle with him the score which I now have against him. I shall shoot him next time he comes as mercilessly as I would a rabid dog; and I should have shot him this time except for my own careless mistake through which I had let my revolver slip to the floor, where I found it. By the bye, we sail for home – that is, England – next week on the steamer *Gladstone*, but I am sorry to say, without my English servant, Beasley. Poor Beasley, since these mysterious occurrences, has been bitten with superstitious terror; the man is in a perfect fright, thinks I am haunted, and does not dare to embark on the same ship with me, for he believes that the *Gladstone* will never reach England in safety if I am aboard. I shall discharge him, of course, but furnish him with

his transportations home and leave him to follow at
his leisure, if he sees fit.'

'This is the first time I have heard of another man in
their party who might possibly be the masquerader, Miss
Waldron;' Trant swung suddenly in his revolving chair
to face the girl again. 'Mr Axton speaks of him as his
English servant – I suppose, from that, he left England
with Mr Axton.'

'Yes, Mr Trant.'

'And therefore was present, though not mentioned, at
Cairo, Calcutta and Cape Town?'

'Yes, Mr Trant; but he was dismissed at that time by
Mr Axton and is now, and also was, at the mysterious
man's next appearance, in the Charing Cross Hospital in
London. He had his leg broken by a cab; and one of the
doctors there wrote Mr Axton two days ago telling him
of Beasley's need of assistance. It could not have been
Beasley.'

'And there was no one else with Mr Axton, except his
friend Lawler who, you say, was drowned in a wreck?'

'No one else but Mr Lawler, Mr Trant; and Howard
himself saw him dead and identified him, as you will see
in that last letter.'

Trant opened the envelope and took out the enclosure
interestedly; but as he unfolded the first page, a printed
sheet dropped out. He spread it upon his desk – a page
from the London *Illustrated News* showing four portraits
with the caption, 'Sole survivors of the ill-fated British
steamer *Gladstone*, wrecked off Cape Blanco, January 24',
the first portrait bearing the name of Howard Axton and
showing the determined, distinctly handsome features
and the full lips and deep-set eyes of the man whom the
girl had defied that morning.

'This is a good portrait?' Trant asked abruptly.

'Very good, indeed,' the girl answered, 'though it was

184

taken almost immediately after the wreck for the *News*. I have the photograph from which it was made at home. I had asked him for a picture of himself in my last previous letter, as my mother had destroyed every picture, even the early pictures, of him and his mother.'

Trant turned to the last letter.

'Wrecked, Miss Waldron. Poor Beasley's prophecy of disaster has come only too true, and I suppose he is already congratulating himself that he was "warned" by my mysterious visitor and so escaped the fate that so many have suffered, including poor Lawler. Of course you will have seen all about it in the staring headlines of some newspaper long before this reaches you. I am glad that when found I was at once identified, though still unconscious, and my name listed first among the very few survivors, so that you were spared the anxiety of waiting for news of me. Only four of us left out of that whole shipload! I had final proof this morning of poor Lawler's death by the finding of his body.

'I was hardly out of bed when a mangy little man – a German trader – came to tell me that more bodies had been found, and, as I have been called upon in every instance to aid in identification, I set out with him down the beach at once. It was almost impossible to recognize that this blue and silver ocean glimmering under the blazing sun was the same white-frothing terror that had swallowed up all my companions of three days before. The greater part of the bodies found that morning had been already carried up the beach. Among those remaining on the sand the first we came upon was that of Lawler. It lay upon its side at the entrance of a ragged sandy cove, half buried in the sand, which here was white as leprosy. His ears, the sockets of his eyes, and every interstice of his clothing were filled with this white and leprous sand by the washing of the waves; his pockets bulged and were distended with it.'

'What! What!' Trant clutched the letter from the desk in excitement and stared at it with eyes flashing with interest.

'It is a horrible picture, Mr Trant,' the girl shuddered.

'Horrible – yes, certainly,' the psychologist assented tensely; 'but I was not thinking of the horror,' he checked himself.

'Of what, then?' asked Caryl pointedly.

But the psychologist had already returned to the letter in his hand, the remainder of which he read with intent and ever-increasing interest:

'Of course I identified him at once. His face was calm and showed no evidence of his last bitter struggle, and I am glad his look was thus peaceful. Poor Lawler! If the first part of his life was not all it should have been – as indeed he frankly told me – he atoned for all in his last hour; for undoubtedly, Miss Waldron, Lawler gave his life for mine.

'I suppose the story of the wreck is already all known to you, for our one telegraph wire that binds this isolated town to the outside world has been labouring for three days under a load of messages. You know then that eighteen hours out of St Vincent fire was discovered among the cargo, that the captain, confident at first that the fire would be got under control, kept on his course, only drawing in somewhat toward the African shore in case of emergency. But a very heavy sea rising, prevented the fire-fighters from doing efficient work among the cargo and in the storm and darkness the *Gladstone* struck several miles to the north of Cape Blanco on a hidden reef at a distance of over a mile from the shore.

'On the night it occurred I awakened with so strong a sense of something being wrong that I rose, partly dressed myself, and went out into the cabin, where I found a white-faced steward going from door to door arousing the passengers. Heavy smoke was billowing up the main companionway in the light of the cabin lamps, and the pitching and reeling of the vessel showed that the sea had greatly increased. I returned and awoke Lawler, and we went out on deck. The sea was a smother of startling whiteness through which the *Gladstone* was staggering at the full power of her engines. No flame as yet was anywhere visible, but huge volumes of smoke were bursting from every opening in the fore part of the vessel. The passengers, in a pale and terrified group, were kept together on the after deck as far as possible from the fire. Now and then some pallid, staring man or woman would break through the guard and rush back to the cabin in search of a missing loved one or valuables. Lawler and I determined that one of us must return to the stateroom for our money, and Lawler successfully made the attempt. He returned in ten minutes with my money and papers and two life preservers. But when I tried to put on my life preserver I found it to be old and in such a condition as made it useless. Lawler then took off the preserver that he himself had on, declaring himself to be a much better swimmer than I – which I knew to be the case – and forced me to wear it. This life preserver was all that brought me safely ashore, and the lack of it was, I believe, the reason for Lawler's death. Within ten minutes afterward the flames burst through the forward deck – a red and awful banner which the fierce wind flattened into a fan-shaped sheet of fire against the night – and the *Gladstone* struck with terrific force, throwing everything and everybody flat upon the deck. The bow was raised high upon the reef, while the stern with its maddened living freight began to sink rapidly into the swirl of foaming waters. The first two boats were overfilled at once in a wild rush, and one was stove immediately against the steamer's side and sank, while the other was badly damaged and made only about fifty yards' progress before it went down also. The remaining boats all were lowered from the starboard davits, and got away in safety; but only to capsize or be stove upon the reef. Lawler and I found places in the last boat – the captain's. At the last moment, just as we were putting off, the fiery maw of the *Gladstone* vomited out the scorched and half-blinded second engineer and a single stoker, whom we took in with difficulty. There was but one woman in our boat – a fragile, illiterate Dutchwoman from the neighbourhood of Johannesburg – who had in her arms a baby. How strange that of our boatload those who alone survived should be the Dutchwoman, but without her baby; the engineer and stoker, whom the fire had already partly disabled, and myself, a very indifferent swimmer – while the strongest among us all perished! Of what happened after leaving the ship I have only the most indistinct recollection. I recall the swamping of our boat, and cruel white waters that rushed out of the night to engulf us; I recall a blind and painful struggle against a power infinitely greater than my own – a struggle which seemed interminable; for, as a matter of fact, I must have been in the water fully four hours and the impact of the waves alone beat my flesh almost to a jelly; and I recall the coming of daylight, and occasional glimpses of a shore which seemed to project itself suddenly above the sea and then at once to sink away and be swallowed by it. I was found unconscious on the sands – I have not the faintest idea how I got there – and I was identified before coming to myself (it may please you to know this) by several of your letters which were found in my pocket. At present, with my three rescued companions – whose names even I probably never should have known if the *Gladstone* had reached England safely – I am a most enthralling centre of interest to the white, black and parti-coloured inhabitants of this region; and I am writing this letter on an antiquated typewriter belonging to the smallest, thinnest, baldest little American that ever left his own dooryard to become a missionary.'

Trant tossed aside the last page and, with eyes flashing with a deep, glowing fire, he glanced across intensely to the girl watching him; and his hands clenched on the table, in the constraint of his eagerness.

'Why – what is it, Mr Trant?' the girl cried.

'This is so taken up with the wreck and the death of Lawler,' the psychologist touched the last letter, 'that there is hardly any more mention of the mysterious man. But you said, since Mr Axton has come home, he has twice appeared and in your room, Miss Waldron. Please give me the details.'

'Of his first appearance – or visit, I should say, since no one really saw him, Mr Trant,' the girl replied, still watching the psychologist with wonder, 'I can't tell you much, I'm afraid. When Mr Axton first came home, I asked him about this mysterious friend; and he put me off with a laugh and merely said he hadn't seen much of him since he last wrote. But even then I could see he wasn't so easy as he seemed. And it was only two days after that – or nights, for it was about one o'clock in the morning – that I was awakened by some sound which seemed to come from my dressing-room. I turned on the light in my room and rang the servant's bell. The butler came almost at once and, as he is not a courageous man, roused Mr Axton before opening the door to my dressing-room. They found no one there and nothing taken or even disturbed except my letters in my writing desk, Mr Trant. My aunt, who has been taking care of me since my mother died, was aroused and came with the servants. She thought I must have imagined everything; but I discovered and showed Mr Axton that it was *his letters to me* that had appeared to be the ones the man was searching for. I found that two of them had been taken and every other typewritten letter in my desk – and only those – had been opened in an apparent search for more of his letters. I could see that this excited him exceedingly, though he tried to conceal it from me; and immediately afterwards he found that a window on the first floor had been forced, so some man had come in, as I said.'

'Then last night.'

'It was early this morning, Mr Trant, but still very dark – a little before five o'clock. It was so damp, you know, that I had not opened the window in my bedroom, which is close to the bed; but had opened the windows of my dressing-room, and so left the door between open. It had been closed and locked before. So when I awoke, I could see directly into my dressing-room.'

'Clearly?'

'Of course not at all clearly. But my writing-desk is directly opposite my bedroom door; and in a sort of silhouette against my shaded desk light, which he was using, I could see his figure – a very vague, monstrous looking figure, Mr Trant. Its lower part seemed plain enough; but the upper part was a formless blotch. I confess at first that enough of my girl's fear for ghosts came to me to make me see him as a headless man, until I remembered how Howard had seen and described him – with a coat wrapped round his head. As soon as I was sure of this, I pressed the bell-button again and this time screamed, too, and switched on my light. But he slammed the door between us and escaped. He went through another window he had forced on the lower floor with a queer sort of dagger-knife which he had broken and left on the sill. And as soon as Howard saw this, he knew it was the same man, for it was then he ordered me not to interfere. He made off after him, and when he came back, he told me he was sure it was the same man.'

'This time, too, the man at your desk seemed rummaging for your correspondence with Mr Axton?'

'It seemed so, Mr Trant.'

'But his letters were all merely personal – like these letters you have given me?'

'Yes.'

'Amazing!' Trant leaped to his feet, with eyes flashing now with unrestrained fire, and took two or three rapid turns up and down the office. 'If I am to believe the obvious inference from these letters, Miss Waldron – coupled with what you have told me – I have not yet come across a case, an attempt at crime more careful, more cold-blooded and, withal, more surprising!'

'A crime – an attempt at crime, Mr Trant?' cried the white and startled girl. 'So there was cause for my belief that something serious underlay these mysterious appearances?'

'Cause?' Trant swung to face her. 'Yes, Miss Waldron – criminal cause, a crime so skilfully carried on, so assisted by unexpected circumstance that you – that the very people against whom it is aimed have not so much as suspected its existence.'

'Then you think Howard honestly believes the man still means nothing?'

'The man never meant "nothing", Miss Waldron; but it was only at first the plot was aimed against Howard Axton,' Trant replied. 'Now it is aimed solely at you!'

The girl grew paler.

'How can you say that so surely, Mr Trant,' Caryl demanded, 'without investigation?'

'Those letters are quite enough evidence for what I say, Mr Caryl,' Trant returned. 'Would you have come to me unless you had known that my training in the methods of psychology enabled me to see causes and motives in such a case as this which others, untrained, cannot see?'

'You have nothing more to tell me which might be of assistance?' he faced the girl again, but turned back at once to Caryl. 'Let me tell you then, Mr Caryl, that I am about to make a very thorough investigation of this for you. Meanwhile, I repeat: a definite, daring crime was planned first, I believe, against Howard Axton and Miss Waldron; but now – I am practically certain – it is aimed against Miss Waldron alone. But there cannot be in it the slightest danger of intentional personal hurt to her. So neither of you need be uneasy while I am taking time to obtain full proof –'

'But, Mr Trant,' the girl interrupted, 'are you not going to tell me – you *must* tell me – what the criminal secret is that these letters have revealed to you?'

'You must wait, Miss Waldron,' the psychologist answered kindly, with his hand on the doorknob, as though anxious for the interview to end. 'What I could tell you now would only terrify you and leave you perplexed how to act while you were waiting to hear from me. No; leave the letters, if you will, and the page from the *Illustrated News*,' he said suddenly, as the girl began gathering up her papers. 'There is only one thing more. You said you expected an interruption here from Howard Axton, Mr Caryl. Is there still a good chance of his coming here or – must I go to see him?'

'Miss Waldron telephoned to me, in his presence, to take her to see you. Afterwards she left the house without his knowledge. As soon as he finds she has gone, he will look up your address, and I think you may expect him.'

'Very good. Then I must set to work at once!' He shook hands with both of them hurriedly and almost forcing them out his door, closed it behind them, and strode back to his desk. He picked up immediately the second of the four letters which the girl had given him, read it through again, and crossed the corridor to the opposite office, which was that of a public stenographer.

'Make a careful copy of that,' he directed, 'and bring it to me as soon as it is finished.'

A quarter of an hour later, when the copy had been brought him, he compared it carefully with the original. He put the copy in a drawer of the desk and was apparently waiting with the four originals before him when he heard a knock on his door, and, opening it, found that his visitor was again young Caryl.

'Miss Waldron did not wish to return home at once; she has gone to see a friend. So I came back,' he explained, 'thinking you might make a fuller statement of your suspicions to me than you would in Miss Waldron's presence.'

'Fuller in what respect, Mr Caryl?'

The young man reddened.

'I must tell you – though you already may have guessed – that before Miss Waldron inherited the estate and came to believe it her duty to do as she has done, there had been an – understanding between us, Mr Trant. She still has no friend to look to as she looks to me. So, if you mean that you have discovered through those letters – though God knows how you can have done it – anything in Axton which shows him unfit to marry her, you must tell me!'

'As far as Axton's past goes,' Trant replied, 'his letters show him a man of high type – moral, if I may make a guess, above the average. There is a most pleasing frankness about him. As to making any further explanation than I have done – but good Lord! what's that?'

The door of the office had been dashed loudly open,

and its still trembling frame was filled by a tall, very angry young man in automobile costume, whose highly coloured, aristocratic looking features Trant recognized immediately from the print in the page of the *Illustrated London News*.

'Ah, Mr Caryl here too? – the village busybody!' the newcomer sneered, with a slight accent which showed his English education. 'You are insufferably mixing yourself in my affairs,' he continued, as Caryl, with an effort, controlled himself and made no answer. 'Keep out of them! That is my advice – take it! Does a woman have to order you off the premises before you can understand that you are not wanted? As for you,' he swung toward Trant, 'you are Trant, I suppose!'

'Yes, that is my name, Mr Axton,' replied the psychologist, leaning against his desk.

The other advanced a step and raised a threatening finger. 'Then that advice is meant for you, too. I want no police, no detectives, no outsider of any sort interfering in this matter. Make no mistake; it will be the worse for anyone who pushes himself in! I came here at once to take the case out of your hands, as soon as I found Miss Waldron had come here. This is strictly my affair – keep out of it!'

'You mean, Mr Axton, that you prefer to investigate it personally?' the psychologist inquired.

'Exactly – investigate and punish!'

'But you cannot blame Miss Waldron for feeling great anxiety even on your account, as your personal risk in making such an investigation will be so immensely greater than anyone's else would be.'

'My risk?'

'Certainly; you may be simply playing into the hand of your strange visitor, by pursuing him unaided. Any other's risk – mine, for instance, if I were to take up the matter – would be comparatively slight, beginning perhaps by questioning the nightwatchmen and stableboys in the neighbourhood with a view to learning what became of the man after he left the house; and besides, such risks are a part of my business.'

Axton halted. 'I had not thought of it in that light,' he said reflectively.

'You are too courageous – foolishly courageous, Mr Axton.'

'Do you mind if I sit down? Thank you. You think, Mr Trant, that an investigation such as you suggest, would satisfy Miss Waldron – make her easier in her mind, I mean?'

'I think so, certainly.'

'And it would not necessarily entail calling in the police? You must appreciate how I shrink from publicity – another story concerning the Axton family exploited in the daily papers!'

'I had no intention of consulting the police, or of calling them in, at least until I was ready to make the arrest.'

'I must confess, Mr Trant,' said Axton easily, 'that I find you a very different man from what I had expected. I imagined an uneducated, somewhat brutal, perhaps talkative fellow; but I find you, if I may say so, a gentleman. Yes, I am tempted to let you continue your investigation – on the lines you have suggested.'

'I shall ask your help.'

'I will help you as much as is in my power.'

'Then let me begin, Mr Axton, with a question – pardon me if I open a window, for the room is rather warm – I want to know whether you can supplement these letters, which so far are the only real evidence against the man, by any further description of him,' and Trant, who had thrown open the window beside him, undisturbed by the roar that filled the office from the traffic-laden street below, took the letters from his pocket and opened them one by one, clumsily, up on the desk.

'I am afraid I cannot add anything to them, Mr Trant.'

'We must get on then with what we have here,' the psychologist hitched his chair near to the window to get a better light on the paper in his hand, and his cuff knocked one of the other letters off the desk onto the windowsill. He turned hastily but clumsily, and touched, but could not grasp it before it slipped from the sill out into the air. He sprang to his feet with an exclamation of dismay, and dashed from the room. Axton and Caryl, rushing to the window, watched the paper, driven by a strong breeze, flutter down the street until lost to sight among wagons; and a minute later saw Trant appear below them, bareheaded and excited, darting in and out among vehicles at the spot where the paper had disappeared; but it had been carried away upon some muddy wagon-wheel or reduced to tatters, for he returned after fifteen minutes' search disheartened, vexed and empty handed.

'It was the letter describing the second visit,' he exclaimed disgustedly as he opened the door. 'It was most essential, for it contained the most minute description of the man of all. I do not see how I can manage well, now, without it.'

'Why should you?' Caryl said in surprise at the evident stupidity of the psychologist. 'Surely, Mr Axton, if he cannot add any other details, can at least repeat those he had already given.'

'Of course!' Trant recollected. 'If you would be so good, Mr Axton, I will have a stenographer take down the statement to give you the least trouble.'

'I will gladly do that,' Axton agreed; and, when the psychologist had summoned the stenographer, he dictated without hesitation the following letter:

'The second time that I saw the man was at Calcutta, in the Great Eastern Hotel. He was the same man I had seen at Cairo – shoeless and turbaned; at least I

believed then that it was a turban, but I saw later, at
Cape Town, that it was his short brown coat wrapped
round his head and tied by the sleeves under his chin.
We had at the Great Eastern two whitewashed communicating rooms opening off a narrow, dirty corridor,
along whose whitewashed walls at a height of some
two feet from the floor ran a greasy smudge gathered
from the heads and shoulders of the dark-skinned,
white-robed native servants who spent the nights
sleeping or sitting in front of their masters' doors.
Though Lawler and I each had a servant also outside
his door, I dragged a trunk against mine after closing
it – a useless precaution, as it proved, as Lawler put no
trunk against his – and though I see now that I must
have been moved by some foresight of danger, I went
to sleep afterward quite peacefully. I awakened somewhat later in a cold and shuddering fright, oppressed
by the sense of some presence in my room – started up
in bed and looked about. My trunk was still against
the door as I had left it; and besides this, I saw at first
only the furniture of the room, which stood as when
I had gone to sleep – two rather heavy and much
scratched mahogany English chairs, a mahogany
dresser with swinging mirror, and the spindle-legged,
four-post canopy bed on which I lay. But presently, I
saw more. He was there – a dark shadow against the
whitewashed wall beside the flat-topped window
marked his position, as he crouched beside my writing
desk and held the papers in a bar of white moonlight
to look at them. For an instant, the sight held me
motionless, and suddenly becoming aware that he was
seen, he leaped to his feet – a short, broad-shouldered,
bulky man – sped across the blue and white straw
matting into Lawler's room and drove the door to
behind him. I followed, forcing the door open with
my shoulder, saw Lawler just leaping out of bed in his

197

pajamas, and tore open Lawler's corridor door, through which the man had vanished. He was not in the corridor, though I inspected it carefully, and Lawler, though he had been awakened by the man's passage, had not seen him. Lawler's servant, pretty well dazed with sleep, told me in blank and open-mouthed amazement at my question, that he had not seen him pass; and the other white-draped Hindoos, gathering about me from the doors in front of which they had been asleep, made the same statement. None of these Hindoos resembled in the least the man I had seen, for I looked them over carefully one by one with this in mind. When I made a light in my room in order to examine it thoroughly, I found nothing had been touched except the writing desk, and even from that nothing had been taken, although the papers had been disturbed. The whole affair was as mysterious and inexplicable as the man's first appearance had been, or as his subsequent appearance proved; for though I carefully questioned the hotel employés in the morning I could not learn that any such man had entered or gone out from the hotel.'

'That is very satisfactory indeed.' Trant's gratification was evident in his tone, as Axton finished. 'It will quite take the place of the letter that was lost. There is only one thing more – so far as I know now – in which you may be of present help to me, Mr Axton. Besides your friend Lawler, who was drowned in the wreck of the *Gladstone*, and the man Beasley – who, Miss Waldron tells me, is in a London hospital – there were only two men in Cape Town with you who had been in Cairo and Calcutta at the same time you were. You do not happen to know what has become of that German freight agent, Schultz?'

'I have not the least idea, Mr Trant.'

'Or Walcott, the American patent medicine man?'

'I know no more of him than of the other. Whether either of them is in Chicago now, is precisely what I would like to know myself, Mr Trant; and I hope you will be able to find out for me.'

'I will do my best to locate them. By the way, Mr Axton, you have no objection to my setting a watch over your family home, provided I employ a man who has no connection with the police?'

'With that condition I think it would be a very good idea,' Axton assented. He waited to see whether Trant had anything more to ask him; then, with a look of partially veiled hostility at Caryl, he went out.

The other followed, but stopped at the door.

'We – that is, Miss Waldron – will hear from you, Mr Trant?' he asked with sudden distrust – 'I mean, you will report to her, as well as to Mr Axton?'

'Certainly; but I hardly expect to have anything for you for two or three days.'

The psychologist smiled, as he shut the door behind Caryl. He dropped into the chair at his desk and wrote rapidly a series of telegrams, which he addressed to the chiefs of police of a dozen foreign and American cities. Then, more slowly, he wrote a message to the Seric Medicine Company, of New York, and another to the Nord Deutscher Lloyd.

The first two days, of the three Trant had specified to Caryl, passed with no other event than the installing of a burly watchman at the Axton home. On the third night this watchman reported to Miss Waldron that he had seen and driven off, without being able to catch, a man who was trying to force a lower window; and the next morning – within half an hour of the arrival of the Overland Limited from San Francisco – Trant called up the Axton home on the telephone with the news that he thought he had at last positive proof of the mysterious man's identity. At least, he had with him a man whom he wanted Mr Axton to see. Axton replied that he would be very glad to see the man, if Trant would make an appointment. In three quarters of an hour at the Axton home, Trant answered; and forty minutes later, having first telephoned young Caryl, Trant with his watchman, escorting a stranger who was broad-shouldered, weasel-eyed, of peculiarly alert and guarded manner, reached the Axton doorstep. Caryl had so perfectly timed his arrival, under Trant's instructions, that he joined them before the bell was answered.

Trant and Caryl, leaving the stranger under guard of the watchman in the hall, found Miss Waldron and Axton in the morning-room.

'Ah! Mr Caryl again?' said Axton sneeringly. 'Caryl was certainly not the man you wanted me to see, Trant!'

'The man is outside,' the psychologist replied. 'But before bringing him in for identification I thought it best to prepare Miss Waldron, and perhaps even more particularly you, Mr Axton, for the surprise he is likely to occasion.'

'A surprise?' Axton scowled questioningly. 'Who is the fellow? – or rather, if that is what you have come to find out from me, where did you get him, Trant?'

'That is the explanation I wish to make,' Trant replied, with his hand still upon the knob of the door, which he had pushed shut behind him. 'You will recall, Mr Axton, that there were but four men whom we know to have been in Cairo, Calcutta, and Cape Town at the same time you were. These were Lawler, your servant Beasley, the German Schultz, and the American Walcott. Through the Seric Medicine Company I have positively located Walcott; he is now in Australia. The Nord Deutscher Lloyd has given me equally positive assurance regarding Schultz. Schultz is now in Bremen. Miss Waldron has accounted for Beasley, and the Charing Cross Hospital corroborates her; Beasley is in London. There remains, therefore, the inevitable conclusion that either there was some other man following Mr Axton – some man whom Mr Axton did not see – or else that the man who so pried into Mr Axton's correspondence abroad and into your letters, Miss Waldron, this last week here in Chicago, was – Lawler; and this I believe to have been the case.'

'Lawler?' the girl and Caryl echoed in amazement, while Axton stared at the psychologist with increasing surprise and wonder. 'Lawler?'

'Oh! I see,' Axton all at once smiled contemptuously. 'You believe in ghosts, Trant – you think it is Lawler's ghost that Miss Waldron saw!'

'I did not say Lawler's ghost,' Trant replied a little testily. 'I said Lawler's self, in flesh and blood. I am trying to make it plain to you,' Trant took from his pocket the letters the girl had given him four days before and indicated the one describing the wreck, 'that I believe the man whose death you so minutely and carefully describe here in this letter as Lawler, was not Lawler at all!'

'You mean to say that I didn't know Lawler?' Axton laughed loudly – 'Lawler, who had been my companion in sixteen thousand miles of travel?'

Trant turned as though to reopen the door into the hall; then paused once more and kindly faced the girl.

'I know, Miss Waldron,' he said, 'that you have believed that Mr Lawler has been dead these six weeks; and it is only because I am so certain that the man who is to be identified here now will prove to be that same Lawler that I have thought best to let you know in advance.'

He threw open the door, and stood back to allow the Irish watchman to enter, preceded by the weasel-faced stranger. Then he closed the door quickly behind him, docked it, put the key in his pocket, and spun swiftly to see the effect of the stranger upon Axton.

That young man's face, despite his effort to control it,

flushed and paled, flushed and went white again; but neither to Caryl nor the girl did it look at all like the face of one who saw a dead friend alive again.

'I do not know him!' Axton's eyes glanced quickly, furtively about. 'I have never seen him before! Why have you brought him here? This is not Lawler!'

'No; he is not Lawler,' Trant agreed; and at his signal the Irishman left his place and went to stand behind Axton. 'But you know him, do you not? You have seen him before! Surely I need not recall to you this special officer Burns of the San Francisco detective bureau! That is right; you had better keep hold of him, Sullivan; and now, Burns, who is this man? Do *you* know *him*? Can you tell us who he is?'

'Do I know him?' the detective laughed. 'Can I tell you who he is? Well, rather! That is Lord George Albany, who got into Claude Shelton's boy in San Francisco for $30,000 in a card game; that is Mr Arthur Wilmering, who came within a hair of turning the same trick on young Stuyvesant in New York; that – first and last – is Mr George Lawler himself, who makes a specialty of cards and rich men's sons!'

'Lawler? George Lawler?' Caryl and the girl gasped again.

'But why, in this affair, he used his own name,' the detective continued, 'is more than I can see; for surely he shouldn't have minded another change.'

'He met Mr Howard Axton in London,' Trant suggested, 'where there was still a chance that the card cheating in the Sussex guards was not forgotten, and he might at any moment meet someone who recalled his face. It was safer to tell Axton all about it, and protest innocence.'

'Howard Axton?' the girl echoed, recovering herself at the name. 'Why, Mr Trant; if this is Mr Lawler, as this man says and you believe, then where is Mr Axton – oh, where is Howard Axton?'

'I am afraid, Miss Waldron,' the psychologist replied, 'that Mr Howard Axton was undoubtedly lost in the wreck of the *Gladstone*. It may even have been the finding of Howard Axton's body that this man described in that last letter.'

'Howard Axton drowned! Then this man –'

'Mr George Lawler's specialty being rich men's sons,' said the psychologist, 'I suppose he joined company with Howard Axton because he was the son of Nimrod Axton. Possibly he did not know at first that Howard had been disinherited, and he may not have found it out until the second Mrs Axton's death, when the estate came to Miss Waldron, and she created a situation which at least promised an opportunity. It was in seeking this opportunity, Miss Waldron, among the intimate family affairs revealed in your letters to Howard Axton that Lawler was three times seen by Axton in his room, as described in the first three letters that you showed to me. That was it, was it not, Lawler?'

The prisoner – for the attitude of Sullivan and Burns left no doubt now that he was a prisoner – made no answer.

'You mean, Mr Trant,' the eyes of the horrified girl turned from Lawler as though even the sight of him shamed her, 'that if Howard Axton had not been drowned, this – this man would have come anyway?'

'I cannot say what Lawler's intentions were if the wreck had not occurred,' the psychologist replied. 'For you remember that I told you that this attempted crime has been most wonderfully assisted by circumstances. Lawler, cast ashore from the wreck of the *Gladstone*, found himself – if the fourth of these letters is to be believed – identified as Howard Axton, even before he had regained consciousness, by your stolen letters to Howard which he had in his pocket. From that time on he did not have to lift a finger, beyond the mere identification of a body – possibly Howard Axton's – as his own. Howard had left America so young that identification here was impossible unless you had a portrait; and Lawler undoubtedly had learned from your letters that you had no picture of Howard. His own picture, published in the *News* over Howard's name, when it escaped identification as Lawler, showed him that the game was safe and prepared you to accept him as Howard without question. He had not even the necessity of counterfeiting Howard's writing, as Howard had the correspondent's habit of using a typewriter. Only two possible dangers threatened him. First, was the chance that, if brought in contact with the police, he might be recognized. You can understand, Miss Waldron, by his threats to prevent your consulting them, how anxious he was to avoid this. And second, that there might be something in Howard Axton's letters to you which, if unknown to him, might lead him to compromise and betray himself in his relations with you. His sole mistake was that, when he attempted to search your desk for these letters, he clumsily adopted once more the same disguise that had proved so perplexing to Howard Axton. For he could have done nothing that would have been more terrifying to you. It quite nullified the effect of the window he had fixed to prove by the man's means of exit and entrance that he was not a member of the household. It sent you, in spite of his objections and threats, to consult me; and, most important of all, it connected these visits at once with the former ones described in Howard's letters, so that you brought the letters to me – when, of course, the nature of the crime, though not the identity of the criminal, was at once plain to me.'

'I see it was plain; but was it merely from these letters – these typewritten letters, Mr Trant?' cried Caryl incredulously.

'From those alone, Mr Caryl,' the psychologist smiled slightly, 'through a most elementary, primer fact of psychology. Perhaps you would like to know, Lawler,' Trant turned, still smiling, to the prisoner, 'just wherein you failed. And, as you will probably never have another chance such as the one just past for putting the information to practical use – even if you were not, as Mr Burns tells me, likely to retire for a number of years from active life – I am willing to tell you.'

The prisoner turned on Trant his face – now grown livid – with an expression of almost superstitious questioning.

'Did you ever happen to go to a light opera with Howard Axton, Mr Lawler,' asked Trant, 'and find after the performance that you remembered all the stage-settings of the piece but could not recall a tune – you know you cannot recall a tune, Lawler – while Axton, perhaps, could whistle all the tunes but could not remember a costume or a scene? Psychologists call that difference between you and Howard Axton a difference in "memory types". In an almost masterly manner you imitated the style, the tricks and turns of expression of Howard Axton in your letter to Miss Waldron describing the wreck – not quite so well in the statement you dictated in my office. But you could not imitate the primary difference of Howard Axton's mind from yours. That was where you failed.

'The change in the personality of the letter writer might easily have passed unnoticed, as it passed Miss Waldron, had not the letters fallen into the hands of one who, like myself, is interested in the manifestations of mind. For different minds are so constituted that inevitably their processes run more easily along certain channels than along others. Some minds have a preference, so to speak, for a particular type of impression; they remember a sight that they have seen, they forget the sound that went with it; or they remember the sound and forget the sight. There are minds which are almost wholly ear-minds or eye-minds. In minds of the visual, or eye, type, all thoughts and memories and imaginations will consist of ideas of sight; if of the auditory type, the impressions of sound predominate and obscure the others.

'The first three letters you handed me, Miss Waldron,' the psychologist turned again to the girl, 'were those really written by Howard Axton. As I read through them I knew that I was dealing with what psychologists call an auditory mind. When, in ordinary memory, he recalled an event he remembered best its sounds. But I had not finished the first page of the fourth letter when I came upon the description of the body lying on the sand – a visual memory so clear and so distinct, so perfect to the pockets distended with sand, that it startled and amazed me – for it was the first distinct visual memory I had found. As I read on I became certain that the man who had written the first three letters – who described a German as guttural and remembered the American as nasal – could never have written the fourth. Would that first man – the man who recalled even the sound of his midnight visitor's shoulders when they rubbed against the wall – fail to remember in his recollection of the shipwreck the roaring wind and roaring sea, the screams of men and women, the crackling of the fire? They would have been his clearest recollection. But the man who wrote the fourth letter recalled most clearly that the sea was white and frothy, the men were pallid and staring!'

'I see! I see!' Caryl and the girl cried as, at the psychologist's bidding, they scanned together the letters he spread before them.

'The subterfuge by which I destroyed the second letter of the set, after first making a copy of it –'

'You did it on purpose? What an idiot I was!' exclaimed Caryl.

'– was merely to obviate the possibility of mistake,' Trant continued, without heeding the interruption. 'The statement this man dictated, as it was given in terms of "sight", assured me that he was not Axton. When, by means of the telegraph, I had accounted for the present whereabouts of three of the four men he might possibly be, it became plain that he must be Lawler. And finding that Lawler was badly wanted in San Francisco, I asked Mr Burns to come on and identify him.'

'And the stationing of the watchman here was a blind also, as well as his report of the man who last tried to force the window?' Caryl exclaimed.

Trant nodded. He was watching the complete dissolution of the swindler's effrontery. Trant had appreciated that Lawler had let him speak on uninterrupted as though, after the psychologist had shown his hand, he held in reserve cards to beat it. But his attempt to sneer and scoff and contemn was so weak, when the psychologist was through, that Ethel Waldron – almost as though to spare him – arose and motioned to Trant to tell her, whatever else he wished, in the next room.

Trant followed her a moment obediently; but at the door he seemed to recollect himself.

'I think there is nothing else now, Miss Waldron,' he said, 'except that I believe I can spare you the reopening of your family affairs here. Burns tells me there is more than enough against him in California to keep Mr Lawler there for some good time. I will go with him now,' and he stood aside for Caryl to go, in his place, into the next room.

8

The Man Who Spoke Latin

Samuel Hopkins Adams

Mementoes of Average Jones' exploits in his chosen field
hang on the walls of his quiet sanctum. Here the favoured
visitor may see the two red-ink dots on a dated sheet of
paper, framed in with the card of a chemist and an
advertised sale of lepidopterae, which drove a famous
millionaire out of the country. Near by are displayed the
exploitation of a lure for black-bass, strangely perforated
(a man's reason hung on those pin-pricks), and a scrawled
legend which seems to spell 'Mercy' (two men's lives were
sacrificed to that); while below them, set in sombre black,
is the funeral notice of a dog worth a million dollars;
facing the call for a trombone-player which made a
mayor, and the mathematical formula which saved a
governor. But nowhere does the observer find any record
of one of the Ad-Visor's most curious cases, running back
two thousand years; for its owner keeps it in his desk
drawer, whence the present chronicler exhumed it, by
accident, one day. Average Jones has always insisted that
he scored a failure on this, because, through no possible
fault of his own, he was unable to restore a document of
the highest historical and literary importance. Of that,
let the impartial reader judge.

It was while Average Jones was awaiting the break of
that deadlock of events which, starting from the flat-
dweller with the poisoned face, finally worked out the
strange fate of Telfik Bey, that he sat, one morning,

breakfasting late. The cool and breezy inner portico of the Cosmic Club, where the small tables overlook a gracious fountain shimmering with the dart and poise of goldfish, was deserted save for himself, a summer-engagement star actor, a specialist in carbohydrates, and a famous adjuster of labour troubles; the four men being fairly typical of the club's catholicity of membership. Contrary to his impeccable habit, Average Jones bore the somewhat frazzled aspect of a man who had been up all night. Further indication of this inhered in the wide yawn, of which he was in mid-enjoyment, when a hand on his shoulder cut short his ecstasy.

'Sorry to interrupt so valuable an exercise,' said a languid voice. 'But –' and the voice stopped.

'Hello, Bert,' returned the Ad-Visor, looking up at the faultlessly clad slenderness of his occasional coadjutor, Robert Bertram. 'Sit down and keep me awake till the human snail who's hypothetically ministering to my wants can get me some coffee.'

'What particular phase of intellectual debauchery have you been up to now?' inquired Bertram, lounging into the chair opposite.

'Trying to forget my troubles by chasing up a promising lead which failed to pan out. "Wanted: a Tin Nose", sounds pretty good, eh?'

'It is music to my untutored ear,' answered Bertram.

'But it turned out to be merely the error of the imbecile, or perhaps facetious printer, who sets up the *Trumpeter*'s personal column. It should have read, "Wanted – a Tea Rose".'

'Even that seems far from commonplace.'

'Only a code summons for a meeting of the Rosicrucians. I suppose you know that the order has been revived here in America.'

'Not the true Rosicrucians, surely!' said Bertram.

'They pretend to be. A stupid lot, who make child's

play of it,' said Average Jones impatiently. 'Never mind them. I'd rather know what's on your mind. You made an observation, when you came in, rather more interesting than your usual output of table-talk. You said "but" and nothing further. The conjunction "but", in polite grammar, ordinarily has a comet-like tail to it.'

'Apropos of polite grammar, do you speak Latin?' asked Bertram carelessly.

'Not enough to be gossipy in it.'

'Then you wouldn't care to give a job to a man who can't speak anything else?'

'On that qualification alone?'

'No-o, not entirely. He is a good military engineer, I believe.'

'So that's the other end of the "but", is it?' asked Average Jones. 'Go on. Elaborate.'

Bertram laid before his friend a printed clipping in clear, large type, saying: 'When I read this, I couldn't resist the notion that somehow or other it was in your line; pursuit of the Adventure of Life, and all that. Let's see what you make of it.'

Average Jones straightened in his chair.

'Latin!' he said. 'And an ad. by the look of it. Can our blind friend, J. Alden Honeywell, have taken to the public prints?'

'Hardly, I think. This is from the *Classical Weekly*, a Baltimore publication of small and select patronage.'

'Hm. Looks ra-a-a-ather alluring,' commented Average Jones with a prolonged drawl. 'Better than the Rosicrucian fakery, anyhow.'

He bent over the clipping, studying these words:

L. Livius M. F. Praenestinus, quodlibet in negotium non inhonestum qui victum meream locare velim. Litteratus sum; scripium facere bene scio. Stipendia multa emeritus, scientiarum belli, praesertim muniendi, sum peritus. Hac de re pro me spondebit M. Agrippa. Latine tantum scio. Siquis me velit

convenire, quovis die mane adesto in publicis hortis urbis
Baltimorianae ad signum apri.

'Can you make it out?' asked Bertram.

'Hm-m-m. Well – the general sense. Livius seems to
yearn in modern print for any honest employment, but
especially scrapping, of the ancient variety, or secretary-
ing. Apply to Agrippa for references. Since he describes
his conversation as being confined to Latin, I take it he
won't find many jobs reaching out eagerly for him. Anybody who wants him can find him in the Park of the Wild
Boar in Baltimore. That's about what I make of it. Now,
what's his little lay, I wonder.'

'Some lay of Ancient Rome, anyhow,' suggested Bertram. 'Association with Agrippa would put him back in
the first century, B.C. wouldn't it? Besides my informant
tells me that Mr Livius, who seems to have been an all-
round sort of person, helped organize fire brigades for
Crassus, and was one of the circle of minor poets who
wrote rhapsodies to the fair but frail Clodia's eyebrows,
ear-lobes and insteps.'

'Your informant? The man's actually been seen, then?'

'Oh, yes. He's on view as per advertisement, I understand.'

Average Jones rose and stretched his well-knit frame.
'Baltimore will be hotter than the Place-as-isn't,' he said
plaintively. 'Martyrdom by fire! However, I'm off by the
five o'clock train. I'll let you know if anything special
comes of it, Bert.'

Barye's splendid bronze boar crouches, semi-shaded, in
the centre of Monument Park, Baltimore's social hill-top.
There Average Jones lounged and strolled through the
longest hour of a glaring July morning. People came and
went; people of all degrees and descriptions, none of
whom suggested in any particular the first century, B.C.
One individual only maintained any permanency of

situation. He was a gaunt, powerful, freckled man of thirty who sprawled on a settee and regarded Average Jones with obvious and amused interest. In time this annoyed the Ad-Visor, who stopped short, facing the settee.

'He's gone,' said the freckled man.

'Meaning Livius the Roman?' asked Average Jones.

'Exactly. Lucius Livius, son of Marcus Praenestinus.'

'Are you the representative of this rather peculiar person, may I ask?'

'It would be a dull world, except for peculiar persons,' observed the man on the settee philosophically. 'I've seen very many peculiar persons lately by the simple process of coming here day after day. No, I'm not Mr Livius' representative. I'm only a town-bound and interested observer of his.'

'There you've got the better of me,' said Average Jones. 'I was rather anxious to see him myself.'

The other looked speculatively at the trim, keen-faced young man. 'Yet you do not look like a Latin scholar,' he observed; 'if you'll pardon the comment.'

'Nor do you,' retorted Jones; 'if the apology is returnable.'

'I suppose not,' owned the other with a sigh. 'I've often thought that my classical capacity would gain more recognition if I didn't have a skin like Bob Fitzsimmons and hands like Ty Cobb. Nevertheless, I'm in and of the department of Latin of Johns Hopkins University. Name, Warren. Sit down.'

'Thanks,' said the other. 'Name, Jones. Profession, advertising advisor. Object, curiosity.'

'A. V. R. E. Jones; better known as Average Jones, I believe?'

'*Experto crede*! Being dog-Latin for "You seem to know all about it".' The new-comer eyed his vis-à-vis. 'Perhaps you – er – know Mr Robert Bertram,' he drawled.

'*Oculus*-the eye-*tauri*-of the bull. Bull's eye!' said the freckled one, with a grin. 'I'd heard of your exploits through Bertram, and thought probably you'd follow the bait contained in my letter to him.'

'Nothing wrong with your nerve-system, is there?' inquired Average Jones with mock anxiety. 'Now that I'm here, where is L. Livius And-so-forth?'

'Elegantly but uncomfortably housed with Colonel Ridgway Graeme in his ancestral barrack on Carteret Street.'

'Is this Colonel Graeme a friend of yours?'

'Friend and foe, tried and true. We meet twice a week, usually at his house, to squabble over his method of Latin pronunciation and his construction of the ablative case. He's got a theory of the ablative absolute,' said Warren with a scowl, 'fit to fetch Tacitus howling from the shades.'

'A scholar, then?'

'A very fine and finished scholar, though a faddist of the rankest type. Speaks Latin as readily as he does English.'

'Old?'

'Over seventy.'

'Rich?'

'Not in money. Taxes on his big place keep him pinched; that and his passion for buying all kinds of old and rare books. He's got, perhaps, an income of five thousand, clear, of which about three thousand goes in book auctions.'

'Any family?'

'No. Lives with two ancient coloured servants who look after him.'

'How did our friend from B.C. connect up with him?'

'Oh, he ran to the old colonel like a chick to its hen. You see, there aren't so very many Latinists in town during the hot weather. Perhaps eighteen or twenty in all came from about here and from Washington to see the prodigy in "the Park of the Boar", after the advertisement appeared. He wouldn't have anything to do with any of us. Pretended he didn't understand our kind of Latin. I offered him a place, myself, at a wage of more *denarii* than I could well afford. I wanted a chance to study him. Then came the colonel and fairly grabbed him. So I sent for you – in my artless professional way.'

'Why such enthusiasm on the part of Colonel Graeme?'

'Simple enough. Livius spoke Latin with an accent which bore out the old boy's contention. I believe they also agreed on the ablative absolute.'

'Yes – er – naturally,' drawled Average Jones. 'Does our early Roman speak pretty ready Latin?'

'He's fairly fluent. Sometimes he stumbles a little on his constructions, and he's apt to be – well – monkish – rather than classical when in full course.'

'Doesn't wear the *toga virilis*, I suppose.'

'Oh, no. Plain American clothes. It's only his inner man that's Roman, of course. He met with a bump on the head – that is his story, and he's got the scar to show for it – and when he came to, he'd lost ground a couple of thousand years and returned to his former existence. No English. No memory of who or what he'd been. No money. No connection whatsoever with the living world.'

'Humph! Wonder if he's been a student of Kipling. You remember "The Greatest Story in the World"; the reincarnated galley slave? Now as to Colonel Graeme; has he ever published?'

'Yes. Two small pamphlets, issued by the Classical Press, which publishes the *Classical Weekly*.'

'Supporting his fads, I suppose.'

'Right. He devoted one pamphlet to each.'

Average Jones contemplated with absorbed attention an ant which was making a laborious spiral ascent of his cane. Not until it had gained a vantage point on the bone handle did he speak again.

'See here, Professor Warren: I'm a passionate devotee of the Latin tongue. I have my deep and dark suspicions of our present modes of pronunciation, all three of 'em. As for the ablative absolute, its reconstruction and regeneration have been the inspiring principle of my studious manhood. Humbly I have sat at the feet of Learning, enshrined in the Ridgway Graeme pamphlets. I must meet Colonel Graeme – after reading the pamphlets. I hope they're not long.'

Warren frowned. 'Colonel Graeme is a gentleman and my friend, Mr Jones,' he said with emphasis. 'I won't have him made a butt.'

'He shan't be, by me,' said Average Jones quietly. 'Has it perhaps struck you, as his friend, that – er – a close daily association with the psychic remnant of a Roman citizen might conceivably be non-conducive to his best interest?'

'Yes, it has. I see your point. You want to approach him on his weak side. But, have you Latin enough to sustain the part? He's shrewd as a weasel in all matters of scholarship, though a child whom any one could fool in practical affairs.'

'No; I haven't,' admitted Average Jones. 'Therefore, I'm a mute. A shock in early childhood paralysed my centres of speech. I talk to you by sign language, and you interpret.'

'But I hardly know the deaf-mute alphabet.'

'Nor I. But I'll waggle my fingers like lightning if he says anything to me requiring an answer, and you'll give the proper reply. Does Colonel Graeme implicitly credit the Romanism of his guest?'

'He does, because he wants to. To have an educated man of the classic period of the Latin tongue, a friend of Caesar, an auditor of Cicero and a contemporary of Virgil, Horace and Ovid come back and speak in the accent he's contended for, makes a powerful support for his theories. He's at work on a supplementary thesis already.'

'What do the other Latin men who've seen Livius think of the metempsychosis claim?'

'They don't know. Livius explained his remote antecedents only after he had got Colonel Graeme's private ear. The colonel has kept it quiet. "Don't want a rabble of psychologists and soul-pokers worrying him to death," he says.'

'Making it pretty plain sailing for the Roman. Well, arrange to take me there as soon as possible.'

At the Graeme house, Average Jones was received with simple courtesy by a thin rosy-cheeked old gentleman with a dagger-like imperial and a dreamy eye, who, on Warren's introduction, made him free of the unkempt old place's hospitality. They conversed for a time, Average Jones maintaining his ends with nods and gestures, and (ostensibly) through the digital mediumship of his sponsor. Presently Warren said to the host:

'And where is your visitor from the past?'

'Prowling among my books,' answered the old gentleman.

'Are we not going to see him?'

The colonel looked a little embarrassed. 'The fact is, Professor Warren, Livius has taken rather an aversion to you.'

'I'm sorry. How so?'

A twinkle of malice shone in the old scholar's eye. 'He says your Latin accent frets his nerves,' he explained.

'In that case,' said Warren, obeying a quick signal from his accomplice, 'I'll stroll in the garden, while you present Mr Jones to Livius.'

Colonel Graeme led the way to a lofty wing, once used as a drawing-room, but now the repository for thousands of books, which not only filled the shelves but were heaped up in every corner.

'I must apologize for this confusion, sir,' said the host. 'No one is permitted to arrange my books but myself.

216

And my efforts, I fear, serve only to make confusion more confounded. There are four other rooms even more chaotic than this.'

At the sound of his voice a man who had been seated behind a tumulus of volumes rose and stood. Average Jones looked at him keenly. He was perhaps forty-five years of age, thin and sinewy, with a close-shaven face, pale blue eyes, and a narrow forehead running high into a mop of grizzled locks. Diagonally across the front part of the scalp a scar could be dimly perceived through the hair. Average Jones glanced at the stranger's hands, to gain, if possible, some hint of his former employment. With his faculty of swift observation, he noticed that the long, slender fingers were not only mottled with dust, but also scuffed, and, in places, scarified, as if their owner had been hurriedly handling a great number of books.

Colonel Graeme presented the new-comer in formal Latin. He bowed. The scarred man made a curious gesture of the hand, addressing Average Jones in an accent which, even to the young man's long-unaccustomed ears, sounded strange and strained.

'*Di illi linguam astrinxere; mutus est,*' said Colonel Graeme, indicating the younger man, and added a sentence in sonorous metrical Greek.

Average Jones recalled the Æschylean line. 'Well, though "a great ox hath stepped on my tongue", it hasn't trodden out my eyes, praises be!' said he to himself as he caught the uneasy glance of the Roman.

By way of allaying suspicion, he scribbled upon a sheet of paper a few complimentary Latin sentences, in which Warren had sedulously coached him for the occasion, and withdrew to the front room, where he was presently joined by the Johns Hopkins man. Fortunately, the colonel gave them a few moments together.

'Arrange for me to come here daily to study in the library,' whispered Jones to the Latin professor.

The other nodded.

'Now, sit tight,' added Jones.

He stepped, soft-footed, on the thick old rug, across to the library door and threw it open. Just inside stood Livius, an expression of startled anger on his thin face. Quickly recovering himself, he explained, in his ready Latin, that he was about to enter and speak to his patron.

'Shows a remarkable interest in possible conversation,' whispered Jones, on his withdrawal, 'for a man who understands no English. Also does me the honour to suspect me. He must have been a wily chap – in the Consulship of Plancus.'

Before leaving, Average Jones had received from Colonel Graeme a general invitation to spend as much time as he chose, studying among the books. The old man-servant, Saul, had orders to admit him at any hour. He returned to his hotel to write a courteous note of acknowledgement.

Many hours has Average Jones spent more tediously than those passed in the cool seclusion of Colonel Ridgway Graeme's treasure-house of print. He burrowed among quaint accumulations of forgotten classics. He dipped with astonishment into the savage and ultra-Rabelaisian satire of Von Hutten's '*Epistolæ Obscurorum Virorum*', which set early sixteenth-century Europe a-roar with laughter at the discomfited monks; and he cleansed himself from that tainted atmosphere in the fresh air and free English of a splendid Audubon 'first' – and all the time he was conscious that the Roman watched, watched, watched. More than once Livius offered aid, seeking to apprise himself of the supposed mute's line of investigation; but the other smilingly fended him off. At the end of four days, Average Jones had satisfied himself that if Livius were seeking anything in particular, he had an indefinite task before him, for the colonel's bound treasures were in indescribable confusion. Apparently he had bought from far and near, without definite theme or purpose. As he bought he read, and having read, cast aside; and where a volume fell, there it had license to lie. No cataloguer had ever sought to restore order to that bibliographic riot. To seek any given book meant a blind voyage, without compass or chart, throughout the mingled centuries.

Often Colonel Graeme spent hours in one or the other of the huge book-rooms talking with his strange protégé and making copious notes. Usually the old gentleman questioned and the other answered. But one morning the attitude seemed, to the listening Ad-Visor, to be reversed. Livius, in the far corner of the room, was speaking in a low tone. To judge from the older man's impatient manner, the Roman was interrupting his host's current of queries with interrogations of his own. Average Jones made a mental note, and, in conference with Warren that evening, asked him to ascertain from Colonel Graeme whether Livius's inquiries had indicated a specific interest in any particular line of reading.

On the following day, however, an event of more immediate import occupied his mind. He had spent the morning in the upstairs library, at the unevadable suggestion of Colonel Graeme, while the colonel and his Roman collogued below. Coming down about noon, Average Jones entered the colonel's small study just in time to see Livius, who was alone in the room, turn away sharply from the desk. His elbow was held close to his ribs in a peculiar manner. He was concealing something under his coat. With a pretence of clumsiness, Average Jones stumbled against him in passing. Livius drew away, his high forehead working with suspicion. The Ad-Visor's expression of blank apology, eked out with a bow and a grimace, belied the busy-working mind within. For, in the moment's contact, he had heard the crisp rustle of paper from beneath the ill-fitting coat.

What paper had the man from B.C. taken furtively from his benefactor's table? It must be large; otherwise he could have readily thrust it into his pocket. No sooner was Livius out of the room than Average Jones scanned the desk. His face lighted with a sudden smile. Colonel Graeme never read a newspaper; boasted, in fact, that he wouldn't have one about the place. But, as Average Jones distinctly recalled, he had, himself, that very morning brought in a copy of the *Globe* and dropped it into the scrap-basket near the writing-table. It was gone. Livius had taken it.

'If he's got the newspaper-reading habit,' said Average Jones to himself, 'I'll set a trap for him. But Warren must furnish the bait.'

He went to look up his aide. The conference between them was long and exhaustive, covering the main points of the case from the beginning.

'Did you find out from Colonel Graeme,' inquired Average Jones, 'whether Livius affected any particular brand of literature?'

'Yes. He seems to be specializing on late seventeenth-century British classicism. Apparently he considers that the flower of British scholarship of that time wrote a very inferior kind of dog-Latin.'

'Late seventeenth-century Latinity,' commented Average Jones. 'That – er – gives us a fair start. Now as to the body-servant.'

'Old Saul? I questioned him about strange callers. He said he remembered only two, besides an occasional pedlar or agent. They were looking for work.'

'What kind of work?'

'Inside the house. One wanted to catalogue the library.'

'What did he look like?'

'Saul says he wore glasses and a worse tall hat than the Colonel's and had a full beard.'

'And the other?'

'Bookbinder and repairer. Wanted to fix up Colonel Graeme's collection. Youngish, smartly dressed, with a small waxed moustache.'

'And our Livius is clean-shaven,' murmured Average Jones. 'How long apart did they call?'

'About two weeks. The second applicant came on the day of the last snowfall. I looked that up. It was March 27.'

'Do you know, Warren,' observed Average Jones, 'I sometimes think that part of your talents, at least, are wasted in a chair of Latin.'

'Certainly, there is more excitement in this hide-and-seek game, as you play it, than in the pursuits of a musty pedant,' admitted the other, crackling his large knuckles. 'But when are we going to spring upon friend Livius and strip him of his fake toga?'

'That's the easiest part of it. I've already caught him filling a fountain-pen as if he'd been brought up on them, and humming the spinning chorus from *The Flying Dutchman*; not to mention the lifting of my newspaper.'

'*Nemo mortalium omnibus horis sapit*,' murmured Warren.

'No. As you say, no fellow can be on the job *all* the time. But our problem is not to catch Livius, but to find out what it is he's been after for the last three months.'

'Three months? You're assuming that it was he who applied for work in the library.'

'Certainly. And when he failed at that he set about a very carefully developed scheme to get at Colonel Graeme's books anyway. By inquiries he found out the old gentleman's fad and proceeded to get in training for it. You don't know, perhaps, that I have a corps of assistants who clip, catalogue and file all unusual advertisements: "Wanted – Daily lessons in Latin speech from competent Spanish scholar. Write, Box 347, *Banner* office." That is from the New York *Banner* of April third, shortly after the strange caller's second abortive attempt to get into the Graeme library.'

'I suppose our Livius figured out that Colonel Graeme's theory of accent was about what a Spaniard would have. But he couldn't have learned all his Latin in four months.'

'He didn't. He was a scholar already; an accomplished one, who went wrong through drink and became a crook, specializing in rare books and prints. His name is Enderby; you'll find it in the Harvard catalogue. He's supposed to be dead. My assistant traced him through his Spanish-Latin teacher, a priest.'

'But even allowing for his scholarship, he must have put in a deal of work perfecting himself in readiness of speech and accent.'

'So he did. Therefore the prize must be big. A man of Enderby's calibre doesn't concoct a scheme of such ingenuity, and go into bondage with it, for nothing. Do you belong to the Cosmic Club?'

The assistant professor stared. 'No,' he said.

'I'd like to put you up there. One advantage of membership is that its roster includes experts in every known line of erudition, from scarabs to skeeing. For example, I am now going to telegraph for aid from old Millington, who seldom misses a book auction and is a human bibliography of the wanderings of all rare volumes. I'm going to find out from him what British publication of the late seventeenth century in Latin is very valuable; also what volumes of that time have changed hands in the last six months.'

'Colonel Graeme went to a big book auction in New York early in March,' volunteered Warren, 'but he told me he didn't pick up anything of particular value.'

'Then it's something he doesn't know about and Livius does. I'm going to take advantage of our Roman's rather un-B.C.-like habit of reading the daily papers by trying him out with this advertisement.'

Average Jones wrote rapidly and tossed the result to his coadjutor who read:

'LOST – Old book printed in Latin. Buff leather binding, a little faded ("It's safe to be that," explained Average Jones). No great value except to owner. Return to Colonel Ridgway Graeme, 11 Carteret Street, and receive reward.'

The advertisement made its appearance in big type on the front pages of the Baltimore paper of the following day. That evening Average Jones met Warren, for dinner, with a puckered brow.

'Did Livius rise to the bait?' asked the scholar.

'Did he!' chuckled Average Jones. 'He's been nervous as a cat all day and hardly has looked at the library. But what puzzles me is this.' He exhibited a telegram from New York.

'Millington says positively no book of that time and description any great value. Enderby at Barclay auction in March and made row over some book which he missed because it was put up out of turn in catalogue. Barclay auctioneer thinks it was one of Percival privately bound books, 1680–1703. An anonymous book of Percival library, *De Meritis Librorum Britannorum*, was sold to Colonel Graeme for $47, a good price. When do I get in on this?

(Signed) Robert Bertram'

'I know that treatise,' said Warren. 'It isn't particularly rare.'

Average Jones stared at the telegram in silence. Finally he drawled: 'There are – er – books and – er – books – and – er – things in books. Wait here for me.'

Three hours later he reappeared with collar wilted, but spirits elate, and abruptly announced:

'Warren, I'm a cobbler.'

'A what?'

'A cobbler. Mend your boots, you know.'

'Are you in earnest?'

'Certainly. Haven't you ever remarked that a serious-minded earnestness always goes with cobbling. Though I'm not really a practical cobbler, but a proprietary one. Our friend, Bertram, will dress and act the principal part. I've wired him and he's replied, collect, accepting the job. You and I will be in the background.'

'Where?'

'No. 27 Jasmine Street. Not a very savoury locality. Why is it, Warren, that the beauty of a city street is generally in inverse ratio to the poetic quality of its name? There I've hired the shop and stock of Mr Hans Fichtel for two days, at the handsome rental of ten dollars per day. Mr Fichtel purposes to take a keg of beer a-fishing. I think two days will be enough.'

'For the keg?'

'For that noble Roman, Livius. He'll be reading the papers pretty keenly now. And in tomorrow's, he'll find this advertisement.'

Average Jones read from a sheet of paper which he took from his pocket:

'Found – Old book in foreign language, probably Latin, marked "Percival". Owner may recover by giving satisfactory description of peculiar and obscure feature and refunding for advertisement. Fichtel, 27 Jasmine Street.'

'What is the peculiar and obscure feature, Jones?' asked Warren.

'I don't know.'

'How do you know there is any?'

'Must be something peculiar about the book or Enderby wouldn't put in four months of work on the chance of stealing it. And it must be obscure, otherwise the auctioneer would have spotted it.'

'Sound enough!' approved the other. 'What could it be? Some interpolated page?'

'Hardly. I've a treatise in my pocket on seventeenth-century book-making, which I'm going to study tonight. Be ready for an early start, to meet Bertram.'

That languid and elegant gentleman arrived by the first morning train. He protested mightily when he was led to the humble shoe-shop. He protested more mightily when invited to don a leather apron and smudge his face appropriately to his trade. His protests, waxing vehement and eventually profane, as he barked his daintily-kept fingers, in rehearsal for giving a correct representation of an honest artisan cobbling a boot, died away when Average Jones explained to him that on pretence of having found a rare book, he was to worm out of a cautious and probably suspicious criminal the nature of some unique and hidden feature of the volume.

'Trust me for diplomacy,' said Bertram airily.

'I will because I've got to,' retorted Average Jones. 'Well, get to work. To you the outer shop: to Warren and me this rear room. And, remember, if you hear me whetting a knife, that means come at once.'

Uncomfortably twisted into a supposedly professional posture, Bertram wrought with hammer and last, while putting off, with lame, blind and halting excuses, such as came to call for their promised footgear. By a triumph of tact he had just disposed of a rancid-tongued female who demanded her husband's boots, a satisfactory explanation, or the arbitrament of the lists, when the bell tinkled and the two watchers in the back room heard a nervous, cultivated voice say:

'Is Mr Fichtel here?'

'That's me,' said Bertram, landing an agonizing blow on his thumb-nail.

'You advertised that you had found an old book.'

'Yes, sir. Somebody left it in the post-office.'

'Ah; that must have been when I went to mail some letters to New York,' said the other glibly. 'From the advertised description, the book is without doubt mine. Now as to the reward –'

'Excuse me, but you wouldn't expect me to give it up without any identification, sir?'

'Certainly not. It was the *De Meritis Libror* –'

'I can't read Latin, sir.'

'But you could make that much out,' said the visitor with rising exasperation. 'Come; if it's a matter of the reward – how much?'

'I wouldn't mind having a good reward; say ten dollars. But I want to be sure it's your book. There's something about it that you could easily tell me sir, for anyone could see it.'

'A very observing shoemaker,' commented the other with a slight sneer. 'You mean the – the half split cover?'

'Whish-swish; whish-swish,' sounded from the rear room.

'Excuse me,' said Bertram, who had not ceased from his pretended work. 'I have to get a piece of leather.'

He stepped into the back room where Average Jones, his face alight, held up a piece of paper upon which he had hurriedly scrawled:

'MSS bound into cover. Get it out of him. Tell him you've a brother who is a Latin scholar.'

Bertram nodded, caught up a strip of calf-skin and returned.

'Yes, sir,' he said, 'the split cover and what's inside?'

The other started. 'You didn't get it out?' he cried. 'You didn't tear it!'

'No, sir. It's there safe enough. But some of it can be made out.'

'You said you didn't read Latin.'

'No, sir; but I have a brother that went through the Academy. He reads a little.' This was thin ice, but Bertram went forward with assumed assurance. 'He thinks the manuscript is quite rare. Oh, Fritz! Come in.'

'Any letter of Bacon's is rare, of course,' returned the other impatiently. 'Therefore, I purpose offering you fifty dollars reward.'

He looked up as Average Jones entered. The young man's sleeves were rolled up, his face was generously smudged, and a strip of cobbler's wax beneath the upper lip, puffed and distorted the firm line of his mouth. Further, his head was louting low on his neck, so that the visitor got no view sufficient for recognition.

'Lord Bacon's letter – er – must be pretty rare, Mister,' he drawled thickly. 'But a letter – er – from Lord Bacon about – er – Shakespeare – *that* ought to be worth a lot of money.'

Average Jones had taken his opening with his customary incisive shrewdness. The mention of Bacon had settled it, to his mind. Only one imaginable character of manuscript from the philosopher-scholar-politician could have value enough to tempt a thief of Enderby's calibre. Enderby's expression told that the shot was a true one. As for Bertram, he had dropped his shoemaker's knife and his shoemaker's rôle.

'Bacon on Shakespeare! Shades of the departed glory of Ignatius Donnelly!'

The visitor drew back. Warren's gaunt frame appeared in the doorway. Jones' head lifted.

'It ought to be as – er – unique,' he drawled, 'as an – er – Ancient Roman speaking perfect English.'

Like a flash, the false Livius caught up the knife from the bench where the false cobbler had dropped it and swung toward Average Jones. At the same moment the ample hand of Professor Warren, bunched into a highly competent fist, flicked across and caught the assailant under the ear. Enderby, alias Livius, fell as if smitten by a cestus. As his arm touched the floor, Average Jones kicked unerringly at the wrist and the knife flew and tinkled in a far corner. Bertram, with a bound, landed on the fallen man's chest and pinned him.

'Did he get you, Average?' he cried.

'Not – er – this time. Pretty good – er – team work,'

drawled the Ad-Visor. 'We've got our man for felonious assault, at least.'

Enderby, panting under Bertram's solid knee, blinked and struggled.

'No use, Livius,' said Average Jones. 'Might as well quiet down and confess. Ease up a little on him, Bert. Take a look at that scar of his first though.'

'Superficial cut treated with make-up paint; a clever job,' pronounced Bertram after a quick examination.

'As I supposed,' said Average Jones.

'Let me in on the deal,' pleaded Livius. 'That letter is worth ten thousand, twelve thousand, fifteen thousand dollars – anything you want to ask, if you find the right purchaser. And you can't manage it without me. Let me in.'

'Think we're crooks, too?' remarked Average Jones. 'Exactly what's in this wonderful letter?'

'It's from Bacon to the author of the book, who wrote about 1610. Bacon prophesies that Shakespeare, "this vagabond and humble mummer", would outshine and outlive in fame all the genius of his time. That's all I could make out by loosening the stitches.'

'Well, that *is* worth anything one could demand,' said Warren in a somewhat awed tone.

'Why didn't you get the letter when you were examining it at the auction room?' inquired Average Jones.

'Some fool of a binder had overlooked the double cover, and sewed it in. I noticed it at the auction, gummed the opening together while no one was watching, and had gone to get cash to buy the book; but the auctioneer put it up out of turn and old Graeme got it. Bring it to me and I'll show you the "pursed" cover. Many of the Percival books were bound that way.'

'We've never had it, nor seen it,' replied Average Jones. 'The advertisement was only a trap into which you stepped.'

Enderby's jaw dropped. 'Then it's still at the Graeme house,' he cried, beating on the floor with his free hand. 'Take me back there!'

'Oh, we'll take you,' said Warren grimly.

Close-packed among them in a cab, they drove him back to Carteret Street. Colonel Ridgway Graeme was at home and greeted them courteously.

'You've found Livius,' he said, with relief. 'I had begun to fear for him.'

'Colonel Graeme,' began Average Jones, 'you have –'

'What! Speech!' cried the old gentleman. 'And you a mute! What does this mean?'

'Never mind him,' broke in Enderby Livius. 'There's something more important.'

But the colonel had shrunk back. 'English from you, Livius!' he cried, setting his hand to his brow.

'All will be explained in time, Colonel,' Warren assured him. 'Meanwhile, you have a document of the utmost importance and value. Do you remember buying one of the Percival volumes at the Barclay auction?'

The collector drew his brows down in an effort to remember.

'An octavo, in fairly good condition?' he asked.

'Yes, yes!' cried Enderby eagerly. 'Where is it? What did you do with it?'

'It was in Latin – very false Latin.' The four men leaned forward, breathless. 'Oh, I remember. It slipped from my pocket and fell into the river as I was crossing the ferry to Jersey.'

There was a dead, flat, stricken silence. Then Average Jones turned hollow eyes upon Warren.

'Professor,' he said, with a rueful attempt at a smile, 'what's the past participle, passive, plural, of the Latin verb, "to sting"?'

9

The Cloud-Bursters

Francis Lynde

It was an article in the news columns of *The Brewster Morning Tribune* which first called attention – the attention of the Brewsterites and the inter-mountain world in general – to the plans and purposes of the Mesquite Valley Land and Irrigation Company.

Connabel, a hard-working reporter on *The Tribune*, had been sent over to Angels, the old head-quarters of the Red Butte Western on the other side of the Timanyonis, to get the story of a shooting affray which had localized itself in Peter Grim's place, the one remaining Angelic saloon. Finding the bar-room battle of little worth as a news story, and having time to kill between trains, Connabel had strolled off up the gulch beyond the old copper mines and had stumbled upon the construction camp of the Mesquite Company.

Being short of 'copy' on the fight story, the reporter had written up the irrigation project, taking the general outlines from a foreman on the job whose tongue he loosened with a handful of Brewster cigars. A big earth dam was in process of construction across the mouth of the rather precipitous valley of Mesquite Creek; and the mesa below, which, to Connabel's unrural eye, seemed to be a very Sahara of infertile desolation, was to be made to blossom like the rose.

Kendall, managing editor of *The Tribune*, had run the story, partly because real news happened to be scarce at the moment, and partly out of sheer astonishment that an enterprise of the magnitude of the Mesquite project had not already flooded the country with the brass-band publicity literature which is supposed to attract investors.

That a land and irrigation company should actually wait until its dam was three-fourths completed before it began to advertise was a thing sufficiently curious to call for editorial comment. Why Editor Kendall did not comment on the news item as a matter of singular interest is a query which had its answer on the loggia porch of the Hotel Topaz in the evening of the day on which Connabel's write-up appeared.

It was Kendall's regular habit to close his desk at seven o'clock and to spend a leisurely hour over his dinner at the Topaz before settling down to his night's work. On the evening in question he had chanced to sit at table with Maxwell, the general superintendent of the railroad, and with Maxwell's friend and college classmate, Sprague. After dinner the three had gone out to the loggia porch to smoke, and it was the big chemistry expert who spoke of the Mesquite news story which had appeared that morning in *The Tribune.*

'Yes,' said the editor; 'Connabel got on to that yesterday. I sent him over to Angels to write up a shooting scrape, and he had more time on his hands than he knew what to do with. We've all known, in a general way, that an Eastern company was doing something over there, but I had no idea that they'd got their dam pretty nearly done and were about ready to open up for business.'

'It's wild-cat, pure and unadulterated!' cut in the railroad man snappily. 'What they are going to do to a lot of woolly investors will be good and plenty. That Mesquite Mesa land is just about as fertile as this street pavement here.'

Kendall was a dried-up little wisp of a man, with tired eyes and a face the colour of old oak-tanned leather.

'That is what you would think – that they are out for the easy money,' he agreed. 'But there is something a little queer about it. They haven't advertised.'

'Not here,' supplemented Maxwell. 'It would be a trifle too rank. Everybody in the Timanyoni knows what that land is over in the edge of the Red Desert.'

'They haven't advertised anywhere, so far as I can ascertain,' put in the editor, quietly. 'What is more, Jennings, who is the engineer in charge of the dam-building and who seems to be the only man in authority on the ground, came in this afternoon and raised sand with me for printing the news story. He said they were not exploiting the scheme here at all; that their money and their investors were all in the East, and they were asking no odds of the Brewster newspapers.'

'Bitter sort of devil, that fellow Jennings,' was Maxwell's comment; but it was the big chemist who followed the main thread of the argument.

'What reason did he give for making such an extra-ordinary break as that, Mr Kendall?'

'Oh, he had his reason pat enough,' rejoined the editor, with his tired smile. 'He said he realized that we have irrigated land of our own over here in the Park upon which we are anxious to get settlers, and that public sentiment here would naturally be against the Mesquite project. He asked, as a matter of fairness, that we simply let the desert project alone. He claimed that it had been financed without taking a dollar out of the Timanyoni, so we could not urge that there were local investors to be protected.'

'Umph! that argument cuts both ways; it's an admission that the Eastern investors might need protection,' scoffed the railroad superintendent. Then he added: 'They certainly will if they expect to get any of the money back that they have been spending in Mesquite Valley. Why, Kendall, Mesquite Creek is bone-dry half the year!'

'And the other half?' inquired Sprague.

'It's a cloud-burst proposition, like a good many of the foothill arroyos,' Maxwell explained. 'Once, in a summer storm, I saw a wall of water ten feet high come down that stream-bed, tumbling twenty-ton boulders in the thick of it as if they had been brook pebbles. Then, for a month, maybe, it would be merely a streak of dry sand.'

'Perhaps they are counting upon storing the cloud-burst water,' commented Kendall dryly. Then as he rose to go back to his work: 'As you say, Maxwell, it has all the earmarks of the wildcat. But so long as it doesn't stick its claws out at us, I suppose we haven't much excuse for butting in. Good night, gentlemen. Drop in on me when you're up my way. Always glad to see you.'

The two who remained on the hotel porch after the editor went away smoked in comradely silence for a time. The night was enchantingly fine, with a first-quarter moon swinging low in a vault of velvety blackness, and a gentle breeze, fragrant with the breath of the mountain forests, creeping down upon the city from the back-grounding highlands. Across the plaza, and somewhere in the yards behind the long two-storeyed railroad head-quarters building and station, a night crew was making up trains, and the clank and crash of coupling cars mingled with the rapid-fire exhausts of the switching engine.

The big-bodied chemistry expert was the first to break the companionable silence, asking a question which had reference to the epidemic of disaster and demoralization which had recently swept over Maxwell's railroad.

'Well, how are things coming by this time, Dick? Are the men responding fairly well to that little circular-letter, man-to-man appeal we concocted?'

'They are, for a fact,' was the hearty assurance. 'I have never seen anything like it in railroading in all my knock-ing about. They've been coming in squads to "fessup and take the pledge", and to assure me that it's the water-wagon for theirs from now on. By George, Calvin, it's the most mellowing experience I've ever had! It proves what you have always said, and what I have always wanted to believe: that the good in the mass definitely outweighs the bad, and that it will come to the front if you only know how to appeal to it.'

'That's right,' averred the chemist. 'It is the strong hope of the country that there is justice and fairness and sane commonsense at the American bottom of us, if you can only get at it. I think you can call the booze-fight and demoralization round-up a trouble past and begin to look around you for the signs and symptoms of the next biff you're going to get.'

The stockily built little man who stood as the railroad company's chief field-officer on the far-western fighting line moved uneasily in his chair.

'I have been hoping there wasn't going to be any "next time",' he said, chewing thoughtfully upon his cigar.

'I should hope with you, Dick, if we had been able, in any of the former scrimmages, to secure good, indubitable court evidence against the men who are backing these buccaneering raids on your securities. The one thing that big money really fears today is the law – the law as the Federal courts are likely to construe and administer it. But to obtain your day in court you've got to have evidence; and thus far we haven't been able to sweat out anything that would implicate the man or men higher up. Therefore, you may continue to sleep on your arms, keeping a sharp eye out for surprises.'

'I guess that is pretty good advice,' was the ready admission; 'but it is rather difficult to put into practice, Calvin. There are five hundred miles of this railroad, and my job of operating them is big enough to keep me busy without doing any detective stunts on the side.'

'I know,' Sprague nodded reflectively, 'and for that

reason I've been half-way keeping an eye out for you myself.'

'You have? Don't tell me you've been finding more grief!'

Sprague thew away his outburned stub and found and lighted a fresh cigar.

'I don't want to pose as an alarmist,' he offered at length, 'but I'd like to dig a little deeper into this Mesquite irrigation scheme. How much or little do you know about it?'

'Next to nothing. About two months ago Jennings, the construction engineer, made application for the through handling, from Copah, of a train-load of machinery, tools, and camp outfit. He asked to have the stuff delivered to the end of the old copper-mine spur above Angels. We put the spur in shape for him and delivered the freight.'

'Well, what else?'

'That is about all we have had to do with them in a business way. Two weeks ago, when we had that wreck at Lobo, they were asking Benson for an extension of the copper-mine spur to a point nearer their job, chiefly, I think, so they could run a hand-car back and forth between the camp and the saloon at Angels. Benson didn't recommend it, and the matter was dropped.'

'Without protest?'

'Oh, yes; Jennings didn't make much of a roar. In fact, I've always felt that he avoided me when he could. He is in town a good bit, but I rarely see him. Somebody told me he tried once to get into the Town and Country Club, and didn't make it. I don't know who would blackball him, or why; but evidently someone did.'

The ash grew a full half-inch longer on Sprague's fresh cigar before he said :

'Doesn't it occur to you that there is something a bit mysterious about this dry-land irrigation scheme, Dick?'

'I had never thought of it as being mysterious. It is a

palpable swindle, of course; but swindles are like the poor – they're always with us.'

'It interests me,' said the big man, half-musingly. 'A company, formed nobody knows where or how, drops down in the edge of the Red Desert and begins – absolutely without any of the clatter and clamour of advertising that usually go with such enterprises – to build what, from all reports, must be a pretty costly dam. If they have acquired a title to the Mesquite Mesa, no one seems to have heard of it; and if they are hoping to sell the land when the dam is completed, that, too, has been kept dark. Now comes this little newspaper puff this morning, and Mr Jennings promptly turns up to ask Kendall to drop it.'

'It is rather queer, when you come to put the odds and ends of it together,' admitted the railroad man.

'Decidedly queer, I should say.' So far the Government man went on the line which he himself had opened. Then he switched abruptly. 'By the way, where is your brother-in-law, Starbuck? I haven't seen him for three or four days.'

'Billy has been in Red Butte, figuring on a little mining deal in which we are both interested. But I am looking for him back tonight.'

'Good. If you should happen to see him when the train comes in, ask him to come over here and smoke a pipe with me. Tell him I'm losing my carefully acquired cow-boy accent and I'd like to freshen it up a bit.'

The superintendent promised; and, since he always had work to do, went across to his office in the second storey of the combined head-quarters and station building.

Some hour or so later the evening train came in from the west, and at the outpouring of passengers from it one, a man whose air of prosperous independence was less in the grave, young-old face and the loosely fitting khaki service clothes than in the way in which he carried his shoulders, was met by a boy from the superintendent's office, and the word passed sent him diagonally across the grass-covered plaza to swing himself lightly over the railing of the hotel porch.

'Dick made motions as if you wanted to smoke a peace pipe with me,' he said, dropping carelessly into the chair which had been Maxwell's.

'Yes,' Sprague assented; and then he went on to explain why. At the end of the explanations Starbuck nodded.

'I reckon we can do it all right; go up on the early morning train to the canyon head, and take a chance on picking up a couple of broncs at Wimberley's ranch. But we could hoof it over from Angels in less than a quarter of the time it'll take us to ride up the river from Wimberley's.'

'For reasons of my own, Billy, I don't want to "hoof it", as you say, from Angels. To mention one of them, I might ask you to remember that I tip the scale at a little over the half of the third hundred, just now, and I'm pretty heavy on my feet.' And therewith the matter rested.

At an early hour the following morning, an hour when the sun was just swinging clear over the far-distant blue horizon line of the Crosswater Hills which marks the eastern limit of the great desert, two men dropped from the halted eastbound train at the Timanyoni Canyon water-tank and made their way around the nearest of the hogbacks to the ranch house of one William Wimberley.

As Starbuck had predicted, two horses were obtainable, though the ranchman looked long and dubiously at the big figure of the Government chemist before he was willing to risk even the heaviest of the horses in his small *remuda*.

'I reckon you'll have ter set sort o' light in the saddle, Mister,' he said at the mounting; and then, apparently as an after-thought: 'By gollies, I wouldn't have you fall

237

over ag'inst me f'r a farm in God's country, stranger! Ef you was to live round here, we'd call you Samson, and take up a c'lection fer the pore, sufferin' Philistines. We shore would.'

Sprague laughed good-naturedly as he followed Starbuck's lead toward the river. He was well used to being joked about his size, and there were times when he rather encouraged the joke. Big men are popularly supposed to be more or less helpless, physically, and Sprague was enough of a humorist to enjoy the upsetting, now and then, of the popular tradition. In his college days he had held the record for the heavy lift and the broad jump; there was no man of his class who could stand up to him with the gloves or on the wrestling-mat; and in the football field he was at once the strongest 'back' and the fastest man on the team – a combination rare enough to be miraculous.

'You say you want to follow the river?' said Starbuck, when they had struck in between the precipitous hills among which the green flood of the Timanyoni made its way toward the canyon portal.

'Yes, if it is at all practicable. I'd like to get some idea of the lay of the land between this and the camp on the Mesquite.'

'I'm anticipatin' that you'll get the idea, good and plenty,' agreed the superintendent's brother-in-law dryly; and during the three-hour jaunt that followed, the prediction was amply confirmed. There was no trail, and for the greater part of the way the river flowed between rocky hogbacks, with only the narrowest of boulder-strewn margins on either hand.

Time and again they were forced to dismount and to lead the horses around or over the natural obstructions; and once they were obliged to leave the river valley entirely, climbing and descending again by a circuitous route among the rugged hills.

It was late in the forenoon when they came finally into the region of upper basins, and, turning to the eastward, threaded a dry arroyo which brought them out upon the level-bottomed valley known as the Mesquite Mesa. It was not a mesa in the proper meaning of the term; it was rather a vast flat wash brought down from the hills by the sluicing of many floods. Here and there its sun-baked surface was cut and gashed by dry gullies all pointing toward the river, and each bearing silent witness to the manner in which the mesa had been formed.

At a point well within this shut-in moraine, Sprague dismounted, tossed his bridle reins to Starbuck, and went to examine the soil in the various gullies. Each dry ditch afforded a perfect cross-section of the different strata, from the thin layer of sandy top-soil to the underlying beds of coarse sandstone pebbles and gravel. Sprague kicked the edges from a dozen of the little ditches, secured a few handfuls of the soil, and came back shaking his head.

'I don't wonder that these people don't want to advertise their land, Billy,' he commented, climbing, with a nimbleness astonishing in so large a man, to the back of his mount. 'As they say down in Tennessee, you couldn't raise a fuss on it. Let's amble along and see what they are doing at the head works.'

At the head of the wash the valley of Mesquite Creek came in abruptly from the right. On a bench above the mouth of the valley they found the construction camp of the irrigation company, a scattered collection of shack sheds and tents, a corral for the working stock, and the usual filth and litter characterizing the temporary home of the 'wop'.

Across the valley mouth a huge earthwork was rising. It was the simplest form of construction known to the dam-building engineer: a mere heaping of earth and gravel moved by two-horse scrapers from the slopes of the contiguous hills on either hand. There was no masonry, no concrete, not even the thin core wall which modern engineering practice prescribes for the strengthening member in an earth embankment designed to retain any considerable body of water.

Moreover, there was no spillway. The creek, carrying at this season of the year its minimum flow, had been stopped off without an outlet; and the embankment upon which the force was heaping the scrapings from the hillsides was already retaining a good-sized lake formed by the checked waters of the stream.

Starbuck and Sprague had drawn rein at the outskirts of the construction camp, and they were not molested until Sprague took a flat black box from his pocket, opened it into a camera, and was preparing to take a snapshot of the dam. At that, a man who had been lounging in the door of the camp commissary, a dark-faced, black-bearded giant in brown duck and service leggings, crossed the camp street and threw up a hand in warning.

'Hey, there; hold on – that don't go!' he shouted gruffly, striding up to stand squarely in the way of the camera. 'You can't take any pictures on this job.'

'Sorry,' Sprague, giving the intruder his most amiable smile, 'but you were just a half-second too late,' and he closed the camera into its box-like shape and dropped it into his pocket.

The black-bearded man advanced threateningly.

'This is company property, and you are trespassers,' he rasped. 'Give me that camera!'

Starbuck's right hand went softly under his coat and stayed there, and his steady grey eyes took on the sleepy look that, in his range-riding days, had been a sufficient warning to those who knew him. Sprague lounged easily in his saddle and ignored the hand extended for the camera.

'You are Mr Jennings, I take it,' he said, as one who would temporize and gain time. 'Fine dam you are building there.'

'Give me that camera!'

Sprague met the angry eyes of the engineer and smiled back into them.

'I'll take it under consideration,' he said, half-jocularly. 'You'll give me a little time to think about it, won't you?'

Jennings's hand dropped to the butt of the heavy revolver sagging at his hip.

'Not a damned minute!' he barked. 'Hand it over!'

Starbuck was closing up slowly on the opposite side of his companion's horse, a movement which he brought about by a steady knee pressure on the bronco's off shoulder. Jennings's fingers were closing around the grip of his pistol when the astounding thing happened. Without so much as a muscle-twitching of warning Sprague's left hand shot out, the fingers grappled an ample breast-hold on the engineer's coat and shirt-bosom, and Jennings was snapped from his feet and flung, back down, across the horn of Sprague's saddle much as if his big body had been a bag of meal. Starbuck reached over, jerked the engineer's weapon from its holster, broke it to eject the cartridges, and flung it away.

'Now you can get down,' said Sprague quietly; and when he loosed the terrible clutch, Jennings slid from the saddle-horn and fell, cursing like a maniac.

'Stand still!' ordered Starbuck, when the engineer bounded to his feet and started to run toward the commissary, and the weapon that made the bidding mandatory materialized suddenly from an inner pocket of the ex-cowman's khaki riding-coat.

But the trouble, it seemed, was just fairly getting under way. Up from the embankment where the scrapers were dumping came two or three foremen armed with pick-handles. The commissary was turning out its quota of rough-looking clerks and time-keepers, and a mob of the foreign labourers – the shift off duty – came pouring out of the bunk houses and shacks.

Sprague had unlimbered and focused his camera again and was calmly taking snapshot after snapshot; of the dam, of the impounded lake, of the up-coming mob, and of the black-bearded man held hands-up in the middle of the camp street. When he shut the box on the last of the exposures he turned to Starbuck with a whimsical smile wrinkling at the corners of his eyes.

'They don't seem to be very enthusiastic about keeping us here, Billy,' he said, with gentle irony. 'Shall we go?'

Starbuck shook the reins over the neck of his mount and the two horses wheeled as one and sprang away down the rough cart-road leading to the end of the copper-mine spur above Angels. At the retreat, someone on the commissary porch began to pump a repeating rifle in the general direction of the pair, but no harm was done.

Starbuck was the first to break the galloping silence when an intervening hill shoulder had cut off the backward view of the camp at the dam, and what he said was purely complimentary.

'You sure have got your nerve with you, and the punch to back it up,' he chuckled. 'I reckon I'm goin' to wake up in the middle of the night laughin' at the way you snatched that rustler out of his tracks and slammed him across the saddle. I'd give a heap to be able to do a thing like that; I sure would.'

'Call it a knack,' rejoined Sprague modestly. 'You pick up a good many of those little tricks when you're training on the squad. Perhaps you've never thought of it, but the human body is easier to handle, weight for weight, than any inanimate object could possibly be. That is one of the first things you learn in tackling on the football field.'

They were jogging along slowly by this time and had

passed the copper-mine switch in the road leading to the station at Angels. Starbuck was not over-curious, but the experiences of the forenoon were a little puzzling. Why had his companion wished to take the long, hard ride up the valley of the Timanyoni? And why, again, had he taken the chance of a fight for the sake of securing a few snapshot pictures of the irrigation company's construction camp and dam? A third query hinged itself upon the decidedly inhospitable, not to say hostile, attitude of Jennings, the irrigation company's field-officer. Why should he object so strenuously to the common sightseer's habit of kodaking anything and everything in sight?

Starbuck was turning these things over in his mind when they reached Angels. As they rode into town Sprague glanced at his watch.

'I have been wondering if we couldn't get this man Dickery at the town corral to take charge of these horses of ours until Wimberley can come and get them?' he said. 'That would make it possible for us to catch the eleven-thirty train for Brewster.'

Starbuck said it was quite feasible, and by the time they had disposed of the horses the train was whistling for the station. When they boarded the train, Sprague proposed that they postpone the midday meal in the diner in order to ride out on the rear platform of the observation-car.

'We'll get to town in time for a late luncheon at the hotel,' was the way he put it; 'and on as fine a day as this I like to ride out of doors and take in the scenery.'

Starbuck acquiesced, and smiled as one well used to the scenery. Truly, the trip through the Timanyoni Canyon was one which usually brought the tourists crowding to the rear platform of the train, but until the morning of this purely sight-seeing jaunt he had been thinking that Maxwell's big friend was altogether superior to the scenic attractions.

Now, however, Sprague seemed greatly interested in the canyon passage. Again and again he called his companion's attention to the engineering difficulties which had been overcome in building the narrow pathway for the rails through the great gorge. Particularly, he dwelt upon the stupendous cost of making the pathway, and upon the temerarious courage of the engineers in adopting a grade so near, in dozens of places, to the level of the foaming torrent at the track-side.

'Yes,' Starbuck agreed; 'it sure did cost a heap of money. Dick says the thirty-six miles are bonded at one hundred thousand dollars a mile, and even that didn't cover the cost of construction on some of the miles.'

'But why did they put the grade so close to the river level?' persisted the expert, when the foam from a midstream boulder breathed a misty breath on them as the train slid past. 'Isn't there constant trouble from high water?'

'No, the Timanyoni's a tolerably dependable creek,' was Starbuck's answer. 'Summer and winter it holds its own, with nothing like the variation you find in the Mississippi Valley rivers. An eight-foot rise is the biggest they've ever recorded at the High Line dam, so J. Montague Smith tells me.'

'They are fixed to take care of that much of a rise at the High Line dam, are they?' queried Sprague.

'Oh, yes; I reckon they could take a bigger one than that, if they had to. That dam is built for keeps. Williams, who was the constructing engineer, says that the dam and plant will stand when the water of the river is pouring through the second-storey windows of the power-house.'

'And that, you would say, would never happen?' put in the expert thoughtfully, adding, 'If it should happen, your brother-in-law would have to build him a new railroad through this canyon, wouldn't he?'

'He sure would. That eight-foot rise I spoke of gave them a heap of trouble up here – washouts to burn!'

'What caused that rise – rains?'

'Rains and cloud-bursts, in the season of the melting snows. It was just as Smith was turning heaven and earth upside down to get the dam completed, and for a little spell they sure was anticipatin' trouble a-plenty; thought they were going to be plumb paralysed.'

'I want to meet that man Smith,' said the expert, going off at a tangent, as his habit was. 'Stillings, your friend the lawyer who has his offices next door to my laboratory, says he's a wonder.'

'Smith is all right,' was Starbuck's verdict. 'He's a first-class fighting man, and he doesn't care much who knows it. He got big rich out of that High Line fight, married old Colonel Baldwin's little peach of a daughter, and is layin' off to live happy ever afterward.'

From that on, the rear-platform talk had to do chiefly with Mr J. Montague Smith and his plucky struggle with the hydro-electric trust which had tried, unsuccessfully as the event proved, to steal the High Line dam and water privilege. In due time the train shot out of the gorge, and after a dodging course among the Park hills, came to the skirting of the High Line reservoir lake lying like a silver mirror in its setting of forested buttes and spurs.

At the lower end of the lake, where the white concrete dam stretched its massive rampart across the river gorge, the train halted for a moment in obedience to an interposing block-signal. It was during the momentary stop that a handsome young fellow, with the healthy tan of the hill country browning his frank boyish face, came out of the nearby power-house, ran up the embankment and swung himself over the railing of the observation platform.

'Hello, John!' said Starbuck; and then he introduced the newcomer to his companion.

'Glad to know you, Mr Sprague,' said the young man, whose hearty hand-grip was an instant recommendation to the good graces of the big expert. 'I've been hearing of you off and on all summer. It's a saying with us out here that any friend of Dick Maxwell's owns Brewster – or as much of it as he cares to make use of.'

'I have certainly been finding it that way, Mr Smith,' Sprague rejoined, in grateful recognition of the Brewster hospitality. And then: 'We were just talking about you and your dam as we came along, Starbuck and I. You have a pretty good head of water on, haven't you?'

'An unusually good head for this time of the year. The heavy storms we have been having in the eastern foothills account for it. Our power plant is working at normal load, and our ranchmen are all using water liberally in their late irrigating, and yet you see the quantity that is going over the splash boards.'

'Yes, I see,' observed Sprague thoughtfully. And when the train began to move onward: 'With this big reservoir behind you, I suppose a sudden flood couldn't hurt you, Mr Smith?'

The young man with the healthy tan on his clean-cut face promptly showed his good business sense.

'We think we have a comfortably safe installation, but we are not specially anxious to try it out merely for the satisfaction of seeing how much it would stand,' was the conservative reply.

Sprague looked up curiously from his solid planting in the biggest of the platform folding chairs.

'And yet, three days ago, Mr Smith, you said, in the presence of witnesses, that a ten-foot rise wouldn't endanger your dam or your power plant,' he put in shrewdly.

Mr J. Montague Smith, secretary and treasurer of the Timanyoni High Line Company, was plainly taken unawares.

'How the dev –' he began; and then he tried again.

'Pardon me, Mr Sprague; you hit me when I wasn't looking for it. I believe I did say something like that; in fact, I've said similar things a good many times.'

'But not in exact feet and inches, I hope,' said Sprague, with a show of mild concern. 'These exactnesses are what murder us, Mr Smith. Now, I presume if somebody should come to you today and threaten to turn another ten feet of river on you, you'd object, wouldn't you?'

'We certainly should – object most strenuously!'

'Yet, if that person were so minded, he might quote you as having said that ten additional feet wouldn't hurt you.'

The young treasurer laughed a trifle uneasily.

'I can't believe that anybody would make a bit of well-meant boasting like that an excuse for – but it's altogether absurd, you know. Your case in unsupposable. Nobody pushes the button for the rains or the cloud-burst storms. When you introduce me to the fellow who really has the making of the weather in the Timanyoni headwaters, I'll be very careful what I say to him.'

'Just so,' said the expert quietly; and then a long-continued blast of the locomotive whistle announced the approach of Brewster.

Sprague took leave of his latest acquaintance at the station entrance, where a trim, high-powered motor car, driven by an exceedingly pretty young woman in leather cap, gauntlets, and driving-coat, was waiting for Smith.

'I am a soil expert, as you may have heard, Mr Smith,' he said at parting, 'and I am interested at the moment in alluvial washes – the detritus brought down from the high lands by the rivers. One of these days I may call upon you for a little information and help.'

'Command me,' said the young financier, with another of the hearty hand-grips; and then he climbed in beside the pretty young woman and was driven away.

Sprague was unusually silent during the tardy luncheon shared with Starbuck in the Topaz café; and Starbuck, who never had much to say unless he was pointedly invited, was correspondingly speechless. Afterward, with a word of caution to his table companion not to mention the morning's adventure to anyone, Sprague went to his laboratory, to test the specimens of soil gathered on the Mesquite Mesa, Starbuck supposed.

But the supposition was wrong. What Mr Calvin Sprague busied himself with during the afternoon was the careful developing of the film taken from his pocket camera, and the printing of several sets of pictures therefrom. These prints he placed in his pocket note-book, and the book and its enclosures went with him when, after the evening meal, at which he had somehow missed both Maxwell and Starbuck, he climbed the three flights of stairs in the Tribune Building and presented himself at the door of Editor Kendall's den.

Kendall was glad to see him, or at least he said he was, and, waving him to a chair at the desk end, produced a box of rather dubious-looking, curiously twisted cigars, at which the visitor shook his head despondently.

'You'd say I was the picture of health, wouldn't you, Kendall, and you wouldn't believe me if I were to tell you that I am smoking a great deal too much?' he said, with a quizzical smile that was on the verge of turning into a grin.

The editor was not fooled; as a matter of fact, it was an exceedingly difficult matter to fool the tired-eyed tyrant of *The Tribune* editorial rooms.

'Cut it out,' he said, with his mirthless laugh. 'You wouldn't expect to find fifty-cent *Rienas* in a newspaper shop – any more than I'd expect you to climb up here with a news story for me. Smoke your own cigars, and be damned to you.' And in sheer defiance he lighted one of his own dubious monstrosities, while Sprague was chuckling and passing his pocket-case of fat black *Maduros*.

'You say, any more than you'd expect a news story.

Perhaps I have a news story for you. Cast your eye over these,' and he threw out the bunch of lately made photographs.

The editor went over the collection carefully, and at the end of the inspection said, 'Well, what's the answer?'

'The construction camp of the Mesquite Land and Irrigation Company at about half past ten this afternoon. The held-up man is Mr Engineer Jennings, posed by Billy Starbuck, who was kindly holding a gun on him for me. The people running are Jennings's workmen, coming to help him obliterate us. The water is the irrigation lake; the heap of dirt is the dam.'

'Still, I don't quite grasp the news value,' said Kendall doubtfully. 'Why should Jennings wish to obliterate you?'

'Because I was taking pictures on his job. He was unreasonable enough to demand my camera, and to make the sham bad man's break of handling his gun without pulling it on me.'

The editor studied the picture long and thoughtfully.

'You've got something up your sleeve, Mr Sprague; what is it?' he asked, after the considering pause.

Sprague drew his chair closer; and for five minutes the city editor, who had come in for a word with his superior, forbore to break in upon the low-toned earnest conference which was going on at the managing-editor's desk. At the end of it, however, he heard Kendall say, 'I'll get Monty Smith on the wire, and if he coincides with you, we'll take a hand in this. I more than half believe you're right, but you'll admit that it sounds rather incredible. *The Tribune*'s motto is "All the news that is news", but we don't want to be classed among the "yellows".'

'You run no risk in the present instance,' was Sprague's confident assurance. 'Of course, there is no direct evidence; if there were, the case would be promptly taken to the courts. As a matter of fact, I'm hoping that Mr Smith will take it to the courts as it stands. But in any event, an appeal to the public will do no harm.'

'All right; we'll see what Smith says,' said Kendall; and then the patient city editor had his inning.

Leaving the Tribune Building, the chemistry expert went to the nearest telephone and called for the house number of Mr Robert Stillings, the attorney who served locally for the railroad company and was also counsel for the High Line people. Happily, it was the young lawyer himself who answered the 'phone.

'This is Sprague,' said the down-town caller. 'How busy are you this evening?'

The answer was apparently satisfactory, since the big man went on: 'All right; I wish you would arrange to meet me in the lobby of the Topaz. Catch the next car if it won't hurry you too much. You'll do it? Thank you. Good-bye.'

Fifteen minutes later the Government man, writing a letter at one of the desks in the hotel lobby, looked up to greet his summoned visitor, a keen-eyed, self-contained young man whose reputation as a fearless fighter in just causes was already spreading from the little inter-mountain city of his adoption and becoming State-wide.

'I'm here,' said Stillings briefly; and Sprague rose and drew him aside into one of the alcoves.

For some little time after they had drawn their chairs together, Sprague held the floor, talking earnestly and exhibiting a set of the snapshot pictures. Stillings listened attentively, examining the pictures by the aid of a small pocket magnifier. But when Sprague finished he was shaking his head doubtfully, unconsciously following the example set by *The Tribune* editor.

'We have nothing definite to go on, Mr Sprague, as you yourself admit. These people are well within their legal rights. As you probably know, there is no statutory provision in this State requiring the builders of a dam to conform to any particular plan of construction; and, as a matter of fact, there are dozens of dams just like this one

– mere earth embankments without masonry of any kind.'

'Do you mean to say that the safety of the entire Timanyoni Valley can be endangered by a structure like this, and that the property owners who are imperilled have no legal recourse?' demanded the expert.

'Recourse, yes; plenty of it after the fact. If the dam should give way and cause damage, the irrigation company would be liable.'

'Humph!' snorted the big-bodied one, half contemptuously. 'Law is one of the few things that I have never dabbled in. What you say amounts to this: if I find a man training a cannon on my house, I have no right to stop him; I can only try to collect damages after the gun has gone off and ripped a hole through my property. I could make a better law than that myself!'

Stillings was staring thoughtfully through the opposite window at the lights in the railroad building across the plaza.

'There are times, Mr Sprague, when we all feel that way; crises which seem to call for something in the way of extra-judicial proceedings,' he admitted. And then: 'Have you told Maxwell about this?'

'Not specifically. Dick has troubles of his own just now; he has had enough of them this summer to turn his hair gray, as you know. I have been hoping that this latest move of the enemy could be blocked without dragging him into it.'

Stillings turned quickly. 'That is the frankest thing you've said this evening. Is it another move of the enemy – the New Yorkers?'

Sprague spread his hands and his big shoulders went up in a shrug.

'You have just as much incriminating evidence as I have. How does it strike you?'

The attorney shook his head in doubtful incredulity,

again unconsciously following Editor Kendall's lead.

'It doesn't seem possible!' he protested. 'Think of the tremendous consequences involved – outside of the crippling of the railroad. The Short Line wouldn't be the only sufferer in case of a dam-break in the Mesquite. The entire valley would be flood-swept, and our High Line dam –' he stopped abruptly and half-rose to his feet. 'Good Lord, Sprague! the breaking of the High Line would mean death and destruction without end!'

Sprague had found a cigar in an overlooked pocket and was calmly lighting it. Though he did not tell Stillings so, the argument had finally gotten around into the field toward which he had been pushing it from the first.

'Three days ago, your High Line treasurer, Mr J. Montague Smith, declared in the presence of witnesses – it was right here in this hotel lobby, and I happened to overhear it – that a ten-foot rise in the river, which, as you know, would submerge and sweep away miles of the railroad track in the canyon, would by no means endanger his dam. There you are, Mr Stillings. Now fish or cut bait.'

'Great Scott! what could Smith have been thinking of!' ejaculated the lawyer.

'It was merely a bit of loyal brag, as he admitted to Starbuck and me on the train this afternoon; and it had been craftily provoked by one of the men who heard it. But he said it, and what is more, he said it to – Jennings!'

This time the attorney's start carried him out of his chair and stood him upon his feet.

'I shall have to see Smith at once,' he said hurriedly. 'Still I can't believe that these New York stock pirates would authorize any such murderous thing as this!'

'Authorize murder of violence? Of course not; big business never does that. What it does is to put a man into the field, telling him in general terms the end that is to be accomplished. The head pushers would turn blue under their finger-nails if you'd charge them with murder.'

'But that is what this would amount to – cold-blooded murder!'

'Hold on a minute,' objected Sprague. 'Let's apply a little scientific reasoning. Suppose this thing has been accurately figured out, engineering-wise. Suppose that, by careful computation, it has been found that a certain quantity of water, turned loose at the mouth of Mesquite Valley, would produce a flood of a certain height in the full length of Timanyoni Canyon – say ten or twelve feet – sufficient to obliterate thirty-five or forty miles of the railroad track. Below its path of the greatest destruction it comes out into your High Line reservoir lake, with some miles farther to go, and a greatly enlarged area over which to diffuse itself.'

Stillings was nodding intelligence. 'I am beginning to see,' he said. 'Ten feet in the canyon wouldn't necessarily mean ten feet at Smith's dam.'

'No; but at the same time Smith is on record as having said that ten feet wouldn't endanger his dam or the power plant. So there you are again.'

Stillings walked the length of the alcove twice with his head down and his hands in his pockets before he stopped in front of the expert to say : 'You've half-convinced me, Mr Sprague. If we could get the barest shred of evidence that these people are building a dam which isn't intended to hold –'

'There spoke the lawyer again,' laughed Sprague. 'If you had the evidence, what would you do?'

'Institute legal proceedings at once.'

'And how long would it take you to get action?'

'Oh, that would depend upon the nature of the evidence I had to offer, of course.'

Sprague laughed again, derisively this time.

'Yes, I thought so; and while you were getting out your

writs and monkeying around – do you know what that piece of canyon track cost, Mr Stillings? I was told today that three million dollars wouldn't replace it – to say nothing of what it would mean to the railroad company to have its through line put out of business indefinitely. No; if we mean to –'

The interruption was the intrusion into the alcove of a huge-framed, hard-faced man who was fumbling in his pocket for a paper.

'Hello, Harding,' said Stillings; and then, jokingly: 'What brings the respected sheriff of Timanyoni County charging in upon us at this time of night?'

'It's a warrant,' said the sheriff, half in apology. And then to Sprague: 'I hate like the mischief to trouble you, Mr Sprague, but duty's duty.'

Sprague smiled up at the big man. 'Tell us about it, Mr Harding. You needn't bother to read the warrant.'

'It's that scrap you had with Jennings up at the Mesquite this morning. He's swore out a warrant against you for assault and battery.'

'And are you going to lock me up over night? I fancy that is what he would like to have you do.'

'Not me,' said the sheriff good-naturedly. 'I got Judge MacFarland out o' bed and made him come down to his office. I'm goin' to ask you to walk around there with me, just to let me out of it whole. I've fixed it with the judge so you won't have to give bail.'

'I'll go with you,' Stillings offered; and a few minutes later, in the magistrate's office, the Government man had bound himself on his own recognisance to appear in court the next morning to answer the charge against him.

On the sidewalk in front of the justice shop, Stillings reverted to the more pressing matter.

'I'm going to see Smith before I sleep, if I have to drive out to the Baldwin ranch to find him,' he declared. 'In the meantime, Mr Sprague, if you can devise any scheme by which we can get a legal hold on these fellows – anything that will serve as an excuse for our asking that an injunction be issued –'

'That would come before Judge Watson, wouldn't it?' Sprague broke in.

'Yes.'

'See Kendall, of *The Tribune*, about that. From what he told me a couple of hours ago, I should say that your petition for an injunction would be only a crude loss of time. We'll try to think of a better way, or at least a more effective way. Good night; and don't omit to throw the gaff into Smith, good and hard.'

On the morning following Sprague's visit to *The Tribune* editorial rooms, the newspaper-reading public of Brewster had a small sensation served, in Starbuck's phrase, 'hot from the skillet'. A good portion of the front page of *The Tribune* was given to a news story of the work which was under way in the Mesquite Valley, and pictures were printed of the camp, the dam, and the growing lake.

On the editorial page there was a caustic arraignment of the Mesquite Company, which was called upon to show cause why it should not be condemned as a public nuisance of a kind which had already brought much reproach upon the West as a field for legitimate investment, and the suggestion was made that a committee of responsible citizens be sent to investigate the Mesquite project, to the end that the charges made might be either substantiated or set aside.

Specifically, these charges were that there was no arable land within reach of the Mesquite dam, and that the dam itself was unsafe. Throughout his editorial Kendall had judiciously refrained from making any mention of a possible disaster to the railroad; but he hinted broadly at the danger to which the High Line dam – the source of the city's power and lights – would be subjected in the event of a flood catastrophe on the distant project.

Maxwell, who was living at the hotel in the absence of

his family, had read the paper before he came down to join Sprague at the breakfast-table and, like every other newspaper reader in Brewster that morning, he was full of the latest sensation.

'By George, Calvin,' he began, 'somebody has been stirring up the mud for those people we were talking about night before last. Have you seen *The Tribune*?'

Sprague nodded assent.

'What do you make of it?' asked the railroad man.

'I should say that somebody – possibly the High Line management – is beginning to sit up and take notice, wouldn't you?'

'Y-yes: but see here – any such thing as Kendall hints at would knock the Nevada Short Line out long before it would get to the High Line dam!'

'Naturally,' said Sprague coolly.

'Great Jehu! was that what you meant when you were making me dig this Mesquite project over for you the other day?'

'I didn't want to drag you into it, and don't yet,' said Sprague quietly. 'You've had grief enough for one summer. But the detective half of me tells me that there is little doubt that this thing is another attempt on the part of the big-money crowd to side-swipe your railroad off the map. It can be done, and you have no preventive recourse; Stillings says you haven't.'

'But, Calvin – something's *got* to be done! Are we going to sit still and –'

'One kind of something is doing itself, right now,' interrupted Sprague. 'It's your play, this time, to keep out of it, if you can. You'd say that the High Line people, J. Montague Smith and his crowd, inspired that blast in *The Tribune* this morning, wouldn't you?'

'It looks that way, yes.'

'Well, let them stir up the mud and make the fight. You sit tight in the boat and say nothing. What kind of an agent or operator have you at Angels?'

'Disbrow? – he's a good man; so good that I'm going to promote him to a better station next week.'

'Let that promotion wait a while. Give this good man instructions to watch every move that Jennings makes, and to report at once anything out of the ordinary that may happen. Do you get that?'

'I'll do it. Anything else?'

'No, not at present. Later on, say after the evening edition of *The Times-Record* comes out, I may want to get you on a quick wire. But the chief thing just now is to post the Angels man, and to have him keep in touch with you.'

After Maxwell had gone the chemistry expert finished his breakfast with epicurean leisure, smoked a reflective cigar in comfortable solitude in the hotel lobby, and, when the court hour arrived, went around to the office of the justice of the peace to answer to the charge of assault. As was to be expected, Jennings was not present; was not even represented by an attorney. Sprague pleaded guilty and paid his nominal fine, which MacFarland took with a quiet smile.

'I don't know what you did to that black-faced bully, Mr Sprague, but I hope you got your money's worth,' he said. 'Every time he turns up here in Brewster he proves himself an undesirable citizen, right from the word go.'

'Tough, is he?' queried Sprague.

'As tough as they make them. I wonder he didn't try to get square with you with a gun. That would be more like him.'

'Perhaps he will, later on,' suggested the fined one, with a good-natured smile; after which he went across to his laboratory, and was invisible for the remainder of the morning.

Just before noon Stillings dropped into the laboratory office. He found the chemist working among his retorts and test-tubes.

'I fell in to give you a pointer,' was the attorney's excuse

257

for the intrusion. 'Jennings is in town. He came over on the ten-o'clock local and went straight to *The Times-Record* office.'

Sprague grinned. 'You were looking out for him were you? Somebody got waked up at last?'

'Yes; the High Line people are on, all right,' was the reply. 'Smith called an emergency meeting of his directors early this morning. Two of them are Red Desert cattle barons, and they know the Mesquite situation like a book. What none of them can understand is the "why"; why the Mesquite outfit should take ninety-nine chances in a hundred of sending a flood down the Timanyoni when there is no money to be made by it.'

'What action did the directors' meeting take?'

'Instructed me to feel Judge Watson on the question of holding things up with an injunction. I did it, and it turned out as you intimated it would; nothing doing. Smith asked me to borrow Maxwell's special officer, Arch Tarbell, suggesting that we ought to keep in touch with Jennings. Archer was going over to Angels on the afternoon train, but Jennings has saved him the trouble by coming to town.'

'Well, what next?' Sprague inquired.

'That is just what I'd like to ask you,' was the lawyer's frank admission. 'We're all looking to you to set the pace. You're the one man with the holy gift of initiative, Mr Sprague. You haven't admitted it in so many words, but I know as well as I know anything that you are the man who started this newspaper talk.'

'Pshaw!' said the expert, in general raillery; 'I'm only a Government chemist, Mr Stillings.'

'That's all right, too; but that isn't why the railroad men call you "Scientific Sprague". Four times this summer you've dug Maxwell and his railroad out of a hole when the rest of us didn't know there was any hole. What I'm most afraid of now is that Jennings will put up some sort of a scheme to get you out of the way. He knows well enough by this time that you are the key to his situation.'

'I'm a tenderfoot,' said the big man, with naïve irony. 'What would you suggest?'

'That you go to Sheriff Harding and get him to swear you in as a special deputy. Then you can be prepared to defend yourself.'

Sprague's mellow laugh rumbled deep in his big body.

'I guess I can take care of myself, if it comes to that, without "packing hardware", as Starbuck would put it,' he averred. 'There won't be more than three or four of them to tackle me at once, will there? But about your campaign, I have been hoping that the High Line people, backed by public sentiment, would be able to head this thing off. I am still hoping it. It will be altogether better if the railroad doesn't have to take a hand on its own account. The New Yorkers would be sure to make capital out of it, holding the Ford-Maxwell management up to public execration as a corporation which deliberately strangles development propositions in its own territory.'

'That's a fact,' the attorney agreed.

'Working along that line, we can afford to wait, for a little while at least, to see how the cat is going to jump. Jennings is over here to get into the newspaper fight himself. In Maxwell's demoralization tussle of two weeks ago, it was demonstrated that *The Times-Record* had been subsidized by the enemy. Now we shall see Higginson and his editor jump in and take up the clubs in defence of the Mesquite Company.'

'I guess that is pretty good advice – to wait,' said Stillings. 'But we have an active crowd in the High Line, and its blood is up. Our people will want to be doing something while they wait.'

'Let them talk,' said Sprague quickly. 'Tell them to resolve themselves into committees of one to throw the big scare into the Brewster public which depends upon the safety of the High Line dam for its own safety. Then pick out a few good, dependable men like Smith, his old fighting father-in-law the colonel, and Williams the engineer, who will hold themselves in readiness to start at a moment's notice, night or day, for the firing line – any firing line that may happen to show up.'

'That is more like it,' rejoined the attorney. 'I'm sworn to uphold the majesty of the law, but –'

'But, as you remarked last night, there are extra-judicial crises now and then which have to be met in any old way that offers. Let it rest at that, and see me at the hotel this evening if you can make it convenient.'

With the appearance on the streets of the evening edition of *The Times-Record*, the Brewster public learned that there were two sides to the Mesquite question. In terms of unmeasured scorn Editor Healy attacked the narrow prejudice which would seek to place stumbling-blocks in the way of a great enterprise designed to benefit, not only the region locally concerned, but the entire West.

In the course of a long and vituperative editorial, the High Line company, the Brewster public-service corporations, and the railroad, each came in for its share of accusation, and their joint lack of public spirit was roundly condemned. It was pointed out that the High Line plant, by the admission of its own officials, would be in no danger even in the unsupposable case of the breaking of the Mesquite dam. Also, it was urged that the penny-wise policy of the railroad in adopting the low grade in Timanyoni Canyon was a matter of its own risk. Was the development of the nation to be halted, it was asked, because a niggardly railroad company was unwilling to spend a little money in raising its grade beyond a possible danger line?

But the sting of the editorial for Maxwell was in its tail. Healy concluded by darkly hinting that certain of the railroad officials were interested financially in sundry

Timanyoni Park lands owned by the High Line Company, and that they were willing to kill the prospects of the new district for the sake of their own pockets.

Maxwell was furiously hot about this blast in the evening paper, as his demeanour at the dinner-table, where he spoke his mind freely to Sprague, sufficiently proved.

'Why, the miserable liars!' he raged. 'There isn't an official on the Short Line from President Ford down who owns a single share of stock in the High Line! We all did help out at first, but Ford made every man of us turn loose the minute the dam was completed and the project was securely on its feet. He insisted that we couldn't afford to work for two dividend accounts!'

'He was quite right,' said Sprague calmly. 'But that is neither here nor there. It was Jennings's turn at bat and he took it. Let it go, and tell me what you hear from that good and reliable man, Disbrow, at Angels.'

'I had him on the wire myself, just a few minutes ago,' was the superintendent's answer. 'He says something has stirred things up over on the Mesquite. They're working night shifts – began last night.'

'Rain?' queried the expert.

'How the devil do you manage to jump at things that way?' demanded Maxwell, half-irritably. 'Yes; there had been cloud-bursts in the eastern foot-hills. The river rose two feet today.'

'Ah? That may bring on more talk – before the stenographers are ready to take it down. Any more items from Angels?'

'Nothing special. The Mesquite people got half a car-load of dynamite this morning. That shows you how careful Disbrow is; he is spotting everything – even the common routine things.'

'Um; dynamite, eh? What use has Jennings for so much high explosive as that?'

'I don't know; uses it in excavating, I suppose. The more he uses, the bigger his rake-off from the powder company.

Where there's a big graft, there are always a lot of little ones.'

Sprague ate in silence for five full minutes before he said, quite without preliminary: 'How long would it take a light special train to run from Brewster to Angels, with a clear track and regardless orders, Dick?'

'I made it once in my own car in two hours and fifty-five minutes, with two stops for water. Why?'

'Oh, I was just curious to know. Two fifty-five, eh? And how long would it take to get the special train ready?'

'Fifteen or twenty minutes, perhaps, on a rush order.'

Sprague sat back and began to fold his napkin carefully in the original creases.

'As I have said before, I don't want to pose as an alarmist, Maxwell; but if I were you, I'd have that special train hooked up and ready to pull out – and I'd keep it that way, on tap, so to speak.'

The railroad man rose to the occasion promptly.

'Beginning tonight?' he asked.

'Yes, beginning tonight.'

'Has Jennings gone back?'

'He has. He went over on the evening train. Your man Tarbell kept cases on him while he was here. He spent most of the day with Higginson and Healy in *The Times-Record* office.'

Maxwell refused his dessert and ordered a second cup of black coffee.

'This suspense is something fierce, Calvin,' he said, when the waiter left them. 'Have we got to sit still and do nothing?'

'That is your part in it,' was the quiet reply. 'If a party of prominent citizens should call upon you for a special train at some odd hour of the day or night, you want to be ready to supply it suddenly. Aside from that, you are to keep hands off.'

For forty-eight hours beyond this evening dinner in the

Topaz café – two days during which the railroad agent at Angels reported increased activities at the Mesquite dam – the newspaper wrangle over the merits and demerits of the irrigation project in the edge of the Red Desert went on with growing acrimony on both sides. But by the end of the second day it was apparent that *The Tribune* had public sentiment with it almost unanimously.

It was also on this second day that further bitterness was engendered by a street report that Judge Watson had enjoined the High Line company from interfering in any way with the operations on the Mesquite. This was the last straw and public indignation found expression that night in a monster mass meeting of protest, in which the speakers, with J. Montague Smith to set them the example, criticized the court sharply in free Western phrase.

After the meeting, adopting all sorts of resolutions condemnatory of everything in sight, adjourned – which was between nine and ten o'clock – there was a street rumour to the effect that Judge Watson would declare some of the speakers in contempt and cinch them accordingly.

Maxwell and Starbuck brought this report to Sprague, who was smoking one of his big, black cigars on the porch of the hotel.

'Going to institute contempt proceedings, is he?' said the expert, with interest apparently only half-aroused.

'Wouldn't that jar you?' commented Starbuck. 'I was telling Dick just now that Judge Watson has about outlived his usefulness in this little old shack town. This injunction of his is about the rawest thing that ever came over the range.'

'Smith is red-hot,' Maxwell put in; 'hot enough to get out and scrap somebody. And his directors are all with him.'

Still the big-bodied expert seemed only mildly interested.

263

'If anybody should happen to get mixed up legally with the Mesquite folks on this job of theirs, it would be pretty hard to get a jury in Brewster which would lean the way the judge does, wouldn't it?' he asked.

Maxwell's verdict was unqualified. 'It would be practically impossible.' He had found his pipe and was filling it when Sprague pointed to the spur track at the end of the railroad building opposite.

'Is that your special train over there, Dick?'

'Yes. You see I've obeyed orders. That train has been standing there for two days, with three shifts of men dividing up the watch in the engine cab.'

'And the committee of prominent citizens hasn't yet materialized, eh? Never mind; you've done your part. What is the latest from Angels?'

'More cloud-bursts in the hills, and more activity up on the Mesquite. Disbrow says that Jennings has been offering all sorts of big pay to the scattered ranchmen to get them to come on the job with scraper-teams.'

'That's bad,' said the chemistry man briefly; adding, 'I don't like that.'

Starbuck got up to stand with his back to a porch pillar. From the new position he could look through the windows into the thronged hotel lobby.

'This town's stirred up some hotter than I've ever seen it before,' he drawled. 'Look at that mob inside – and every blame' man of it chewing the rag over this water proposition.'

'I don't like that,' Sprague repeated, thus proving that he had entirely missed Starbuck's comment on the excitement. Then he sat up suddenly. 'There's a boy just coming down from your offices, Maxwell; it's the night watchman's boy, isn't it? Run across and head him, Starbuck, I believe that's a telegram he has in his hand.'

Starbuck swung himself over the railing and caught the lad before he could disappear in the street throngs.

'You were plumb right,' he said, when he came back to take his place on the porch. 'He did have a message; it's for Dick. Here you are.'

Maxwell tore the envelope across and held the telegram up to the ceiling light.

'Here's news,' he announced. 'It's from our man at Angels. He says: "Jennings's force disbanded, and most of it gone east on Limited. Been shipping teams and outfit all afternoon. Too busy to wire sooner".' The superintendent crumpled the telegram and smote fist into palm. 'Bully for you, Sprague!' he exulted. 'You pushed the right button just right! Jennings couldn't stand the pressure; he's given up the job and quit!'

There was no answering enthusiasm on the part of the big man who rose suddenly out of his chair and reached for the telegram. Quite the contrary, the hand which took the crumpled bit of paper was trembling a little.

'Dick,' he began, in his deepest chest tone, 'you hike over to the dispatcher's office on the dead run and have Connolly clear for that special train. Don't lose a minute! Starbuck, it's up to you to find Smith, Tarbell, Williams, Colonel Baldwin, and two or three more good men whom you can trust – trust absolutely, mind you. Herd your crowd at the station in the quickest possible time; and you, Maxwell, make it your first business to tell the agent at Angels that there is a special train coming over the road. Don't tell him its destination; just say it will leave Brewster, going east, in a few minutes. Don't slip up on that – it may mean a dozen human lives! Get busy, both of you!'

After he was left alone, Sprague shouldered a path through the crowd in the lobby and had himself lifted to his rooms. When he came down a few minutes later he had changed his business clothes for the field rig which he wore on his soil-collecting expeditions. He had scarcely worked his way through the throng to the comparative freedom of the porch when Maxwell came hurrying across from the railroad building.

'Bad luck,' said the superintendent, with brittle emphasis. 'There's a freight-train off the steel half-way between Corona and Timanyoni, this side of the canyon, and the track is blocked.'

'And we can't get by? There is nothing on the other side of the wreck that you could order down to meet us at the block?'

'Nothing nearer than Angels. There is an eastbound freight held there, loading the last of Jennings's outfit. To order the engine back from that would add at least an hour and a half to the two-hour-and-fifty-minute running schedule I gave you the other day.'

Sprague swore out of a full heart, which, since he was the least profane of men, was an accurate measure of his growing disquietude.

'That's on me!' he grated. 'I had it all figured out to the tenth decimal place, *and I didn't put in the factor of chance*! Dick, I want the biggest automobile in this town, and the one man among all your thousands who is least afraid to drive it.'

Maxwell was able to answer without hesitation. 'The car will be Colonel Baldwin's big "six", with Starbuck for your reckless chauffeur. But I doubt if you can get over the range in anything that goes on wheels.' Then he added: 'What is it, Calvin? What have you figured out?'

Sprague ignored the anxious query and spoke only to the fact.

'Can't get over the range? I tell you, we've *got* to get over the range! Good Lord! why in Heaven's name doesn't Starbuck hurry?'

Starbuck had hurried. He had looked to find most, if not all, of the men he had been told to summon, closeted in conference with Stillings, and his guess had gone true to the mark. Only Tarbell was missing, and him they picked up in front of *The Tribune* office as they were hurrying to the rendezvous in the colonel's big touring-car.

Maxwell saw the car as it came under the corner electrics. 'There's a little luck, anyway!' he exclaimed. 'That is the Colonel's car, now, and Billy is driving it.'

'Tools and arms; half a dozen picks and shovels, and anything you can find that will shoot,' commanded Sprague, vaulting the porch railing to the sidewalk as easily as Starbuck had vaulted it a little while before. 'See to that part of the outfit yourself, Dick, while I'm looking after the human end of it.'

One minute afterward the big man was standing beside the touring-car which had been drawn up at the town-side platform of the railroad building. Sprague shot the emergency at the five men in the car in bullet-like sentences.

'Gentlemen, we've got to get over to the Mesquite as quick as the Lord'll let us. The railroad is blocked, and it's an auto or nothing. Maxwell says we can't do it. I say we've got to do it. What do you say?'

'I reckon we can do it,' drawled Starbuck, speaking for all. Then he turned to Smith, who was in the tonneau. 'How about the tanks, Monty?'

'I filled them tonight, before we left the ranch,' said the High Line treasurer. 'Also, there is an extra gallon of oil aboard – we always carry it.'

'How about it, colonel?' Sprague demanded of the erect, white-moustached old man in the back seat.

'Sure!' was the quick reply. 'You haven't told us yet whether it's a fight or a frolic, but we're all with you, either way, Mr Sprague. Hop in, and we'll be jogging along.'

It was at this moment that Maxwell, followed by a couple of yard men, came up. The men were carrying the picks and shovels, which were hastily stowed in the car, and the superintendent handed over a small arsenal of weapons, three of them being sawed-off Winchesters.

'I had to raid the express office,' he explained, 'and I

took what I could find.' Then to Sprague, who had mounted to the seat beside Starbuck, 'Don't you want me along?'

'No; you can do a great deal more good right here. Listen, now, and follow my directions to the letter. Go upstairs to the wire and get in touch with your man at Angels. It will be your job to keep him in doubt as to what is on the road *between his station and the lower end of the canyon.* Lie to him if you have to; tell him a part of the wrecked freight is on its way up the canyon, or something of that sort, and keep him believing it as long as you possibly can. Don't fall down on it! Everything depends now upon the length of time you can keep some such story as that going over the wires.'

Starbuck had adjusted a pair of goggles to his eyes, and had his foot on the clutch-pedal. 'All set?' he asked.

'Go!' said Sprague; and at the word the big car shot away from the platform, rounded the end of the plaza, and bore away through a cross street to the eastward, gathering headway until, when the city limits were passed, its cut-out exhausts were blending in a deafening roar.

Sprague was the only member of the party who had not at some time in the past had experience with Starbuck's driving. But before the first ten-mile lap on the mesa road had been covered he, too, had had his initiation. There was a little lamp on the dash which poured its tiny ray on the dial of the speedometer. Sprague saw the index pointer go up to thirty-five, jump to forty, crawl steadily onward until it had passed the forty-five and was mounting to the fifty. After that he saw no more, for the simple reason that he was obliged to close his unprotected eyes against the hurricane speed blast. The big man from Washington had asked for the fastest car in Brewster and for a man who was not afraid to drive it. He had got both.

At the same time, alarming as the pace might seem, Starbuck was not taking any needless chances. He knew his road, and knew also that there were many miles of it among the mountains that would have to be taken at slower speed. None the less, when the long mesa stretch was covered, and the big car was making zigzags up the precipitous slopes of Mount Cornell to reach the gap called Nevajo Notch, the pace was still terrific, and the sober-faced driver was leaning over his wheel and pushing the motor like a true speed-maniac.

There was an hour of this risky zigzagging, and then the pass, lying cold and grim in the half moonlight at altitude ten thousand feet, was reached and threaded. Following the summit-gaining came the down-mountain rush on the eastern slope, and again Sprague closed his eyes, confessing inwardly that the steadiest nerve may have its limitations. With precipices shooting skyward on the right, and plunging sheer to unknown depths on the left, and with a man at the wheel who had apparently hypnotised himself until he had become a mere machine driving a machine –

When Sprague opened his eyes the great car was once more on an even keel and its wheels were spurning the hard red sand of the desert. In the far distance ahead a light was twinkling, the lamp in the station office at Angels. Sprague spoke to the iron-nerved driver at his side.

'Hold on, Billy; can you make the remainder of the run without the lamps?'

Starbuck brought the big machine to a stand, and leaned over and extinguished the lights. A little later, under Sprague's directions, he was making a silent circuit of the town, with the muffler in and the engine speeded at its quietest.

Since it was far past midnight, the better part of Angels was abed and asleep, with lights showing only at the railroad station and in Pete Grim's dance-hall, where, arguing from the row of hitched horses, a round-up of Red Desert cowboys made merry. Sprague stopped the car by a sign to Starbuck and turned to Tarbell.

'Get out, Archer, and make a quick run over to the station. I want to know what's going on in Disbrow's office.'

Tarbell made the reconnaissance and was back in a few minutes.

'Disbrow is at his wire, with a man walkin' the floor behind him; and there's a piebald bronc' hitched out beyond the freight shed,' was the brief report.

'Who is the floor-walker?' asked Sprague.

'I couldn't get a fair squint at him, but he looked mightily like the fellow I been keepin' cases on for the last two or three days.'

'Gentlemen, we're in luck, for once,' Sprague said impressively. 'That's Jennings, without doubt; and he is waiting for a wire – the right kind of wire – to come from Brewster. You remember what I told Maxwell, as we were leaving? That was one time when a guess was as good as a prophecy. Go on, Billy, and head straight for the Mesquite. And you gentlemen back there, get your weapons ready. If there happens to be a guard at the dam, we'll have to rush it.'

Singularly enough, when the short run was accomplished they found that there was no guard. The shack camp was deserted, with all the disorder of a hasty evacuation strewn broadcast. But in the valley itself there was a startling change. The lake, which, three days earlier, had reached only halfway up the earth embankment, was now lapping within a foot of the dam top, the result of the continued storms and cloud-bursts reported by the Brewster weather station.

Starbuck eased the big car up to the dam head, and Williams and Tarbell made a quick quartering of the deserted camp. 'Nobody here,' the engineer reported, when they came back to the car; and then Sprague asked Starbuck to relight the head-lamps.

With the acetylenes flinging their broad white beam across the earthwork, another change was made apparent. In the centre of the dam a square pit, plank-lined like the shaft of a mine, had been either sunk or left in the building. Over this pit stood a three-legged hoist, with the block-and-tackle still hanging from its apex.

'What is that thing out there?' queried the colonel, shading his eyes with his hand.

'Jennings would probably tell you that it is a new kind of spillway, by which, in case of need, the reservoir lake can be emptied,' suggested Sprague. 'But we haven't time to investigate it just now. Our job at the present moment is to take the law into our hands and empty this lake, and to do it, if we can, without bringing on the catastrophe it was designed to accomplish.'

'Heavens!' ejaculated Colonel Baldwin. 'That's a criminal offence, isn't it? – and in the face of Judge Watson's injunction, at that!'

'It is criminal,' was the calm reply; 'unless we shall find sufficient justification for it as we go along. There is one chance in a dozen that we may find it first. Tarbell, take this little flash-light of mine and skip out there and look into that pit.'

Tarbell paused scarcely a moment at the mouth of the mid-dam shaft. 'It's filled up to within a few feet of the top with dirt,' he said, when he returned.

'That is what I expected. We might find another warrant for what we are about to do, but we haven't time to search for it. Jennings may come back at any minute, and if he suspects anything wrong, he'll bring that bunch of dance-hall cowmen with him. If you'd like to hide the car and stand aside to see what he will do when he comes –'

'By Jove! I'm with you, injunction or no injunction!' cried Smith, and he began to take the picks and shovels out of the car.

'Go to it,' said the colonel; and Sprague turned to Williams.

'Mr Williams, you're an engineer. Our problem is to drain this lake in the shortest possible time in which it can be done without raising a dangerous flood-level in the Timanyoni River. We're under your orders.'

Williams took the job as a dog snaps at a fly, barking out his directions with the curt precision of a man who knew his business. Planks were brought from the dismantled shacks to be thrust down on the inward face of the dam as a protection, and these were weighted in place with a make-shift buttressing built out of the bags of sand which had been used as temporary coffer-dams in the construction work. When all was ready, a small ditch was opened across the protected end of the dam and the water began to pour through.

Immediately the wisdom of Williams's precaution became evident. Instantly the rushing stream began to eat into the loosely built dam, threatening to turn the ditch into a gully and the gully into a chasm, and quick work was necessary with more planks and sand-bags to check the rapid widening of the spillway. Even at that, the ditch grew swiftly deeper and more cavernous as the torrent emptied itself through it, and the roar of the artificial cataract filled the air with a note of sustained thunder.

'Jennings'll be deaf if he doesn't hear this plumb down at the railroad!' shouted Tarbell. But there was no time to consider the consequences Jennings-wise. Every man of the six, including the colonel, was constrained to work like mad to prevent the catastrophe they were trying to avert.

It was when the flood was pouring through the gap in a solid six-foot stream that shot itself far out to fall in a thunderous deluge upon the barren Mesquite Mesa, and the planking and sand-bagging was sufficing to hold it measurably within bounds, that Sprague took steps looking toward a defensive battle should the need arise. Under his direction the auto was drawn out to one side and the lamps were extinguished. Then a hasty breastwork was made of the remaining bags of sand, and Tarbell and Starbuck were sent out as skirmishers to keep watch on the Angels road while the others renewed their efforts to hold the pouring torrent within safe limits.

A toiling half-hour, during which the spillway flood had slowly grown in volume until it threatened to become a destroying crevasse, slipped away, and at the end of it the two scouts came hurrying in.

'They're coming!' yelled Starbuck; and once again the big man from the East took the command.

'Down behind the sand-bags!' he shouted. 'If Jennings gets near enough to strike a match on this hillside, we'll all go to glory!'

Sprague had predicted that if Jennings suspected trouble he would not return to the dam alone. The prediction was verified when a squad of mounted men came in view at the turn in the road leading around the hill shoulder. The moon declining to its setting behind the Timanyonis, flung ghostly shadows across the valley, and the watchers behind the sand-bag breastwork saw only the dark blot of blacker shadow – sweeping up the road.

'Give 'em a volley over their heads!' Sprague ordered and the three sawed-off Winchesters barked spitefully.

'That means war,' said the colonel, when the charging cavalcade stopped abruptly and a dropping fusillade of revolver-shots spatted into the sand breastwork and whined overhead. 'We're strictly in for it, now.'

'If those fool cow-punch's only knew what they're fightin' for, they'd turn their artillery the other way,' growled Starbuck. 'I reckon they're the "Lazy X" outfit, and

Cummings, their owner, is one of the High Line directors.'

'It's a pity we can't get word to them some way,' said Smith. 'We're not out to kill anybody if we can help it.'

'No, but they're out to kill us,' grunted Williams, as a second shower of bullets thudded into the breastwork and tore up the gravel on either hand. Then: 'What are they doing now?'

The defenders of the breastwork were not left long in doubt as to what was doing. The horsemen in front were deploying in a thin line which rapidly bent itself into a semi-circle across the hill slope. To let any one of these skilled marksmen gain the rear meant death for somebody, and again Sprague gave the word of command.

'Better kill horses than men,' he said. 'We've got to stop that manoeuvre,' and again the Winchesters spoke, this time to deadlier purpose. At the third volley two of the horses were down, and the scattering line was drawing together again and galloping out of range.

In the lull which succeeded, Williams dropped his weapon and crawled quickly away to the edge of the spillway torrent. When he came back there was a new note of alarm in his voice.

'That spillway of ours is eating away the dam at the rate of a foot a minute!' he announced. 'If we can't get to work on it again, the whole business will go out with a rush!'

It was a cruel dilemma, and it was quickly made worse by a new movement on the part of the attackers. Jennings's party was closing in again, and flashes of red fire were appearing here and there on the hillside to herald a dropping hail of pistol bullets. Under cover of the irregular firing, a man was worming his way down toward the edge of the ravine through which the wasting torrent was rushing out upon the mesa. It was Sprague who first saw the crawling man and divined his purpose.

'That's Jennings!' he exclaimed, 'and if he reaches the

edge of that gully, we're all dead men! Stop him, Star-buck! don't kill him if you can help it, but stop him!'

Starbuck levelled his short rifle over the top of the breastwork and took careful aim. The light was bad and he could scarcely see the sights. At the trigger-pulling, those who were watching saw a little cloud of dust and gravel spring up directly in front of the crawling man; saw this, and heard above the roaring of the torrent his yell of pain as he doubled up and clapped his hands to his face.

'Good shot, Billy!' gritted the white-haired colonel. 'You've blinded him! Now if we could only choke those crazy range-riders off ... Tarbell, can't you – where's Tarbell gone?'

Tarbell's place at the end of the breastwork was empty, and Smith, who was next in the line, accounted for him.

'Archer dropped out a minute or two ago. I think he's trying to make a dodge-around to get at those cow-punchers.'

The firing had ceased for the moment, and the man who had tried to creep down to the ravine was stumbling back up the hill. Williams nervously thrust in his plea again.

'I tell you, we've got to get to work on this thing behind us and do it quick!' he urged. 'There is still water enough in the lake to tear the heart out of Timanyoni Canyon if it all goes at once!'

Sprague set the temerarious example by springing to his feet, and the others followed him. There was no answering volley from the hillside. On the contrary, the black blot of things animate on the slope was melting away, and a minute later Tarbell came running back.

'The boys have got their hunch!' he cried. 'A couple of them are taking Jennings back to Angels, and the rest of 'em'll be here in a minute to help us. They didn't know what was up.'

As one man the half-dozen flung themselves upon the

task of keeping the roaring crevasse under control; and a little later eight of the cowmen came racing down to swell the working force. But even for the augmented numbers, it proved to be a fiercely fought battle, with the issue hanging perilously in the balance for a long time.

Hour by hour they toiled, making plank bulkheads out of the shack lumber, piling sand-bags against the crumbling embankment, and fighting inch by inch with the gnawing flood as the night wore away.

And it was thus that the graying dawn found them; soaked, muddied, gasping, and haggard with fatigue, but with the victory fairly won. The flood was still pouring through the gap which had by now widened to the cutting away of a full half of the dam; but the great body of water had already passed out and there was no longer any danger.

When the sun was just beginning to redden on the higher peaks of the western mountains, a shout from the hillside road broke upon the morning stillness. A moment later Maxwell and Stillings came running to the brink of hazard.

Sprague stumbled up out of the crevasse chasm and pointed down to the washed-out heart of the dam. There, piled in the bottom of what had once been the plank-lined pit with the hoisting-tackle over it, and laid bare now by the scouring flood, was a great pile of dynamite stacked solidly in its shipping-boxes. And, half-buried in the sand and detritus of the outflow, lay the iron pipe through which the firing fuse had been carried to the gully edge Jennings had tried to reach.

'There is the warrant for what we've been doing, gentlemen,' said the big expert wearily. 'Take a good look at it, all of you, so that if the courts have anything to say about this night's work –'

Maxwell cut in quickly.

'There's nobody left to make the fight. Jennings went

east from Angels on the first train that got through. He was badly blinded, so Disbrow says; got a fall from his horse, was the story he told. We'll fix this lay-out so it will stand just as it is until everybody who wants to has seen it!'

'You couldn't stay away, could you?' said the white-haired colonel, grinning up from his seat on the last of the sand-bags. 'I told the boys here you'd be turning up as soon as your railroad track was open.'

'We've had a mighty anxious night,' Stillings put in. 'The river is up five feet, and we couldn't tell what was happening over here. Great Jonah! but you men must have had your hands full!'

'We did,' said Smith; 'but it's all over now.'

'All but the shouting,' said Maxwell. 'But post your guards and let's get back to town. My car is at Angels, and we came up special. When we left Brewster the plaza was black with people waiting for news.'

It was on the way down the flood-swollen canyon that the chemistry expert explained to the private-car company at the breakfast-table how he had been able to diagnose the case of the cloud-bursters.

'It was merely a bit of what you might call constructive reasoning,' he said modestly. 'I knew by personal investigation in the line of my proper work – soil-testing – that there was no arable land within reach of the Mesquite project. The other steps followed, as a matter of course. Starbuck, here, is wondering why I risked his life and mine to get a few photographs for *The Tribune*, but if any of you will examine the snapshots carefully under a magnifier, you will see that they prove the existence of the central pit in the dam, and that one of them shows the pipe-line through which the fuse was to run. For the possible legal purpose I was anxious to have this evidence in indisputable form. That's all, I believe.'

'Not quite all,' Maxwell broke in. 'How did you know

that Jennings would be hanging over the wire at Angels while you people were making your flying trip across the mountain in the auto?'

Sprague laughed good-naturedly.

'Call it a guess,' he said. 'It was evident that Jennings wasn't anxious to kill a lot of innocent people. His inquiries about the strength of the High Line dam proved that. It ran in my mind that he wouldn't touch off his earthquake until he could be reasonably sure that the flood wouldn't catch a train in transit in the canyon. That would have been a little too horrible, even for him. Now you've got it all, I guess.'

'But you haven't got yours yet,' laughed Stillings. 'When this thing gets out in Brewster the whole town will mob you and want to make you the next mayor, or send you to Congress, or something of that sort.'

'Not this year,' said the big man, with another mellow laugh. 'And I'll tell you why. Just before this train reaches town it's going to stop and let us law-breakers get off, scatter and drop into town as best we can without calling attention to ourselves. And tomorrow morning you'll read in *The Tribune* how the Mesquite dam, weakened by the recent storms and cloud-bursts, went out by littles during the night, watched over and kept from going as a disastrous whole by a brave little bunch of cowboys from the "Lazy X".' Then, with sudden soberness: 'Promise me that you won't give it away, gentlemen all. It's the only fee I shall exact for my small part in the affair.'

And the promise was given while the locomotive whistle was sounding for the Brewster yard limits, and Maxwell was pulling the air-cord for the out-of-town stop.

10

The Affair of Lamson's Cook

Charles Felton Pidgin and J. M. Taylor

Quincy sauntered slowly along the street, enjoying the sunny warmth of an early June morning. Few cases had been presented to him of late, and the resulting inactivity had served to stock him, both mentally and physically, with unusual energy. His keen eyes, restless with inaction, flashed hither and thither over the small throng of hurrying pedestrians, as though in search of something on which to exercise his peculiar talents. But the people surrounding him seemed productive of anything other than mysteries. They comprised mainly the usual throng of hurrying clerks, stenographers and other employees, all rushing toward their individual desks or stations, and whatever secrets might be buried in their minds were for the present, at least, successfully forgotten or covered. With a deep sigh at the possibility of another day of quiet and solitude, Quincy turned slowly in the direction of his own office, but paused sharply as the sound of a call reached his ears.

'Sawyer! Oh, I say, Sawyer!' came the half-suppressed shout, and Quincy's eyes, flashing sharply over the street, instantly picked out the source of the call.

Slowly bearing down on him, through the press of market wagons, trucks and other early morning vehicles, came a handsome touring car. At the wheel sat an impassive French chauffeur and in the tonneau a fat, puffy little man danced frantically about for all the world like a huge bullfrog in a net. Quincy recognized the man as Herbert Lamson, prominent clubman, first-nighter, and society leader in general, and wondered vaguely what unseemly occurrence could have brought Lamson out at that early hour of the morning. He halted and stood smiling interrogatively as the machine drew up at the curb.

'Oh, I say, Sawyer!' Lamson puffed, as soon as the car had been brought to a halt. 'It's lucky I found you, you know. I want you to come right out to my house without a moment's delay. We've had a frightful occurrence there. Frightful!'

'Which house?' Quincy inquired, ignoring the door which Lamson held invitingly open.

'My country house, Sawyer. The one at Beverly. Come right away, won't you? It's an awful thing and I simply must have help!'

'But what is it? What has happened?' Quincy questioned, not relishing the idea of being dragged down to Beverly to discover who had thrown a pebble through one of Lamson's plate glass windows, which possibility, knowing Lamson as well as he did, Quincy deemed not improbable.

'It's murder, Sawyer, murder!' Lamson spluttered, spitting out the word as though it choked him and gazing helplessly at Quincy through his round, sheep-like eyes. 'Somebody brutally murdered my cook last night – and she could cook the best fish dinners I ever tasted.'

Quincy barely repressed a desire to laugh at the incongruity of the two statements, knowing well that the only method of endearing oneself to Lamson was through the medium of the latter's digestive system. For a moment only he hesitated, then, swinging into the car beside Lamson, he settled back for the ride to Beverly.

'Now, Lamson,' he said, when the car had drawn away from the mid-city tumult, 'give me some of the details of this case, so that I may be prepared to act when we arrive.

Just when, so far as you can tell, did the murder take place?'

'I can't say just when,' Lamson informed him. 'I was away from the house from five o'clock in the afternoon until late last night. It might have been done while I was away, or after I returned, because she was not discovered until early this morning. One of the maids, according to custom, went to call her in time to prepare breakfast, and found her dead. I was immediately notified and, not knowing what else to do, I hurried up after you. I'll catch that murderer, Sawyer, if it costs me my entire fortune,' he broke off savagely. 'That woman was a downright shrew, but she could cook – Lord bless you! she could cook! And now I must spend a year or two hunting another cook, and I shall probably be obliged to live on all manner of horrible dishes during my search. I know I can never find another who will be able to cook fish the way she could!' He seemed saddened, almost to the point of breaking down, at the last thought.

'I understand, Lamson,' said Quincy, after a protracted coughing fit behind his hand. 'But I want to get the facts of the case itself, the murder. How was she murdered, and do you suspect anybody? Now, give me something of that sort to work on. First, what was her name, where did she come from, and how long had she been with you?'

'Her name,' said Lamson in a saddened voice, apparently engendered by the thought of the fish dinners which were to be his no more, 'was Mrs Elizabeth Buck. She had been with me as cook for about twelve years, but I have no idea where she came from originally. You see, I was obliged to hire her rather hastily at a time when I was giving a dinner and my other cook –'

'Yes, yes,' Quincy hurriedly interrupted, 'but had she any relatives or friends who wrote to her, or with whom she visited?'

'Nobody of whom I ever heard. In fact, from the time

when I first engaged her, I do not believe she has been away from my house a single day. Her sharp temper would rather preclude the possibility of her having any friends, and I doubt if there was a person in the world, outside myself, in whom she felt the slightest interest.'

'Now,' said Quincy approvingly, 'you are started right. Give me all the details you can up to the time when the body was discovered.'

'Well, she was a woman who, as I said, apparently had neither friends nor acquaintances. Therefore, I do not think that the affair occurred because of some old grudge a previous associate may have owed her. Since I have been talking with you a possibility, which hitherto had not occurred to me, has come into my mind. I paid her well, very well, and, as I never knew of her spending much money at a time, she must have been able to lay by quite a bit in the last twelve years. Of course she may have kept her money in a savings bank, but it is equally possible that her distrustful nature led her to hide it somewhere about her house. She did not room in my house, but in a little cottage which stood on the grounds, living by herself. Now the possibility I mentioned, and which, at the time when I left, had not been investigated, is that somebody may have murdered her for her money. Damn 'em! I'd have given them an equal amount gladly, if they'd only have let her live to cook for me.

'In person she was a small woman of perhaps fifty, although she was so wizened and dried-up by nature that she might have been either more or less. In fact, her appearance has never changed since I have known her. She was very small in stature, and, although I think she would have been capable of putting up a stiff fight, she would have been no match, of course, for an ordinarily strong man. Last night, the servants say, she retired to her cottage at her usual time, and nothing was heard of her during the evening. Very early this morning one of the maids went to call her and, receiving no response to her knock, pushed open the door and found the body.

'The woman had been stabbed, and the place was in a terrible state of disorder; but that part of it you can see for yourself when we get there. I left orders that nobody should enter the building, and that nothing was to be disturbed until I returned. On making the discovery, the maid rushed from the house screaming, and fell on the lawn in a dead faint. I was at once called, and by the time the maid had regained her senses, I was on the spot. As soon as she had told her story I looked hastily into the woman's house to verify the facts, and hurried to Boston to secure your services. You are, of course, to do whatever you think best in the matter, and I give you full authority to act in any way you may deem necessary on my premises.'

For a few moments, following the recital, Quincy was silent, knowing well that little further information was to be gained until he should arrive at the grounds and be able to examine the premises in person.

'How did you come to employ the woman when you had absolutely no knowledge of her, or of her previous state of life?' he asked, after a time.

'Why, I told you that I was obliged to have a cook in great haste at that time,' Lamson protested. 'She was well recommended as a cook by the employment agency and consequently I hired her with very little question. I have never had any trouble whatever with her and in the twelve years I had come to look on her as being scrupulously honest and trustworthy in every way. But wait, we are nearly there now, and you will soon have an opportunity to judge this matter at first hand.'

Quincy stared unseeingly at the low and dirty wooden buildings which lined the street along which the machine was speeding. The case appealed strongly to him as it had been rehearsed, and he could not suppress a certain intangible feeling that it would grow yet more interesting as it progressed. Of course, he considered, in case of a murder for the purpose of robbery, at the possibility of which Lamson hinted, the case would undoubtedly degenerate into a mere police routine affair in which he could take no part. But, on the other hand, the very air of mystery which appeared to surround the woman, herself, gave a vague promise of possibilities into which he would be able to dig and search to his heart's content. He glanced once more at his surroundings, and discovered that they were now in more open country and that the dirty little buildings had given place to the more imposing residences of Beverly's summer colony. The machine turned abruptly, and he discovered that they were rolling up a curved driveway to what was undoubtedly Lamson's house.

A much agitated servant hurried up to the machine as they alighted and, after a somewhat doubtful glance at Quincy, reported in a rapid undertone:

'The police are here, sir, and the medical examiner. I told them of my orders against allowing anybody to enter the cook's house until you had returned with a detective, and they consented to wait. They are down under the tree by the house now.'

'All right, Higgins,' Lamson replied, turning once more toward Quincy. 'Now, Mr Sawyer, if you will come right down we can all examine the rooms together. I am somewhat surprised that the police consented to await my return. They are usually little inclined to await the convenience of a private detective, are they not?'

'Unfortunately, they are,' Quincy replied with a dry smile. 'The police in a large city would not have done so, under any circumstances; but it is probable that in these smaller towns the police and all other municipal officials are more ready to pay heed to the wishes of their wealthy residents. It is out of respect to you, and through no regard for me, that they are waiting.'

Quincy carefully examined the exterior of the cook's former place of residence as they approached. It was a pretty little cottage, painted a conservative white and standing in a location considerably removed from the residence of Lamson himself. The cottage was of fair dimensions, containing, he judged, about six rooms; but it appeared dwarfed because of the giant horse-chestnut trees which towered above it on every side. From beneath one of these trees three men arose and came forward to meet them, Quincy having an excellent opportunity to examine the officials as they advanced.

The foremost of the trio he judged, by reason of the bountiful supply of gold braid sprinkled over his uniform, to be the chief of the local department. The second, who followed at a respectful distance, was evidently a member of the force, while the last, a rather small, dark-faced man in plain clothes, was undoubtedly the medical examiner. As Quincy and Lamson halted before the house, the chief bustled up to them, a smile, which was evidently intended to be courteous, playing across his ordinarily pompous features.

'We have been waiting some time for you, Mr Lamson,' he remarked; 'but under the circumstances we were willing to delay our work until your return. The affair undoubtedly will prove a simple one, and it is too bad you have gone to the expense of importing a private detect-ive.' With the concluding words he shot a brief, but un-friendly, glance in Quincy's direction.

Lamson made no reply to the speech, other than by a brief nod of recognition, and, stepping quickly to the door, he unlocked it and threw it open, standing aside to allow the entrance of the officials. Like a pack of hounds unleashed the local men dived through the door, and into what was apparently a living room, Quincy and Lamson following in their rear. On entering the room all paused abruptly and stared about them, the scene well warrant-ing the sudden halt.

The room was, indeed, in a terrible state of disorder. Furniture had been overturned, some had been broken, all had been misplaced, and on every hand were to be seen signs of violence and confusion. The main feature, however, was to be found in the figure of a little woman who lay almost in the very middle of the room. The body lay face down, the hair dishevelled and the clothing disarranged from the struggle, while from its side and several inches below the left armpit protruded the hilt of a heavy and strong-bladed knife. There were very few signs of blood, as the wound had evidently bled inwardly; but the scene was ghastly enough without that.

Exercising the prerogative of his office, the medical examiner strode forward and knelt at the side of the body, gently turning it over. As he did so the watchers instinctively started, for on the woman's face was revealed such an expression of fierce and malignant hatred as it is seldom the misfortune of any person to gaze on. The lips were drawn back in a snarl of rage which left exposed the worn and ragged teeth, and the eyes, fixed and staring, seemed to hold in their depths a fury scarcely human.

'Lord!' muttered Lamson, repressing a shudder. 'She didn't die with any love of man in her heart.'

The medical examiner grimly held up the knife. 'From here on it's your work, gentlemen,' he observed. 'Make what you can of this.'

The chief took the knife, and all stared curiously at it. It was an ordinary wooden-hilted knife of the kind to be found in any market and, from the thinness of the blade, it had evidently known long service and many grindings. After nodding his head over it several times, the chief passed the knife on to Quincy with the air of a man wishing to be courteous, although hardly recognizing the possibility of any value in the act. To Quincy, judging from his expression, the knife meant much or nothing.

He glanced at it keenly, turned it over several times and then, without comment, returned it to the chief.

The search for clues then started in earnest, the two members of the regular force burrowing amidst the debris in the room like terriers after a rat. They pulled open every drawer, peered under or through every article of furniture, and minutely examined every square inch of space in the room. Now and then the chief would pause to glance speculatively at Quincy, as though in fear that the private detective might stumble on a clue that the regulars had overlooked. After each scrutiny, however, he invariably returned to his search, appearing satisfied that Quincy's aimless wanderings would net him nothing of value in the way of clues.

'By the way, Chief,' Quincy interrupted at length, 'may I inquire as to what it is that you expect to find in this room?'

The chief eyed him suspiciously before replying. 'Well, it's not customary to hand our suspicions to outsiders, but, as you are, in a way, one of us, I don't mind telling you. Of course we are looking for possible clues which the murderer may have left behind, but primarily I want to discover whether or not the old woman's hoard of money is missing.'

'I see, Chief; but, unless we know, which we do not, where the money was hidden, how are we to be able to tell whether or not it is gone? We suspect, of course, but we do not know, that there was money hidden in the house. It is hardly likely that the woman would have kept any quantity of it hidden away in a bureau drawer. It strikes me that if she had money to hide she would have placed it in a more secret hiding-place – under the floor boards, behind a stone in the cellar wall, or in some similar crevice. We might search a week and still not find the place. And, even if we should chance to find the money, all we should have gained would be a knowledge that the murderer did not take it. Look over the room. There was no search for money previous to our coming. That furniture was all disarranged during the struggle. Either the murderer knew exactly where the money was hidden, and took it from its hiding-place, or else he was actuated by some other motive, entirely and had neither thought nor regard for the money that might be here.'

The chief listened stolidly to Quincy's summing up of the matter; but he seemed unimpressed. 'You are at liberty to follow any method you please in the conduct of your search,' he said coldly; 'but the regular police must act under my orders, and I see no necessity for changing the orders because of your ingenious theory. I am experienced in these matters, Mr Sawyer, and I judge that you are not; so please don't confuse my men by advancing any other theories. This murder was for the purpose of robbery, and for no other purpose under the sun.'

Quincy meekly accepted the rebuff without reply, but there was a peculiar smile playing about his lips as he turned away. Apparently undisturbed, he wandered nonchalantly out of the room, with Lamson, angered at the treatment his special representative had received, trailing behind. To the remaining rooms on the first floor Quincy paid only the most casual notice, doing little more than to glance in each before ascending the stairs. On the second floor, however, his interest appeared to awaken, especially when the woman's chamber had been reached.

Once within the chamber his aimless wandering ceased, and his every movement appeared to take on a definite purpose. He glanced sharply over the walls, carefully scrutinizing the few pictures with which they were adorned, after which he stepped briskly to the bureau, where he conducted a most minute examination of the contents of every drawer. Once he paused and held up a small packet before the gaze of Lamson, grinning as he did so.

'I imagine our friends downstairs would be interested in this,' he remarked.

'What are they?' Lamson questioned eagerly.

'Bank books. Your late cook evidently patronized several savings banks, instead of hoarding her money as has been suspected. I'll place them back where they were, and let the police discover them when they reach this point in their search. At their present rate of speed they should reach this room in a day or two.'

For some little time, after the discovery of the books, he remained before the bureau, searching every nook and cranny of it. At last, appearing vastly dissatisfied with the result, he arose and stood meditatively in the middle of the room, allowing his eyes to run rapidly over first one article of furniture and then another.

'Did your cook have a trunk when she came here?' he questioned abruptly.

'I don't think so,' said Lamson slowly, as he strived to remember the event of twelve years previous. 'No, I am sure she brought with her one of those old-fashioned canvas extension bags. It must be around here somewhere.'

Quincy's interest appeared to renew itself at the information, and he was immediately deep in his search again. At last, with much shuffling and scuffling of his feet, he emerged backward from a dark nook in the closet, dragging after him the described bag. Placing it on the floor, he arose and stared at Lamson through eyes shining with eagerness.

'Lamson,' he said, 'I expect to find the clue I want in that bag. There is one thing that no woman, and few men for that matter, regardless of station in life, is without in these days. It may be only the most tantalizing of clues which I shall be able to make nothing of, but I'll stake my reputation that it's there.'

With no further explanation he threw back the cover

of the bag, dropped on his knees before it, and dug into its contents. For several moments there was no sound save his eager breathing, echoed by the puffing breaths of Lamson, and the swishing of articles being hastily over-turned in the bag. Then, with an almost explosive ex-halation, he started back and sprang to his feet, three small articles in his hand.

'I have it, Lamson,' he exclaimed. 'I have it. Now, what can we make of it?'

He strode to the nearest window, with Lamson scuttl-ing at his heels, and held up to the light three small, un-mounted photographs, 'You see, Lamson,' he said, 'every woman has a certain degree of sentiment in her make-up. Consequently, in these days of plentiful photographs, there is scarcely a woman anywhere who does not possess photographs of her early home, or associations surround-ing it. Here we have the photographs, but, as they are not mounted, and bear no photographer's seal, their value to us will depend on our ability to recognize the places represented.'

Lamson stared incredulously. 'But my dear Sawyer,' he protested, 'those photographs may represent scenes hun-dreds or thousands of miles from here. How are we to recognize them?'

Quincy lowered the photographs and turned impres-sively. 'Lamson,' he said, 'I have not yet looked at these photographs closely, but mark my words when I tell you that they will represent scenes within a radius of fifty miles. That woman was not a traveller.'

Without further comment he raised the photographs once more and studied them carefully. The first depicted a woman, beyond doubt Mrs Buck at a period much earlier in her life, standing before a small cottage of the style of architecture most frequently seen among the houses of the ocean fishermen. The second showed a large open boat, a trawler, fully manned, and lying just below a wharf with the wharf's buildings visible in the background. The last showed two fishermen standing on the steps of a hotel, and holding between them a strange monster of the deep, while, from above, curious guests, peered down from over the balcony rail.

'There, Lamson, I think we have our clue.'

'But how? What in the deuce is there to all that stuff that shows you anything?' Lamson was fairly staggered with bewilderment.

'Look here!' Quincy flipped the second photograph into view. 'That trawler indicates, as do all three photographs, a fishing community. Now look at the buildings in the background. On the central building you can dimly distinguish the sign of the fishing company: The Bay State Codfish Company. Now look at this third photograph. Above the fishermen's heads is the sign of the Puritan Hotel. By coupling those two names we have our clue. Both the Bay State Codfish Company and the Puritan Hotel are located in Gloucester. In the photograph of Mrs Buck herself we find her standing before a typical fisherman's cottage. Therefore, does our clue not point toward Gloucester as a starting-point in our search for the woman's identity and that of her murderer? I also have another clue, but I shall leave that out of the matter for the present.'

'Then you will go to Gloucester?' Lamson questioned.

'At once, although I would suggest that you do not mention the fact to the police. It might only serve to further muddle their brains, and they are sufficiently at sea in regard to this case already.'

'You may use my car for the trip if you want to,' Lamson volunteered immediately.

'No, I thank you. I prefer to go in the train. I shall be pleased to have your car to take me to the station, though, if that will not inconvenience you.'

As the pair descended the stairs they paused a moment

to gaze at the activities of the police. The room remained in much the same condition as when they had originally viewed it, except for the fact that the body had been removed, thus doing away with the most gruesome feature of the case. Seeing them, the chief paused for a moment.

'Giving up so early in the game, Mr Sawyer?' he inquired, a slightly sneering accent in his voice.

'Not exactly giving up, Chief,' Quincy replied, ignoring the tone. 'But my business temporarily calls me elsewhere, and, for the present, I shall be obliged to absent myself. I expect to return here later on, though, unless in the meantime you have been able to solve the mystery. You have found no trace of hidden wealth as yet, I suppose?'

'No, we have found nothing, but there must be some clue to it somewhere. I am about to act on your suggestion and search the cellar.'

'Before you do that, Chief,' said Quincy, smiling frankly, 'I would suggest that you search the woman's chamber. There are some bank-books there which will be of interest to you.'

'You mean that her money was deposited in a bank?' the chief demanded sharply.

'It was, and still is, in a bank, or in banks, to be more exact. I fear you will be wasting your time if you search farther for it here.'

For a moment the chief stared silently, but at last a slow grin began to relieve the hard lines of his face. 'Mr Sawyer,' he said, 'you have put one across on us. I held you lightly in the beginning because, several times of late, my department has been considerably hindered by the actions of amateur detectives, and I took you to belong to the same class. I see you know your business, and I apologize for my former abruptness of speech.'

The speech came as a complete surprise to Quincy, but he was not to be outdone in courtesy. 'Chief,' he said, 'I accept your remarks in the spirit in which they were intended. Frankly, I am now starting out on a clue which I think will prove valuable. If I am successful I shall notify you of the fact on my return, and it is highly probable that we may be able to act together in the final scenes.'

The chief regarded him with increased respect. 'I shall be pleased to act with you if you are successful,' he said simply.

In ten minutes' time Quincy was seated in Lamson's car and hurrying toward the railroad station. Shortly afterward he was aboard a train for Gloucester and, bending over the three photographs, was carefully arranging his plans for the campaign he intended to wage in that peculiar city.

All that day, and throughout the night, Lamson and the chief anxiously awaited the return of Quincy or the coming of some word which would indicate his progress. The affair by that time had been spread broadcast through the medium of the press, and the grounds swarmed with reporters, to the disgust of Lamson, who cordially hated the notoriety which was thus being brought to his door. The second forenoon following the murder passed away without result in the desired direction, and Lamson, unused to the necessary tedium of a police investigation, and suffering from the strain involved, was at his wits' end when Quincy suddenly reappeared as unostentatiously as he had departed. Lamson rushed eagerly from the house to greet him, the chief, no less eager, hurrying after, while the handful of reporters clustered around, listening intently for the first hint which might be incorporated in their several stories. Quincy waved them laughingly aside.

'Not yet, boys,' he adjured them. 'I have a good story for you, and you shall have it very shortly, but I must first make my report to Mr Lamson.'

Obediently the reporters fell back, accepting his assurance without question. Lamson and the chief reached him simultaneously and, above the hurried hum of the reporters' voices, rose Lamson's appeal:

'What luck, Sawyer? For heaven's sake tell me the result quickly.'

Quincy took him soothingly by the arm. 'It's settled, Lamson,' he said quietly; 'but my investigation has had a most remarkable result. A most surprising result! Come into the house, and I'll tell you all about it.'

When they were seated in the library, or at least when the chief and Quincy were seated, Lamson being too nervous to do anything other than to fidget about the room, Quincy digressed slightly from the point of the matter in hand.

'I notice that you have gained considerable notoriety, Lamson,' he said.

'Notoriety!' Lamson snorted the word furiously. 'Notoriety! Yes, I certainly have, thanks to the press and its representatives outside! Look at the headlines which have been running. "Wealthy Epicurean's Cook Murdered", "Lamson's Elysium Wrecked by Murderer", and so on without end! Why in the world must I be dragged into the case in that manner?'

Quincy allowed himself a smile at Lamson's expense before proceeding. 'You are merely the victim of circumstances, Lamson; but that was not what I intended to tell you. I wish to warn you that you are to receive still more notoriety because this case is about to produce one of the greatest sensations the press has had for years.'

Lamson paled at the words, and his agitation increased perceptibly. 'You don't mean,' he stammered, 'that you suspect me of the murder?'

'Oh, no, Lamson, great Scott, no!' Quincy hastened to assure him. 'I have the murderer, and he has confessed. I merely wish to warn you that Mrs Buck, regardless of her own identity, will still continue in the eyes of the public to be Lamson's cook, and as such she will be handled by the press. But sit down, man, nobody suspects you. I'll tell you my story at once, so that your mind may be placed at rest in that direction at least. You know of the photographs which I discovered before going to Gloucester?' he inquired, turning toward the chief.

'Yes, Mr Lamson told me of them,' the chief informed him.

'Very well, then, I wished you to know of them before telling my story, because I desire you to be in possession of the several clues which led me to Gloucester. As you are aware, one of those pictures showed the wharf of the Bay State Codfish Company. Now, Chief, remember. Do you not recall that the knife with which the murder was committed was stamped on the hilt with the letter "B.S.C.Co."? From that fact I argued that the person connected with the Bay State Codfish Company in whom Mrs Buck was interested years ago must still be there, and that Gloucester was the spot which I must search for the murderer. As I said before, I found him; but in order to place you thoroughly in possession of the facts I am going to retrogress twelve years and begin my story at that point. The discovery of the man after I reached Gloucester was a very simple act, so simple as to hardly be worthy of recognition in the story, while his confession followed almost as a matter of course. He is at present being held by the Gloucester police. I recognized him, Lamson, from his photograph. He is the man on the right of that sea monster in the third picture; he also appears in the second photograph and, as the other does not, I naturally settled on him at once as the man whom I desired to find.

'But now for the story. Twelve years ago Amos Buck and his shrewish wife, Elizabeth – your cook, Lamson – lived in a small cottage at the far end of the Gloucester water-front. Amos was a trawler in the employ of the Bay State Codfish Company and, being a steady, temperate man, was regarded by the heads of his department as being one of their most reliable employees. But in his case, as in that of every other man, his home environment played a great part in the matter of his value to his employers. His wife's shrewish nature developed, and her constant nagging eventually began to play its part in his ultimate downfall, the result being that he finally became a steady patron of the nearest groggery, and it appeared that his complete degeneration would be merely a matter of time. Daily indulgence soon became protracted into sprees of a week's duration, and Mrs Buck became more vituperative than ever.

'Then another link in the peculiar chain of circumstances was forged. Amos brought to his home a widowed cousin, Emma Bray by name, and insisted upon her taking up her permanent residence with himself and his wife. Mrs Bray greatly resembled Mrs Buck in figure, although their features were vastly dissimilar, and their dispositions were as far separated as the poles. The cousin proved to be a pleasant even-tempered woman, and she showed every desire to alleviate the constant friction between Buck and his wife.

'Her attempts at intervention only added to Mrs Buck's fury, and within a few weeks Mrs Buck had developed a hatred for both her husband and his cousin that was almost inhuman in its intensity. The demeanour of his wife at last had its effect on Buck himself, and, instead of meekly submitting to her verbal assaults, as he had done in the past, he soon commenced to reply in kind, with the result that the house became a veritable inferno. This continued until one day Buck's temper, grown ragged from the constant warfare, gave way entirely and he struck his wife, knocking her down. Then, overcome by the deed, and by the scenes which had led up to it, he rushed from the house to his favourite haunt in a cheap saloon.

'Although naturally a reticent man, his tongue soon

became loosened by liquor and, when one of his associates pointed to a fresh cut on the side of Buck's head, inquiring as to its origin, he replied that his wife had made it, but that he had fixed her so she wouldn't do it again. The savage look with which he accompanied the words, and the dark hint which seemed to be contained in them, caused the speech to be remembered. Shortly afterward Buck purchased a quart of raw rum and disappeared, going nobody knew where.

'The next morning he was aroused by the chief of police from the drunken slumber into which he had sunk behind the sheltering piles of a lumber wharf. The rough handling by the chief, together with the black looks and muttered threats of the small body of men who accompanied him, completely sobered Buck, and he demanded the reason of his arrest. The reply was unsatisfactory, being merely a gruff "Guess you know", from the chief, and a volley of threats from the crowd, which was constantly growing larger.

'To Buck's surprise he was taken directly to his own house, and, when led indoors, the last trace of liquor was driven out of him, and his surprise was turned to horror. The main room of the cottage was indeed in a terrible state, its floor and walls being covered with blood, its meagre furnishings broken and scattered, and its every appearance being as if a terrific battle had been waged within it. To make the nature of the crime which had been committed doubly sure, a bloodstained axe lay at one side of the room, where it had evidently been thrown by the fleeing murderer. But, whatever hopes the chief may have had of securing a confession from Buck by taking him to the place were speedily dashed, for Buck, instead of breaking down, appeared too utterly stupefied by the scene for speech of any kind.

'No trace of either woman had been found, and there was consequently nothing to do save to hold Buck on suspicion while the search for the bodies was being conducted. The search speedily bore fruit, for, within an hour of Buck's arrest, the body of a woman was found floating in the harbour. The features had been obliterated, being so badly hacked and battered as to make recognition impossible, but the clothing on the body was speedily identified as being that of Mrs Buck. As no trace of the cousin was found it was decided that her body must have floated out to sea on the tide, and Buck was held, charged with the murder of both women.

'At the trial circumstantial evidence figured strongly in securing Buck's conviction, but there was also a beautiful train of circumstantial evidence in his favor. He pointed out that no blood-stains had been found on his clothing, and defied the prosecution to demonstrate a way in which he could have hacked a body as his wife's had been mangled and then have conveyed it to the water without having become stained with blood. He also showed a streak of genius by defying the police to show conclusively that his cousin Emma Bray, was really dead, as no trace of her body had been found. This part of the indictment was shortly dropped, and he stood accused of only the one murder, that of his wife.

'Of course his rash words in the saloon played an important part against him, but in his favor was the absense of blood-stains upon him and that fact, together with his drunkenness and the well-known frequency with which his wife had assaulted him, both orally and physically, saved him from execution. He was, however, convicted of murder in the second degree, and sentenced to imprisonment for life; but, even after Buck had been imprisoned, there remained many people who did not believe him guilty of the crime. Consequently, after he had served a term of years, a movement was set on foot to have him pardoned, the movement being eventually successful.

'After his release Buck returned to Gloucester and

quietly resumed his old life, taking up his residence in his former house and again entering the employ of the Bay State Codfish Company. For two years he lived quietly and then, like a sudden thunderclap, came a piece of news which entirely upset his every thought. An associate came to him, giving him positive assurance that he had seen Mrs Buck in Beverly, and had been told that she was employed by a rich man as a cook. For days Buck brooded over that information, striving to make himself realize that he had not only been sent to prison for a crime which he had never committed, but also, for one which, possibly, had never been committed at all.

'At last he could stand the strain no longer, and so set out one night for Beverly, to prove for himself the truth or falsity of the weird rumour. Before starting, moved by some instinct which even he himself cannot define, he secreted one of the company's knives in his coat, giving it no more thought after his departure from Gloucester.

'On his arrival in Beverly he had no difficulty in locating Lamson's estate and, proceeding here at once, he slipped about in the darkness, searching for the woman who might or might not prove to be his wife. He soon stumbled on the cook's cottage, and, peering through one of the lighted windows, he was able to clearly view the woman within and his feelings cannot be described when he realized that she was indeed his wife. Overcome by a blind, insensate fury, he made his way quickly to the front of the house, burst open the door and confronted her.

'According to his story the woman showed no surprise at seeing him, but merely sat staring into his face with a smile of contempt on her lips. She made no reply when he accused her of allowing him to be falsely imprisoned, but continued to gloat over him with an air that aroused his already nearly uncontrollable fury to a pitch which it had never hitherto reached. He broke into savage de-

nunciation of her, and, at last, stung her into replying to
his charges. To his intense surprise she admitted them to
be true. Not only that, but she boastfully asserted that she
had killed his cousin out of revenge, and had then dressed
the body in her own clothes to throw suspicion on him,
had dragged it into the water and had then fled from
the place in disguise. As she warmed up to the recital she
added almost fiendish details, and through it all she continued to glory in her own success and Buck's resulting
conviction.

'Naturally such a scene could have but one ending.
Buck's temper became more and more savage and at the
conclusion of her story he had reached a point but little,
if anything, short of insanity. He told her he was going to
kill her and that he would be justified in the act. The
announcement sobered her and silenced her tongue; but,
instead of screaming for help as he had expected her to
do, she launched herself fiercely at his throat. You know
the result. The struggle was short-lived, and at its conclusion Buck hurried from the place, making his way
immediately back to Gloucester, where I found him.

'Now, gentlemen,' and with the words Quincy straightened impressively, 'now we come to the sensational part
of the whole affair. The question to be decided, and it is
an important one, is: *Can Buck be punished for the
murder?*

'At first glance the natural reply would be that he can;
but, can he? Can the courts touch him in any way? When
a man is tried and acquitted he cannot again be brought
to trial for the same offence, even though it may afterwards be shown conclusively that he is guilty. Therefore,
can Buck be twice punished for the same offence? He has
already paid the penalty, has paid in advance, so to speak,
for the privilege of killing his wife. He was convicted
when innocent, and, now that he is guilty, can he be
again convicted of the same crime for which he has

already paid the penalty which was legally demanded of him?

'I freely admit, gentlemen, that it is a question which I cannot answer, and you may rest assured that the press will eagerly await the decision of the Supreme Court if it is considered necessary to carry the matter that far.'

11

The Campaign Grafter

Arthur B. Reeve

'What a relief it will be when this election is over and the newspapers print news again,' I growled as I turned the first page of the *Star* with a mere glance at the headlines.

'Yes,' observed Kennedy, who was puzzling over a note which he had received in the morning mail. 'This is the bitterest campaign in years. Now, do you suppose that they are after me in a professional way or are they trying to round me up as an independent voter?'

The letter which had called forth this remark was headed, 'The Travis Campaign Committee of the Reform League,' and, as Kennedy evidently intended me to pass an opinion on it, I picked it up. It was only a few lines, requesting him to call during the morning, if convenient, on Wesley Travis, the candidate for governor and the treasurer of his campaign committee, Dean Bennett. It had evidently been written in great haste in longhand the night before.

'Professional,' I hazarded. 'There must be some scandal in the campaign for which they require your services.'

'I suppose so,' agreed Craig. 'Well, if it is business instead of politics it has at least this merit – it is current business. I suppose you have no objection to going with me?'

Thus it came about that not very much later in the morning we found ourselves at the campaign headquarters, in the presence of two nervous and high-keyed gentlemen in frock coats and silk hats. It would have taken no great astuteness, even without seeing the surroundings, to deduce instantly that they were engaged in the annual struggle of seeking the votes of their fellow-citizens for something or other, and were nearly worn out by the arduous nature of that process.

Their headquarters were in a tower of a skyscraper, whence poured forth a torrent of appeal to the moral sense of the electorate, both in printed and oral form. Yet there was a different tone to the place from that which I had ordinarily associated with political headquarters in previous campaigns. There was an absence of the old-fashioned politicians and of the air of intrigue laden with tobacco. Rather, there was an air of earnestness and efficiency which was decidedly prepossessing. Maps of the state were hanging on the walls, some stuck full of various coloured pins denoting the condition of the canvass. A map of the city in colours, divided into all sorts of districts, told how fared the battle in the stronghold of the boss, Billy McLoughlin. Huge systems of card indexes, loose-leaf devices, labour-saving appliances for getting out a vast mass of campaign 'literature' in a hurry, in short a perfect system, such as a great, well-managed business might have been proud of were in evidence everywhere.

Wesley Travis was a comparatively young man, a lawyer who had early made a mark in politics and had been astute enough to shake off the thraldom of the bosses before the popular uprising against them. Now he was the candidate of the Reform League for governor and a good stiff campaign he was putting up.

His campaign manager, Dean Bennett, was a business man whose financial interests were opposed to those usually understood to be behind Billy McLoughlin, of the regular party to which both Travis and Bennett might naturally have been supposed to belong in the old days. Indeed the Reform League owed its existence to a fortunate conjunction of both moral and economic conditions demanding progress.

'Things have been going our way up to the present,' began Travis confidentially, when we were seated democratically with our campaign cigars lighted. 'Of course we haven't such a big "barrel" as our opponents, for we are not frying the fat out of the corporations. But the people have supported us nobly, and I think the opposition of the vested interests has been a great help. We seem to be winning, and I say "seem" only because one can never be certain how anything is going in this political game nowadays.

'You recall, Mr Kennedy, reading in the papers that my country house out on Long Island was robbed the other day? Some of the reporters made much of it. To tell the truth, I think they had become so satiated with sensations that they were sure that the thing was put up by some muckrakers and that there would be an exposé of some kind. For the thief, whoever he was, seems to have taken nothing from my library but a sort of scrapbook or album of photographs. It was a peculiar robbery, but as I had nothing to conceal it didn't worry me. Well, I had all but forgotten it when a fellow came into Bennett's office here yesterday and demanded – tell us what it was, Bennett. You saw him.'

Bennett cleared his throat. 'You see, it was this way. He gave his name as Harris Hanford and described himself as a photographer. I think he has done work for Billy McLoughlin. At any rate, his offer was to sell us several photographs, and his story about them was very circumstantial. He hinted that they had been evidently among those stolen from Mr Travis and that in a roundabout way they had come into the possession of a friend of his without his knowing who the thief was. He said that he had not made the photographs himself, but had an idea by whom they were made, that the original plates had been destroyed, but that the person who made them was ready to swear that the pictures were taken after the nominating convention this fall which had named Travis. At any rate the photographs were out and the price for them was $25,000.'

'What are they that he should set such a price on them?' asked Kennedy, keenly looking from Bennett quickly to Travis.

Travis met his look without flinching. 'They are supposed to be photographs of myself,' he replied slowly. 'One purports to represent me in a group on McLoughlin's porch at his farm on the south shore of the island, about twenty miles from my place. As Hanford described it, I am standing between McLoughlin and J. Cadwalader Brown, the trust promoter who is backing McLoughlin to save his investments. Brown's hand is on my shoulder and we are talking familiarly. Another is a picture of Brown, McLoughlin and myself riding in Brown's car, and in it Brown and I are evidently on the best of terms. Oh, there are several of them, all in the same vein. Now,' he added, and his voice rose with emotion as if he were addressing a cart-tail meeting which must be convinced that there was nothing criminal in riding in a motor-car, 'I don't hesitate to admit that a year or so ago I was not on terms of intimacy with these men, but at least acquainted with them. At various times, even as late as last spring, I was present at conferences over the presidential outlook in this state, and once I think I did ride back to the city with them. But I know that there were no pictures taken, and even if there had been I would not care if they told the truth about them. I have frankly admitted in my speeches that I knew these men, that my knowledge of them and breaking from them is my chief qualification for waging an effective war on them if I am elected. They hate me cordially. You know that. What I do care about is the sworn allegation that now accompanies these – these fakes. They were not, could not have been taken after the independent convention that nominated me. If the photographs were true I would be a fine traitor. But I haven't even seen McLoughlin or Brown since last spring. The whole thing is a –'

'Lie from start to finish,' put in Bennett emphatically. 'Yes, Travis, we all know that. I'd quit right now if I didn't believe in you. But let us face the facts. Here is this story, sworn to as Hanford says and apparently acquiesced in by Billy McLoughlin and Cad. Brown. What do they care anyhow as long as it is against you? And there, too, are the pictures themselves – at least they will be in print or suppressed, according as we act. Now, you know that nothing could hurt the reform ticket worse than to have an issue like this raised at this time. We were supposed at least to be on the level, with nothing to explain away. There may be just enough people to believe that there is some basis for this suspicion to turn the tide against us. If it were earlier in the campaign I'd say accept the issue, fight it out to a finish, and in the turn of events we should really have the best campaign material. But it is too late now to expose such a knavish trick of theirs on the Friday before election. Frankly, I believe discretion is the better part of valour in this case and without abating a jot of my faith in you, Travis, well, I'd pay first and expose the fraud afterward, after the election, at leisure.'

'No, I won't,' persisted Travis, shutting his square jaw doggedly. 'I won't be held up.'

The door had opened and a young lady in a very stunning street dress, with a huge hat and a tantalizing veil, stood in it for a moment, hesitated, and then was about to shut it with an apology for intruding on a conference.

'I'll fight it if it takes my last dollar,' declared Travis, 'but I won't be blackmailed out of a cent. Good morning, Miss Ashton. I'll be free in a moment. I'll see you in your office directly.'

The girl, with a portfolio of papers in her hand, smiled, and Travis quickly crossed the room and held the door deferentially open as he whispered a word or two. When she had disappeared he returned and remarked, 'I suppose you have heard of Miss Margaret Ashton, the suffragette leader, Mr Kennedy? She is the head of our press bureau.' Then a heightened look of determination set his fine face in hard lines, and he brought his fist down on the desk. 'No, not a cent,' he thundered.

Bennett shrugged his shoulders hopelessly and looked at Kennedy in mock resignation as if to say, 'What can you do with such a fellow?' Travis was excitedly pacing the floor and waving his arms as if he were addressing a meeting in the enemy's country. 'Hanford comes at us in this way,' he continued, growing more excited as he paced up and down. 'He says plainly that the pictures will of course be accepted as among those stolen from me, and in that, I suppose, he is right. The public will swallow it. When Bennett told him I would prosecute he laughed and said, "Go ahead. I didn't steal the pictures. That would be a great joke for Travis to seek redress from the courts he is criticizing. I guess he'd want to recall the decision if it went against him – hey?" Hanford says that a hundred copies have been made of each of the photographs and that this person, whom we do not know, has them ready to drop into the mail to the one hundred leading papers of the state in time for them to appear in the Monday editions just before Election Day. He says no amount of denying on our part can destroy the effect – or at least he went further and said "shake their validity."

'But I repeat. They are false. For all I know, it is a plot

of McLoughlin's, the last fight of a boss for his life, driven into a corner. And it is meaner than if he had attempted to forge a letter. Pictures appeal to the eye and mind much more than letters. That's what makes the thing so dangerous. Billy McLoughlin knows how to make the best use of such a roor-back on the eve of an election, and even if I not only deny but prove that they are a fake, I'm afraid the harm will be done. I can't reach all the voters in time. Ten see such a charge to one who sees the denial.'

'Just so,' persisted Bennett coolly. 'You admit that we are practically helpless. That's what I have been saying all along. Get control of the prints first, Travis, for God's sake. Then raise any kind of a howl you want – before election or after. As I say, if we had a week or two it might be all right to fight. But we can make no move without making fools of ourselves until they are published Monday as the last big thing of the campaign. The rest of Monday and the Tuesday morning papers do *not* give us time to reply. Even if they were published today we should hardly have time to expose the plot, hammer it in and make the issue an asset instead of a liability. No, you must admit it yourself. There isn't time. We must carry out the work we have so carefully planned to cap the campaign, and if we are diverted by this it means a let-up in our final efforts, and that is as good as McLoughlin wants anyhow. Now, Kennedy, don't you agree with me? Squelch the pictures now at any cost, then follow the thing up and, if we can, prosecute after election?'

Kennedy and I, who had been so far little more than interested spectators, had not presumed to interrupt. Finally Craig asked, 'You have copies of the pictures?'

'No,' replied Bennett. 'This Hanford is a brazen fellow, but he was too astute to leave them. I saw them for an instant. They look bad. And the affidavits with them look worse.'

'H'm,' considered Kennedy, turning the crisis over in his mind. 'We've had alleged stolen and forged letters before, but alleged stolen and forged photographs are new. I'm not surprised that you are alarmed, Bennett – nor that you want to fight, Travis.'

'Then you will take up the case?' urged the latter eagerly, forgetting both his campaign manager and his campaign manners, and leaning forward almost like a prisoner in the dock to catch the words of the foreman of the jury. 'You will track down the forger of those pictures before it is too late?'

'I haven't said I'll do that – yet,' answered Craig measuredly. 'I haven't even said I'd take up the case. Politics is a new game to me, Mr Travis. If I go into this thing I want to go into it and stay in it – well, you know how you lawyers put it, with clean hands. On one condition I'll take the matter up, and on only one.'

'Name it,' cried Travis anxiously.

'Of course, having been retained by you,' continued Craig with provoking slowness, 'it is not reasonable to suppose that if I find – how shall I put it – bluntly, yes? – if I find that the story of Hanford has some – er – foundation, it is not reasonable to suppose that I should desert you and go over to the other side. Neither is it to be supposed that I will continue and carry such a thing through for you regardless of truth. What I ask is to have a free hand, to be able to drop the case the moment I cannot proceed further in justice to myself, drop it, and keep my mouth shut. You understand? These are my conditions and no less.'

'And you think you can make good?' questioned Bennett rather sceptically. 'You are willing to risk it? You don't think it would be better to wait until after the election is won?'

'You have heard my conditions,' reiterated Craig.

'Done,' broke in Travis. 'I'm going to fight it out, Bennett. If we get in wrong by dickering with them at the start it may be worse for us in the end. Paying amounts to confession.'

Bennett shook his head dubiously. 'I'm afraid this will suit McLoughlin's purpose just as well. Photographs are like statistics. They don't lie unless the people who make them do. But it's hard to tell what a liar can accomplish with either in an election.'

'Say, Dean, you're not going to desert me?' reproached Travis. 'You're not offended at my kicking over the traces, are you?'

Bennett rose, placed a hand on Travis's shoulder, and grasped his other. 'Wesley,' he said earnestly. 'I wouldn't desert you even if the pictures were true.'

'I knew it,' responded Travis heartily. 'Then let Mr Kennedy have one day to see what he can do. Then if we make no progress we'll take your advice, Dean. We'll pay, I suppose and ask Mr Kennedy to continue the case after next Tuesday.'

'With the proviso,' put in Craig.

'With the proviso, Kennedy,' repeated Travis. 'Your hand on that. Say, I think I've shaken hands with half the male population of this state since I was nominated, but this means more to me than any of them. Call on us, either Bennett or myself, the moment you need aid. Spare no reasonable expense, and – and get the goods, no matter whom it hits higher up, even if it is Cadwalader Brown himself. Good-bye, and a thousand thanks – oh, by the way, wait. Let me take you around and introduce you to Miss Ashton. She may be able to help you.'

The office of Bennett and Travis was in the centre of the suite. On one side were the cashier and clerical force as well as the speakers' bureau, where spellbinders of all degrees were getting instruction, tours were being laid out, and reports received from meetings already held.

On the other side was the press bureau with a large and active force in charge of Miss Ashton, who was supporting Travis because he had most emphatically declared for 'Votes for Women' and had insisted that his party put this plank in its platform. Miss Ashton was a clever girl, a graduate of a famous woman's college, and had had several years of newspaper experience before she became a leader in the suffrage cause. I recalled having read and heard a great deal about her, though I had never met her. The Ashtons were well known in New York society, and it was a sore trial to some of her conservative friends that she should reject what they considered the proper 'sphere' for women. Among those friends, I understood, was Cadwalader Brown himself.

Travis had scarcely more than introduced us, yet already I scented a romance behind the ordinarily prosaic conduct of a campaign press bureau. It is far from my intention to minimise the work or the ability of the head of the press bureau, but it struck me, both then and later, that the candidate had an extraordinary interest in the newspaper campaign, much more than in the speakers' bureau, and I am sure that it was not solely accounted for by the fact that publicity is playing a more and more important part in political campaigning.

Nevertheless such innovations as her card index system by election districts all over the state, showing the attitude of the various newspaper editors, of local political leaders, and changes of sentiment, were very full and valuable. Kennedy, who had a regular pigeon-hole mind for facts, was visibly impressed by this huge mechanical memory built up by Miss Ashton. Though he said nothing to me I knew he had also observed the state of affairs between the reform candidate and the suffrage leader.

It was at a moment when Travis had been called back to his office that Kennedy, who had been eyeing Miss Ashton with marked approval, leaned over and said in a low voice, 'Miss Ashton, I think I can trust you. Do you want to do a great favour for Mr Travis?'

She did not betray even by a fleeting look on her face what the true state of her feelings was, although I fancied that the readiness of her assent had perhaps more meaning than she would have placed in a simple 'Yes' otherwise.

'I suppose you know that an attempt is being made to blackmail Mr Travis?' added Kennedy quickly.

'I know something about it,' she replied in a tone which left it for granted that Travis had told her before even we were called in. I felt that not unlikely Travis's set determination to fight might be traceable to her advice or at least to her opinion of him.

'I suppose in a large force like this it is not impossible that your political enemies may have a spy or two,' observed Kennedy, glancing about at the score or more clerks busily engaged in getting out 'literature'.

'I have sometimes thought that myself,' she agreed. 'But of course I don't know. Still, I have to be pretty careful. Someone is always over here by my desk or looking over here. There isn't much secrecy in a big room like this. I never leave important stuff lying about where any of them could see it.'

'Yes,' mused Kennedy. 'What time does the office close?'

'We shall finish tonight about nine, I think. Tomorrow it may be later.'

'Well, then, if I should call here tonight at, say, half-past nine, could you be here? I need hardly say that your doing so may be of inestimable value to – to the campaign.'

'I shall be here,' she promised, giving her hand with a peculiar straight arm shake and looking him frankly in the face with those eyes which even the old guard in the legislature admitted were vote winners.

Kennedy was not quite ready to leave yet, but sought out Travis and obtained permission to glance over the financial end of the campaign. There were few large contributors to Travis's fund, but a host of small sums ranging from ten and twenty-five dollars down to dimes and nickels. Truly it showed the depth of the popular uprising. Kennedy also glanced hastily over the items of expense – rent, salaries, stenographer and office force, advertising, printing and stationery, postage, telephone, telegraph, automobile and travelling expenses, and miscellaneous matters.

As Kennedy expressed it afterwards, as against the small driblets of money coming in, large sums were going out for expenses in lumps. Campaigning in these days costs money even when done honestly. The miscellaneous account showed some large indefinite items, and after a hasty calculation Kennedy made out that if all the obligations had to be met immediately the committee would be in the hole for several thousand dollars.

'In short,' I argued as we were leaving, 'this will either break Travis privately or put his fund in hopeless shape. Or does it mean that he foresees defeat and is taking this way to recoup himself under cover of being held up?'

Kennedy said nothing in response to my suspicions, though I could see that in his mind he was leaving no possible clue unnoted.

It was only a few blocks to the studio of Harris Hanford, whom Kennedy was now bent on seeing. We found him in an old building on one of the side streets in the thirties which business had captured. His was a little place on the top floor, up three flights of stairs, and I noticed as we climbed up that the room next to his was vacant.

Our interview with Hanford was short and unsatisfactory. He either was or at least posed as representing a third party in the affair, and absolutely refused to permit us to have even a glance at the photographs.

'My dealings,' he asserted airily, 'must all be with Mr

313

Bennett, or with Mr Travis, direct, not with emissaries.
I don't make any secret about it. The prints are not here.
They are safe and ready to be produced at the right time,
either to be handed over for the money or to be published in the newspapers. We have found out all about
them; we are satisfied, although the negatives have been
destroyed. As for their having been stolen from Travis,
you can put two and two together. They are out and
copies have been made of them, good copies. If Mr Travis
wishes to repudiate them, let him start proceedings. I told
Bennett all about that. Tomorrow is the last day, and I
must have Bennett's answer then, without any interlopers
coming into it. If it is yes, well and good; if not, then they
know what to expect. Good-bye.'

It was still early in the forenoon, and Kennedy's next
move was to go out on Long Island to examine the library
at Travis's from which the pictures were said to have been
stolen. At the laboratory Kennedy and I loaded ourselves
with a large oblong black case containing a camera and
a tripod.

His examination of the looted library was minute,
taking in the window through which the thief had apparently entered, the cabinet he had forced, and the situation in general. Finally Craig set up his camera with
most particular care and took several photographs of the
window, the cabinet, the doors, including the room from
every angle. Outside he snapped the two sides of the
corner of the house in which the library was situated.
Partly by trolley and partly by carriage we crossed the
island to the south shore, and finally found McLoughlin's
farm, where we had no trouble in getting half a dozen
photographs of the porch and house. Altogether the proceedings seemed tame to me, yet I knew from previous
experience that Kennedy had a deep laid purpose.

We parted in the city, to meet just before it was time
to visit Miss Ashton. Kennedy had evidently employed

the interval in developing his plates, for he now had ten or a dozen prints, all of exactly the same size, mounted on stiff cardboard in a space with scales and figures on all four sides. He saw me puzzling over them.

'Those are metric photographs such as Bertillon of Paris takes,' he explained. 'By means of the scales and tables and other methods that have been worked out we can determine from those pictures distances and many other things almost as well as if we were on the spot itself. Bertillon has cleared up many crimes with this help, such as the mystery of the shooting in the Hotel Quai d'Orsay and other cases. The metric photograph, I believe, will in time rank with the portrait parlé, finger prints, and the rest.

'For instance, in order to solve the riddle of a crime the detective's first task is to study the scene topographically. Plans and elevations of a room or house are made. The position of each object is painstakingly noted. In addition, the all-seeing eye of the camera is called into requisition. The plundered room is photographed, as in this case. I might have done it by placing a foot rule on a table and taking that in the picture, but a more scientific and accurate method has been devised by Bertillon. His camera lens is always used at a fixed height from the ground and forms its image on the plate at an exact focus. The print made from the negative is mounted on a card in a space of definite size, along the edges of which a metric scale is printed. In the way he has worked it out the distance between any two points in the picture can be determined. With a topographical plan and a metric photograph one can study a crime as a general studies the map of a strange country. There were several peculiar things that I observed today, and I have here an indelible record of the scene of the crime. Preserved in this way it cannot be questioned.

'Now the photographs were in this cabinet. There are

other cabinets, but none of them has been disturbed. Therefore the thief must have known just what he was after. The marks made in breaking the lock were not those of a jemmy but of a screwdriver. No amazing command of the resources of science is needed so far. All that is necessary is a little scientific common sense, Walter.

'Now, how did the robber get in? All the windows and doors were supposedly locked. It is alleged that a pane was cut from this window at the side. It was, and the pieces were there to show it. But take a glance at this outside photograph. To reach that window even a tall man must have stood on a ladder or something. There are no marks of a ladder or of any person in the soft soil under the window. What is more, that window was cut from the inside. The marks of the diamond which cut it plainly show that. Scientific common sense again.'

'Then it must have been someone in the house or at least someone familiar with it?' I exclaimed.

Kennedy nodded. 'One thing we have which the police greatly neglect,' he pursued, 'a record. We have made some progress in reconstructing the crime, as Bertillon calls it. If we only had those Hanford pictures we should be all right.'

We were now on our way to see Miss Ashton at headquarters and as we rode downtown I tried to reason out the case. Had it really been a put-up job? Was Travis himself faking, and was the robbery a 'plant' by which he might forestall exposure of what had become public property in the hands of another, no longer disposed to conceal it? Or was it after all the last desperate blow of the Boss?

The whole thing began to assume a suspicious look in my mind. Although Kennedy seemed to have made little real progress, I felt that, far from aiding Travis, it made things darker. There was nothing but his unsupported word that he had not visited the Boss subsequent to the nominating convention. He admitted having done so before the Reform League came into existence. Besides it seemed tacitly understood that both the Boss and Cadwalader Brown acquiesced in the sworn statement of the man who said he had made the pictures. Added to that the mere existence of the actual pictures themselves was a graphic clincher to the story. Personally, if I had been in Kennedy's place I think I should have taken advantage of the proviso in the compact with Travis to back out gracefully. Kennedy, however, now started on the case, hung to it tenaciously.

Miss Ashton was waiting for us at the press bureau. Her desk was at the middle of one end of the room in which, if she could keep an eye on her office force, the office force also could keep an eye on her.

Kennedy had apparently taken in the arrangement during our morning visit, for he set to work immediately. The side of the room toward the office of Travis and Bennett presented an expanse of blank wall. With a mallet he quickly knocked a hole in the rough plaster, just above the baseboard about the room. The hole did not penetrate quite through to the other side. In it he placed a round disc of vulcanized rubber, with insulated wires leading down back of the baseboard, then out underneath it, and under the carpet. Some plaster quickly closed up the cavity in the wall, and he left it to dry.

Next he led the wires under the carpet to Miss Ashton's desk. There they ended, under the carpet and a rug, eighteen or twenty huge coils several feet in diameter disposed in such a way as to attract no attention by a curious foot on the carpet which covered them.

'That is all, Miss Ashton,' he said as we watched for his next move. 'I shall want to see you early tomorrow, and – might I ask you to be sure to wear that hat which you have on?'

It was a very becoming hat, but Kennedy's tone clearly

indicated that it was not his taste in inverted basket millinery that prompted the request. She promised, smiling, for even a suffragette may like pretty hats.

Craig had still to see Travis and report on his work. The candidate was waiting anxiously at his hotel after a big political mass meeting on the East Side, at which capitalism and the bosses had been hissed to the echo, if that is possible.

'What success?' inquired Travis eagerly.

'I'm afraid,' replied Kennedy, and the candidate's face fell at the tone, 'I'm afraid you will have to meet them, for the present. The time limit will expire tomorrow, and I understand Hanford is coming up for a final answer. We must have copies of those photographs, even if we have to pay for them. There seems to be no other way.'

Travis sank back in his chair and regarded Kennedy hopelessly. He was actually pale. 'You – you don't mean to say that there is no other way, that I'll have to admit even before Bennett – and others that I'm in bad?'

'I wouldn't put it that way,' said Kennedy mercilessly, I thought.

'It is that way,' Travis asserted almost fiercely. 'Why, we could have done that anyhow. No, no – I don't mean that. Pardon me. I'm upset by this. Go ahead,' he sighed.

'You will direct Bennett to make the best terms he can with Hanford when he comes up tomorrow. Have him arrange the details of payment and then rush the best copies of the photographs to me.'

Travis seemed crushed.

We met Miss Ashton the following morning entering her office. Kennedy handed her a package, and in a few words, which I did not hear, explained what he wanted, promising to call again later.

When we called, the girls and other clerks had arrived, and the office was a hive of industry in the rush of winding up the campaign. Typewriters were clicking, clippings were being snipped out of a huge stack of newspapers and pasted into large scrap-books, circulars were being folded and made ready to mail for the final appeal. The room was indeed crowded, and I felt that there was no doubt, as Kennedy had said, that nothing much could go on there unobserved by any one to whose interest it was to see it.

Miss Ashton was sitting at her desk with her hat on directing the work. 'It works,' she remarked enigmatically to Kennedy.

'Good,' he replied. 'I merely dropped in to be sure. Now if anything of interest happens, Miss Ashton, I wish you would let me know immediately. I must not be seen up here, but I shall be waiting downstairs in the corridor of the building. My next move depends entirely on what you have to report.'

Downstairs Craig waited with growing impatience. We stood in an angle in which we could see without being readily seen, and our impatience was not diminished by seeing Hanford enter the elevator.

I think that Miss Ashton would have made an excellent woman detective, that is, on a case in which her personal feelings were not involved as they were here. She was pale and agitated as she appeared in the corridor, and Kennedy hurried toward her.

'I can't believe it. I won't believe it,' she managed to say.

'Tell me, what happened?' urged Kennedy soothingly.

'Oh, Mr Kennedy, why did you ask me to do this?' she reproached. 'I would almost rather not have known at all.'

'Believe me, Miss Ashton,' said Kennedy, 'you ought to know. It is on you that I depend most. We saw Hanford go up. What occurred?'

She was still pale, and replied nervously, 'Mr Bennett came in about quarter to ten. He stopped to talk to me and looked about the room curiously. Do you know, I felt very uncomfortable for a time. Then he locked the door leading from the press bureau to his office, and left word that he was not to be disturbed. A few minutes later a man called.'

'Yes, yes,' prompted Kennedy. 'Hanford, no doubt.'

She was racing on breathlessly, scarcely giving one a chance to inquire how she had learned so much.

'Why,' she cried with a sort of defiant ring in her tone, 'Mr Travis is going to buy those pictures after all. And the worst of it is that I met him in the hall coming in as I was coming down here, and he tried to act toward me in the same old way – and that after all I know now about him. They have fixed it all up, Mr Bennett acting for Mr Travis, and this Mr Hanford. They are even going to ask me to carry the money in a sealed envelope to the studio of this fellow Hanford, to be given to a third person who will be there at two o'clock this afternoon.'

'You, Miss Ashton?' inquired Kennedy, a light breaking on his face as if at last he saw something.

'Yes, I,' she repeated. 'Hanford insisted that it was part of the compact. They – they haven't asked me openly yet to be the means of carrying out their dirty deals, but when they do, I – I won't –'

'Miss Ashton,' remonstrated Kennedy, 'I beg you to be calm. I had no idea you would take it like this, no idea. Please, please. Walter, you will excuse us if we take a turn down the corridor and out in the air. This is most extraordinary.'

For five or ten minutes Kennedy and Miss Ashton appeared to be discussing the new turn of events earnestly, while I waited impatiently. As they approached again she seemed calmer, but I heard her say, 'I hope you're right. I'm all broken up by it. I'm ready to resign. My faith in human nature is shaken. No, I won't expose Wesley Travis for his sake. It cuts me to have to admit it, but Cadwalader used always to say that every man has his price. I am afraid this will do great harm to the cause of reform and through it to the woman suffrage cause which cast its lot with this party. I – I can hardly believe –'

Kennedy was still looking earnestly at her. 'Miss Ashton,' he implored, 'believe nothing. Remember one of the first rules of politics is loyalty. Wait until –'

'Wait?' she echoed. 'How can I? I hate Wesley Travis for giving in – more than I hate Cadwalader Brown for his cynical disregard of honesty in others.'

She bit her lip at thus betraying her feelings, but what she had heard had evidently affected her deeply. It was as though the feet of her idol had turned to clay. Nevertheless it was evident that she was coming to look on it more as she would if she were an outsider.

'Just think it over,' urged Kennedy. 'They won't ask you right away. Don't do anything rash. Suspend judgement. You won't regret it.'

Craig's next problem seemed to be to transfer the scene of his operations to Hanford's studio. He was apparently doing some rapid thinking as we walked uptown after leaving Miss Ashton, and I did not venture to question him on what had occurred when it was so evident that everything depended on being prepared for what was still to occur.

Hanford was out. That seemed to please Kennedy, for with a brightening face, which told more surely than words that he saw his way more and more clearly, he asked me to visit the agent and hire the vacant office next to the studio while he went uptown to complete his arrangements for the final step.

I had completed my part and was waiting in the empty room when he returned. He lost no time in getting to work, and it seemed to me as I watched him curiously in silence that he was repeating what he had already done at the Travis headquarters. He was boring into the wall, only this time he did it much more carefully, and it was evident that if he intended putting anything into this cavity it must be pretty large. The hole was square, and as I bent over I could see that he had cut through the plaster and laths all the way to the wallpaper on the other side, though he was careful to leave that intact. Then he set up a square black box in the cavity, carefully poising it and making measurements that told of the exact location of its centre with reference to the partitions and walls.

A skeleton key took us into Hanford's well-lighted but now empty studio. For Miss Ashton's sake I wished that the photographs had been there. I am sure Kennedy would have found slight compunction in a larceny of them, if they had been. It was something entirely different that he had in mind now, however, and he was working quickly for fear of discovery. By his measurements I guessed that he was calculating as nearly as possible the centre of the box which he had placed in the hole in the wall on the other side of the dark wallpaper. When he had quite satisfied himself he took a fine pencil from his pocket and made a light cross on the paper to indicate it. The dot fell to the left of a large calendar hanging on the wall.

Kennedy's appeal to Margaret Ashton had evidently had its effect, for when he saw her a few moments after these mysterious preparations she had overcome her emotion.

'They have asked me to carry a note to Mr Hanford's studio,' she said quietly, 'and without letting them know that I know anything about it I have agreed to do so.'

'Miss Ashton,' said Kennedy, greatly relieved, 'you're a trump.'

'No,' she replied, smiling faintly, 'I'm just feminine enough to be curious.'

Craig shook his head, but did not dispute the point.

'After you have handed the envelope to the person, whoever it may be, in Hanford's studio, wait until he does
something – er – suspicious. Meanwhile look at the wall
on the side toward the next vacant office. To the left of
the big calendar you will see a light pencil mark, a cross.
Somehow you must contrive to get near it, but don't
stand in front of it. Then if anything happens stick this
little number 10 needle in the wall right at the intersec-
tion of the cross. Withdraw it quickly, count fifteen, then
put this little sticker over the cross, and get out as best
you can, though we shan't be far away if you should
need us. That's all.'

We did not accompany her to the studio for fear of
being observed, but waited impatiently in the next office.
We could hear nothing of what was said, but when a door
shut and it was evident that she had gone, Kennedy
quickly removed something from the box in the wall
covered with a black cloth.

As soon as it was safe Kennedy had sent me posting
after her to secure copies of the incriminating photographs which were to be carried by her from the studio,
while he remained to see who came out. I thought a
change had come over her as she handed me the package
with the request that I carry it to Mr Bennett and get
them from him.

The first inkling I had that Kennedy had at last been
able to trace back something in the mysterious doings of
the past two days came the following evening, when Craig
remarked casually that he would like to have me call on
Billy McLoughlin if I had no engagement. I replied that
I had none – and managed to squirm out of the one I
really had.

The Boss's office was full of politicians, for it was the eve
of 'dough day', when the purse strings were loosed and a
flood of potent argument poured forth to turn the tide of
election. Hanford was there with the other ward heelers.

'Mr McLoughlin,' began Kennedy quietly, when we were seated alone with Hanford in the little sanctum of the Boss, 'you will pardon me if I seem a little slow in coming to the business that has brought me here tonight. First of all, I may say, and you, Hanford, being a photographer will appreciate it, that ever since the days of Daguerre photography has been regarded as the one infallible means of portraying faithfully any object, scene, or action. Indeed a photograph is admitted in court as irrefutable evidence. For when everything else fails, a picture made through the photographic lens almost invariably turns the tide. However, such a picture upon which the fate of an important case may rest should be subjected to critical examination for it is an established fact that a photograph may be made as untruthful as it may be reliable. Combination photographs change entirely the character of the initial negative and have been made for the past fifty years. The earliest, simplest, and most harmless photographic deception is the printing of clouds into a bare sky. But the retoucher with his pencil and etching tool today is very skilful. A workman of ordinary skill can introduce a person taken in a studio into an open-air scene well blended and in complete harmony without a visible trace of falsity.

'I need say nothing of how one head can be put on another body in a picture, nor need I say what a double exposure will do. There is almost no limit to the changes that may be wrought in form and feature. It is possible to represent a person crossing Broadway or walking on Riverside Drive, places he may never have visited. Thus a person charged with an offence may be able to prove an alibi by the aid of a skilfully prepared combination photograph.

'Where, then, can photography be considered as irrefutable evidence? The realism may convince all, will convince all, except the expert and the initiated after careful

study. A shrewd judge will insist that in every case the
negative be submitted and examined for possible altera-
tions by a clever manipulator.'

Kennedy bent his gaze on McLoughlin. 'Now, I do not
accuse you, sir, of anything. But a photograph has come
into the possession of Mr Travis in which he is represented as standing on the steps of your house with yourself and Mr Cadwalader Brown. He and Mr Brown are
in poses that show the utmost friendliness. I do not hesitate to say that that was originally a photograph of yourself, Mr Brown, and your own candidate. It is a pretty raw
deal, a fake in which Travis has been substituted by very
excellent photographic forgery.'

McLoughlin motioned to Hanford to reply.

'A fake?' repeated the latter contemptuously. 'How
about the affidavits? There's no negative. You've got to
prove that the original print stolen from Travis, we'll say,
is a fake. You can't do it.'

'September 19th was the date alleged, I believe?' asked
Kennedy quietly, laying down the bundle of metric
photographs and the alleged photographs of Travis. He
was pointing to a shadow of a gable on the house as it
showed in the metric photographs and the others.

'You see that shadow of the gable? Perhaps you never
heard of it, Hanford, but it is possible to tell the exact
time at which a photograph was taken from a study of
the shadows. It is possible in principle and practice and
can be trusted. Almost any scientist may be called on to
bear testimony in court nowadays, but you would say the
astronomer is one of the least likely. Well, the shadow in
this picture will prove an alibi for someone.

'Notice. It is seen very prominently to the right, and
its exact location on the house is an easy matter. You
could almost use the metric photograph for that. The
identification of the gable casting the shadow is easy. To
be exact it is 19·62 feet high. The shadow is 14·23 feet

down, 13·10 feet east, and 3·43 feet north. You see I am exact. I have to be. In one minute it moved 0·080 feet upward, 0·053 feet to the right, and 0·096 feet in its apparent path. It passes the width of a weatherboard, 0·37 foot, in four minutes and thirty-seven seconds.'

Kennedy was talking rapidly of data which he had derived from his metric photograph, from plumb line, level, compass and tape, astrononomical triangle, vertices, zenith, pole and sun, declination, azimuth, solar time, parallactic angles, refraction, and a dozen bewildering terms.

'In spherical trigonometry,' he concluded, 'to solve the problem three elements must be known. I knew four. Therefore I could take each of the known, treat it as unknown, and have four ways to check my result. I find that the time might have been either three o'clock, twenty-one minutes and twelve seconds, in the afternoon, or 3:21:31, or 3:21:29, or 3:21:33. The average is 3:21:26, and there can therefore be no appreciable error except for a few seconds. For that date must have been one of two days, either May 22 or July 23. Between these two dates we must decide on evidence other than the shadow. It must have been in May, as the immature condition of the foliage shows. But even if it had been in July, that is far from being September. The matter of the year I have also settled. Weather conditions, I find, were favourable on all these dates except that in September. I can really answer, with an assurance and accuracy superior to that of the photographer himself – even if he were honest – as to the real date. The real picture, aside from being doctored, was actually taken last May. Science is not fallible, but exact in this matter.'

Kennedy had scored a palpable hit. McLoughlin and Hanford were speechless. Still Craig hurried on.

'But, you may ask, how about the automobile picture? That also is an unblushing fake. Of course I must prove that. In the first place, you know that the general public has come to recognize the distortion of a photograph as denoting speed. A picture of a car in a race that doesn't lean is rejected – people demand to see speed, speed, and more speed even in pictures. Distortion does indeed show speed, but that, too, can be faked.

'Hanford knows that the image is projected upside down by the lens on the plate, and that the bottom of the picture is taken before the top. The camera mechanism admits light, which makes the picture, in the manner of a roller blind curtain. The slit travels from the top to the bottom and the image on the plate being projected upside down, the bottom of the object appears on the top of the plate. For instance, the wheels are taken before the head of the driver. If the car is moving quickly the image moves on the plate and each successive part is taken a little in advance of the last. The whole leans forward. By widening the slit and slowing the speed of the shutter, there is more distortion.

'Now, this is what happened. A picture was taken of Cadwalader Brown's automobile, probably at rest, with Brown in it. The matter of faking Travis or anyone else by his side is simple. If with an enlarging lantern the image of this faked picture is thrown on the paper like a lantern slide, and if the right hand side is a little further away than the left, the top further away than the bottom, you can print a fraudulent high speed ahead picture. True, everything else in the picture, even if motionless, is distorted, and the difference between this faking and the distortion of the shutter can be seen by an expert. But it will pass. In this case, however, the faker was so sure of that that he was careless. Instead of getting the plate further from the paper on the right he did so on the left. It was further away on the bottom than on the top. He got distortion all right, enough still to satisfy the uninitiated. But it was distortion in the wrong way! The top

327

of the wheel, which goes fastest and ought to be most indistinct, is, in the fake, as sharp as any other part. It is a
small mistake, but fatal. That picture is really at high
speed – backwards! It is too raw, too raw.'

'You don't think people are going to swallow all that
stuff, do you?' asked Hanford coolly, in spite of the exposure.

Kennedy paid no attention. He was looking at Mc-
Loughlin. The Boss was regarding him surlily. 'Well,' he
said at length, 'what of all this? I had nothing to do with
it. Why do you come to me? Take it to the proper
parties.'

'Shall I?' asked Kennedy quietly.

He had uncovered another picture carefully. We could
not see it, but as he looked at it McLoughlin fairly staggered.

'Wh – where did you get that?' he gasped.

'I got it where I got it, and it is no fake,' replied Kennedy enigmatically. Then he appeared to think better of
it. 'This,' he explained, 'is what is known as a pinhole
photograph. Three hundred years ago della Porta knew
the camera obscura, and but for the lack of a sensitive
plate would have made photographs. A box, thoroughly
light-tight, slotted inside to receive plates, covered with
black, and glued tight, a needle hole made by a number
10 needle in a thin sheet of paper – and you have the
apparatus for lensless photography. It has a correctness
such as no image-forming means by lenses can have. It
is literally rectigraphic, rectilinear, it needs no focusing,
and it takes a wide angle with equal effect. Even pinhole
snapshots are possible where the light is abundant, with
a ten to fifteen second exposure.

'That picture, McLoughlin, was taken yesterday at
Hanford's. After Miss Ashton left I saw who came out,
but this picture shows what happened before. At a critical
moment Miss Ashton stuck a needle in the wall of the
studio, counted fifteen, closed the needle-hole, and there

is the record. Walter, Hanford – leave us alone an instant.'

When Kennedy passed out of the Boss's office there was a look of quiet satisfaction on his face which I could not fathom. Not a word could I extract from him either that night or on the following day, which was the last before the election.

I must say that I was keenly disappointed by the lack of developments, however. The whole thing seemed to me to be a mess. Everybody was involved. What had Miss Ashton overheard and what had Kennedy said to McLoughlin? Above all, what was his game? Was he playing to spare the girl's feelings by allowing the election to go on without a scandal for Travis?

At last election night arrived. We were all at the Travis headquarters, Kennedy, Travis, Bennett, and myself. Miss Ashton was not present, but the first returns had scarcely begun to trickle in when Craig whispered to me to go out and find her, either at her home or club. I found her at home. She had apparently lost interest in the election, and it was with difficulty that I persuaded her to accompany me.

The excitement of any other night in the year paled to insignificance before this. Distracted crowds everywhere were cheering and blowing horns. Now a series of wild shouts broke forth from the dense mass of people before a newspaper bulletin board. Now came sullen groans, hisses, and catcalls, or all together with cheers as the returns swung in another direction. Not even baseball could call out such a crowd as this. Lights blazed everywhere. Automobiles honked and ground their gears. The lobster palaces were thronged. Police were everywhere. People with horns and bells and all manner of noise-making devices pushed up one side of the thoroughfares and down the other. Hungrily, ravenously they were feeding on the meagre bulletins of news.

Yet back of all the noise and human energy I could

only think of the silent, systematic gathering and editing
of the news. High up in the League headquarters, when
we returned, a corps of clerks was tabulating returns,
comparing official and semi-official reports. As first the
state swung one way, then another, our hopes rose and
fell. Miss Ashton seemed cold and ill at ease, while Travis
looked more worried and paid less attention to the returns than would have seemed natural. She avoided him
and he seemed to hesitate to seek her out.

Would the up-state returns, I had wondered at first, be
large enough to overcome the hostile city vote? I was
amazed now to see how strongly the city was turning to
Travis.

'McLoughlin has kept his word,' ejaculated Kennedy
as district after district showed that the Boss's pluralities
were being seriously cut into.

'His word? What do you mean?' we asked almost together.

'I mean that he has kept his word given to me at a conference which Mr Jameson saw but did not hear. I told
him I would publish the whole thing, not caring whom or
where or when it hit if he did not let up on Travis. I
advised him to read his Revised Statutes again about
money in elections, and I ended up with the threat,
"There will be no dough day, McLoughlin, or this will
be prosecuted to the limit." There was no dough day.
You see the effect in the returns.'

'But how did you do it?' I asked, not comprehending.
'The faked photographs did not move him, that I could
see.'

The words, 'faked photographs', caused Miss Ashton
to glance up quickly. I saw that Kennedy had not told
her or anyone yet, until the Boss had made good. He had
simply arranged one of his little dramas.

'Shall I tell, Miss Ashton?' he asked, adding. 'Before I
complete my part of the compact and blot out the whole
affair?'

'I have no right to say no,' she answered tremulously, but with a look of happiness that I had not seen since our first introduction.

Kennedy laid down a print on a table. It was the pinhole photograph, a little blurry, but quite convincing. On a desk in the picture was a pile of bills. McLoughlin was shoving them away from him toward Bennett. A man who was facing forward in the picture was talking earnestly to someone who did not appear. I felt intuitively, even before Kennedy said so, that the person was Miss Ashton herself as she stuck the needle into the wall. The man was Cadwalader Brown.

'Travis,' demanded Kennedy, 'bring the account books of your campaign. I want the miscellaneous account particularly.'

The books were brought, and he continued, turning the leaves, 'It seemed to me to show a shortage of nearly twenty thousand dollars the other day. Why, it has been made up. How was that, Bennett?'

Bennett was speechless. 'I will tell you,' Craig proceeded inexorably. 'Bennett, you embezzled that money for your business. Rather than be found out, you went to Billy McLoughlin and offered to sell out the Reform campaign for money to replace it. With the aid of the crook, Hanford, McLoughlin's tool, you worked out the scheme to extort money from Travis by forged photographs. You knew enough about Travis's house and library to frame up a robbery one night when you were staying there with him. It was inside work, I found, at a glance. Travis, I am sorry to have to tell you that your confidence was misplaced. It was Bennett who robbed you – and worse.

'But Cadwalader Brown, always close to his creature, Billy McLoughlin, heard of it. To him it presented another idea. To him it offered a chance to overthrow a political enemy and a hated rival for Miss Ashton's hand. Perhaps into the bargain it would disgust her with politics, disillusion her, and shake her faith in what he believed to be some of her "radical" notions. All could be gained at one blow. They say that a check-book knows no politics, but Bennett has learned some, I venture to say, and to save his reputation he will pay back what he has tried to graft.'

Travis could scarcely believe it yet. 'How did you get your first hint?' he gasped.

Kennedy was digging into the wall with a bill file at the place where he had buried the little vulcanized disc. I had already guessed that it was a dictograph, though I could not tell how it was used or who used it. There it was, set squarely in the plaster. There also were the wires running under the carpet. As he lifted the rug under Miss Ashton's desk there also lay the huge circles of wire. That was all.

At this moment Miss Ashton stepped forward.

'Last Friday,' she said in a low tone, 'I wore a belt which concealed a coil of wire about my waist. From it a wire ran under my coat, connecting with a small dry battery in a pocket. Over my head I had an arrangement such as the telephone girls wear with a receiver at one ear connected with the battery. No one saw it, for I wore a large hat which completely hid it. If anyone had known, and there were plenty of eyes watching, the whole thing would have fallen through. I could walk around; no one could suspect anything; but when I stood or sat at my desk I could hear everything that was said in Mr Bennett's office.'

'By induction,' explained Kennedy. 'The impulses set up in the concealed dictograph set up currents in these coils of wire concealed under the carpet. They were wirelessly duplicated by induction in the coil about Miss Ashton's waist and so affected the receiver under her very becoming hat. Tell the rest, Miss Ashton.'

'I heard the deal arranged with this Hanford,' she added, almost as if she were confessing something, 'but not

understanding it as Mr Kennedy did, I very hastily condemned Mr Travis. I heard talk of putting back twenty
thousand into the campaign accounts, of five thousand
given to Hanford for his photographic work, and of the
way Mr Travis was to be defeated whether he paid or not.
I heard them say that one condition was that I should
carry the purchase money. I heard much that must have
confirmed Mr Kennedy's suspicion in one way, and my
own in an opposite way, which I know now was wrong.
And then Cadwalader Brown in the studio taunted me
cynically and – and it cut me, for he seemed right. I hope
that Mr Travis will forgive me for thinking that Mr
Bennett's treachery was his –'

A terrific cheer broke out among the clerks in the
outer office. A boy rushed in with a still unblotted report.
Kennedy seized it and read: 'McLoughlin concedes the
city by a small majority to Travis, fifteen election districts
estimated. This clinches the Reform League victory in
the state.'

I turned to Travis. He was paying no attention except
to the pretty apology of Margaret Ashton.

Kennedy drew me to the door. 'We might as well con-
cede Miss Ashton to Travis,' he said, adding gaily, 'by
induction of an arm about the waist. Let's go out and
watch the crowd.'

12

The Infallible Godahl

Frederick Irving Anderson

Oliver Armiston never was much of a sportsman with a rod or gun – though he could do fancy work with a pistol in a shooting gallery. He had, however, one game from which he derived the utmost satisfaction. Whenever he went travelling, which was often, he invariably caught his trains by the tip of the tail, so to speak, and hung on till he could climb aboard. In other words he believed in close connections. He had a theory that more valuable dollars-and-cents time and good animal heat are wasted warming seats in stations waiting for trains than by missing them. The sum of joy to his methodical mind was to halt the slamming gates at the last fraction of the last second with majestic upraised hand, and to stroll aboard his parlour car with studied deliberation, while the train crew were gnashing their teeth in rage and swearing to get even with the gateman for letting him through.

Yet Mr Armiston never missed a train. A good many of them tried to miss him, but none ever succeeded. He reckoned time and distance so nicely that it really seemed as if his trains had nothing else half so important as waiting until Mr Oliver Armiston got aboard.

On this particular June day he was due in New Haven at two. If he failed to get there at two o'clock he could very easily arrive at three. But an hour is sixty minutes, and a minute is sixty seconds; and, further,

Mr Armiston having passed his word that he would be there at two o'clock, surely would be.

On this particular day, by the time Armiston finally got to the Grand Central the train looked like an odds-on favourite. In the first place he was still in his bed at an hour when another and less experienced traveller would have been watching the clock in the station waiting room. In the second place, after kissing his wife in that absent-minded manner characteristic of true love, he became tangled in a Broadway traffic crush at the first corner. Scarcely was he extricated from this when he ran into a Socialist mass meeting at Union Square. It was due only to the wits of his chauffeur that the taxicab was extricated with very little damage to the surrounding human scenery. But our man of method did not fret. Instead he buried himself in his book, a treatise on Cause and Effect, which at that moment was lulling him with soothing sentiment:

'There is no such thing as accident. The so-called accidents of everyday life are due to the preordained action of correlated causes, which is inevitable and over which man has no control.'

This was comforting, but not much to the point, when Oliver Armiston looked up and discovered he had reached 23rd Street and had come to a halt. A sixty-foot truck, with an underslung burden consisting of a sixty-ton steel girder, had at this point suddenly developed weakness in its off hind-wheel and settled down on the pavement across the right of way like a tired elephant. This, of course, was not an accident. It was due to a weakness in the construction of that wheel – a weakness that had from the beginning been destined to block street cars and taxicabs at this particular spot at this particular hour.

Mr Armiston dismounted and walked a block. Here he hailed a second taxicab and soon was spinning north

again at a fair speed, albeit the extensive building operations in Fourth Avenue had made the street well-nigh
impassable.

The roughness of the pavement merely shook up his
digestive apparatus and gave it zest for the fine luncheon
he was promising himself the minute he stepped aboard
his train. His new chauffeur got lost three times in the
maze of traffic about the Grand Central Station. This,
however, was only human, seeing that the railroad company changed the map of 42nd Street every twenty-four
hours during the course of the building of its new
terminal.

Mr Armiston at length stepped from his taxicab, gave
his grip to a porter and paid the driver from a huge roll
of bills. This same roll was no sooner transferred back
to his pocket than a nimble-fingered pickpocket removed
it. This again was not an accident. That pickpocket had
been waiting there for the last hour for that roll of bills.
It was preordained, inevitable. And Oliver Armiston had
just thirty seconds to catch his train by the tail and
climb aboard. He smiled contentedly to himself.

It was not until he called for his ticket that he discovered his loss. For a full precious second he gazed at
the hand that came away empty from his money pocket,
and then:

'I find I left my purse at home,' he said with a grand
air he knew how to assume on occasions. 'My name is
Mr Oliver Armiston.'

Now Oliver Armiston was a name to conjure with.

'I don't doubt it,' said the ticket agent dryly. 'Mr
Andrew Carnegie was here yesterday begging car fare
to 125th Street, and Mr John D. Rockefeller quite frequently drops in and leaves his dollar watch in hock.
Next!'

And the ticket agent glared at the man blocking the
impatient line and told him to move on.

Armiston flushed crimson. He glanced at the clock. For once in his life he was about to experience that awful feeling of missing his train. For once in his life he was about to be robbed of that delicious sensation of hypnotizing the gate-keeper and walking majestically down that train platform that extends northwards under the train-shed a considerable part of the distance toward Yonkers. Twenty seconds. Armiston turned round, still holding his ground, and glared concentrated malice at the man next in line. That man was in a hurry. In his hand he held a bundle of bills. For a second, the thief instinct that is latent in us all suggested itself to Armiston. There within reach of his hand was the money, the precious paltry dollar bills that stood between him and his train. It scared him to discover that he, an upright and honoured citizen, was almost in the act of grabbing them like a common pickpocket.

Then a truly remarkable thing happened. The man thrust his handful of bills at Armiston.

'The only way I can raise this blockade is to bribe you,' he said, returning Armiston's glare. 'Here – take what you want – and give the rest of us a chance.'

With the alacrity of a blind beggar miraculously cured by the sight of much money, Armiston grabbed the handful, extracted what he needed for his ticket, and thrust the rest back into the waiting hand of his unknown benefactor. He caught the gate by a hair. So did his unknown friend. Together they walked down the platform, each matching the other's leisurely pace with his own. They might have been two potentates, so deliberately did they catch this train. Armiston would have liked very much to thank this person, but the other presented so forbidding an exterior that it was hard to find a point of attack. By force of habit Armiston boarded the parlour car, quite forgetting he did not have money for a seat. So did the other. The unknown thrust a bill at the porter. 'Get me two chairs,' he said. 'One is for this gentleman.'

Once inside and settled, Armiston renewed his efforts to thank this strange person. That person took a card from his pocket and handed it to Armiston.

'Don't run away with the foolish idea,' he said tartly, 'that I have done you a service willingly. You were making me miss my train, and I took this means of bribing you to get you out of my way. That is all, sir. At your leisure you may send me your cheque for the trifle.'

'A most extraordinary person!' said Armiston to himself. 'Let me give you my card,' he said to the other. 'As to the service rendered, you are welcome to your own ideas on that. For my part I am very grateful.'

The unknown took the proffered card and thrust it in his waistcoat pocket without glancing at it. He swung his chair round and opened a magazine, displaying a pair of broad unneighbourly shoulders. This was rather disconcerting to Armiston, who was accustomed to have his card act as an Open Sesame!

'Damn his impudence!' he said to himself. 'He takes me for a mendicant. I'll make copy of him!'

This was the popular author's way of getting even with those who offended his tender sensibilities.

Two things worried Armiston: One was his luncheon – or rather the absence of it; and the other was his neighbour. This neighbour, now that Armiston had a chance to study him, was a young man, well set up. He had a fine bronzed face that was not half so surly as his manner. He was now buried up to his ears in a magazine, oblivious of everything about him, even the dining-car porter, who strode down the aisle and announced the first call to lunch in the dining car.

'I wonder what the fellow is reading,' said Armiston to himself. He peeped over the man's shoulder and was interested at once, for the stranger was reading a copy of a magazine called by the vulgar 'The Whited Sepulchre'. It was the pride of this magazine that no man on earth could read it without the aid of a dictionary. Yet this person seemed to be enthralled. And what was more to the point, and vastly pleasing to Armiston, the man was at that moment engrossed in one of Armiston's own effusions. It was one of his crime stories that had won him praise and lucre. It concerned the Infallible Godahl.

These stories were pure reason incarnate in the person of a scientific thief. The plot was invariably so logical that it seemed more like the output of some machine than of a human mind. Of course the plots were impossible, because the fiction thief had to be an incredible genius to carry out the details. But nevertheless they were highly entertaining, fascinating and dramatic at one and the same time.

And this individual read the story through without winking an eyelash – as though the mental effort cost him nothing – and then, to Armiston's delight, turned back to the beginning and read it again. The author threw out his chest and shot his cuffs. It was not often that such unconscious tribute fell to his lot. He took the card of his unknown benefactor. It read:

> MR. J. BORDEN BENSON
> THE TOWERS
> NEW YORK CITY

'Humph!' snorted Armiston. 'An aristocrat – and a snob too!'

At this moment the aristocrat turned in his chair and handed the magazine to his companion. All his bad humour was gone.

'Are you familiar,' he asked, 'with this man Armiston's work? I mean these scientific thief stories that are runing now.'

'Ye-yes. Oh, yes,' sputtered Armiston, hastily putting the other's card away. 'I – in fact, you know – I take them every morning before breakfast.'

In a way this was the truth, for Armiston always began his day's writing before breakfasting.

Mr Benson smiled – a very fine smile at once boyish and sophisticated.

'Rather a heavy diet early in the morning, I should say,' he replied. 'Have you read this last one then?'

'Oh, yes,' said the delighted author.

'What do you think of it?' asked Benson.

The author puckered his lips.

'It is on a par with the others,' he said.

'Yes,' said Benson thoughtfully, 'I should say the same thing. And when we have said that there is nothing left to say. They are truly a remarkable product. Quite unique, you know. And yet,' he said, frowning at Armiston, 'I believe that this man Armiston is to be ranked as the most dangerous man in the world today.'

'Oh, I say –' began Armiston. But he checked himself, chuckling. He was very glad Mr Benson had not looked at his card.

'I mean it,' said the other decidedly. 'And you think so yourself, I fully believe. No thinking man could do otherwise.'

'In just what way? I must confess I have never thought of his work as anything but pure invention.'

It was truly delicious. Armiston would certainly make copy of this person.

'I will grant,' said Benson, 'that there is is not a thief in the world today clever enough – brainy enough – to take advantage of the suggestions put forth in these stories. But some day there will arise a man to whom they will be as simple as an ordinary blueprint, and he will profit accordingly. This magazine, by printing these stories, is merely furnishing him with his tools, showing him how to work. And the worst of it is –'

'Just a minute,' said the author. 'Agreeing for the moment that these stories will be the tools of Armiston's hero in real life some day, how about the popular magazines? They print ten such stories to one of these by Armiston.'

'Ah, my friend,' said Benson, 'you forget one thing: the popular magazines deal with real life – the possible, the usual. And in that very thing they protect the public against sharpers, by exposing the methods of those same sharpers. But with Armiston – no. Much as I enjoy him as an intellectual treat, I am afraid –'

He didn't finish his sentence. Instead he fell to shaking his head, as though in amazement at the devilish ingenuity of the author under discussion.

'I am certainly delighted,' thought that author, 'that my disagreeable benefactor did not have the good grace to look at my card. This really is most entertaining.' And then aloud, and treading on thin ice. 'I should be very glad to tell Oliver what you say and see what he has to say about it.'

Benson's face broke into a wreath of wrinkles:

'Do you know him? Well, I declare! That is a privilege. I heartily wish you would tell him.'

'Would you like to meet him? I am under obligation to you. I can arrange a little dinner for a few of us.'

'No,' said Benson, shaking his head; 'I would rather go on reading him without knowing him. Authors are so disappointing in real life. He may be some puny, anaemic little half-portion, with dirty fingernails and all the rest that goes with genius. No offence to your friend! Besides, I am afraid I might quarrel with him.'

'Last call for lunch in the dinin' cy-yah-aa,' sang the porter. Armiston was looking at his fingernails as the porter passed. They were manicured once a day.

'Come lunch with me,' said Benson heartily. 'I should be pleased to have you as my guest. I apologize for being rude to you at the ticket window, but I did want to catch this train mighty bad.'

Armiston laughed. 'Well, you have paid my car fare,' he said, 'and I won't deny I am hungry enough to eat a hundred-and-ten-pound rail. I will let you buy me a meal, being penniless.'

Benson arose, and as he drew out his handkerchief the card Armiston had given him fluttered into that worthy's lap. Armiston closed his hand over it, chuckling again. Fate had given him the chance of preserving his incognito with this person as long as he wished. It would be a rare treat to get him ranting again about the author Armiston.

But Armiston's host did not rant against his favourite author. In fact he was so enthusiastic over that man's genius that the same qualities which he decried as a danger to society in his opinion only added lustre to the work. Benson asked his guest innumerable questions as to the personal qualities of his ideal, and Armiston shamelessly constructed a truly remarkable person. The other listened entranced.

'No, I don't want to know him,' he said. 'In the first place I haven't the time, and in the second I'd be sure to start a row. And then there is another thing: if he is half the man I take him to be from what you say, he wouldn't stand for people fawning on him and telling him what a wonder he is. That's about what I should be doing, I am afraid.'

'Oh,' said Armiston, 'he isn't so bad as that. He is a – well, a sensible chap, with clean fingernails and all that, you know, and he gets a haircut once every three weeks, the same as the rest of us.'

'I am glad to hear you say so, Mr – er . . .'

Benson fell to chuckling.

342

'By gad,' he said, 'here we have been talking with each other for an hour, and I haven't so much as taken a squint at your card to see who you are!'

He searched for the card Armiston had given him.

'Call it Brown,' said Armiston, lying gorgeously and with a feeling of utmost righteousness. 'Martin Brown, single, read-and-write, colour, white, laced shoes and derby hat, as the police say.'

'All right, Mr Brown; glad to know you. We will have some cigars. You have no idea how much you interest me, Mr Brown. How much does Armiston get for his stories?'

'Every word he writes brings him the price of a good cigar. I should say he makes forty thousand a year.'

'Humph! That is better than Godahl, his star creation, could bag as a thief, I imagine, let alone the danger of getting snipped with a pistol ball on a venture.'

Armiston puffed up his chest and shot his cuffs again.

'How does he get his plots?'

Armiston knitted his ponderous brows. 'There's the rub,' he said. 'You can talk about so-and-so much a word until you are deaf, dumb and blind. But, after all, it isn't the number of words or how they are strung together that makes a story. It is the idea. And ideas are scarce.'

'I have an idea that I have always wanted to have Armiston get hold of, just to see what he could do with it. If you will pardon me, to my way of thinking the really important thing isn't the ideas, but how to work out the details.'

'What's your idea?' asked Armiston hastily. He was not averse to appropriating anything he encountered in real life and dressing it up to suit his taste. 'I'll pass it on to Armiston, if you say so.'

'Will you? That's capital. To begin with,' Mr Benson said as he twirled his brandy glass with long, lean, silky fingers – a hand Armiston thought he would not like to have handle him in a rage – 'to begin with, Godahl, this thief, is not an ordinary thief, he is a high-brow. He has made some big hauls. He must be a very rich man now – eh? You see that he is quite real to me. By this time, I should say, Godahl has acquired such a fortune that thieving for mere money is no longer an object. What does he do? Sit down and live on his income? Not much. He is a person of refined tastes with an eye for the aesthetic. He desires art objects, rare porcelains, a gem of rare cut or colour set by Benvenuto Cellini, a Leonardo da Vinci – did Godahl steal the Mona Lisa, by the way? He is the most likely person I can think of – or perhaps a Gutenberg Bible. Treasures, things of exquisite beauty to look at, to enjoy in secret, not to show to other people. That is the natural development of this man Godahl, eh?'

'Splendid!' exclaimed Armiston, his enthusiasm getting the better of him.

'Have you ever heard of Mrs Billy Wentworth?' asked Benson.

'Indeed, I know her well,' said Armiston, his guard down.

'Then you must surely have seen her white ruby?'

'White ruby! I never heard of such a thing. A white ruby?'

'Exactly. That's just the point. Neither have I. But if Godahl heard of a white ruby the chances are he would possess it – especially if it were the only one of its kind in the world.'

'Gad! I do believe he would, from what I know of him.'

'And especially,' went on Benson, 'under the circumstances. You know the Wentworths have been round a good deal. They haven't been over-scrupulous in getting things they wanted. Now Mrs Wentworth – but before I go on with this weird tale I want you to understand me.

344

It is pure fiction – an idea for Armiston and his wonderful Godahl. I am merely suggesting the Wentworths as fictitious characters.'

'I understand,' said Armiston.

'Mrs Wentworth might very well possess this white ruby. Let us say she stole it from some potentate's household in the Straits Settlements. She gained admittance by means of the official position of her husband. They can't accuse her of theft. All they can do is to steal the gem back from her. It is a sacred stone of course. They always are in fiction stories. And the usual tribe of jugglers, rug-peddlers, and so on – all disguised, you understand – have followed her to America, seeking a chance, not on her life, not to commit violence of any kind, but to steal that stone.

'She can't wear it,' went on Benson. 'All she can do is to hide it away in some safe place. What is a safe place? Not a bank. Godahl could crack a bank with his little finger. So might those East Indian fellows, labouring under the call of religion. Not in a safe. That would be folly.'

'How then?' put in Armiston eagerly.

'Ah, there you are! That's for Godahl to find out. He knows, let us say, that these foreigners in one way or another have turned Mrs Wentworth's apartments upside down. They haven't found anything. He knows that she keeps that white ruby in that house. Where is it? Ask Godahl! Do you see the point? Has Godahl ever cracked a nut like that? No. Here he must be the cleverest detective in the world and the cleverest thief at the same time. Before he can begin thieving he must make his blue-prints.

'When I read Armiston,' continued Benson, 'that is the kind of problem that springs up in my mind. I am always trying to think of some knot this wonderful thief would have to employ his best powers to unravel. I think of some weird situation like this one. I say to myself: "Good! I will write that. I will be as famous as Armiston. I will create another Godahl." But,' he said with a wave of his hands, 'what is the result? I tie the knot, but I can't untie it. The trouble is, I am not a Godahl. And this man Armiston, as I read him, is Godahl. He must be, or else Godahl could not be made to do the wonderful things he does. Hello! New Haven already? Mighty sorry to have you go, old chap. Great pleasure. When you get to town let me know. Maybe I will consent to meet Armiston.'

Armiston's first care on returning to New York was to remember the providential loan by which he had been able to keep clean his record of never missing a train. He counted out the sum in bills, wrote a polite note, signed it 'Martin Brown', and dispatched it by messenger to J. Borden Benson, The Towers. The Towers, the address Mr Benson's card bore, is an ultra-fashionable apartment hotel in Lower Fifth Avenue. It maintains all the pomp and solemnity of an English ducal castle. Armiston remembered having on a remote occasion taken dinner there with a friend and the recollection always gave him a chill. It was like dining among ghosts of kings, so grand and funereal was the air that pervaded everything.

Armiston, who could not forbear curiosity as to his queer benefactor, took occasion to look him up in the Blue Book and the Club Directory, and found that J. Borden Benson was quite some personage, several lines being devoted to him. This was extremely pleasing. Armiston had been thinking of that white-ruby yarn. It appealed to his sense of the dramatic. He would work it up in his best style, and on publication have a fine laugh on Benson by sending him an autographed copy and thus waking that gentleman up to the fact that it really had been the great Armiston in person he had befriended and entertained. What a joke it would be on Benson, thought the author; not without an intermixture of personal vanity, for even a genius such as he was not blind to flattery properly applied, and Benson unknowingly had laid it on thick.

'And, by gad,' thought the author, 'I will use the Wentworths as the main characters, as the victims of Godahl! They are just the people to fit into such a romance. Benson put money in my pocket, though he didn't suspect it. Lucky he didn't know what shifts we popular authors are put to for plots.'

Suiting the action to the word, Armiston and his wife accepted the next invitation they received from the Wentworths.

Mrs Wentworth, be it understood, was a lion hunter. She was forever trying to gather about her such celebrities as Armiston the author, Brackens the painter, Johanssen the explorer, and others. Armiston had always withstood her wiles. He always had some excuse to keep him away from her gorgeous table, where she exhibited her lions to her simpering friends.

There were many undesirables sitting at the table, idle-rich youths, girls of the fast hunting set, and so on, and they all gravely shook the great author by the hand and told him what a wonderful man he was. As for Mrs Wentworth, she was too highly elated at her success in roping him for sane speech, and she fluttered about him like a hysterical bridesmaid. But, Armiston noted with relief, one of his pals was there – Johanssen. Over cigars and cognac he managed to buttonhole the explorer.

'Johanssen,' he said, 'you have been everywhere.'

'You are mistaken there,' said Johanssen. 'I have never before tonight been north of 59th Street in New York.'

'Yes, but you have been in Java and Ceylon and the Settlements. Tell me, have you ever heard of such a thing as a white ruby?'

The explorer narrowed his eyes to a slit and looked queerly at his questioner. 'That's a queer question,' he said in a low voice, 'to ask in this house.'

Armiston felt his pulse quicken. 'Why?' he asked, assuming an air of surprised innocence.

'If you don't know,' said the explorer shortly, 'I certainly will not enlighten you.'

'All right; as you please. But you haven't answered my question yet. Have you ever heard of a white ruby?'

'I don't mind telling you that I have heard of such a thing – that is, I have heard there is a ruby in existence that is called the white ruby. It isn't really white, you know; it has a purplish tinge. But the old heathen who rightly owns it likes to call it white, just as he likes to call his blue and grey elephants white.'

'Who owns it?' asked Armiston, trying his best to make his voice sound natural. To find in this manner that there was some parallel for the mystical white ruby of which Benson had told him appealed strongly to his superdeveloped dramatic sense. He was now as keen on the scent as a hound.

Johanssen took to drumming on the tablecloth. He smiled to himself and his eyes glowed. Then he turned and looked sharply at his questioner.

'I suppose,' he said, 'that all things are grist to a man of your trade. If you are thinking of building a story round a white ruby I can think of nothing more fascinating. But, Armiston,' he said, suddenly altering his tone and almost whispering, 'if you are on the track of *the* white ruby let me advise you now to call off your dogs and keep your throat whole. I think I am a brave man. I have shot tigers at ten paces – held my fire purposely to see how charmed a life I really did bear. I have been charged by mad rhinos and by wounded buffaloes, have walked across a clearing where the air was being punctured with bullets as thick as holes in a mosquito screen. But,' he said, laying his hand on Armiston's arm, 'I have never had the nerve to hunt the white ruby.'

Capital!' exclaimed the author.

'Capital, yes, for a man who earns his bread and gets his excitement by sitting at a typewriter and dreaming about these things. But take my word for it, it isn't capital for a man who gets his excitement by doing this thing. Hands off, my friend!'

'It really does exist then?'

Johanssen puckered his lips. 'So they say,' he said.

'What's it worth?'

'Worth? What do you mean by worth? Dollars and cents? What is your child worth to you. A million, a billion – how much? Tell me. No, you can't. Well, that's just what the miserable stone is worth to the man who rightfully owns it. Now let's quit talking nonsense. There's Billy Wentworth shooing the men into the drawing-room. I suppose we shall be entertained this evening by some of the hundred-dollar-a-minute songbirds, as usual. It's amazing what these people will spend for mere vulgar display when there are hundreds of families starving within a mile of this spot!'

Two famous singers sang that night. Armiston did not have much opportunity to look over the house. He was now fully determined to lay the scene of his story in this very house. At leavetaking the sugar-sweet Mrs Billy Wentworth drew Armiston aside and said:

'It's rather hard on you to ask you to sit through an evening with these people. I will make amends by asking you to come to me some night when we can be by ourselves. Are you interested in rare curios? Yes, we all are. I have some really wonderful things I want you to see. Let us make it next Tuesday, with a little informal dinner, just for ourselves.'

Armiston then and there made the lion hunter radiantly happy by accepting her invitation to sit at her board as a family friend instead of as a lion.

As he put his wife into their automobile he turned and looked at the house. It stood opposite Central Park. It was a copy of some French château in gray sandstone, with a barbican, and overhanging towers, and all the rest of it. The windows of the street floor peeped out through deep embrasures and were heavily guarded with iron latticework.

'Godahl will have the very devil of a time breaking in there,' he chuckled to himself. Late that night his wife awakened him to find out why he was tossing about so.

'That white ruby has got on my nerves,' he said cryptically, and she, thinking he was dreaming, persuaded him to try to sleep again.

Great authors must really live in the flesh, at times at least, the lives of their great characters. Otherwise these great characters would not be so real as they are. Here was Armiston, who had created a superman in the person of Godahl the thief. For ten years he had written nothing else. He had laid the life of Godahl out in squares, thought for him, dreamed about him, set him to new tasks, gone through all sorts of queer adventures with him. And this same Godahl had amply repaid him. He had raised the author from the ranks of struggling amateurs to a position among the most highly paid fiction writers in the United States. He had brought him ease and luxury. Armiston did not need the money any more. The serial rights telling of the exploits of this Godahl had paid him handsomely. The book of Godahl's adventures had paid him even better, and had furnished him yearly with a never-failing income, like government bonds, but at a much higher rate of interest. Even though the crimes this Godahl had committed were all on paper, nevertheless Godahl was a living being to his creator. More – he was Armiston, and Armiston was Godahl.

It was not surprising, then, that when Tuesday came Armiston awaited the hour with feverish impatience. Here, as his strange friend had so thoughtlessly and casually told him, was an opportunity for the great

Godahl to outdo even himself. Here was an opportunity for Godahl to be the greatest detective in the world, in the first place, before he could carry out one of his sensational thefts.

So it was Godahl, not Armiston, who helped his wife out of their automobile that evening and mounted the splendid steps of the Wentworth mansion. He cast his eyes aloft; took in every inch of the façade.

'No,' he said, 'Godahl cannot break in from the street. I must have a look at the back of the house.'

He cast his eyes on the ironwork that guarded the deep windows giving on the street.

It was not iron after all, but chilled steel sunk into armoured concrete. The outposts of this house were as safely guarded as the vault of the United States Mint.

'It's got to be from the inside,' he said, making mental note of this fact.

The butler was stone-deaf. This was rather singular. Why should a family of the standing of the Wentworths employ a man as head of their city establishment who was stone-deaf? Armiston looked at the man with curiosity. He was still in middle age. Surely, then, he was not retained because of years of service. No, there was something more than charity behind this. He addressed a casual word to the man as he handed him his hat and cane. His back was turned and the man did not reply. Armiston turned and repeated the sentence in the same tone. The man watched his lips in the bright light of the hall.

'A lip-reader, and a dandy,' thought Armiston, for the butler seemed to catch every word he said.

'Fact Number 2!' said the creator of Godahl the thief.

He felt no compunction at thus noting the most intimate details of the Wentworth establishment. An accident had put him on the track of a rare good story, and it was all copy. Besides, he told himself, when he came to write the story he would disguise it in such a way that no-one reading it would know it was about the Wentworths. If their establishment happened to possess the requisite setting for a great story, surely there was no reason why he should not take advantage of that fact.

The great thief – he made no bones of the fact to himself that he had come here to help Godahl – accepted the flattering greeting of his hostess with the grand air that so well fitted him. Armiston was tall and thin, with slender fingers and a touch of grey in his wavy hair, for all his youthful years, and he knew how to wear clothes. Mrs Wentworth was proud of him as a social ornament, even aside from his glittering fame as an author. And Mrs Armiston was well born, so there was no jar in their being received in the best house of the town.

The dinner was truly delightful. Here Armiston saw, or thought he saw, one of the reasons for the deaf butler. The hostess had him so trained that she was able to catch her servant's eye and instruct him in this or that trifle by merely moving her lips. It was almost uncanny, thought the author, this silent conversation the deaf man and his mistress were able to carry on unnoticed by the others.

'By gad, it's wonderful! Godahl, my friend, underscore that note of yours referring to the deaf butler. Don't miss it. It will take a trick.'

Armiston gave his undivided attention to his hostess as soon as he found Wentworth entertaining Mrs Armiston and thus properly dividing the party. He persuaded her to talk by a cleverly pointed question here and there; and as she talked, he studied her.

'We are going to rob you of your precious white ruby, my friend,' he thought humorously to himself; 'and while we are laying our wires there is nothing about you too small to be worthy of our attention.'

Did she really possess the white ruby? Did this man

Benson know anything about the white ruby? And what was the meaning of the strange actions of his friend Johanssen when approached on the subject in this house? His hostess came to have a wonderful fascination for him. He pictured this beautiful creature so avid in her lust for rare gems that she actually did penetrate the establishment of some heathen potentate in the Straits simply for the purpose of stealing the mystic stone. 'Have you ever, by any chance, been in the Straits?' he asked indifferently.

'Wait,' Mrs Wentworth said with a laugh as she touched his hand lightly; 'I have some curios from the Straits, and I will venture to say you have never seen their like.'

Half an hour later they were all seated over coffee and cigarettes in Mrs Wentworth's boudoir. It was indeed a strange place. There was scarcely a single corner of the world that had not contributed something to its furnishing. Carvings of teak and ivory; hangings of sweet-scented vegetable fibres; lamps of jade; queer little gods, all sitting like Buddha with their legs drawn up under them, carved out of jade or sardonyx; scarfs of baroque pearls; Darjeeling turquoises – Armiston had never before seen such a collection. And each item had its story. He began to look on this frail little woman with different eyes. She had been and seen and done, and the tale of her life, what she had actually lived, outshone even that of the glittering rascal Godahl, who was standing beside him now and directing his ceaseless questions. 'Have you any rubies?' he asked.

Mrs Wentworth bent before a safe in the wall. With swift fingers she whirled the combination. The keen eyes of Armiston followed the bright knob like a cat.

'Fact Number 3!' said the Godahl in him as he mentally made note of the numbers. 'Five – eight – seven – four – six. That's the combination.'

Mrs Wentworth showed him six pigeon-blood rubies.

'This one is pale,' he said carelessly, holding a particularly large stone up to the light. 'Is it true that occasionally they are found white?'

His hostess looked at him before answering. He was intent on a deep-red stone he held in the palm of his hand. It seemed a thousand miles deep.

'What a fantastic idea!' she said. She glanced at her husband, who had reached out and taken her hand in a naturally affectionate manner.

'Fact Number 4!' mentally noted Armiston. 'Are not you in mortal fear of robbery with all this wealth?'

Mrs Wentworth laughed lightly.

'That is why we live in a fortress,' she said.

'Have you never, then, been visited by thieves?' asked the author boldly.

'Never!' she said.

'A lie,' thought Armiston. 'Fact Number 5! We are getting on swimmingly.'

'I do not believe that even your Godahl the Infallible could get in here,' Mrs Wentworth said. 'Not even the servants enter this room. That door is not locked with a key; yet it locks. I am not much of a housekeeper,' she said lazily, 'but such housekeeping as is done in this room is all done by these poor little hands of mine.'

'No! Most amazing! May I look at the door?'

'Yes, Mr Godahl,' said the woman, who had lived more lives than Godahl himself.

Armiston examined the door, this strange device that locked without a key, apparently indeed without a lock, and came away disappointed.

'Well, Mr Godahl?' his hostess said tauntingly. He shook his head in perplexity.

'Most ingenious,' he said; and then suddenly: 'Yet I will venture that if I turned Godahl loose on this problem he would solve it.'

'What fun!' she cried, clapping her hands.

'You challenge him?' asked Armiston.

'What nonsense is this!' cried Wentworth, coming forward.

'No nonsense at all,' said Mrs Wentworth. 'Mr Armiston has just said that his Godahl could rob me. Let him try. If he can – if mortal man can gain the secrets of ingress and egress of this room – I want to know it. I don't believe mortal man can enter this room.'

Armiston noted a strange glitter in her eyes.

'Gad! She was born to the part! What a woman!' he thought. And then aloud:

'I will set him to work. I will lay the scene of his exploit in – say – Hungary, where this room might very well exist in some feudal castle. How many people have entered this room since it was made the storehouse of all this wealth?'

'Not six besides yourself,' replied Mrs Wentworth.

'Then no-one can recognize it if I describe it in a story – in fact, I will change the material details. We will say that it is not jewels Godahl is seeking. We will say that it is a –'

Mrs Wentworth's hand touched his own. The tips of her fingers were cold. 'A white ruby,' she said.

'Gad! What a thoroughbred!' he exclaimed to himself – or to Godahl. And then aloud: 'Capital! I will send you a copy of the story autographed.'

The next day he called at The Towers and sent up his card to Mr Benson's apartments. Surely a man of Benson's standing could be trusted with such a secret. In fact it was evidently not a secret to Benson, who in all probability was one of the six Mrs Wentworth said had entered that room. Armiston wanted to talk the matter over with Benson. He had given up his idea of having fun with him by sending him a marked copy of the magazine containing his tale. His story had taken complete possession of him, as always had been the case when he was at work dispatching Godahl on his adventures.

'If that ruby really exists,' Armiston said, 'I don't know whether I shall write the story or steal the ruby for myself. Benson is right. Godahl should not steal any more for mere money. He is after rare, unique things now. And I am Godahl. I feel the same way myself.'

A valet appeared, attired in a gorgeous livery. Armiston wondered why any self-respecting American would consent to don such raiment, even though it was the livery of the great Benson family.

'Mr Armiston, sir,' said the valet, looking at the author's card he held in his hand. 'Mr Benson sailed for Europe yesterday morning. He is spending the summer in Norway. I am to follow on the next steamer. Is there any message I can take to him, sir? I have heard him speak of you, sir.'

Armiston took the card and wrote on it in pencil:

I called to apologize. I am Martin Brown. The chance was too good to miss. You will pardon me, won't you?

For the next two weeks Armiston gave himself over to his dissipation, which was accompanying Godahl on this adventure. It was a formidable task. The secret room he placed in a Hungarian castle, as he had promised. A beautiful countess was his heroine. She had seen the world, mostly in man's attire, and her escapades had furnished vivacious reading for two continents. No-one could possibly connect her with Mrs Billy Wentworth. So far it was easy. But how was Godahl to get into this wonderful room where the countess had hidden this wonderful rare white ruby? The room was lined with chilled steel. Even the door – this he had noted when he was examining that peculiar portal – was lined with layers of steel. It could withstand any known tool.

However, Armiston was Armiston, and Godahl was Godahl. He got into that room. He got the white ruby!

The manuscript went to the printers, and the publishers said that Armiston had never done anything like it since he started Godahl on his astonishing career.

He banked the cheque for his tale, and as he did so he said: 'Gad I would a hundred times rather possess that white ruby. Confound the thing! I feel as if I had not heard the last of it.'

Armiston and his wife went to Maine for the summer without leaving their address. Along in the early fall he received by registered mail, forwarded by his trusted servant at the town house, a package containing the envelope he had addressed to J. Borden Benson, The Towers. Furthermore it contained the dollar bills he had dispatched to that individual, together with his note which he had signed 'Martin Brown'. And across the note, in the most insulting manner, was written in coarse, greasy blue-pencil lines:

Damnable impertinence. I'll cane you the first time I see you.

And no more. That was enough of course – quite sufficient.

In the same mail came a note from Armiston's publishers, saying that his story 'The White Ruby' was scheduled for publication in the October number, out September 25th. This cheered him up. He was anxious to see it in print. Late in September they started back to town.

'Aha!' he said as he sat reading his paper in the parlour car. He had caught this train by the veriest tip of its tail and upset the running schedule in the act. 'Aha! I see my genial friend, J. Borden Benson, is in town, contrary to custom at this time of year. Life must be a great bore to that snob.'

A few days after arriving in town he received a package of advance copies of the magazine containing his story, and he read the tale of 'The White Ruby' as if he had never seen it before. On the cover of one copy, which he was to dispatch to his grumpy benefactor, J. Borden Benson, he wrote:

Charmed to be caned. Call any time. See contents.
                                        Oliver Armiston.

On another he wrote:

Dear Mrs Wentworth,
    See how simple it is to pierce your fancied security!

He dispatched these two magazines with a feeling of glee. No sooner had he done so, however, than he learned that the Wentworths had not yet returned from Newport. The magazine would be forwarded to them no doubt. The Wentworths' absence made the tale all the better, in fact, for in his story Armiston had insisted on Godahl's breaking into the castle and solving the mystery of the keyless door during the season when the château was closed and strung with a perfect network of burglar alarms connecting with the *Gendarmerie* in the near-by village.

That was the twenty-fifth day of September. The magazine was put on sale that morning.

On the twenty-sixth day of September Armiston bought a late edition of an afternoon paper from a leather-lunged boy who was hawking 'Extra!' in the street. Across the first page the headlines met his eye:

ROBBERY AND MURDER IN THE WENTWORTH MANSION!

Private watchmen, summoned by burglar alarm at ten o'clock this morning, find servant with skull crushed on floor of mysterious steel-doored room. Murdered man's pockets filled with rare jewels. Police believe he was murdered by a confederate who escaped.

*

It was ten o'clock that night when an automobile drew up at Armiston's door, and a tall man with a square jaw, square shoes and a square moustache alighted. This was Deputy Police Commissioner Byrnes, a professional detective whom the new administration had drafted into the city's service from the government secret service.

Byrnes was admitted and as he advanced to the middle of the drawing-room, without so much as a nod to the ghostlike Armiston who stood shivering before him, he drew a package of papers from his pocket.

'I presume you have seen all the evening papers,' he said, spitting his words through his half-closed teeth with so much show of personal malice that Armiston – never a brave man in spite of his Godahl – cowered before him.

Armiston shook his head dumbly at first, but at length he managed to say: 'Not all; no.'

The Deputy Commissioner with much deliberation drew out the latest extra and handed it to Armiston without a word.

It was the *Evening News*. The first page was divided down its entire length by a black line. On one side, and occupying four columns, was a word-for-word reprint of Armiston's story, 'The White Ruby'.

On the other, the facts in deadly parallel, was a graphic account of the robbery and murder at the home of Billy Wentworth. The parallel was glaring in the intensity of its dumb accusation. On the one side was the theoretical Godahl, working his masterly way of crime, step by step; and on the other was the plagiarism of Armiston's story, following the intricacies of the master mind with copy-book accuracy.

The editor, who must have been a genius in his way, did not accuse. He simply placed the fiction and the fact side by side and let the reader judge for himself. It was masterly. If, as the law says, the mind that conceives, the intelligence that directs, a crime is more guilty than the very hand that acts, then Armiston here was both thief and murderer. Thief, because the white ruby had actually been stolen. Mrs Billy Wentworth, rushed to the city by special train, attended by doctors and nurses, now confirmed the story of the theft of the ruby. Murderer, because in the story Godahl had for once in his career stooped to murder as the means, and had triumphed over the dead body of his confederate, scorning, in his joy at possessing the white ruby, the paltry diamonds, pearls and red rubies with which his confederate had crammed his pockets.

Armiston seized the police official by his lapels.

'The butler!' he screamed. 'The butler! Yes, the butler. Quick, or he will have flown.'

Byrnes gently disengaged the hands that had grasped him.

'Too late,' he said. 'He has already flown. Sit down and quiet your nerves. We need your help. You are the only man in the world who can help us now.'

When Armiston was himself again he told the whole tale, beginning with his strange meeting with J. Borden Benson on the train, and ending with his accepting Mrs Wentworth's challenge to have Godahl break into the room and steal the white ruby. Byrnes nodded over the last part. He had already heard that from Mrs Wentworth, and there was the autographed copy of the magazine to show for it.

'You say that J. Borden Benson told you of this white ruby in the first place.'

Armiston again told, in great detail, the circumstances, all the humour now turned into grim tragedy.

'That is strange,' said the ex-secret-service chief. 'Did you leave your purse at home or was your pocket picked?'

'I thought at first that I had absent-mindedly left it at home. Then I remembered having paid the chauffeur out of the roll of bills, so my pocket must have been picked.'

'What kind of a looking man was this Benson?'

'You must know him,' said Armiston.

'Yes, I know him; but I want to know what he looked like to you. I want to find out how he happened to be so handy when you were in need of money.'

Armiston described the man minutely.

The Deputy sprang to his feet. 'Come with me,' he said; and they hurried into the automobile and soon drew up in front of The Towers.

Five minutes later they were ushered into the magnificent apartment of J. Borden Benson. That worthy was in his bath preparing to retire for the night.

'I don't catch the name,' Armiston and the Deputy heard him cry through the bathroom door to his valet.

'Mr Oliver Armiston, sir.'

'Ah, he has come for his caning, I expect. I'll be there directly.'

He did not wait to complete his toilet, so eager was he to see the author. He strode out in a brilliant bathrobe and in one hand he carried an alpenstock. His eyes glowed in anger. But the sight of Byrnes surprised as well as halted him.

'Do you mean to say this is J. Borden Benson?' cried Armiston to Byrnes, rising to his feet and pointing at the man.

'The same,' said the Deputy; 'I swear to it. I know him well! I take it he is not the gentleman who paid your car fare to New Haven.'

'Not by a hundred pounds!' exclaimed Armiston as he surveyed the huge bulk of the elephantine clubman.

The forced realization that the stranger he had hitherto regarded as a benefactor was not J. Borden Benson at all, but someone who had merely assumed that worthy's name while he was playing the conceited author as an easy dupe, did more to quiet Armiston's nerves than all the sedatives his doctor had given him. It was a badly dashed popular author who sat down with the Deputy Commissioner in his library an hour later. He would gladly have consigned Godahl to the bottom of the sea; but it was too late. Godahl had taken the trick.

'How do you figure it?' Armiston asked, turning to the Deputy.

'The beginning is simple enough. It is the end that bothers me,' said the official. 'Your bogus J. Borden Benson is, of course, the brains of the whole combination. Your infernal Godahl has told us just exactly how this crime was committed. Now your infernal Godahl must bring the guilty parties to justice.'

It was plain to be seen that the police official hated Godahl worse than poison, and feared him too.

'Why not look in the Rogues' Gallery for this man who befriended me on the train?'

The chief laughed.

'For the love of Heaven, Armiston, do you, who pretend to know all about scientific thievery, think for a moment that the man who took your measure so easily is of the class of crooks who get their pictures in the Rogues' Gallery? Talk sense!'

'I can't believe you when you say he picked my pocket.'

'I don't care whether you believe me or not; he did, or one of his pals did. It all amounts to the same thing, don't you see? First, he wanted to get acquainted with you. Now the best way to get into your good graces was

to put you unsuspectingly under obligation to him. So
he robs you of your money. From what I have seen of
you in the last few hours it must have been like taking
candy from a child. Then he gets next to you in line.
He pretends that you are merely some troublesome toad
in his path. He gives you money for your ticket, to get
you out of his way so he won't miss his train. His train!
Of course his train is your train. He puts you in a position where you have to make advances to him. And then,
grinning to himself all the time at your conceit and
gullibility, he plays you through your pride, your
Godahl. Think of the creator of the great Godahl falling
for a trick like that!'

Byrnes's last words were the acme of biting sarcasm.

'You admit yourself that he is too clever for you to put
your hands on.'

'And then,' went on Byrnes, not heeding the interruption, 'he invites you to lunch and tells you what he
wants you to do for him. And you follow his lead like
a sheep at the tail of the bellwether! Great Scott,
Armiston! I would give a year's salary for one hour's
conversation with that man.'

Armiston was beginning to see the part this queer
character had played; but he was in a semi-hysterical
state, and, like a woman in such a position, he wanted a
calm mind to tell him the whole thing in words of one
syllable, to verify his own dread.

'What do you mean?' he asked. 'I don't quite follow.
You say he tells me what he wants me to do.'

Byrnes shrugged his shoulders in disgust; then, as if
resigned to the task before him, he began his explanation.

'Here, man, I will draw a diagram for you. This
gentleman friend of yours – we will call him John
Smith for convenience – wants to get possession of this
white ruby. He knows that it is in the keeping of Mrs

Billy Wentworth. He knows you know Mrs Wentworth
and have access to her house. He knows that she stole
this bauble and is frightened to death all the time. Now
John Smith is a pretty clever chap. He handled the great
Armiston like hot putty. He had exhausted his resources.
He is baffled and needs help. What does he do? He
reads the stories about the great Godahl. Confidentially,
Mr Armiston, I will tell you that I think your great
Godahl is mush. But that is neither here nor there. If
you can sell him as a gold brick, all right. But Mr John
Smith is struck by the wonderful ingenuity of this
Godahl. He says, "Ha! I will get Godahl to tell me how
to get this gem!"

'So he gets hold of yourself, sir, and persuades you
that you are playing a joke on him by getting him to
rant and rave about the great Godahl. Then – and here
the villain enters – he says: "Here is a thing the great
Godahl cannot do. I dare him to do it." He tells you
about the gem, whose very existence is quite fantastic
enough to excite the imagination of the wonderful
Armiston. And by clever suggestion he persuades you
to play the plot at the home of Mrs Wentworth. And all
the time you are chuckling to yourself, thinking what a
rare joke you are going to have on J. Borden Benson
when you send him an autographed copy and show him
that he was talking to the distinguished genius all the
time and didn't know it. That's the whole story, sir.
Now wake up!'

Byrnes sat back in his chair and regarded Armiston
with the smile a pedagogue bestows on a refractory boy
whom he has just flogged soundly.

'I will explain further,' he continued. 'You haven't
visited the house yet. You can't. Mrs Wentworth, for all
she is in bed with four dozen hot-water bottles, would
tear you limb from limb if you went there. And don't
you think for a minute she isn't able to. That woman is
a vixen.'

Armiston nodded gloomily. The very thought of her now sent him into a cold sweat.

'Mr Godahl, the obliging,' continued the Deputy, 'notes one thing to begin with: the house cannot be entered from the outside. So it must be an inside job. How can this be accomplished? Well, there is the deaf butler. Why is he deaf? Godahl ponders. Ha! He has it! The Wentworths are so dependent on servants that they must have them round at all times. This butler is the one who is constantly about them. They are worried to death by their possession of this white ruby. Their house has been raided from the inside a dozen times. Nothing is taken, mind you. They suspect their servants. This thing haunts them, but the woman will not give up this foolish bauble. So she has as her major domo a man who cannot understand a word in any language unless he is looking at the speaker and is in a bright light. He can only understand the lips. Handy, isn't it? In a dull light or with their backs turned they can talk about anything they want. This is a jewel of a butler.

'But,' added Byrnes, 'one day a man calls. He is a lawyer. He tells the butler he is heir to a fortune – fifty thousand dollars. He must go to Ireland to claim it. Your friend on the train – he is the man of course – sends your butler to Ireland. So this precious butler is lost. They must have another. Only a deaf one will do. And they find just the man they want – quite accidentally, you understand. Of course it is Godahl, with forged letters saying he has been in service in great houses. Presto! The great Godahl himself is now the butler. It is simple enough to play deaf. You say this is fiction. Let me tell you this: six weeks ago the Wentworths actually changed butlers. That hasn't come out in the papers yet.'

Armiston, who had listened to the Deputy's review of his story listlessly, now sat up with a start. He suddenly exclaimed gleefully:

'But my story didn't come out till two days ago!'

'Ah, yes; but you forget that it has been in the hands of your publishers for three months. A man who was clever enough to dupe the great Armiston wouldn't shirk the task of getting hold of a proof of that story.'

Armiston sank deeper into his chair.

'Once Godahl got inside the house the rest was simple. He corrupted one of the servants. He opened the steel-lined door with the flame of an oxyacetylene blast. As you say in your story that flame cuts steel like wax; he didn't have to bother about the lock. He simply cut the door down. Then he put his confederate in a good humour by telling him to fill his pockets with the diamonds and other junk in the safe, which he obligingly opens. One thing bothers me, Armiston. How did you find out about that infernal contraption that killed the confederate?'

Armiston buried his face in his hands. Byrnes rudely shook him.

'Come,' he said; 'you murdered that man, though you are innocent. Tell me how.'

'Is this the third degree?' said Armiston.

'It looks like it,' said the Deputy grimly as he gnawed at his stubby moustache. Armiston drew a long breath, like one who realizes how hopeless is his situation. He began to speak in a low tone. All the while the Deputy glared at Godahl's inventor with his accusing eye.

'When I was sitting in the treasure room with the Wentworths and my wife, playing auction bridge, I dismissed the puzzle of the door as easily solved by means of the brazing flame. The problem was not to get into the house, or into this room, but to find the ruby. It was not in the safe.'

'No, of course not. I suppose your friend on the train was kind enough to tell you that. He had probably looked there himself.'

'Gad! He did tell me that, come to think of it. Well, I studied that room. I was sure the white ruby, if it really existed, was within ten feet of me. I examined the floor, the ceiling, the walls. No result. But,' he said, shivering as if in a draught of cold air, 'there was a chest in that room made of Lombary oak.' The harassed author buried his face in his hands. 'Oh, this is terrible!' he moaned.

'Go on,' said the Deputy in his colourless voice.

'I can't. I tell it all in the story, Heaven help me!'

'I know you tell it all in the story,' came the rasping voice of Byrnes, 'but I want you to tell it to me. I want to hear it from your own lips – as Armiston; you understand, whose devilry has just killed a man; not as your damnable Godahl.'

'The chest was not solid oak,' went on Armiston. 'It was solid steel covered with oak to disguise it.'

'How did you know that?'

'I had seen it before.'

'Where?'

'In Italy fifteen years ago, in a decayed castle, back through the Soldini Pass from Lugano. It was the possession of an old nobleman, a friend of a friend of mine.'

'Humph!' grunted the Deputy. And then: 'Well, how did you know it was the same one?'

'By the inscription carved on the front. It was – but I have told all this in print already. Why need I go over it all again?'

'I want to hear it again from your own lips. Maybe there are some points you did not tell in print. Go on!'

'The inscription was "*Sanctus Dominus*".'

The Deputy smiled grimly.

'Very fitting, I should say. Praise the Lord with the most diabolical engine of destruction I have ever seen.'

'And then,' said Armiston, 'there was the owner's name – "Arno Petronii". Queer name that.'

'Yes,' said the Deputy dryly. 'How did you hit on this as the receptacle for the white ruby?'

'If it were the same one I saw in Lugano – and I felt sure it was – it was certain death to attempt to open it – that is, for one who did not know how. Such machines were common enough in the Middle Ages. There was an obvious way to open it. It was meant to be obvious. To open it that way was inevitable death. It released tremendous springs that crushed anything within a radius of five feet. You saw that?'

'I did,' said the Deputy, and he shuddered as he spoke. Then, bringing his fierce face within an inch of the cowering Armiston, he said:

'You knew the secret spring by which that safe could be opened as simply as a shoebox, eh?'

Armiston nodded his head.

'But Godahl did not,' he said. 'Having recognized this terrible chest,' went on the author, 'I guessed it must be the hiding place of the jewel – for two reasons: in the first place Mrs Wentworth had avoided showing it to us. She passed it by as a mere bit of curious furniture. Second, it was too big to go through the door or any one of the windows. They must have gone to the trouble of taking down the wall to get that thing in there. Something of a task, too, considering it weighs about two tons.'

'You didn't bring out that point in your story.'

'Didn't I? I fully intended to.'

'Maybe,' said the Deputy, watching his man sharply, 'it so impressed your friend who paid your car fare to New Haven that he clipped it out of the manuscript when he borrowed it.'

'There is no humour in this affair, sir, if you will pardon me,' said Armiston.

'That is quite true. Go ahead.'

'The rest you know. Godahl, in my story – the thief

in real life – had to sacrifice a life to open that chest. So he corrupted a small kitchen servant, filling his pockets with these other jewels, and told him to touch the spring.'

'You murdered that man in cold blood,' said the Deputy, rising and pacing the floor. 'The poor deluded devil, from the looks of what's left of him, never let out a whimper, never knew what hit him. Here, take some more of this brandy. Your nerves are in a bad way.'

'What I can't make out is this,' said Armiston after a time. 'There was a million dollars' worth of stuff in that room that could have been put into a quart measure. Why did not this thief, who was willing to go to all the trouble to get the white ruby, take some of the jewels? Nothing is missing besides the white ruby, as I understand it. Is there?'

'No,' said the Deputy. 'Not a thing. Here comes a messenger boy.'

'For Mr Armiston? Yes,' he said to the entering maid. The boy handed him a package for which the Deputy signed.

'This is for you,' he said, turning to Armiston as he closed the door. 'Open it.'

When the package was opened the first object to greet their eyes was a roll of bills.

'This grows interesting,' said Byrnes. He counted the money. 'Thirty-nine dollars. Your friend evidently is returning the money he stole from you at the station. What does he have to say for himself? I see there is a note.'

He reached over and took the paper out of Armiston's hands. It was ordinary bond stationery, with no identifying marks of any consequence. The note was written in bronze ink, in a careful copperplate hand, very small and precise. It read:

Most Excellency Sir:

Herewith, most honoured dollars I am dispatching complete. Regretful extremely of sad blood being not to be prevented. Accept trifle from true friend.

That was all.

'There's a jeweller's box,' said Byrnes. 'Open it.'

Inside the box was a lozenge-shaped diamond about the size of a little fingernail. It hung from a tiny bar of silver, highly polished and devoid of ornament. On the back under the clasp-pin were several microscopic characters.

There were several obvious clues to be followed – the messenger boy, the lawyers who induced the deaf butler to go to Ireland on what later proved to be a wild-goose chase, the employment agency through which the new butler had been secured, and so on. But all of these avenues proved too respectable to yield results. Deputy Byrnes had early arrived at his own conclusions, by virtue of the knowledge he had gained as government agent, yet to appease the popular indignation he kept up a desultory search for the criminal.

It was natural that Armiston should think of his friend Johanssen at this juncture. Johanssen possessed that wonderful Oriental capacity of aloofness which we Westerners are so ready to term indifference or lack of curiosity.

'No, I thank you,' said Johanssen. 'I'd rather not mix in.'

The pleadings of the author were in vain. His words fell on deaf ears.

'If you will not lift a hand because of your friendship for me,' said Armiston bitterly, 'then think of the law. Surely there is something due to justice, when both robbery and bloody murder have been committed!'

'Justice!' cried Johanssen in scorn. 'Justice, you say! My friend, if you steal from me, and I reclaim by force that which is mine, is that injustice? If you cannot see the idea behind that surely, then, I cannot explain it to you.'

'Answer one question,' said Armiston. 'Have you any idea who the man was I met on the train?'

'For your own peace of mind – yes. As a clue leading to what you so glibly term justice – pshaw! Tonight's sundown would be easier for you to catch than this man if I know him. Mind you, Armiston, I do not know. But I believe. Here is what I believe:

'In a dozen courts of kings and petty princelings that I know of in the East there are Westerners retained as advisers – fiscal agents they usually call them. Usually they are American or English, or occasionally German.

'Now I ask you a question. Say that you were in the hire of a heathen prince, and a grievous wrong were done that prince, say, by a thoughtless woman who had not the least conception of the beauty of an idea she has outraged, Merely for the possession of a bauble, valueless to her except to appease vanity, she ruthlessly rode down a superstition that was as holy to this prince as your own belief in Christ is to you. What would you do?'

Without waiting for Armiston to answer, Johanssen went on:

'I know a man – You say this man you met on the train had wonderful hands, did he not? Yes, I thought so. Armiston, I know a man who would not sit idly by and smile to himself over the ridiculous fuss occasioned by the loss of an imperfect stone – off-colour, badly cut, and everything else. Neither would he laugh at the superstition behind it. He would say to himself: "This superstition is older by several thousand years than I or my people." And this man, whom I know, is brave enough to right that wrong himself if his underlings failed.'

'I follow,' said Armiston dully.

'But,' said Johanssen, leaning forward and tapping the author on the knee – 'but the task proves too big for him. What did he do? He asked the cleverest man in the world to help him. And Godahl helped him. That,' said Johans-

371

sen, interrupting Armiston with a raised finger, 'is the story of the white ruby. The Story of the White Ruby, you see, is something infinitely finer than mere vulgar robbery and murder, as the author of Godahl the Infallible conceived it.'

Johanssen said a great deal more. In the end he took the lozenge-shaped diamond pendant and put the glass on the silver bar, that his friend might see the inscription on the back. He told him what the inscription signified – 'Brother of a King,' and, furthermore, how few men alive possessed the capacity for brotherhood.

'I think,' said Armiston as he was about to take his leave, 'that I will travel in the Straits this winter.'

'If you do,' said Johanssen, 'I earnestly advise you to leave your Godahl and his decoration at home.'

13

The Frame-Up

Richard Harding Davis

When the voice over the telephone promised to name the man who killed Hermann Banf, District Attorney Wharton was uptown lunching at Delmonico's. This was contrary to his custom and a concession to Hamilton Cutler, his distinguished brother-in-law. That gentleman was interested in a State constabulary bill and had asked State Senator Bissell to father it. He had suggested to the senator that, in the legal points involved in the bill, his brother-in-law would undoubtedly be charmed to advise him. So that morning, to talk it over, Bissell had come from Albany and, as he was forced to return the same afternoon, had asked Wharton to lunch with him uptown near the station.

That in public life there breathed a man with soul so dead who, were he offered a chance to serve Hamilton Cutler, would not jump at the chance, was outside the experience of the county chairman. And in so judging his fellow men, with the exception of one man, the senator was right. The one man was Hamilton Cutler's brother-in-law.

In the national affairs of his party Hamilton Cutler was one of the four leaders. In two cabinets he had held office. At a foreign court as an ambassador his dinners, of which the diplomatic corps still spoke with emotion, had upheld the dignity of ninety million Americans. He was rich. The history of his family was the history of the

State. When the Albany boats drew abreast of the old Cutler mansion on the east bank of the Hudson the passengers pointed at it with deference. Even when the search-lights pointed at it, it was with deference. And on Fifth Avenue, as the 'Seeing New York' car passed his town house it slowed respectfully to half speed. When, apparently for no other reason than that she was good and beautiful, he had married the sister of a then un-known up-State lawyer, every one felt Hamilton Cutler had made his first mistake. But, like everything else into which he entered, for him matrimony also was a success. The prettiest girl in Utica showed herself worthy of her distinguished husband. She had given him children as beautiful as herself; as what Washington calls 'a cabinet lady' she had kept her name out of the newspapers; as Madame l'Ambassadrice she had put arch-duchesses at their ease; and after ten years she was an adoring wife, a devoted mother, and a proud woman. Her pride was in believing that for every joy she knew she was indebted entirely to her husband. To owe everything to him, to feel that through him the blessings flowed, was her ideal of happiness.

In this ideal her brother did not share. Her delight in a sense of obligation left him quite cold. No one better than himself knew that his rapid-fire rise in public favour was due to his own exertions, to the fact that he had worked very hard, had been independent, had kept his hands clean, and had worn no man's collar. Other people believed he owed his advancement to his brother-in-law. He knew they believed that, and it hurt him When, at the annual dinner of the Amen Corner, they burlesqued him as singing to 'Ham' Cutler, 'You made me what I am today, I hope you're sat-isfied,' he found that to laugh with the others was something of an effort. His was a difficult position. He was a party man; he had always worked inside the organization. The fact that whenever he ran for an elective office the reformers indorsed him and the best elements in the opposition parties voted for him did not shake his loyalty to his own people. And to Hamilton Cutler, as one of his party leaders, as one of the bosses of the 'invisible government', he was willing to defer. But while he could give allegiance to his party leaders, and from them was willing to receive the rewards of office, from a rich brother-in-law he was not at all willing to accept anything. Still less was he willing that of the credit he deserved for years of hard work for the party, of self-denial, and of efficient public service the rich brother-in-law should rob him.

His pride was to be known as a self-made man, as the servant only of the voters. And now that he had fought his way to one of the goals of his ambition, now that he was district attorney of New York City, to have it said that the office was the gift of his brother-in-law was bitter. But he believed the injustice would soon end. In a month he was coming up for re-election, and night and day was conducting a campaign that he hoped would result in a personal victory so complete as to banish the shadow of his brother-in-law. Were he re-elected by the majority on which he counted, he would have the party leaders on their knees. Hamilton Cutler would be forced to come to him. He would be in line for promotion. He knew the leaders did not want to promote him, that they considered him too inclined to kick over the traces; but were he now re-elected, at the next election, either for mayor or governor, he would be his party's obvious and legitimate candidate.

The re-election was not to be an easy victory. Outside his own party, to prevent his succeeding himself as district attorney, Tammany Hall was using every weapon in her armoury. The commissioner of police was a Tammany man, and in the public prints Wharton had repeatedly declared that Banf, his star witness against the police, had been killed by the police, and that they had prevented the discovery of his murderer. For this the wigwam wanted his scalp, and to get it had raked his public and private life, had used threats and bribes, and with women had tried to trap him into a scandal. But 'Big Tim' Mehan, the lieutenant the Hall had detailed to destroy Wharton, had reported back that for their purpose his record was useless, that bribes and threats only flattered him, and that the traps set for him he had smilingly side-stepped. This was the situation a month before election day when, to oblige his brother-in-law, Wharton was uptown at Delmonico's lunching with Senator Bissell.

Downtown at the office, Rumson, the assistant district attorney, was on his way to lunch when the telephone-girl halted him. Her voice was lowered and betrayed almost human interest.

From the corner of her mouth she whispered: 'This man has a note for Mr Wharton – says if he don't get it quick it'll be too late – says it will tell him who killed "Heimie" Banf!'

The young man and the girl looked at each other and smiled. Their experience had not tended to make them credulous. Had he lived, Hermann Banf would have been, for Wharton, the star witness against a ring of corrupt police officials. In consequence his murder was more than the taking off of a shady and disreputable citizen. It was a blow struck at the high office of the district attorney, at the grand jury, and the law. But, so far, whoever struck the blow had escaped punishment, and though for a month, ceaselessly, by night and day 'the office' and the police had sought him, he was still at large, still 'unknown'. There had been hundreds of clews. They had been furnished by the detectives of the city and county and of the private agencies, by amateurs, by newspapers, by members of the underworld with a score to pay off or to gain favour. But no clew had led any-

where. When, in hoarse whispers, the last one had been
confided to him by his detectives, Wharton had protested
indignantly.

'Stop bringing me clews!' he exclaimed. 'I want the
man. I can't electrocute a clew!'

So when, after all other efforts, over the telephone a
strange voice offered to deliver the murderer, Rumson
was sceptical. He motioned the girl to switch to the desk
telephone.

'Assistant District Attorney Rumson speaking,' he said.
'What can I do for you?'

Before the answer came, as though the speaker were
choosing his words, there was a pause. It lasted so long
that Rumson exclaimed sharply:

'Hello,' he called. 'Do you want to speak to me, or
don't you want to speak to me?'

'I've gotta letter for the district attorney,' said the voice.
'I'm to give it to nobody but him. It's about Banf. He
must get it quick, or it'll be too late.'

'Who are you?' demanded Rumson. 'Where are you
speaking from?'

The man at the other end of the wire ignored the questions.

'Where'll Wharton be for the next twenty minutes?'

'If I tell you,' parried Rumson, 'will you bring the letter
at once?'

The voice exclaimed indignantly:

'Bring nothing! I'll send it by district messenger.
You're wasting time trying to reach me. It's the *letter*
you want. It tells' – the voice broke with an oath and instantly began again: 'I can't talk over a phone. I tell you,
it's life or death. If you lose out, it's your own fault.
Where can I find Wharton?'

'At Delmonico's,' answered Rumson. 'He'll be there
until two o'clock.'

'Delmonico's! That's Forty-fourth Street?'

'Right,' said Rumson. 'Tell the messenger –'

He heard the receiver slam upon the hook.

With the light of the hunter in his eyes, he turned to the girl.

'They can laugh,' he cried, 'but I believe we've hooked something. I'm going after it.'

In the waiting-room he found the detectives.

'Hewitt,' he ordered, 'take the subway and whip up to Delmonico's. Talk to the taxi-starter till a messenger-boy brings a letter for the D.A. Let the boy deliver the note, and then trail him till he reports to the man he got it from. Bring the man here. If it's a district messenger and he doesn't report, but goes straight back to the office, find out who gave him the note; get his description. Then meet me at Delmonico's.'

Rumson called up that restaurant and had Wharton come to the phone. He asked his chief to wait until a letter he believed to be of great importance was delivered to him. He explained, but, of necessity, somewhat sketchily.

'It sounds to me,' commented his chief, 'like a plot of yours to get a lunch up-town.'

'Invitation!' cried Rumson. 'I'll be with you in ten minutes.'

After Rumson had joined Wharton and Bissell the note arrived. It was brought to the restaurant by a messenger-boy, who said that in answer to a call from a saloon on Sixth Avenue he had received it from a young man in ready-to-wear clothes and a green hat. When Hewitt, the detective, asked what the young man looked like, the boy said he looked like a young man in ready-to-wear clothes and a green hat. But when the note was read the identity of the man who delivered it ceased to be of importance. The paper on which it was written was without stamped address or monogram, and carried with it the mixed odours of the drug-store at which it had been

purchased. The handwriting was that of a woman, and
what she had written was: 'If the district attorney will
come at once, and alone, to Kessler's Café, on the Boston
Post Road, near the city line, he will be told who killed
Hermann Banf. If he don't come in an hour, it will be
too late. If he brings anybody with him, he won't be told
anything. Leave your car in the road and walk up the
drive. Ida Earle.'

Hewitt, who had sent away the messenger-boy and had
been called in to give expert advice, was enthusiastic.

'Mr District Attorney,' he cried, 'that's no crank letter.
This Earle woman is wise. You got to take her as a serious proposition. She wouldn't make that play if she
couldn't get away with it.'

'Who is she?' asked Wharton.

To the police, the detective assured them, Ida Earle
had been known for years. When she was young she had
been under the protection of a man high in the ranks of
Tammany, and, in consequence, with her different ven-
tures the police had never interfered. She now was pro-
prietress of the road-house in the note described as
Kessler's Café. It was a place for joy-riders. There was a
cabaret, a hall for public dancing, and rooms for very
private suppers.

In so far as it welcomed only those who could spend
money it was exclusive, but in all other respects its reputation was of the worst. In situation it was lonely, and
from other houses separated by a quarter of a mile of
dying trees and vacant lots.

The Boston Post Road upon which it faced was the old
post road, but lately, through this back yard and dump-
ing-ground of the city, had been relaid. It was patrolled
only and infrequently by bicycle policemen.

'But this,' continued the detective eagerly, 'is where we
win out. The road-house is an old farmhouse built over,
with the barns changed into garages. They stand on the

edge of a wood. It's about as big as a city block. If we come in through the woods from the rear, the garages will hide us. Nobody in the house can see us, but we won't be a hundred yards away. You've only to blow a police whistle and we'll be with you.'

'You mean I ought to go?' said Wharton.

'You *got* to go!'

'It looks to me,' objected Bissell, 'like a plot to get you there alone and rap you on the head.'

'Not with that note inviting him there,' protested Hewitt, 'and signed by Earle herself.'

'You don't know she signed it,' objected the senator.

'I know *her*,' returned the detective. 'I know she's no fool. It's her place, and she wouldn't let them pull off any rough stuff there – not against the D.A., anyway.'

The D.A. was rereading the note.

'Might this be it?' he asked. 'Suppose it's a trick to mix me up in a scandal? You say the place is disreputable. Suppose they're planning to compromise me just before election. They've tried it already several times.'

'You've still got the note,' persisted Hewitt. 'It proves *why* you went there. And the senator, too. He can testify. And we won't be a hundred yards away. And,' he added grudgingly, 'you have Nolan.'

Nolan was the spoiled child of 'the office'. He was the district attorney's pet. Although still young, he had scored as a detective and as a driver of racing-cars. As Wharton's chauffeur he now doubled the parts.

'What Nolan testified wouldn't be any help,' said Wharton. 'They would say it was just a story he invented to save me.'

'Then square yourself this way,' urged Rumson. 'Send a note now by hand to Ham Cutler and one to your sister. Tell *them* you're going to Ida Earle's – and why – tell them you're afraid it's a frame-up and for them to keep your notes as evidence. And enclose the one from her.'

Wharton nodded in approval, and, while he wrote, Rumson and the detective planned how, without those inside the road-house being aware of their presence, they might be near it.

Kessler's Café lay in the Seventy-ninth Police Precinct. In taxi-cabs they arranged to start at once and proceed down White Plains Avenue, which parallels the Boston Road, until they were on a line with Kessler's, but from it hidden by the woods and the garages. A walk of a quarter of a mile across lots and under cover of the trees would bring them to within a hundred yards of the house.

Wharton was to give them a start of half an hour. That he might know they were on watch, they agreed, after they dismissed the taxi-cabs, to send one of them into the Boston Post Road past the road-house. When it was directly in front of the café, the chauffeur would throw away into the road an empty cigarette-case.

From the cigar-stand they selected a cigarette box of a startling yellow. At half a mile it was conspicuous.

'When you see this in the road,' explained Rumson, 'you'll know we're on the job. And after you're inside, if you need us, you've only to go to a rear window and wave.'

'If they mean to do him up,' growled Bissell, 'he won't get to a rear window.'

'He can always tell them we're outside,' said Rumson – 'and they are extremely likely to believe him. Do you want a gun?'

'No,' said the D.A.

'Better have mine,' urged Hewitt.

'I have my own,' explained the D.A.

Rumson and Hewitt set off in taxi-cabs and, a half-hour later, Wharton followed. As he sank back against the cushions of the big touring-car he felt a pleasing thrill of excitement, and as he passed the traffic police, and they saluted mechanically, he smiled. Had they

guessed his errand their interest in his progress would
have been less perfunctory. In half an hour he might
know that the police killed Banf; in half an hour he himself might walk into a trap they had, in turn, staged for
him. As the car ran swiftly through the clean October
air, and the wind and sun alternately chilled and warmed
his blood, Wharton considered these possibilities.

He could not believe the woman Earle would lend herself to any plot to do him bodily harm. She was a responsible person. In her own world she was as important
a figure as was the district attorney in his. Her allies were
the men 'higher up' in Tammany and the police of the
upper ranks of the uniformed force. And of the higher
office of the district attorney she possessed an intimate
and respectful knowledge. It was not to be considered
that against the prosecuting attorney such a woman
would wage war. So the thought that upon his person
any assault was meditated Wharton dismissed as unintelligent. That it was upon his reputation the attack
was planned seemed much more probable. But that con-
tingency he had foreseen and so, he believed, forestalled.
There then remained only the possibility that the offer
in the letter was genuine. It seemed quite too good to be
true. For, as he asked himself, on the very eve of an election, why should Tammany, or a friend of Tammany,
place in his possession the information that to the Tammany candidate would bring inevitable defeat. He felt
that the way they were playing into his hands was too
open, too generous. If their object was to lead him into a
trap, of all baits they might use the promise to tell him
who killed Banf was the one certain to attract him. It
made their invitation to walk into the parlour almost too
obvious. But were the offer not genuine, there was a condition attached to it that puzzled him. It was not the
condition that stipulated he should come alone. His experience had taught him many will confess, or betray, to
the district attorney who, to a deputy, will tell nothing.

The condition that puzzled him was the one that insisted he should come at once or it would be 'too late'.

Why was haste so imperative? Why, if he delayed, would he be 'too late'? Was the man he sought about to escape from his jurisdiction, was he dying, and was it his wish to make a death-bed confession; or was he so reluctant to speak that delay might cause him to reconsider and remain silent?

With these questions in his mind, the minutes quickly passed, and it was with a thrill of excitement Wharton saw that Nolan had left the Zoological Gardens on the right and turned into the Boston Road. It had but lately been completed and to Wharton was unfamiliar. On either side of the unscarred roadway still lay scattered the uprooted trees and bowlders that had blocked its progress, and abandoned by the contractors were empty tar-barrels, cement-sacks, tool-sheds, and forges. Nor was the surrounding landscape less raw and unlovely. Toward the Sound stretched vacant lots covered with ash heaps; to the left a few old and broken houses set among the glass-covered cold frames of truck-farms.

The district attorney felt a sudden twinge of loneliness. And when an automobile sign told him he was '10 miles from Columbus Circle,' he felt that from the New York he knew he was much farther. Two miles up the road his car overhauled a bicycle policeman, and Wharton halted him.

'Is there a road-house called Kessler's beyond here?' he asked.

'On the left, farther up,' the officer told him, and added: 'You can't miss it, Mr Wharton; there's no other house near it.'

'You know me,' said the D.A. 'Then you'll understand what I want you to do. I've agreed to go to that house alone. If they see you pass they may think I'm not playing fair. So stop here.'

The man nodded and dismounted.

'But,' added the district attorney, as the car started forward again, 'if you hear shots, I don't care how fast you come.'

The officer grinned.

'Better let me trail along now,' he called; 'that's a tough joint.'

But Wharton motioned him back; and when again he turned to look the man still stood where they had parted.

Two minutes later an empty taxi-cab came swiftly toward him and, as it passed, the driver lifted his hand from the wheel and with his thumb motioned behind him.

'That's one of the men,' said Nolan, 'that started with Mr Rumson and Hewitt from Delmonico's.'

Wharton nodded; and, now assured that in their plan there had been no hitch, smiled with satisfaction. A moment later, when ahead of them on the asphalt road Nolan pointed out a spot of yellow, he recognized the signal and knew that within call were friends.

The yellow cigarette-box lay directly in front of a long wooden building of two storeys. It was linked to the road by a curving driveway marked on either side by white-washed stones. On verandas enclosed in glass Wharton saw white-covered tables under red candle-shades and, protruding from one end of the house and hung with electric lights in paper lanterns, a pavilion for dancing. In the rear of the house stood sheds and a thick tangle of trees on which the autumn leaves showed yellow. Painted fingers and arrows pointing, and an electric sign, proclaimed to all who passed that this was Kessler's. In spite of its reputation, the house wore the aspect of the commonplace. In evidence nothing flaunted, nothing threatened. From a dozen other inns along the Pelham Parkway and the Boston Post Road it was in no way to be distinguished.

As directed in the note, Wharton left the car in the

road. 'For five minutes stay where you are,' he ordered
Nolan; 'then go to the bar and get a drink. Don't talk to
anyone or they'll think you're trying to get information.
Work around to the back of the house. Stand where I
can see you from the window. I may want you to carry a
message to Mr Rumson.'

On foot Wharton walked up the curving driveway, and
if from the house his approach was spied upon, there was
no evidence. In the second storey the blinds were drawn
and on the first floor the verandas were empty. Nor, not
even after he had mounted to the veranda and stepped
inside the house, was there any sign that his visit was
expected. He stood in a hall, and in front of him rose a
broad flight of stairs that he guessed led to the private
supper-rooms. On his left was the restaurant.

Swept and garnished after the revels of the night previous, and as though resting in preparation for those to
come, it wore an air of peaceful inactivity. At a table a
maitre d'hôtel was composing the menu for the evening,
against the walls three coloured waiters lounged sleepily,
and on a platform at a piano a pale youth with drugged
eyes was with one hand picking an accompaniment. As
Wharton paused uncertainly the young man, disdaining
his audience, in a shrill, nasal tenor raised his voice and
sang:

> 'And from the time the rooster calls
> I'll wear my overalls,
>   And you, a simple gingham gown.
> So, if you're strong for a shower of rice,
> We two could make a paradise
>   Of any One-Horse Town.'

At the sight of Wharton the head waiter reluctantly
detached himself from his menu and rose. But before he
could greet the visitor, Wharton heard his name spoken
and, looking up, saw a woman descending the stairs. It

was apparent that when young she had been beautiful, and, in spite of an expression in her eyes of hardness and distrust, which seemed habitual, she was still handsome. She was without a hat and wearing a house dress of decorous shades and in the extreme of fashion. Her black hair, built up in artificial waves, was heavy with brilliantine; her hands, covered deep with rings, and of an unnatural white, showed the most fastidious care. But her complexion was her own; and her skin, free from paint and powder, glowed with that healthy pink that is supposed to be the perquisite only of the simple life and a conscience undisturbed.

'I am Mrs Earle,' said the woman. 'I wrote you that note. Will you please come this way?'

That she did not suppose he might not come that way was obvious, for, as she spoke, she turned her back on him and mounted the stairs. After an instant of hesitation, Wharton followed.

As well as his mind, his body was now acutely alive and vigilant. Both physically and mentally he moved on tiptoe. For whatever surprise, for whatever ambush might lie in wait, he was prepared. At the top of the stairs he found a wide hall along which on both sides were many doors. The one directly facing the stairs stood open. At one side of this the woman halted and with a gesture of the jewelled fingers invited him to enter.

'My sitting-room,' she said. As Wharton remained motionless she substituted: 'My office.'

Peering into the room, Wharton found it suited to both titles. He saw comfortable chairs, vases filled with autumn leaves, in silver frames photographs, and between two open windows a businesslike roller-top desk on which was a hand telephone. In plain sight through the windows he beheld the garage and behind it the tops of trees. To summon Rumson, to keep in touch with Nolan, he need only step to one of these windows and beckon. The strategic position of the room appealed, and with a bow of the head he passed in front of his hostess and entered it. He continued to take note of his surroundings.

He now saw that from the office in which he stood doors led to rooms adjoining. These doors were shut, and he determined swiftly that before the interview began he first must know what lay behind them. Mrs Earle had followed and, as she entered, closed the door.

'No!' said Wharton.

It was the first time he had spoken. For an instant the woman hesitated, regarding him thoughtfully, and then without resentment pulled the door open. She came toward him swiftly, and he was conscious of the rustle of silk and the stirring of perfumes. At the open door she cast a frown of disapproval and then, with her face close to his, spoke hurriedly in a whisper.

'A man brought a girl here to lunch,' she said: 'they've been here before. The girl claims the man told her he was going to marry her. Last night she found out he has a wife already, and she came here today meaning to make trouble. She brought a gun. They were in the room at the far end of the hall. George, the waiter, heard the two shots and ran down here to get me. No one else heard. These rooms are fixed to keep out noise, and the piano was going. We broke in and found them on the floor. The man was shot through the shoulder, the girl through the body. His story is that after she fired, in trying to get the gun from her, she shot herself – by accident. That's right, I guess. But the girl says they came here to die together – what the newspapers call a "suicide pact" – because they couldn't marry, and that he first shot her, intending to kill her and then himself. That's silly. She framed it to get him. She missed him with the gun, so now she's trying to get him with this murder charge. I know her. If she'd been sober she wouldn't have shot him; she'd have blackmailed him. She's *that* sort. I know her, and –'

With an exclamation the district attorney broke in

upon her. 'And the man,' he demanded eagerly; 'was it *he* killed Banf?'

In amazement the woman stared. 'Certainly *not*!' she said.

'Then what *has* this to do with Banf?'

'Nothing!' Her tone was annoyed, reproachful. 'That was only to bring you here –'

His disappointment was so keen that it threatened to exhibit itself in anger. Recognizing this, before he spoke Wharton forced himself to pause. Then he repeated her words quietly.

'Bring me here?' he asked. 'Why?'

The woman exclaimed impatiently: 'So you could beat the police to it,' she whispered. 'So you could *hush it up*!'

The surprised laugh of the man was quite real. It bore no resentment or pose. He was genuinely amused. Then the dignity of his office, tricked and insulted, demanded to be heard. He stared at her coldly; his indignation was apparent.

'You have done extremely ill,' he told her. 'You know perfectly well you have no right to bring me up here; to drag me into a row in your road-house. "Hush it up"!' he exclaimed hotly. This time his laugh was contemptuous and threatening.

'I'll show you how I'll hush it up!' He moved quickly to the open window.

'Stop!' commanded the woman. 'You can't do that!'

She ran to the door.

Again he was conscious of the rustle of silk, of the stirring of perfume.

He heard the key turn in the lock. It had come. It was a frame-up. There would be a scandal. And to save himself from it they would force him to 'hush up' this other one. But, as to the outcome, in no way was he concerned. Through the window standing directly below it, he had seen Nolan. In the sunlit yard the chauffeur, his cap on the back of his head, his cigarette drooping from his lips, was tossing the remnants of a sandwich to a circle of excited hens. He presented a picture of bored indolence, of innocent preoccupation. It was almost *too* well done.

Assured of a witness for the defense, he greeted the woman with a smile. 'Why can't I do it?' he taunted.

She ran close to him and laid her hands on his arm. Her eyes were fixed steadily on his. 'Because,' she whispered, 'the man who shot that girl – is your brother-in-law, Ham Cutler!'

For what seemed a long time Wharton stood looking down into the eyes of the woman, and the eyes never faltered. Later he recalled that in the sudden silence many noises disturbed the lazy hush of the Indian-summer afternoon: the rush of a motor-car on the Boston Road, the tinkle of the piano and the voice of the youth with the drugged eyes singing, 'And you'll wear a simple gingham gown', from the yard below the cluck-cluck of the chickens and the cooing of pigeons.

His first thought was of his sister and of her children, and of what this bomb, hurled from the clouds, would mean to her. He thought of Cutler, at the height of his power and usefulness, by this one disreputable act dragged into the mire, of what disaster it might bring to the party, to himself.

If, as the woman invited, he helped to 'hush it up', and Tammany learned the truth, it would make short work of him. It would say, for the murderer of Banf he had one law and for the rich brother-in-law, who had tried to kill the girl he deceived, another. But before he gave voice to his thoughts he recognized them as springing only from panic. They were of a part with the acts of men driven by sudden fear, and of which acts in their sane moments they would be incapable.

The shock of the woman's words had unsettled his traditions. Not only was he condemning a man unheard, but a man who, though he might dislike him, he had for years, for his private virtues, trusted and admired. The panic passed and with a confident smile he shook his head.

'I don't believe you,' he said quietly.

The manner of the woman was equally calm, equally assured.

'Will you see her?' she asked.

'I'd rather see my brother-in-law,' he answered.

The woman handed him a card.

'Doctor Muir took him to his private hospital,' she said. 'I loaned them my car because it's a limousine. The address is on that card. But,' she added, 'both your brother and Sammy – that's Sam Muir, the doctor – asked you wouldn't use the telephone; they're afraid of a leak.'

Apparently Wharton did not hear her. As though it were 'Exhibit A' presented in evidence by the defense, he was studying the card she had given him. He stuck it in his pocket.

'I'll go to him at once,' he said.

To restrain or dissuade him, the woman made no sudden move. In level tones she said: 'Your brother-in-law asked especially that you wouldn't do that until you'd fixed it with the girl. Your face is too well known. He's afraid someone might find out where he is – and for a day or two no one must know that.'

'This doctor knows it,' retorted Wharton.

The suggestion seemed to strike Mrs Earle as humorous. For the first time she laughed.

'Sammy!' she exclaimed. 'He's a lobbygow of mine. He's worked for me for years. I could send him up the river if I liked. He knows it.' Her tone was convincing. 'They both asked,' she continued evenly, 'you should keep off until the girl is out of the country, and fixed.'

Wharton frowned thoughtfully.

And, observing this, the eyes of the woman showed

that, so far, toward the unfortunate incident the attitude of the district attorney was to her most gratifying.

Wharton ceased frowning.

'How fixed?' he asked.

Mrs Earle shrugged her shoulders.

'Cutler's idea is money,' she said; 'but, believe *me*, he's wrong. This girl is a vampire. She'll only come back to you for more. She'll keep on threatening to tell the wife, to tell the papers. The way to fix *her* is to throw a scare into her. And there's only one man can do that; there's only one man that can hush this thing up – that's you.'

'When can I see her?' asked Wharton.

'Now,' said the woman, 'I'll bring her.'

Wharton could not suppress an involuntary start.

'Here?' he exclaimed.

For the shade of a second Mrs Earle exhibited the slightest evidence of embarrassment.

'My room's in a mess,' she explained; 'and she's not hurt so much as Sammy said. He told her she was in bad just to keep her quiet until you got here.'

Mrs Earle opened one of the doors leading from the room. 'I won't be a minute,' she said. Quietly she closed the door behind her.

Upon her disappearance the manner of the district attorney underwent an abrupt change. He ran softly to the door opposite the one through which Mrs Earle had passed, and pulled it open. But, if beyond it he expected to find an audience of eavesdroppers, he was disappointed. The room was empty – and bore no evidence of recent occupation. He closed the door, and, from the roller-top desk, snatching a piece of paper, scribbled upon it hastily. Wrapping the paper around a coin, and holding it exposed to view, he showed himself at the window. Below him, to an increasing circle of hens and pigeons, Nolan was still scattering crumbs. Without withdrawing his gaze from them the chauffeur nodded. Wharton opened his hand and the note fell into the yard. Behind him he heard the murmur of voices, the sobs of a woman in pain, and the rattle of a door-knob. As from the window he turned quickly, he saw that toward the spot where his note had fallen Nolan was tossing the last remnants of his sandwich.

The girl who entered with Mrs Earle, leaning on her and supported by her, was tall and fair. Around her shoulders her blonde hair hung in disorder, and around her waist, under the kimono Mrs Earle had thrown about her, were wrapped many layers of bandages. The girl moved unsteadily and sank into a chair.

In a hostile tone Mrs Earle addressed her.

'Rose,' she said, 'this is the district attorney.' To him she added : 'She calls herself Rose Gerard.'

One hand the girl held close against her side, with the other she brushed back the hair from her forehead. From half-closed eyes she stared at Wharton defiantly.

'Well,' she challenged, 'what about it?'

Wharton seated himself in front of the roller-top desk.

'Are you strong enough to tell me?' he asked.

His tone was kind, and this the girl seemed to resent.

'Don't you worry,' she sneered. 'I'm strong enough. Strong enough to tell *all* I know – to you, and to the papers, and to a jury – until I get justice.' She clinched her free hand and feebly shook it at him. '*That's* what I'm going to get,' she cried, her voice breaking hysterically, 'justice.'

From behind the armchair in which the girl half-reclined Mrs Earle caught the eye of the district attorney and shrugged her shoulders.

'Just what *did* happen?' asked Wharton.

Apparently with an effort the girl pulled herself together.

'I first met your brother-in-law –' she began.

Wharton interrupted quietly.

'Wait!' he said. 'You are not talking to me as anybody's brother-in-law, but as the district attorney.'

The girl laughed vindictively.

'I don't wonder you're ashamed of him!' she jeered.

Again she began: 'I first met Ham Cutler last May. He wanted to marry me then. He told me he was not a married man.'

As her story unfolded, Wharton did not again interrupt; and speaking quickly, in abrupt, broken phrases, the girl brought her narrative to the moment when, as she claimed, Cutler had attempted to kill her. At this point a knock at the locked door caused both the girl and her audience to start. Wharton looked at Mrs Earle inquiringly, but she shook her head, and with a look at him also of inquiry, and of suspicion as well, opened the door.

With apologies her head waiter presented a letter.

'For Mr Wharton,' he explained, 'from his chauffeur.'

Wharton's annoyance at the interruption was most apparent. 'What the devil –' he began.

He read the note rapidly, and with a frown of irritation raised his eyes to Mrs Earle.

'He wants to go to New Rochelle for an inner tube,' he said. 'How long would it take him to get there and back?'

The hard and distrustful expression upon the face of Mrs Earle, which was habitual, was now most strongly in evidence. Her eyes searched those of Wharton.

'Twenty minutes,' she said.

'He can't go,' snapped Wharton.

'Tell him,' he directed the waiter, 'to stay where he is. Tell him I may want to go back to the office any minute.' He turned eagerly to the girl. 'I'm sorry,' he said. With impatience he crumpled the note into a ball and glanced about him. At his feet was a waste-paper basket. Fixed upon him he saw, while pretending not to see, the eyes of Mrs Earle burning with suspicion. If he destroyed the note, he knew suspicion would become certainty. Without an instant of hesitation, carelessly he tossed it intact into the waste-paper basket. Toward Rose Gerard he swung the revolving chair.

'Go on, please,' he commanded.

The girl had now reached the climax of her story, but the eyes of Mrs Earle betrayed the fact that her thoughts were elsewhere. With an intense and hungry longing, they were concentrated upon her own waste-paper basket.

The voice of the girl in anger and defiance recalled Mrs Earle to the business of the moment.

'He tried to kill me,' shouted Miss Rose. 'And his shooting himself in the shoulder was a bluff. *That's* my story; that's the story I'm going to tell the judge' – her voice soared shrilly 'that's the story that's going to send your brother-in-law to Sing Sing!'

For the first time Mrs Earle contributed to the general conversation.

'You talk like a fish,' she said.

The girl turned upon her savagely.

'If he don't like the way I talk,' she cried, 'he can come across!'

Mrs Earle exclaimed in horror. Virtuously her hands were raised in protest.

'Like hell he will!' she said. 'You can't pull that under my roof!'

Wharton looked disturbed.

' "Come across"?' he asked.

'Come across?' mimicked the girl. 'Send me abroad and keep me there. And I'll swear it was an accident. Twenty-five thousand, that's all I want. Cutler told me he was going to make you governor. He can't make you governor if he's in Sing Sing, can he? Ain't it worth twenty-five thousand to you to be governor? Come on,' she jeered, 'kick in!'

With a grave but untroubled voice Wharton addressed Mrs Earle.

'May I use your telephone?' he asked. He did not wait

for her consent, but from the desk lifted the hand telephone.

'Spring, three one hundred!' he said. He sat with his
legs comfortably crossed the stand of the instrument
balanced on his knee, his eyes gazing meditatively at the
yellow tree-tops.

If with apprehension both women started, if the girl
thrust herself forward, and by the hand of Mrs Earle was
dragged back, he did not appear to know it.

'Police headquarters?' they heard him ask. 'I want to
speak to the commissioner. This is the district attorney.'

In the pause that followed, as though to torment her,
the pain in her side apparently returned, for the girl
screamed sharply.

'Be still!' commanded the older woman. Breathless,
across the top of the armchair, she was leaning forward.
Upon the man at the telephone her eyes were fixed in
fascination.

'Commissioner,' said the district attorney, 'this is Wharton speaking. A woman has made a charge of attempted
murder to me against my brother-in-law, Hamilton Cutler. On account of our relationship, I want *you* to make
the arrest. If there were any slip, and he got away, it
might be said I arranged it. You will find him at the
Winona apartments on the Southern Boulevard, in the
private hospital of a Doctor Samuel Muir. Arrest them
both. The girl who makes the charge is at Kessler's Café,
on the Boston Post Road, just inside the city line. Arrest
her too. She tried to blackmail me. I'll appear against
her.'

Wharton rose and addressed himself to Mrs Earle.

'I'm sorry,' he said, 'but I had to do it. You might have
known I could not hush it up. I am the only man who
can't hush it up. The people of New York elected me to
enforce the laws.' Wharton's voice was raised to a loud
pitch. It seemed unnecessarily loud. It was almost as
though he were addressing another and more distant

audience. 'And,' he continued, his voice still soaring, 'even if my own family suffer, even if I suffer, even if I lose political promotion, those laws I will enforce!'

In the more conventional tone of everyday politeness, he added:

'May I speak to you outside, Mrs Earle?'

But, as in silence that lady descended the stairs, the district attorney seemed to have forgotten what it was he wished to say.

It was not until he had seen his chauffeur arouse himself from apparently deep slumber and crank the car that he addressed her.

'That girl,' he said, 'had better go back to bed. My men are all around this house and, until the police come, will detain her.'

He shook the jewelled fingers of Mrs Earle warmly. 'I thank you,' he said; 'I know you meant well. I know you wanted to help me, but –' he shrugged his shoulders – 'my duty!'

As he walked down the driveway to his car his shoulders continued to move.

Mrs Earle did not wait to observe this phenomenon. Rid of his presence, she leaped, rather than ran, up the stairs and threw open the door of her office.

As she entered, two men followed her. One was a young man who held in his hand an open note-book, the other was Tim Meehan of Tammany. The latter greeted her with a shout.

'We heard everything he said!' he cried. His voice rose in torment. 'An' we can't use a word of it! He acted just like we'd oughta knowed he'd act. He's *honest*! He's so damned honest he ain't human; he's a – gilded saint!'

Mrs Earle did not heed him. On her knees she was tossing to the floor the contents of the waste-paper basket. From them she snatched a piece of crumpled paper.

'Shut up!' she shouted. 'Listen! His chauffeur brought

him this.' In a voice that quivered with indignation, that sobbed with anger, she read aloud:

' "As directed by your note from the window, I went to the booth and called up Mrs Cutler's house and got herself on the phone. Your brother-in-law lunched at home today with her and the children and they are now going to the Hippodrome.

' "Stop, look, and listen! Back of the bar I see two men in a room, but they did not see me. One is Tim Meehan, the other is a stenographer. He is taking notes. Each of them has on the ear-muffs of a dictagraph. Looks like you'd better watch your step and not say nothing you don't want Tammany to print." ' The voice of Mrs Earle rose in a shrill shriek.

'Him – a gilded saint?' she screamed; 'you big stiff! He knew he was talking into a dictagraph all the time – and he double-crossed us!'

Sources

1 Hugh C. Weir: *Miss Madelyn Mack, Detective.* (Boston, The Page Co., 1914)

2 & 3 Rodriguez Ottolengui: *The Final Proof.* (N.Y., G. P. Putnam, 1898)

4 Josiah Flynt & Francis Walton: *Powers That Prey.* (N.Y., McClure, Philips, 1900)

5 Jacques Futrelle: *The Thinking Machine.* (N.Y., Dodd Mead, 1907)

6 & 7 William MacHarg & Edwin Balmer: *The Adventures of Luther Trant.* (Boston, Small Maynard, 1910)

8 Samuel Hopkins Adams: *Average Jones.* (Indianapolis, Bobbs Merrill, 1911)

9 Francis Lynde: *Scientific Sprague.* (N.Y., Scribner, 1912)

10 Charles Felton Pidgin & J. M. Taylor: *The Chronicles of Quincy Adams Sawyer, Detective.* (Boston, L. C. Page, 1912)

11 Arthur B. Reeve: *The Poisoned Pen.* (N.Y., Dodd Mead, 1913)

12 Frederick Irving Anderson: *Adventures of the Infallible Godahl.* (N.Y., Thomas Y. Crowell, 1914)

13 Richard Harding Davis: *'Somewhere in France'.* (N.Y., A. L. Burt by arrangement with Charles Scribner, 1915)